# A Certain Scientific Accelerator 09

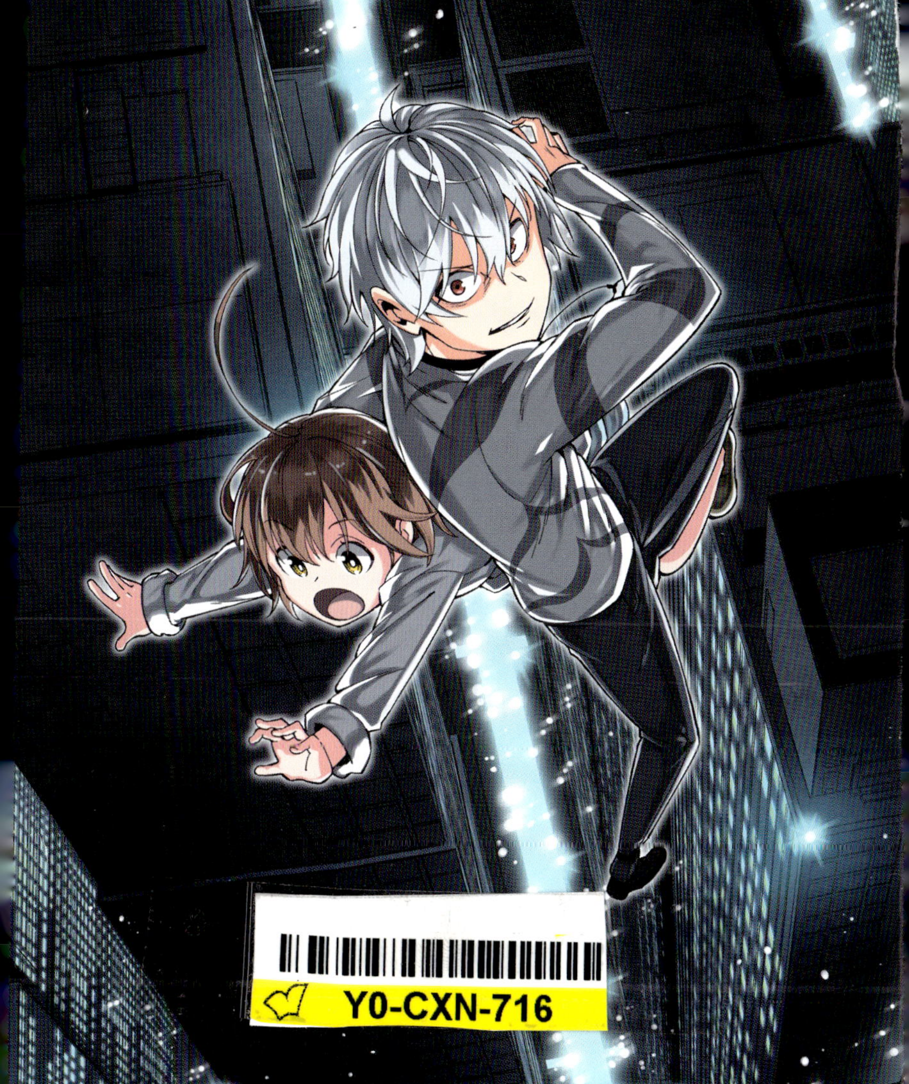



STORY BY KAZUMA KAMACHI
ART BY ARATA YAMAJI
CHARACTER DESIGN BY KIYOTAKA HAIMURA & ARATA YAMAJI

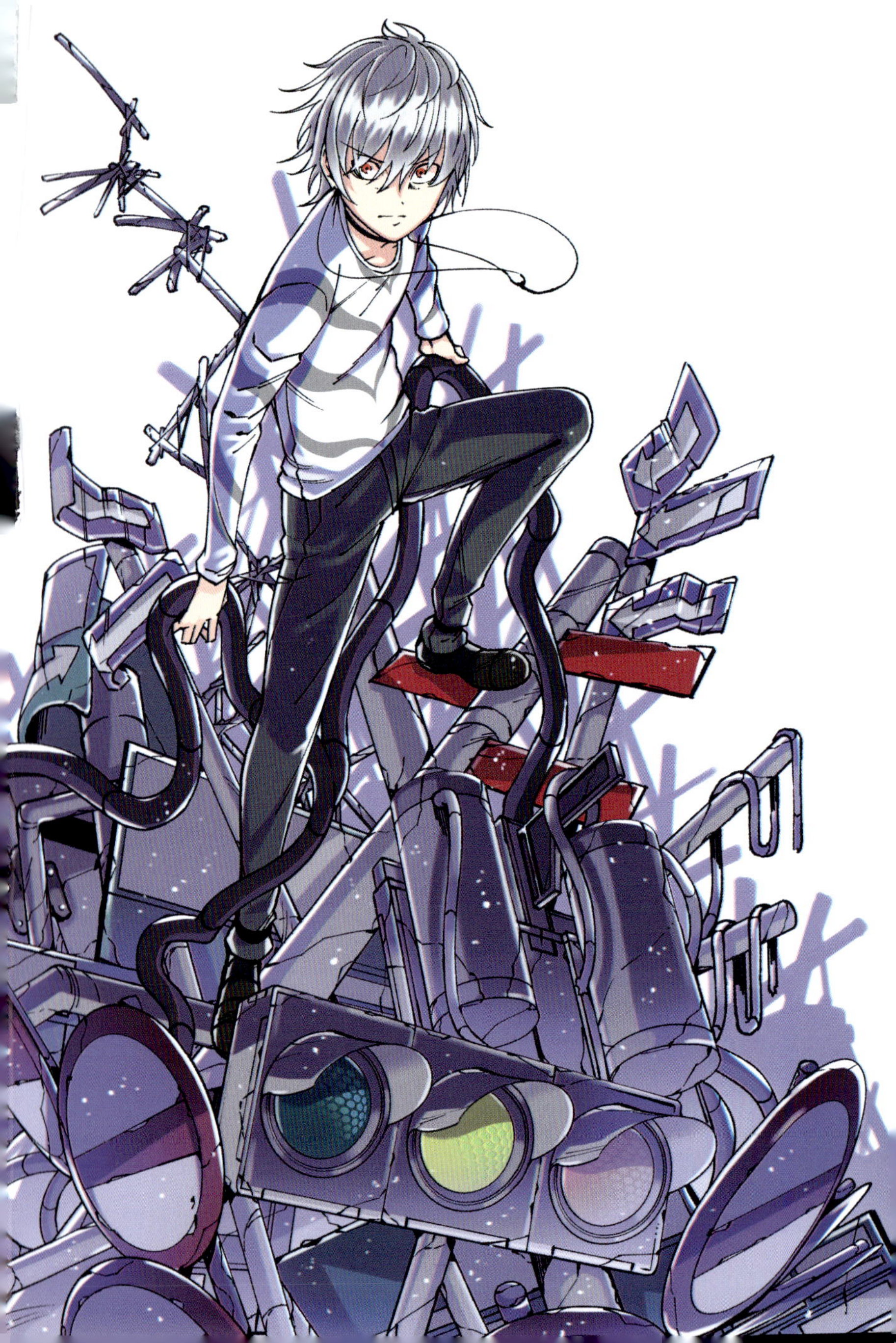

# CHAPTER 44

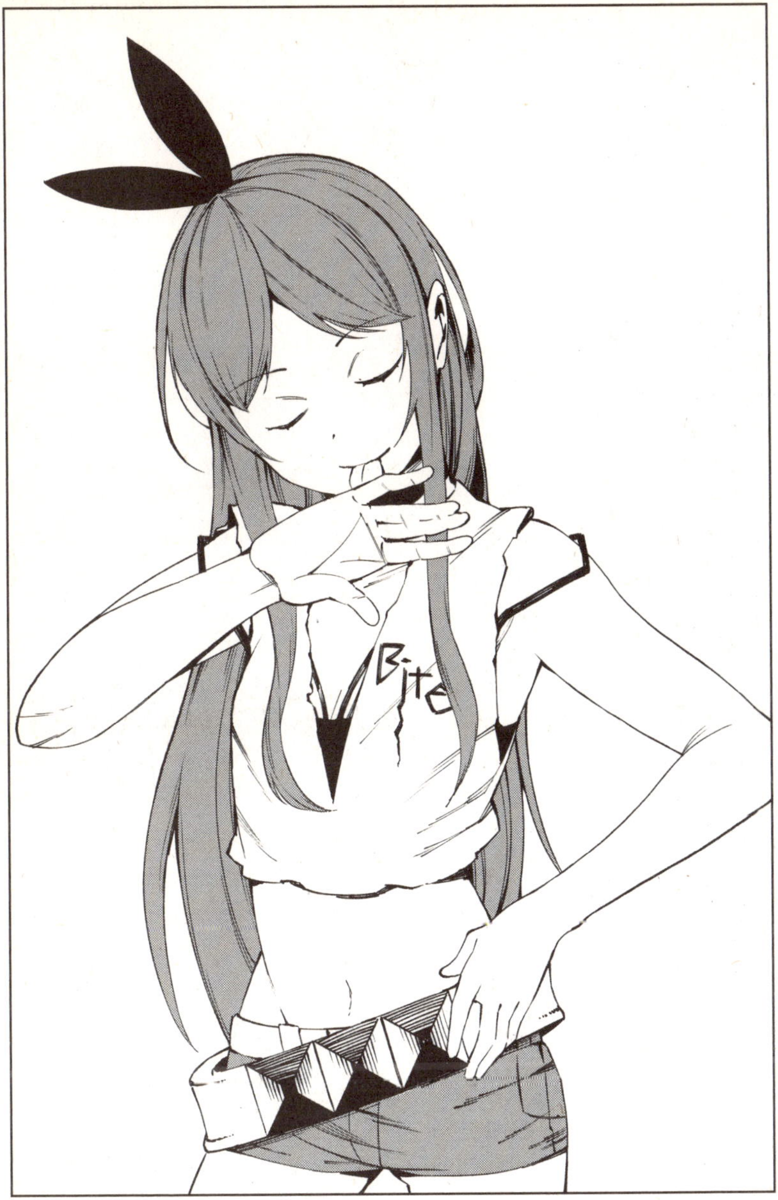
Bite

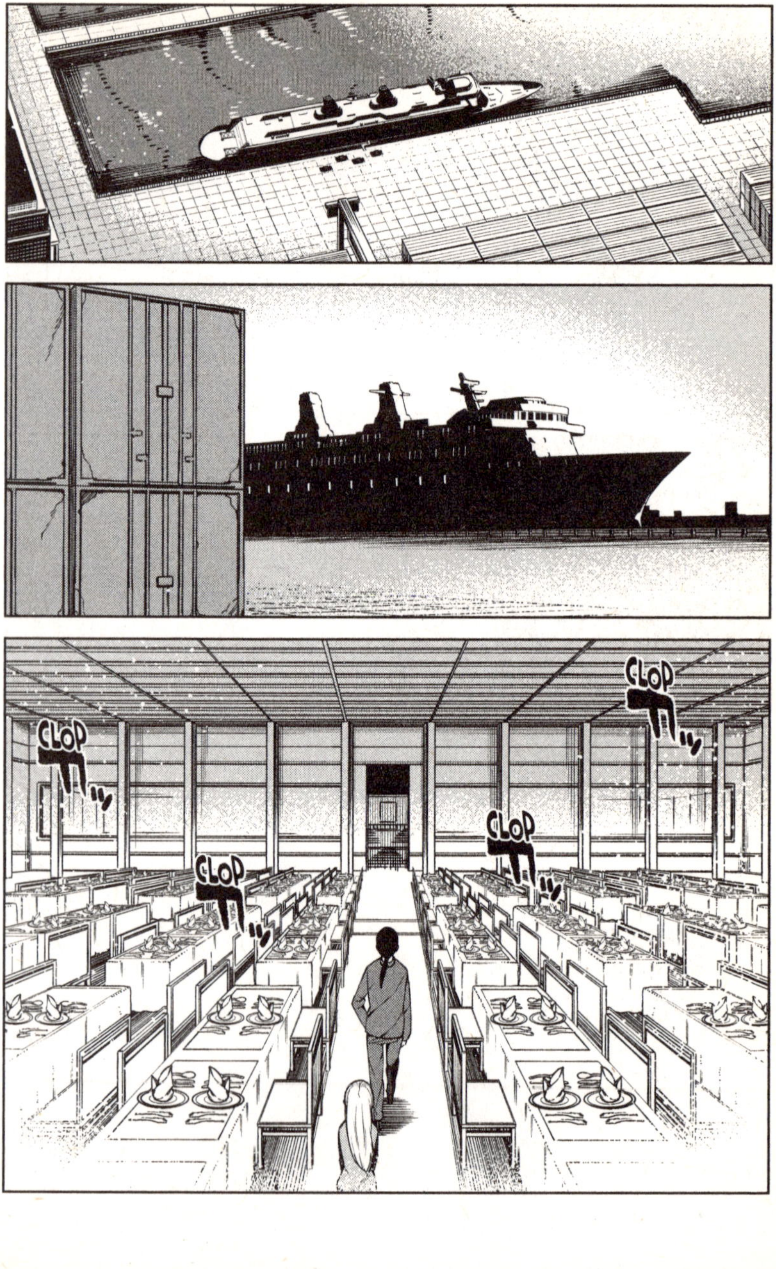
CLOP
CLOP
CLOP
CLOP

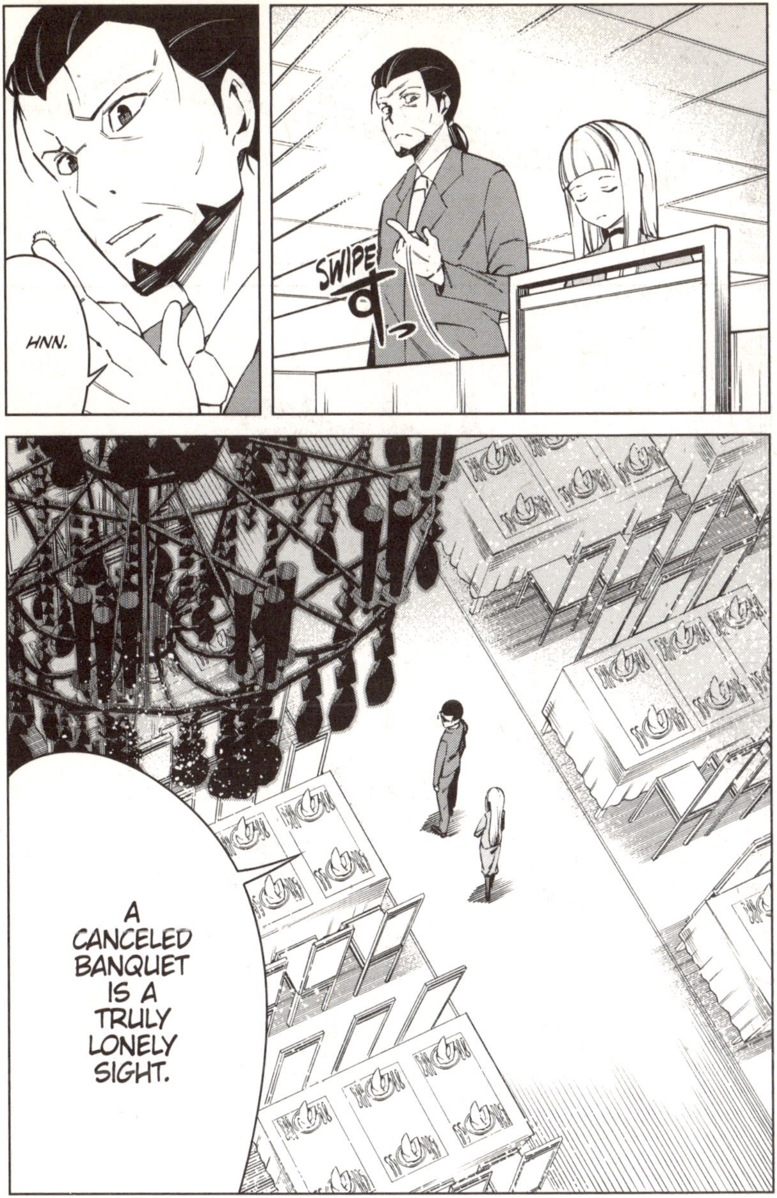
SWIPE
すっ
HNN.
A CANCELED BANQUET IS A TRULY LONELY SIGHT.

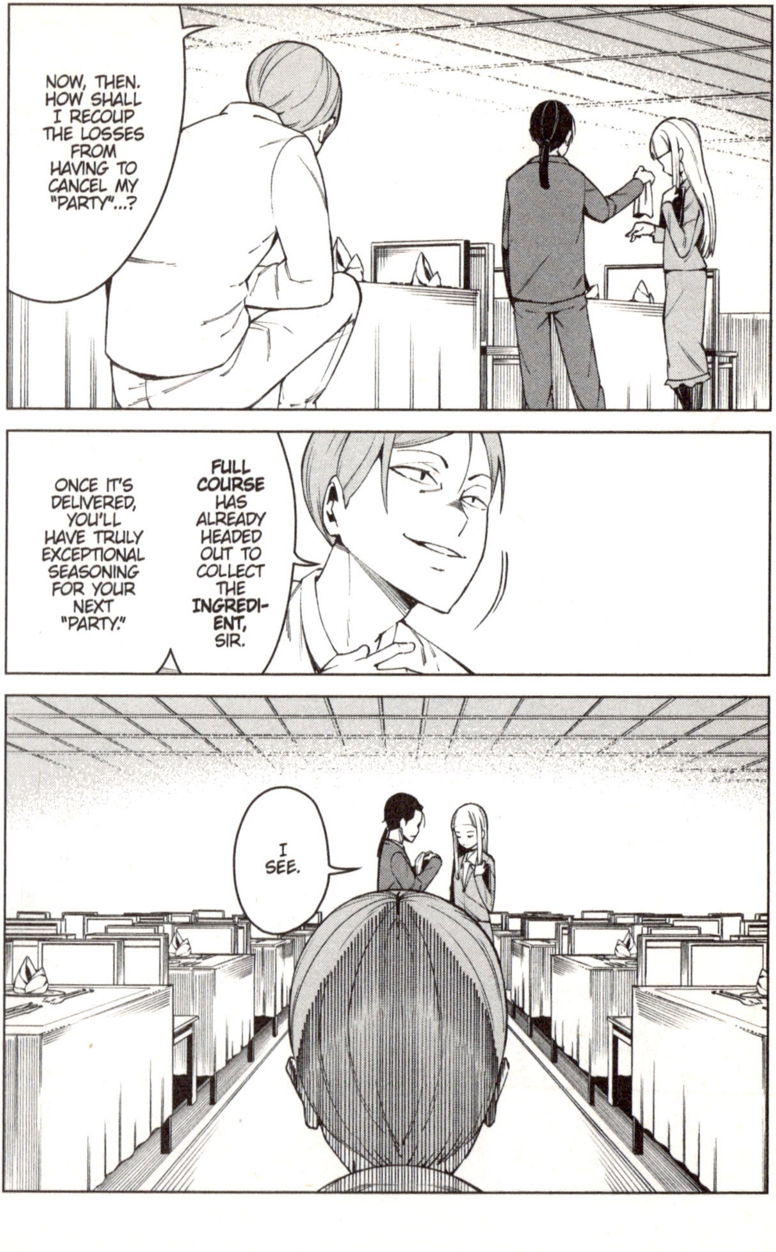
NOW, THEN. HOW SHALL I RECOUP THE LOSSES FROM HAVING TO CANCEL MY "PARTY"...?
**FULL COURSE** HAS ALREADY HEADED OUT TO COLLECT THE **INGREDIENT,** SIR.
ONCE IT'S DELIVERED, YOU'LL HAVE TRULY EXCEPTIONAL SEASONING FOR YOUR NEXT "PARTY."
I SEE.

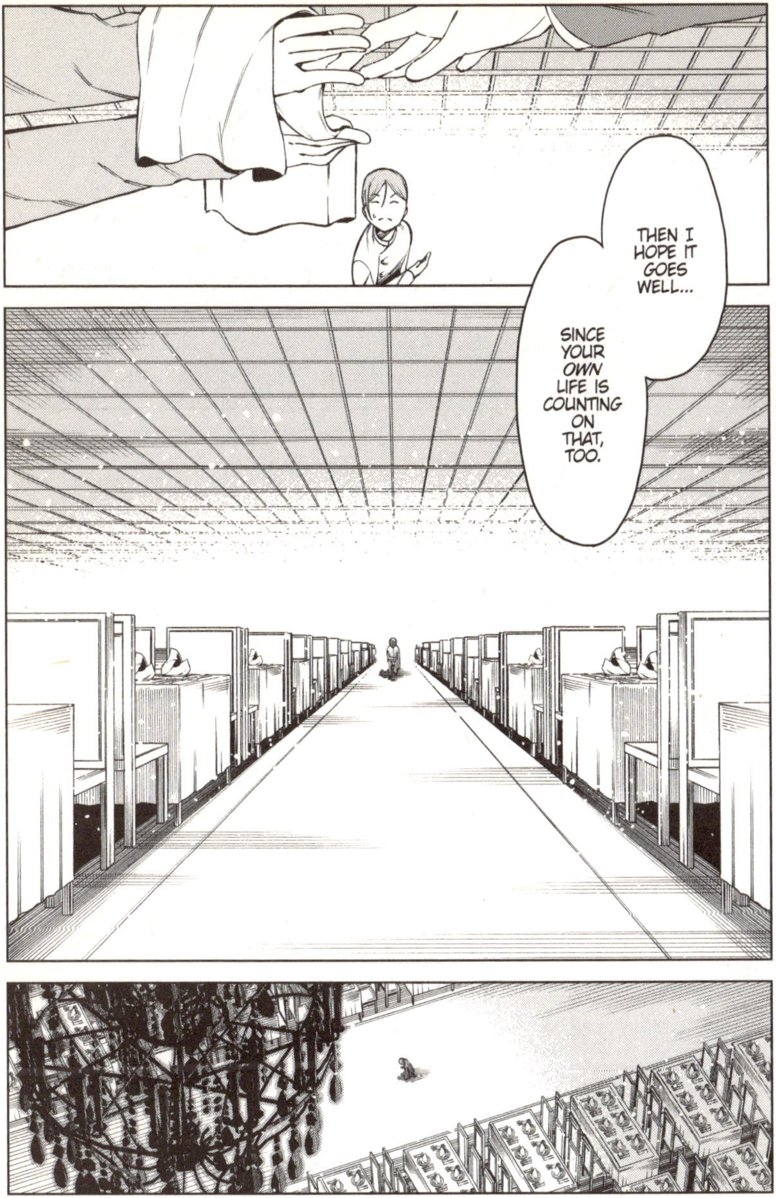
THEN I HOPE IT GOES WELL...
SINCE YOUR *OWN* LIFE IS COUNTING ON THAT, TOO.

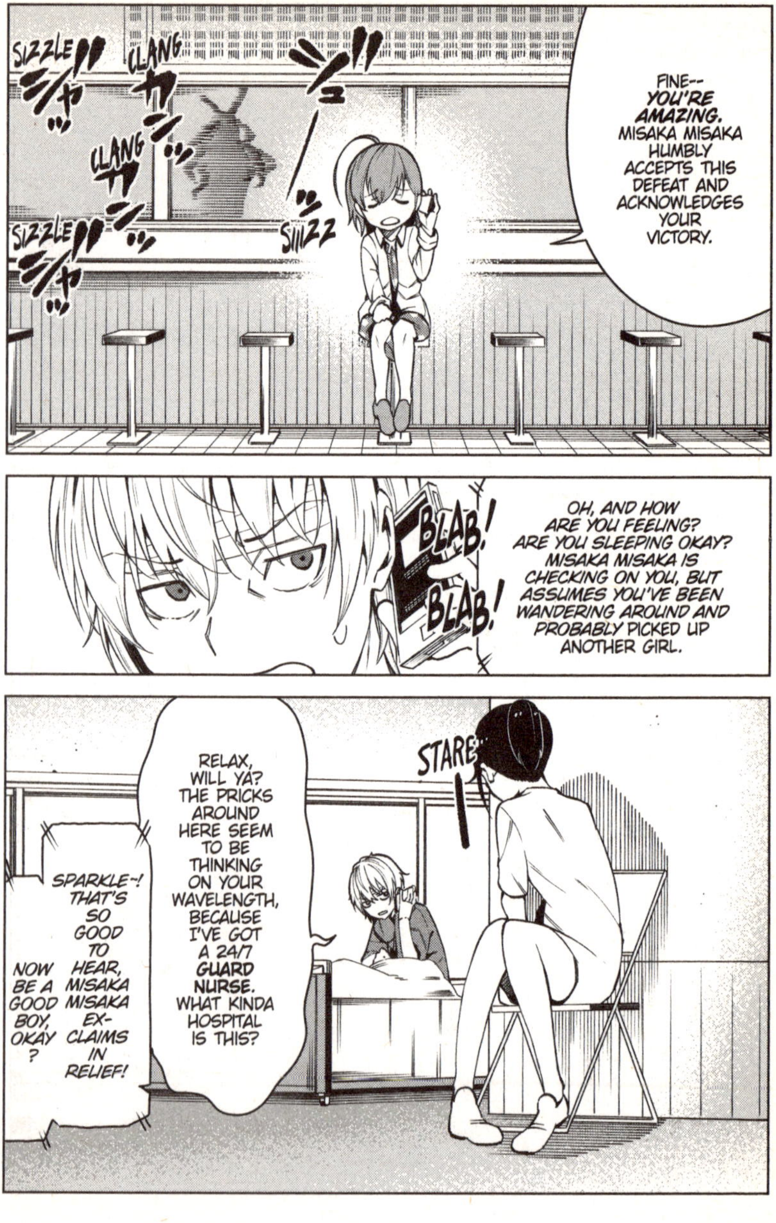
FINE-- YOU'RE AMAZING. MISAKA MISAKA HUMBLY ACCEPTS THIS DEFEAT AND ACKNOWLEDGES YOUR VICTORY.
SIIZZ
CLANG
CLANG
SIZZLE
SIZZLE
OH, AND HOW ARE YOU FEELING? ARE YOU SLEEPING OKAY? MISAKA MISAKA IS CHECKING ON YOU, BUT ASSUMES YOU'VE BEEN WANDERING AROUND AND PROBABLY PICKED UP ANOTHER GIRL.
BLAB! BLAB!
STARE
RELAX, WILL YA? THE PRICKS AROUND HERE SEEM TO BE THINKING ON YOUR WAVELENGTH, BECAUSE I'VE GOT A 24/7 GUARD NURSE. WHAT KINDA HOSPITAL IS THIS?
SPARKLE~! THAT'S SO GOOD TO HEAR, MISAKA MISAKA EX-CLAIMS IN RELIEF!
NOW BE A GOOD BOY, OKAY?

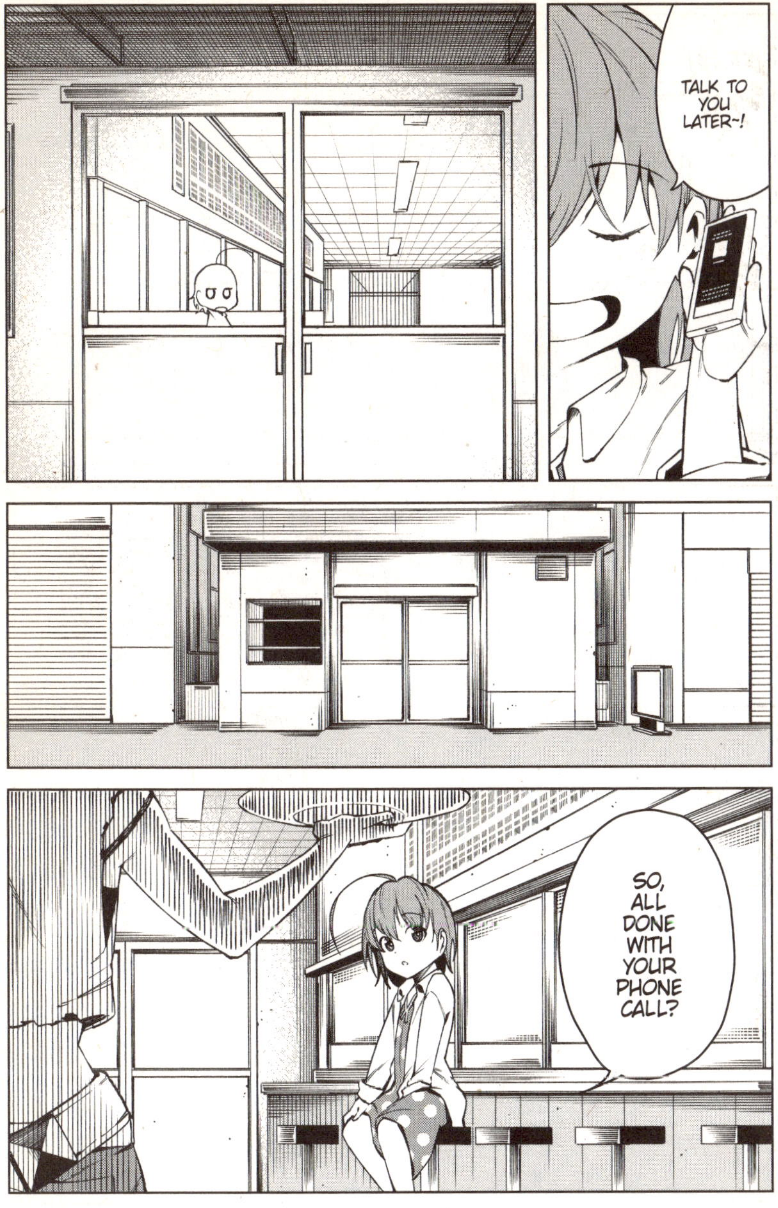
TALK TO YOU LATER~!
SO, ALL DONE WITH YOUR PHONE CALL?

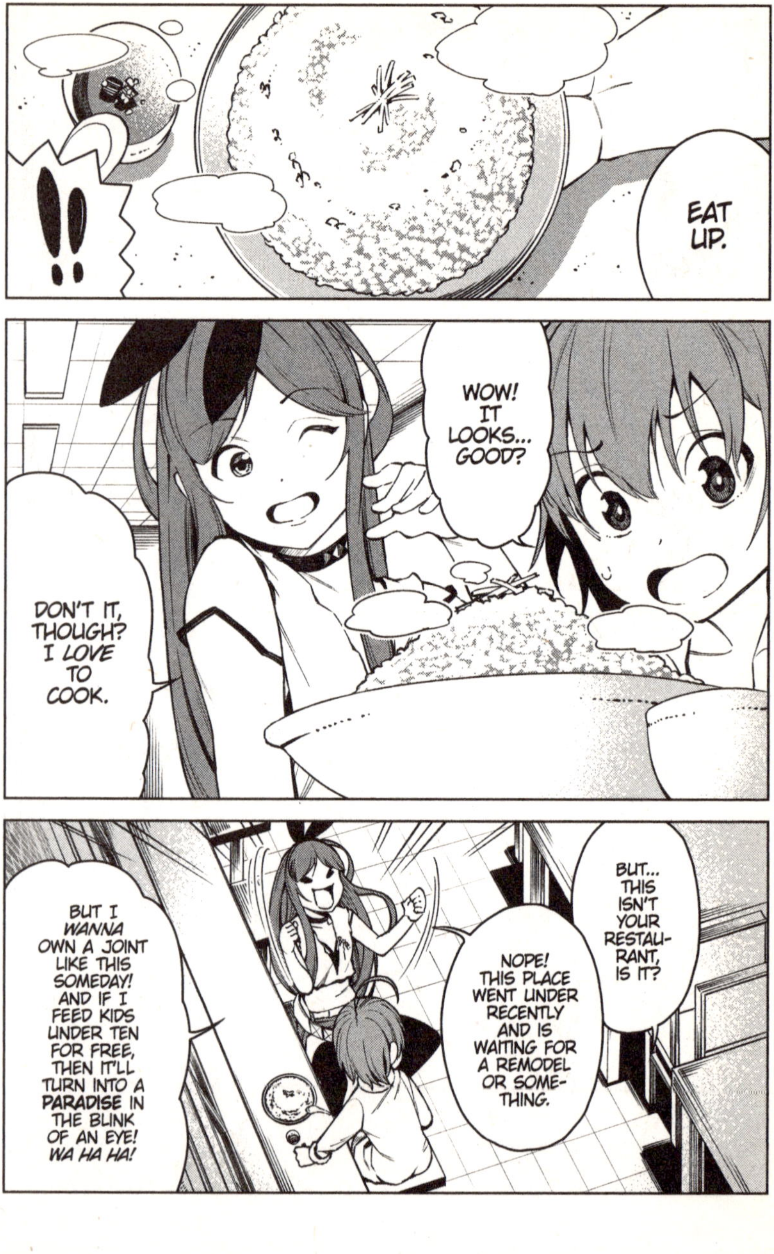
EAT UP.
!!
WOW! IT LOOKS... GOOD?
DON'T IT, THOUGH? I *LOVE* TO COOK.
BUT... THIS ISN'T YOUR RESTAU-RANT, IS IT?
NOPE! THIS PLACE WENT UNDER RECENTLY AND IS WAITING FOR A REMODEL OR SOME-THING.
BUT I *WANNA* OWN A JOINT LIKE THIS SOMEDAY! AND IF I FEED KIDS UNDER TEN FOR FREE, THEN IT'LL TURN INTO A **PARADISE** IN THE BLINK OF AN EYE! *WA HA HA!*

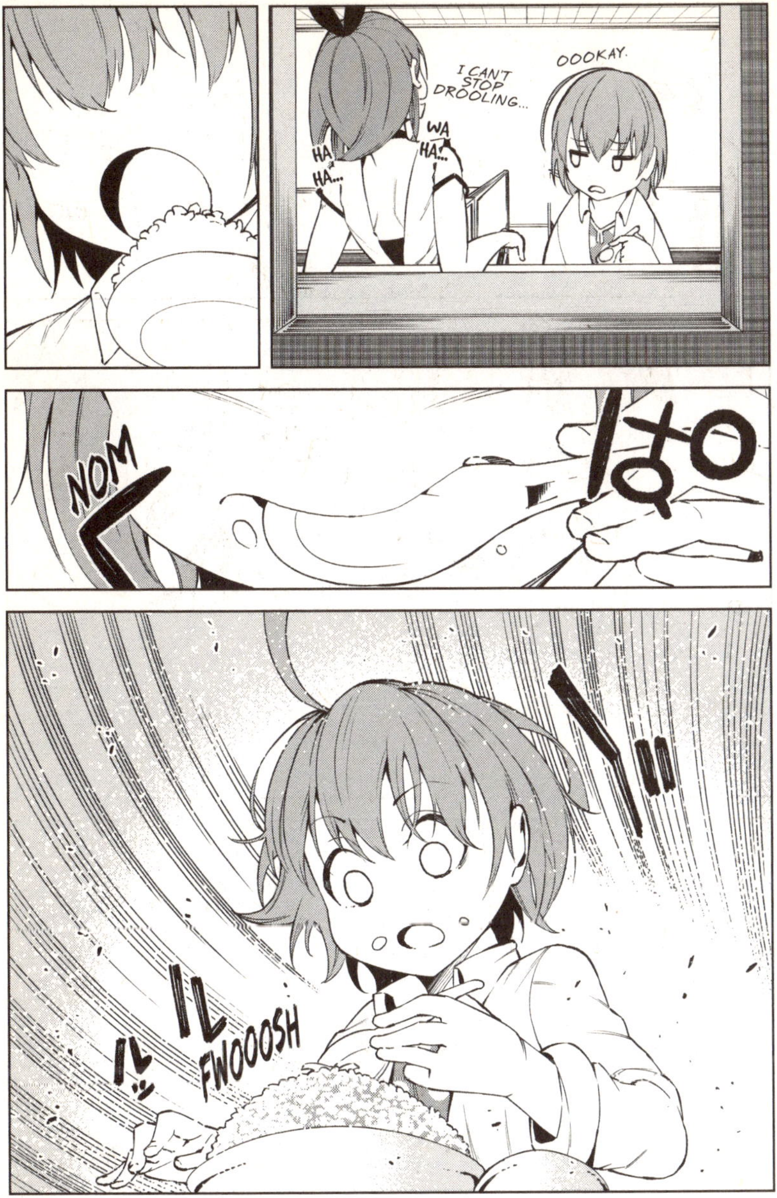
OOOKAY.
I CAN'T STOP DROOLING...
WA HA...
HA HA...
は
NOM
FWOOOSH
ハッ

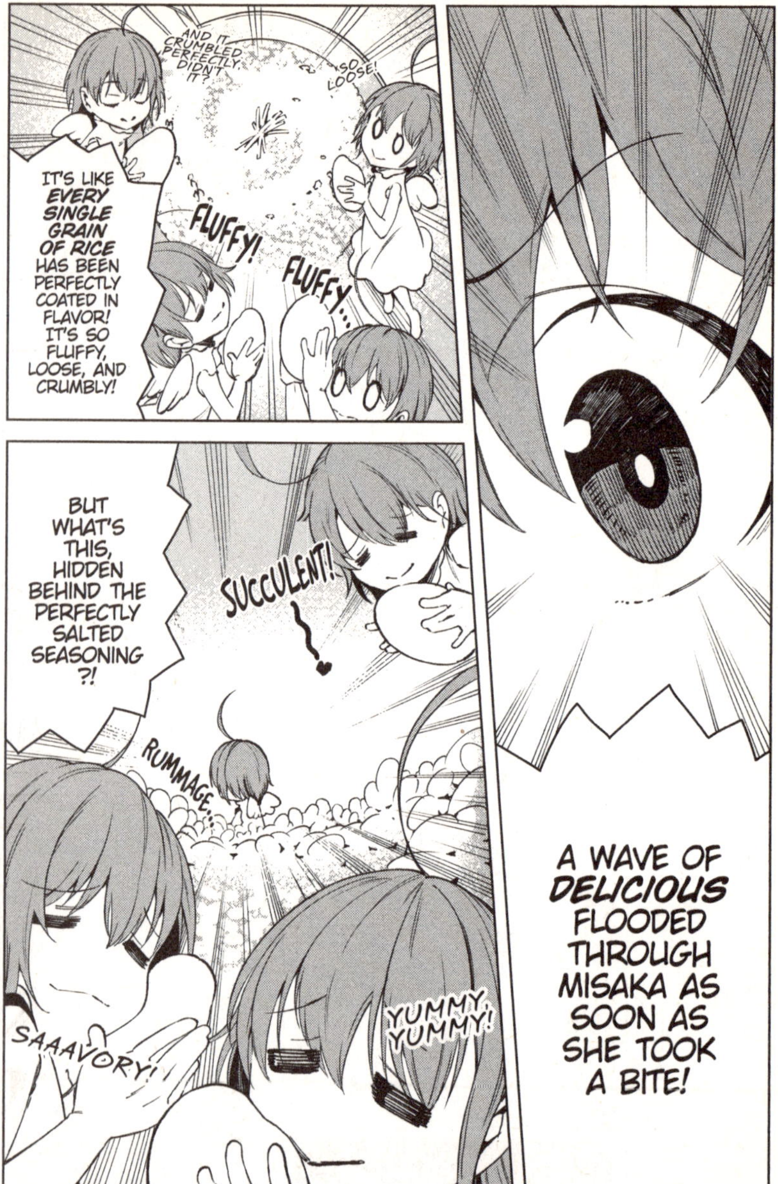
A WAVE OF DELICIOUS FLOODED THROUGH MISAKA AS SOON AS SHE TOOK A BITE!
SO LOOSE!
AND IT CRUMBLED PERFECTLY, DIDN'T IT?
FLUFFY...
FLUFFY!
IT'S LIKE EVERY SINGLE GRAIN OF RICE HAS BEEN PERFECTLY COATED IN FLAVOR! IT'S SO FLUFFY, LOOSE, AND CRUMBLY!
SUCCULENT!
BUT WHAT'S THIS, HIDDEN BEHIND THE PERFECTLY SALTED SEASONING?!
RUMMAGE...
YUMMY, YUMMY!
SAAAVORY!

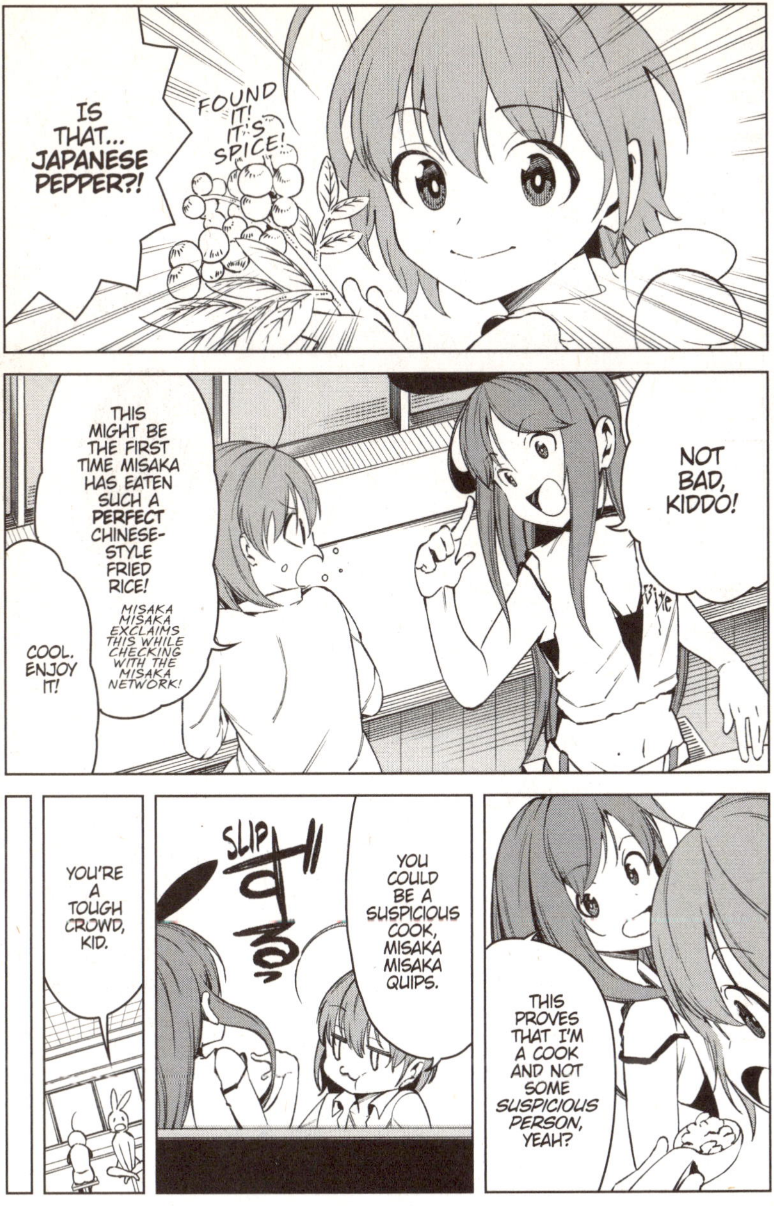
FOUND IT! IT'S SPICE!
IS THAT... JAPANESE PEPPER?!
NOT BAD, KIDDO!
THIS MIGHT BE THE FIRST TIME MISAKA HAS EATEN SUCH A PERFECT CHINESE-STYLE FRIED RICE!
MISAKA MISAKA EXCLAIMS THIS WHILE CHECKING WITH THE MISAKA NETWORK!
COOL. ENJOY IT!
THIS PROVES THAT I'M A COOK AND NOT SOME SUSPICIOUS PERSON, YEAH?
YOU COULD BE A SUSPICIOUS COOK, MISAKA MISAKA QUIPS.
SLIP
YOU'RE A TOUGH CROWD, KID.

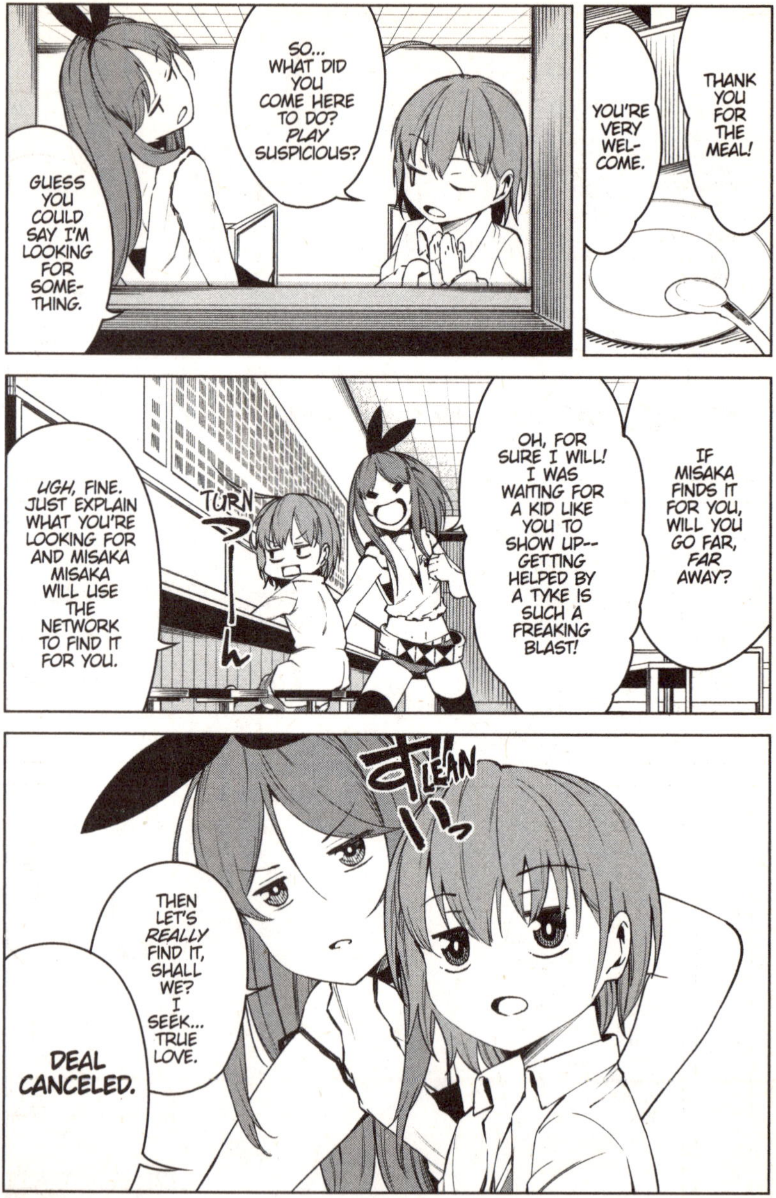
THANK YOU FOR THE MEAL!
YOU'RE VERY WEL-COME.
SO... WHAT DID YOU COME HERE TO DO? *PLAY* SUSPICIOUS?
GUESS YOU COULD SAY I'M LOOKING FOR SOME-THING.
IF MISAKA FINDS IT FOR YOU, WILL YOU GO FAR, *FAR* AWAY?
OH, FOR SURE I WILL! I WAS WAITING FOR A KID LIKE YOU TO SHOW UP-- GETTING HELPED BY A TYKE IS SUCH A FREAKING BLAST!
TURN
*UGH*, FINE. JUST EXPLAIN WHAT YOU'RE LOOKING FOR AND MISAKA MISAKA WILL USE THE NETWORK TO FIND IT FOR YOU.
LEAN
THEN LET'S *REALLY* FIND IT, SHALL WE? I SEEK... TRUE LOVE.
DEAL CANCELED.

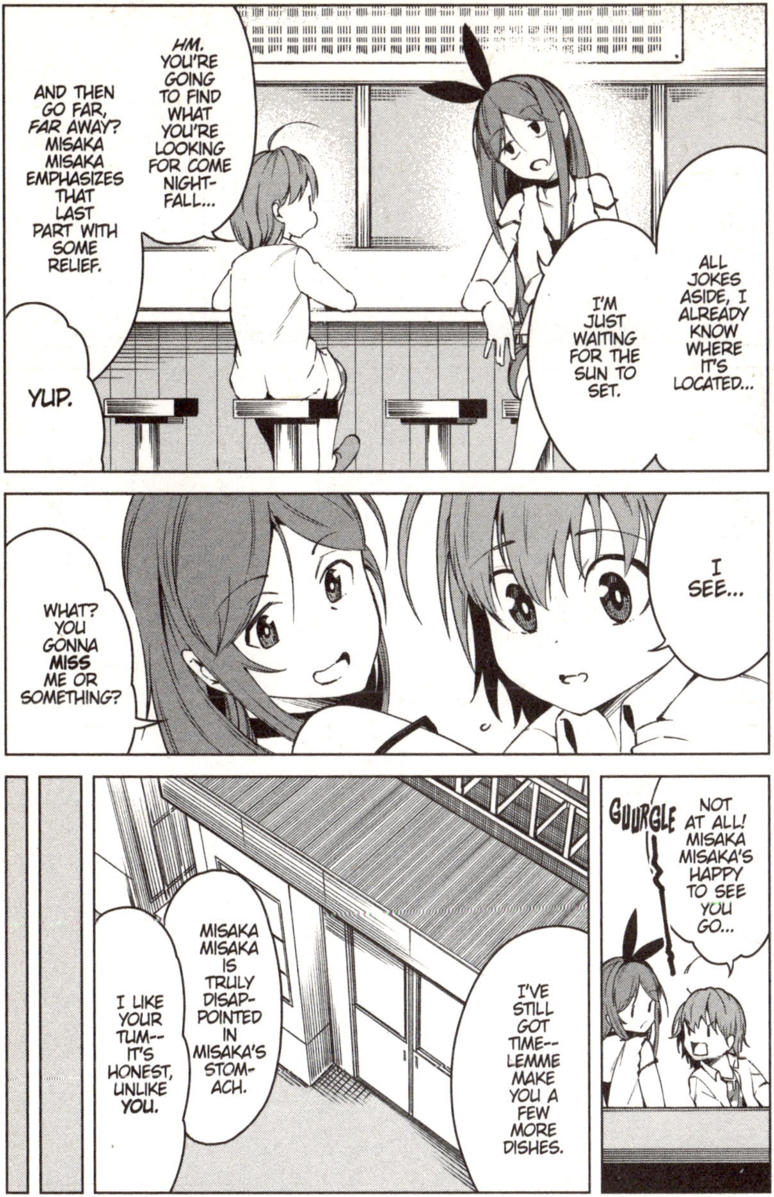
ALL JOKES ASIDE, I ALREADY KNOW WHERE IT'S LOCATED...
I'M JUST WAITING FOR THE SUN TO SET.
*HM.* YOU'RE GOING TO FIND WHAT YOU'RE LOOKING FOR COME NIGHTFALL...
AND THEN GO FAR, *FAR AWAY?* MISAKA MISAKA EMPHASIZES THAT LAST PART WITH SOME RELIEF.
YUP.
I SEE...
WHAT? YOU GONNA **MISS** ME OR SOMETHING?
NOT AT ALL! MISAKA MISAKA'S HAPPY TO SEE YOU GO...
GUURGLE
I'VE STILL GOT TIME--LEMME MAKE YOU A FEW MORE DISHES.
MISAKA MISAKA IS TRULY DISAPPOINTED IN MISAKA'S STOMACH.
I LIKE YOUR TUM--IT'S HONEST, UNLIKE **YOU.**

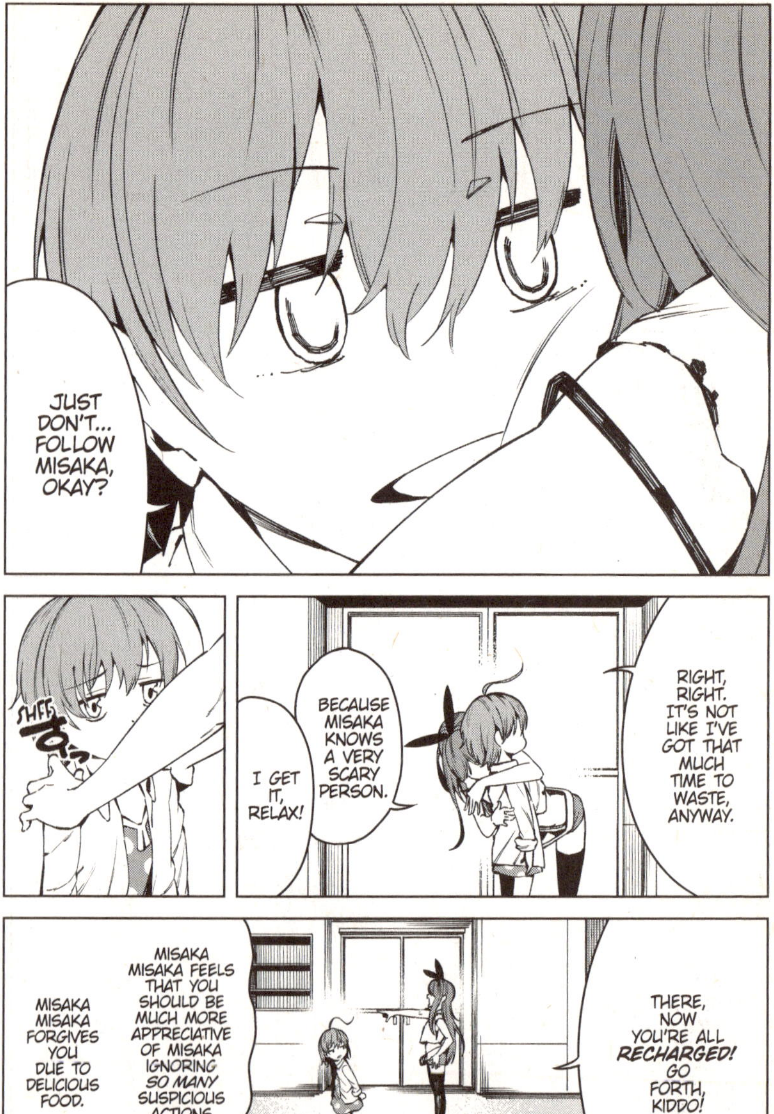
JUST DON'T... FOLLOW MISAKA, OKAY?
RIGHT, RIGHT. IT'S NOT LIKE I'VE GOT THAT MUCH TIME TO WASTE, ANYWAY.
BECAUSE MISAKA KNOWS A VERY SCARY PERSON.
I GET IT, RELAX!
SHFF
THERE, NOW YOU'RE ALL RECHARGED! GO FORTH, KIDDO!
MISAKA MISAKA FEELS THAT YOU SHOULD BE MUCH MORE APPRECIATIVE OF MISAKA IGNORING SO MANY SUSPICIOUS ACTIONS FROM YOU, BUT...
MISAKA MISAKA FORGIVES YOU DUE TO DELICIOUS FOOD.

SEE YAAA~!

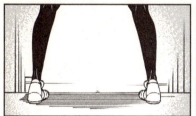

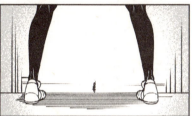

ALL RIGHT... TIME TO GET THIS SHOW ON THE ROAD.

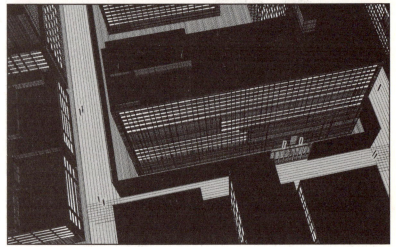

THEY SAY A PERSON YAWNS WHEN THEY'RE FEELING TOO RELAXED.

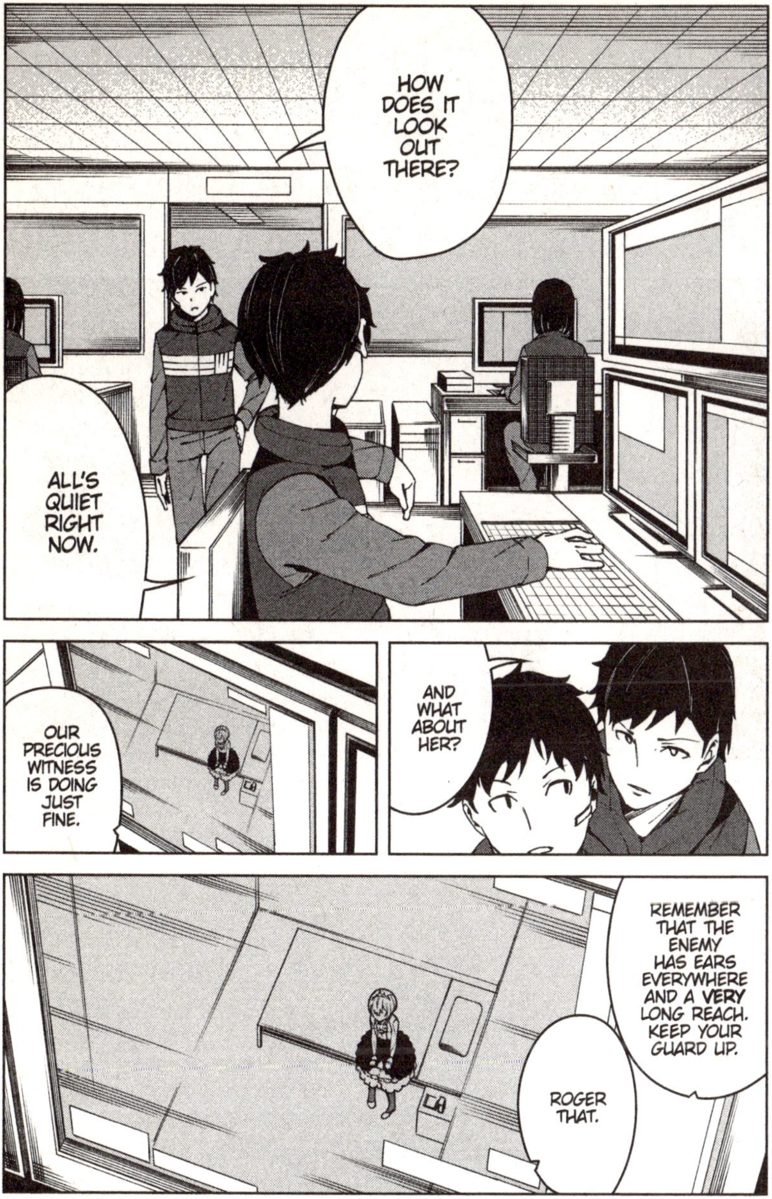
HOW DOES IT LOOK OUT THERE?
ALL'S QUIET RIGHT NOW.
AND WHAT ABOUT HER?
OUR PRECIOUS WITNESS IS DOING JUST FINE.
REMEMBER THAT THE ENEMY HAS EARS EVERYWHERE AND A **VERY** LONG REACH. KEEP YOUR GUARD UP.
ROGER THAT.

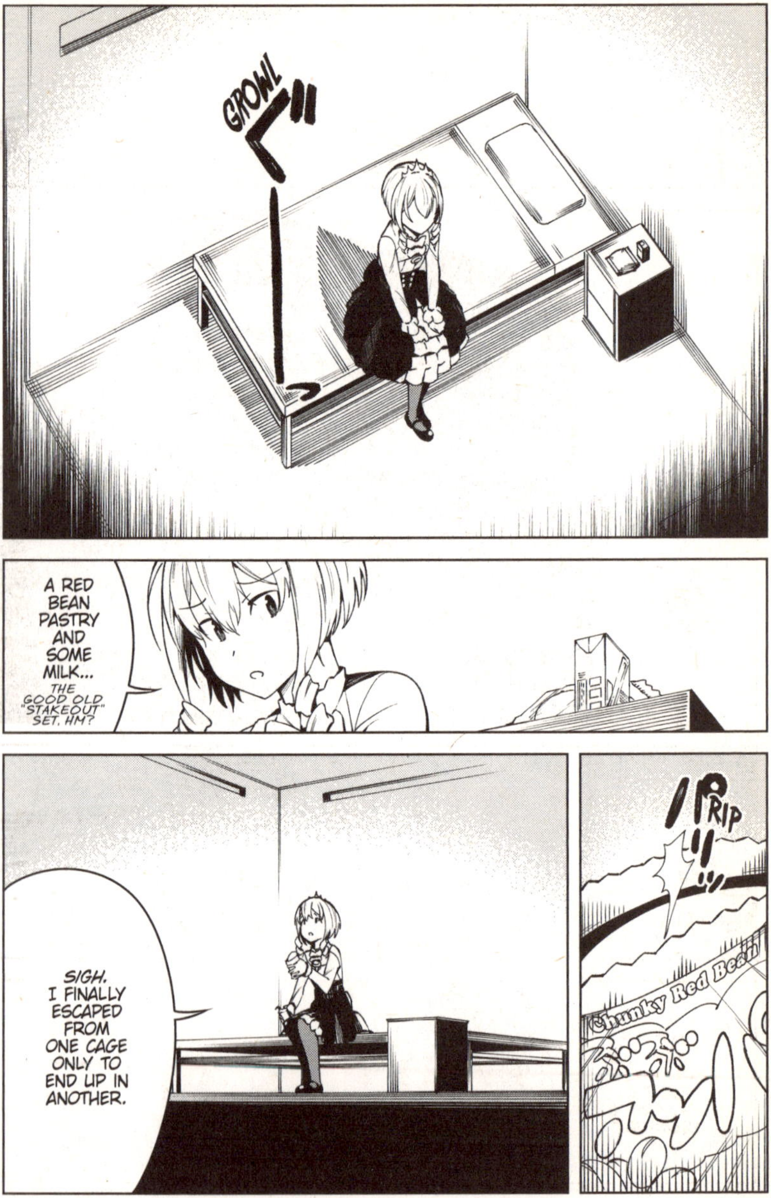
GROWL
A RED BEAN PASTRY AND SOME MILK...
THE GOOD OLD "STAKEOUT" SET, HM?
RIP
Chunky Red Bean
SIGH. I FINALLY ESCAPED FROM ONE CAGE ONLY TO END UP IN ANOTHER.

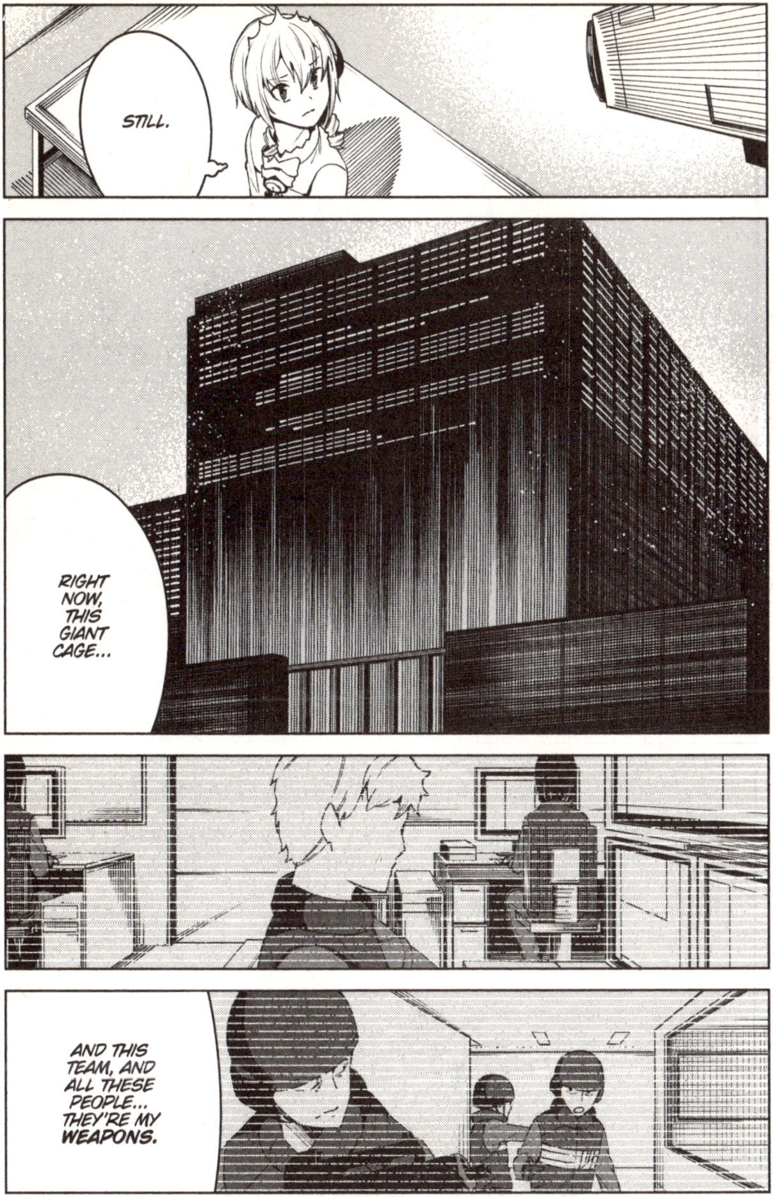
STILL.
RIGHT NOW, THIS GIANT CAGE...
AND THIS TEAM, AND ALL THESE PEOPLE... THEY'RE MY WEAPONS.

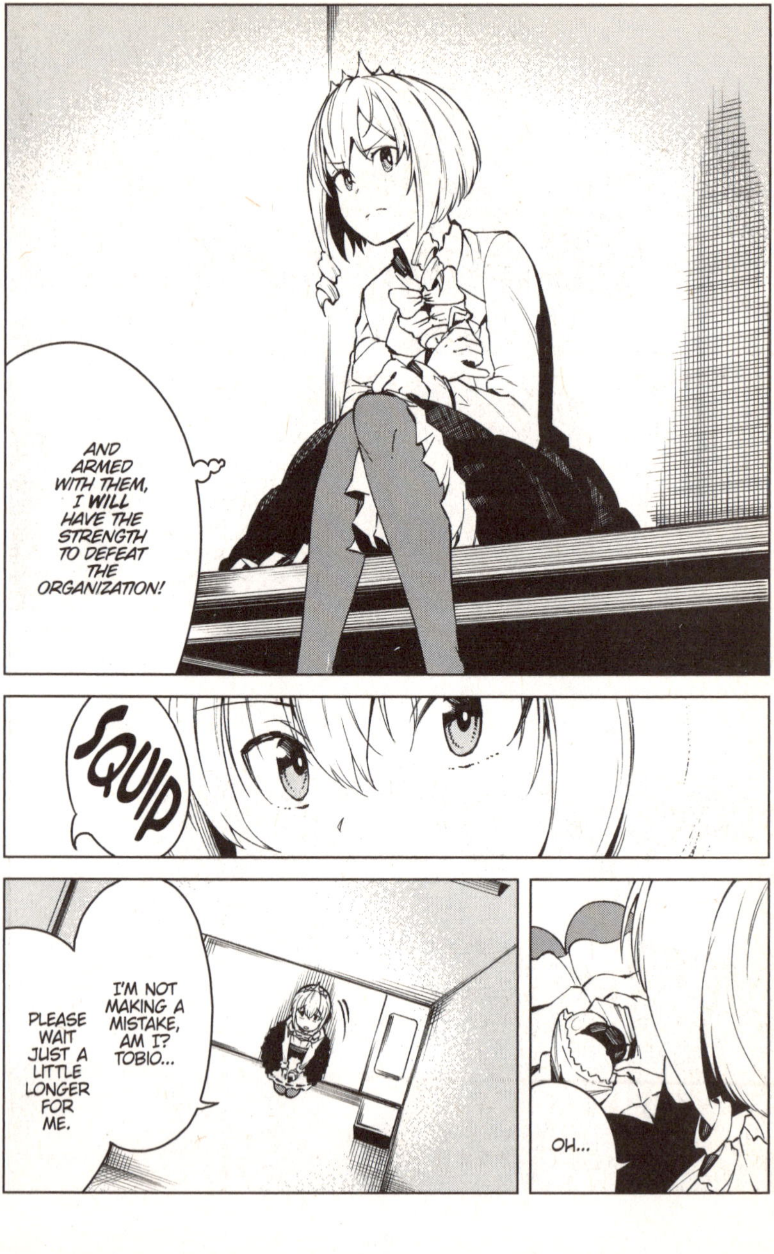
AND ARMED WITH THEM, I WILL HAVE THE STRENGTH TO DEFEAT THE ORGANIZATION!
SQUIP
OH...
I'M NOT MAKING A MISTAKE, AM I? TOBIO...
PLEASE WAIT JUST A LITTLE LONGER FOR ME.

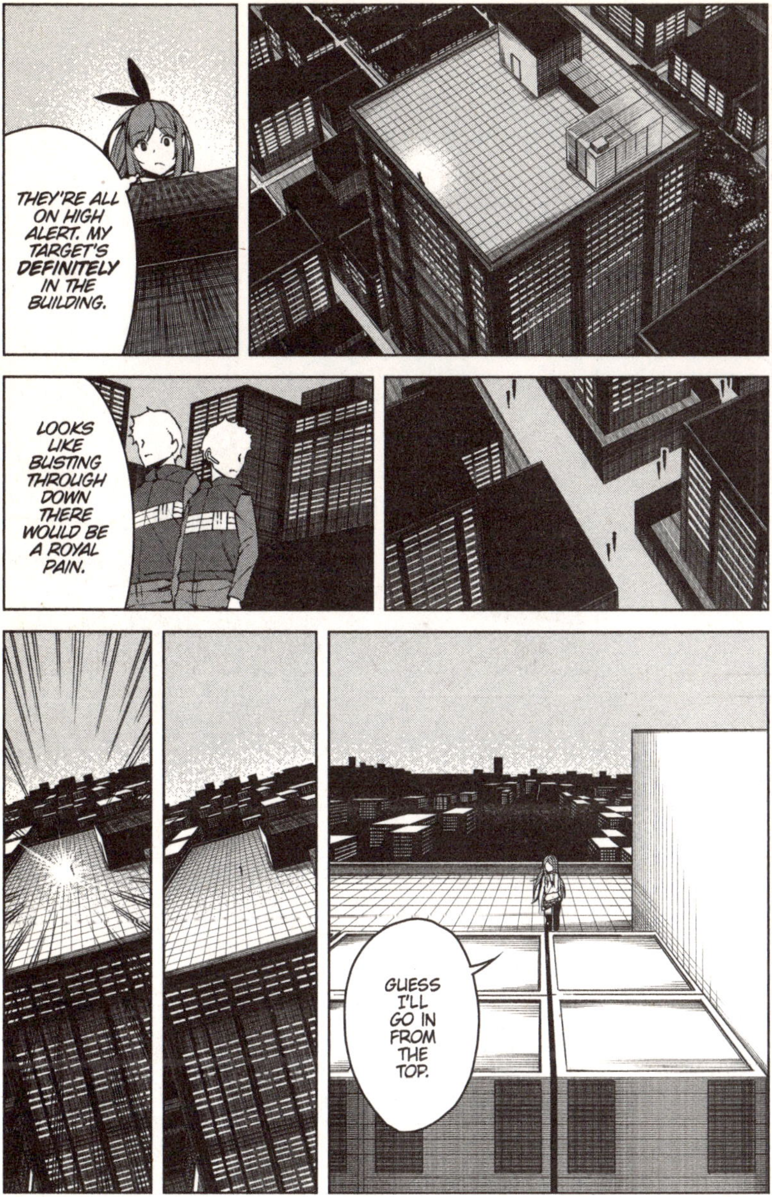
THEY'RE ALL ON HIGH ALERT. MY TARGET'S DEFINITELY IN THE BUILDING.
LOOKS LIKE BUSTING THROUGH DOWN THERE WOULD BE A ROYAL PAIN.
GUESS I'LL GO IN FROM THE TOP.

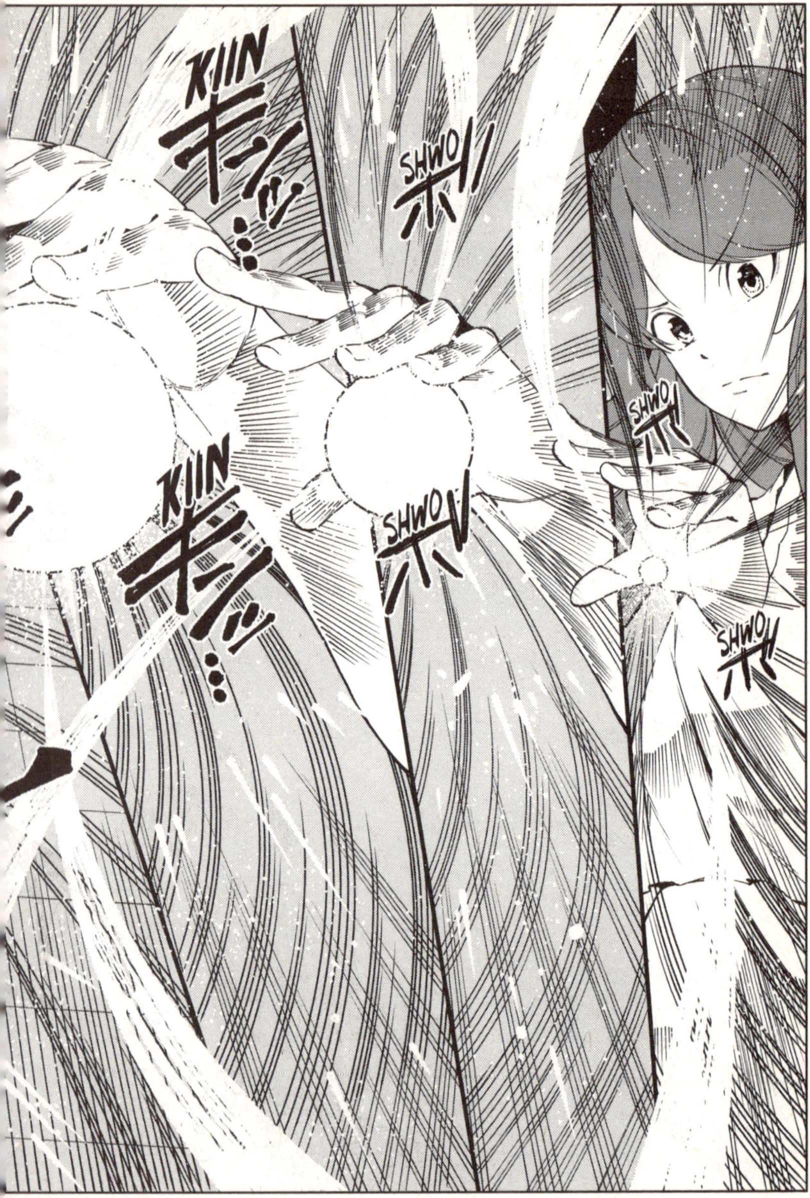
SHWO
KIIN
SHWO
SHWO
SHWO
KIIN

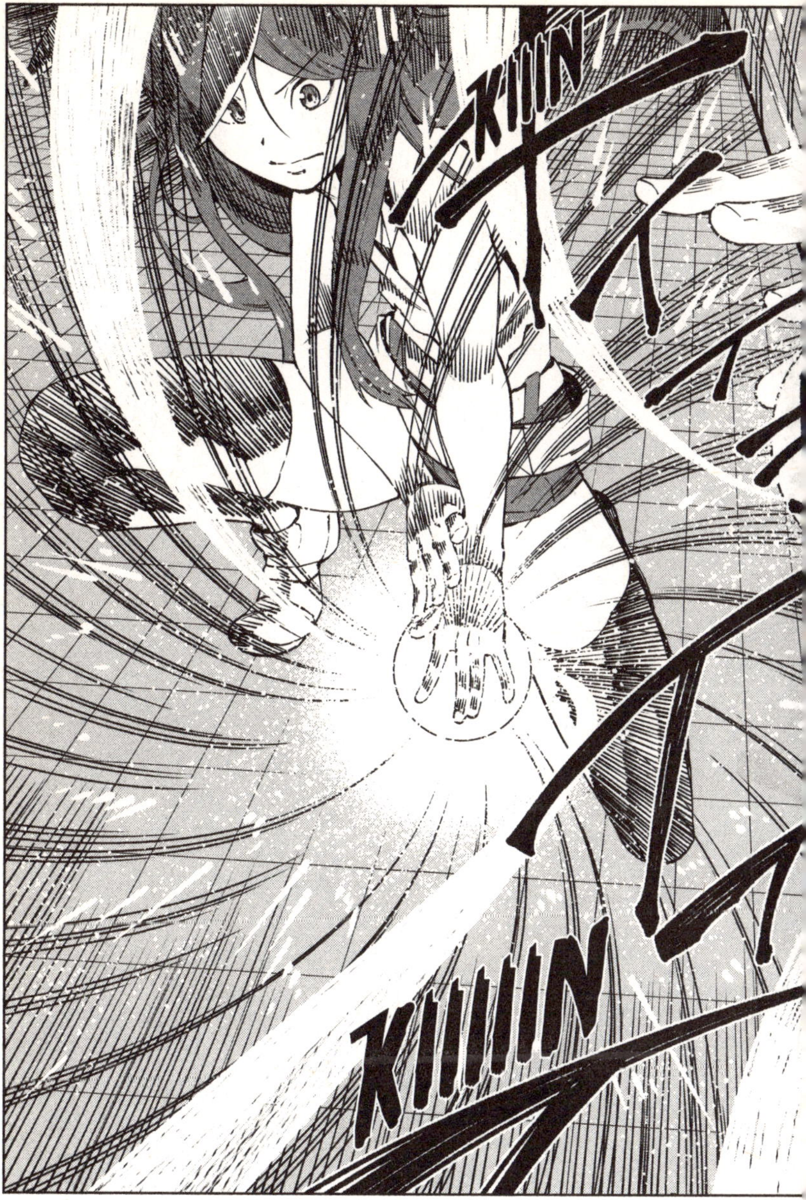
KIIIN
KIIIIN

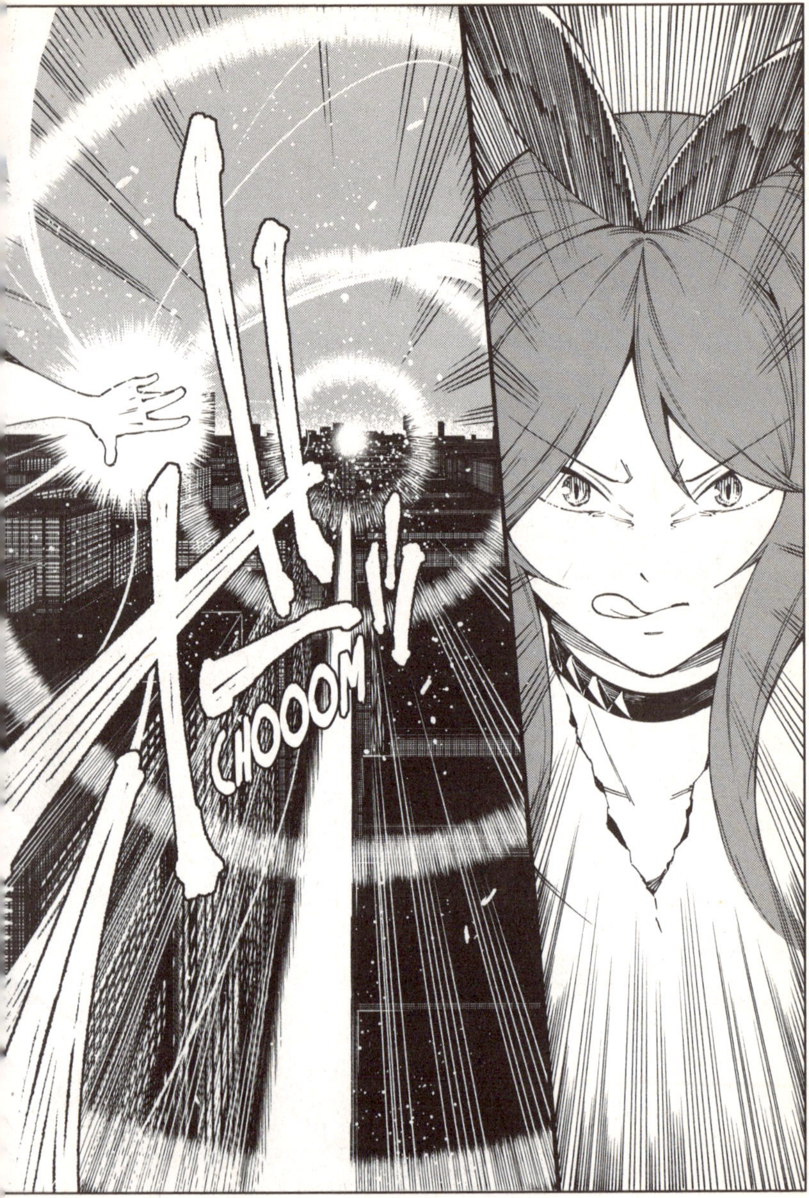
CHOOOM

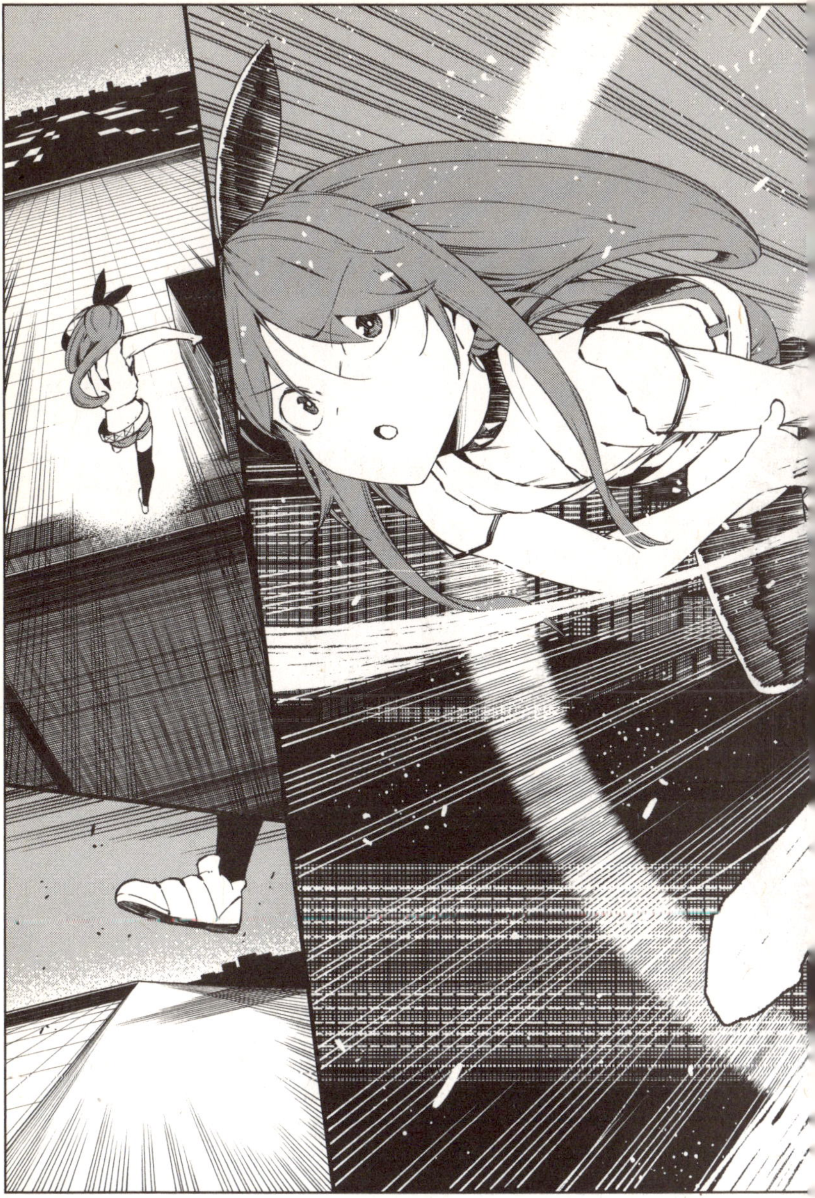

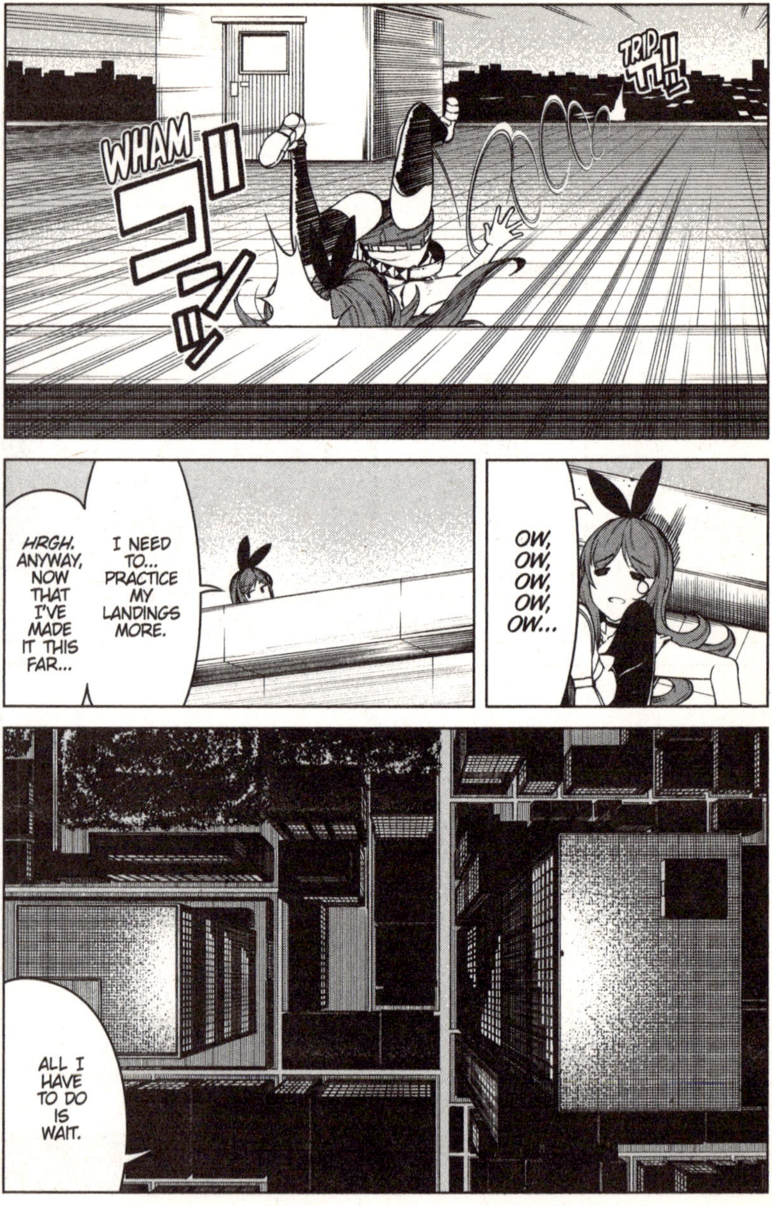

TRIP
WHAM
OW, OW, OW, OW, OW...
I NEED TO... PRACTICE MY LANDINGS MORE.
HRGH. ANYWAY, NOW THAT I'VE MADE IT THIS FAR...
ALL I HAVE TO DO IS WAIT.

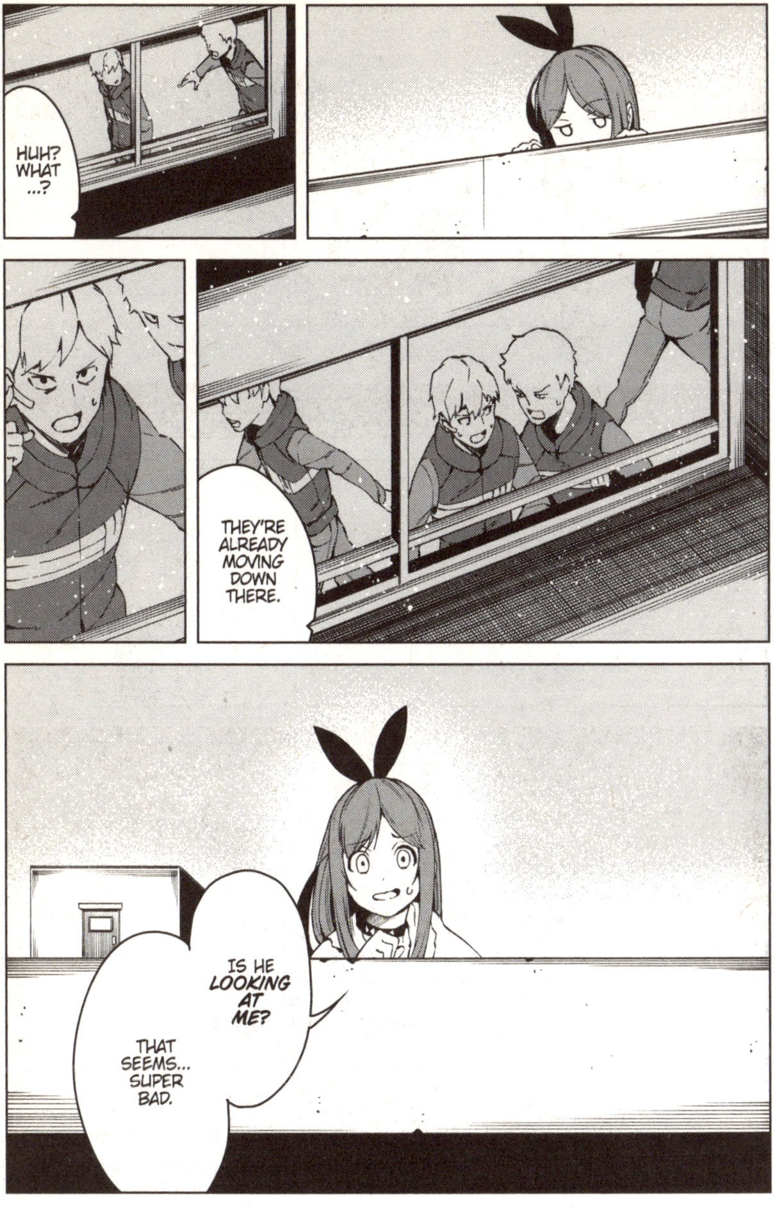
HUH? WHAT ...?
THEY'RE ALREADY MOVING DOWN THERE.
IS HE *LOOKING AT ME?*
THAT SEEMS... SUPER BAD.

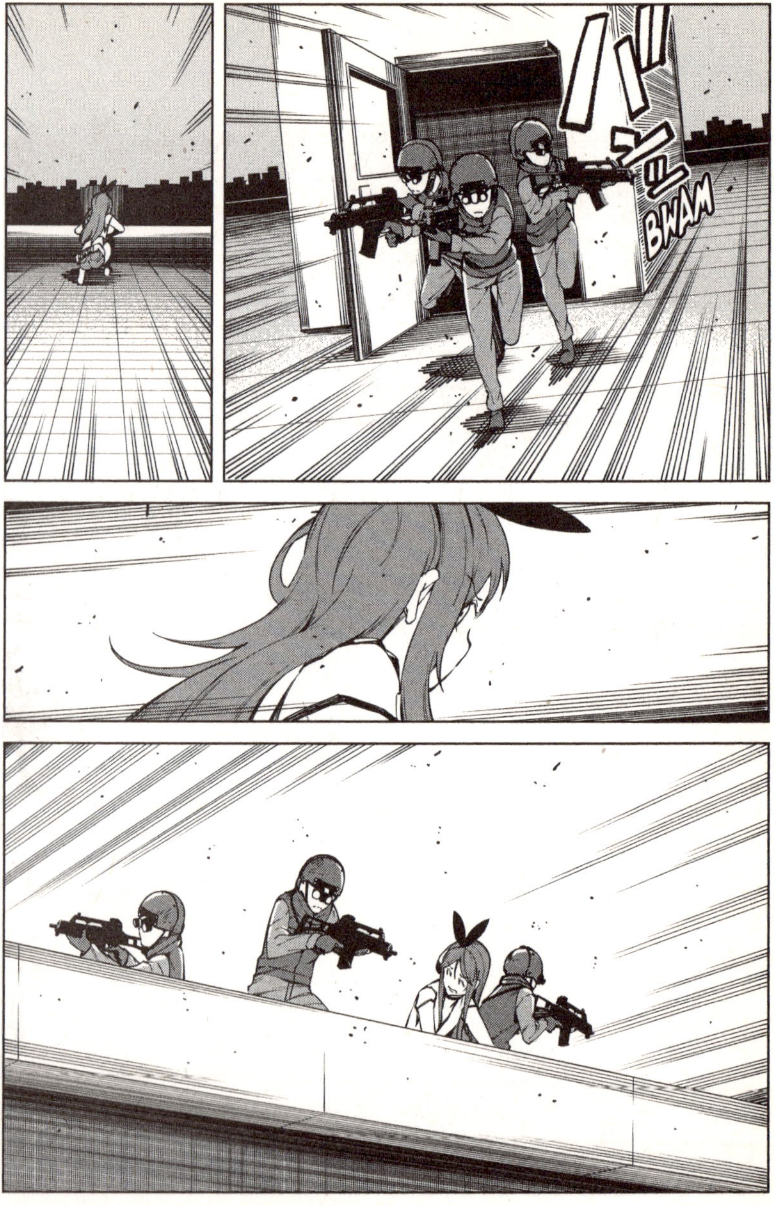
BWAM

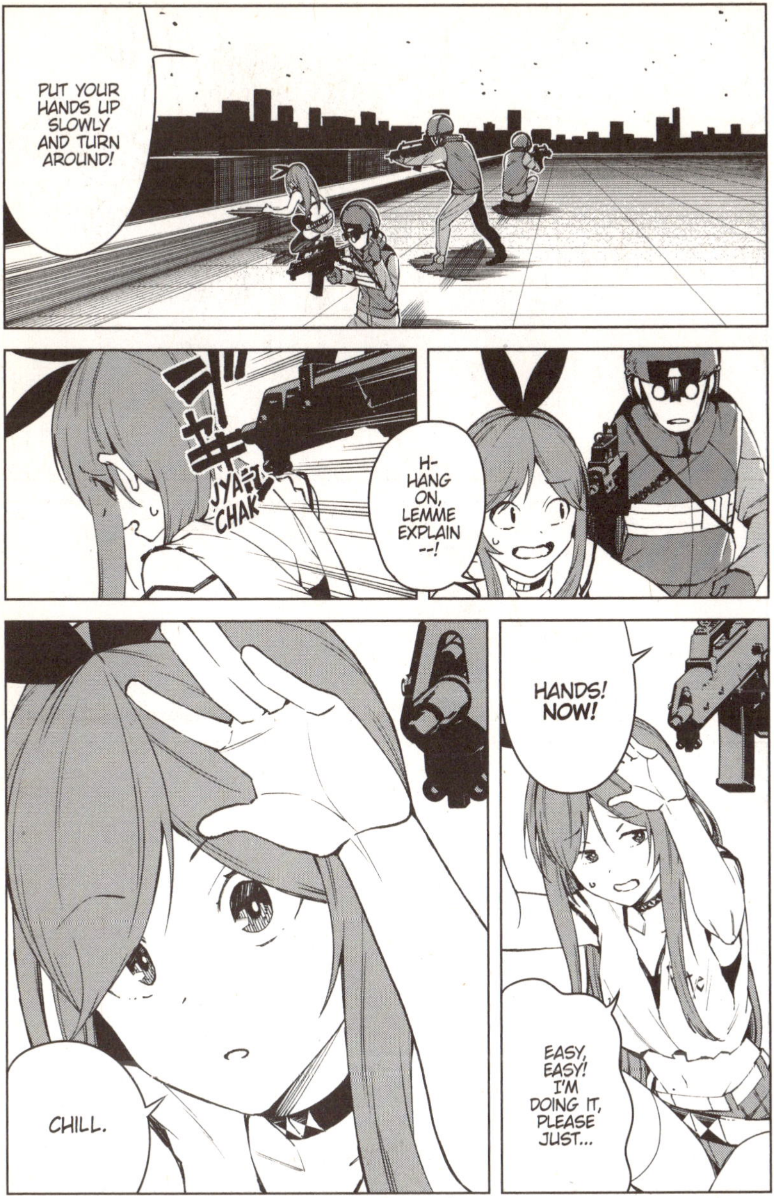
PUT YOUR HANDS UP SLOWLY AND TURN AROUND!
H-HANG ON, LEMME EXPLAIN --!
JYA CHAK
HANDS! NOW!
EASY, EASY! I'M DOING IT, PLEASE JUST...
CHILL.

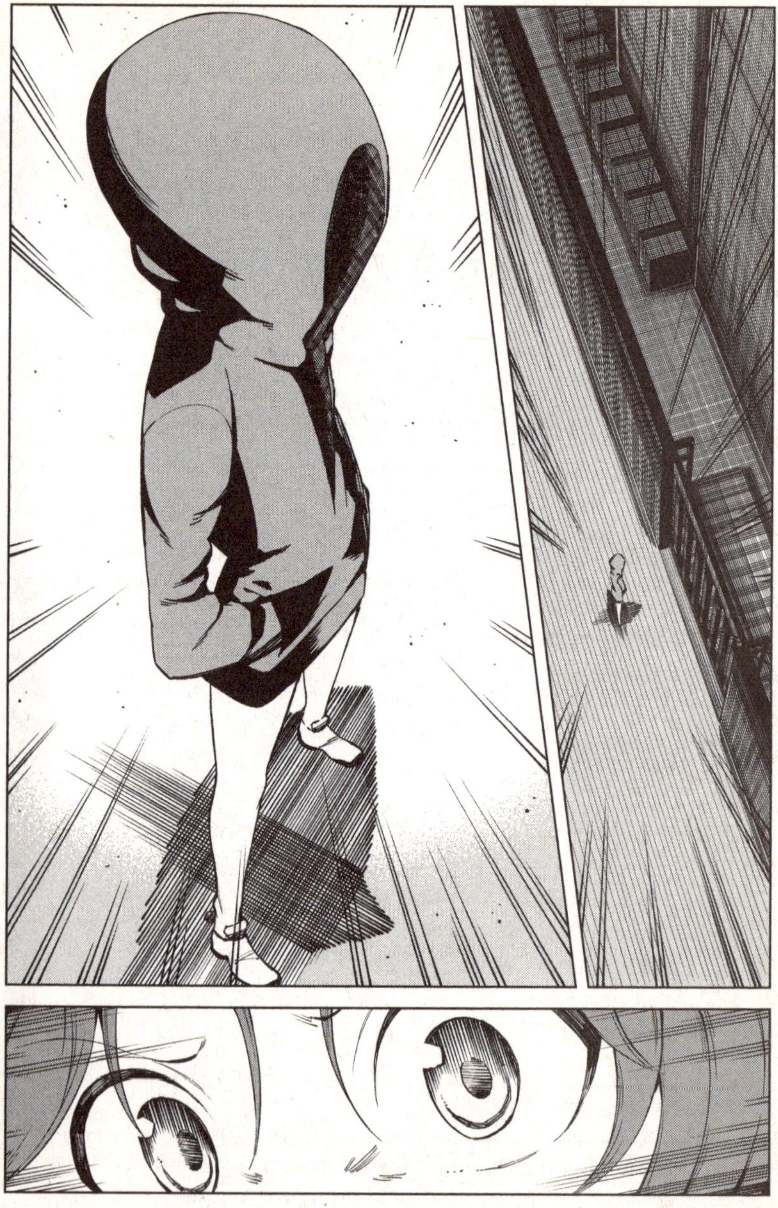

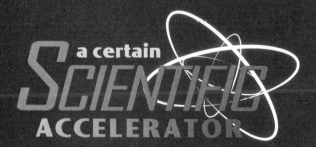

a certain
SCIENTIFIC
ACCELERATOR

とある科学の一方通行

アクセラレータ

とある魔術の禁書目録外伝

# CHAPTER 45

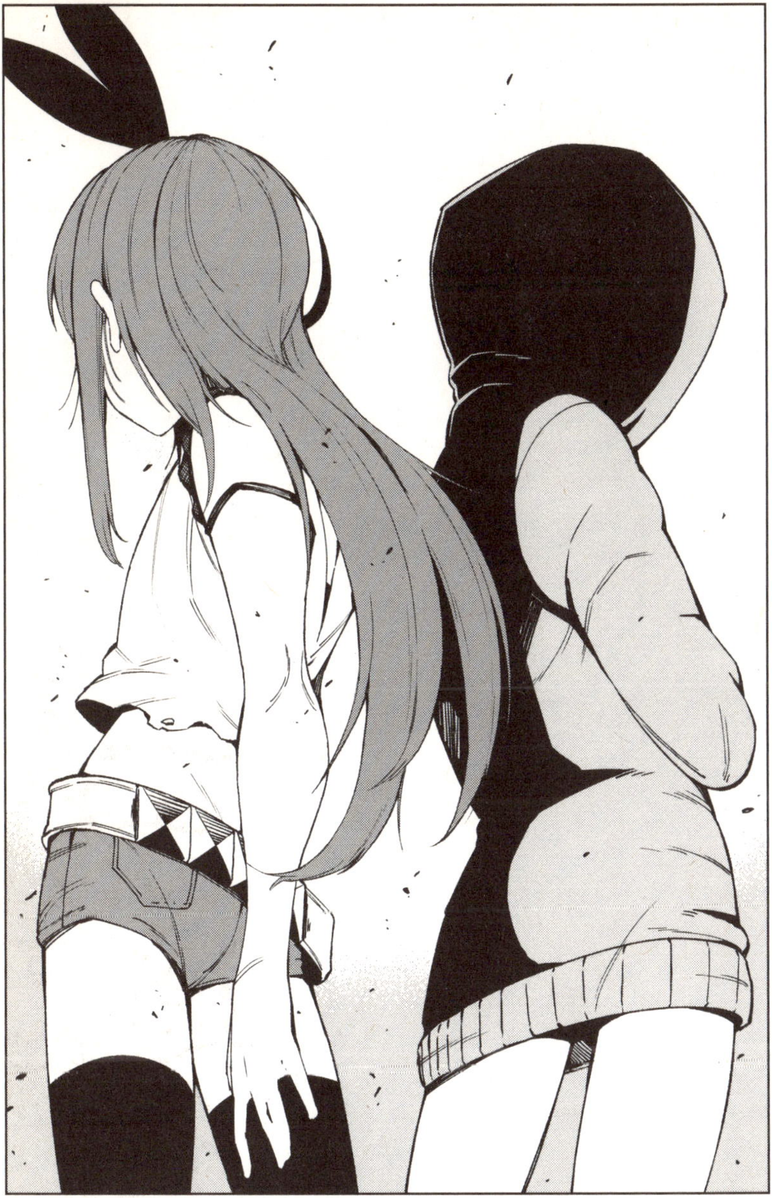

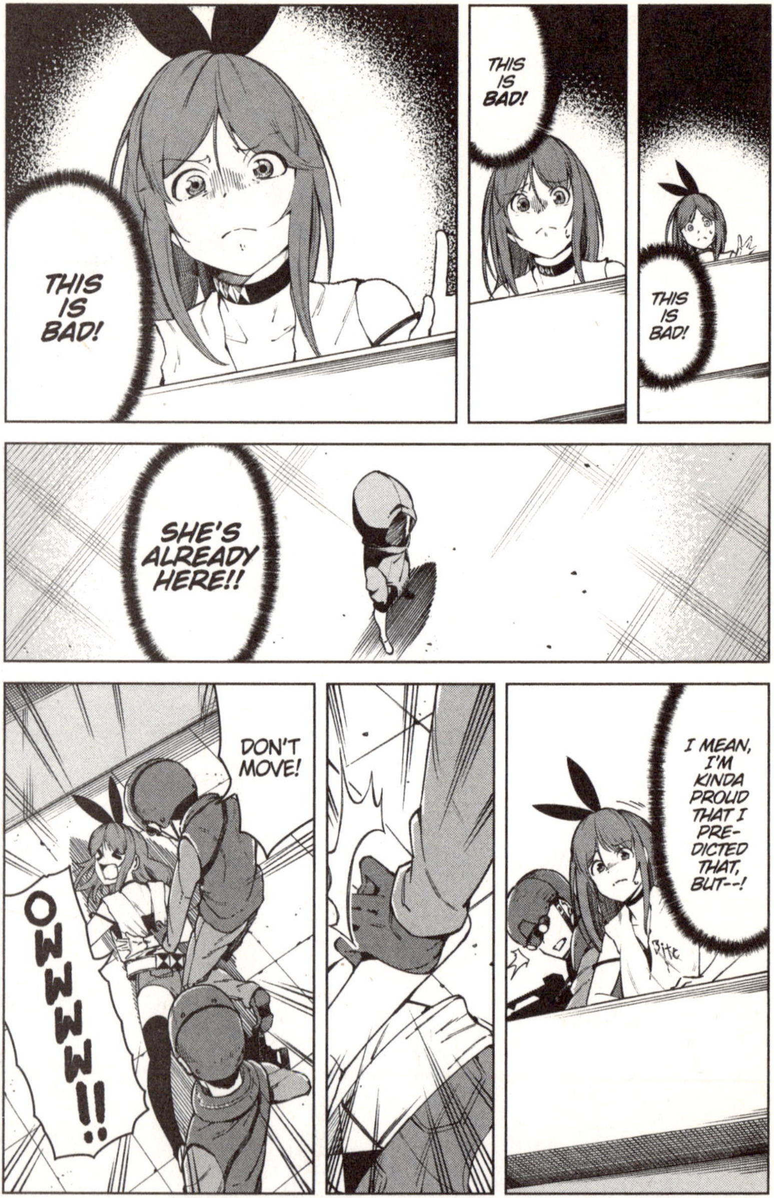
THIS IS BAD!
THIS IS BAD!
THIS IS BAD!
SHE'S ALREADY HERE!!
I MEAN, I'M KINDA PROUD THAT I PRE-DICTED THAT, BUT--!
DON'T MOVE!
OWWWW!!

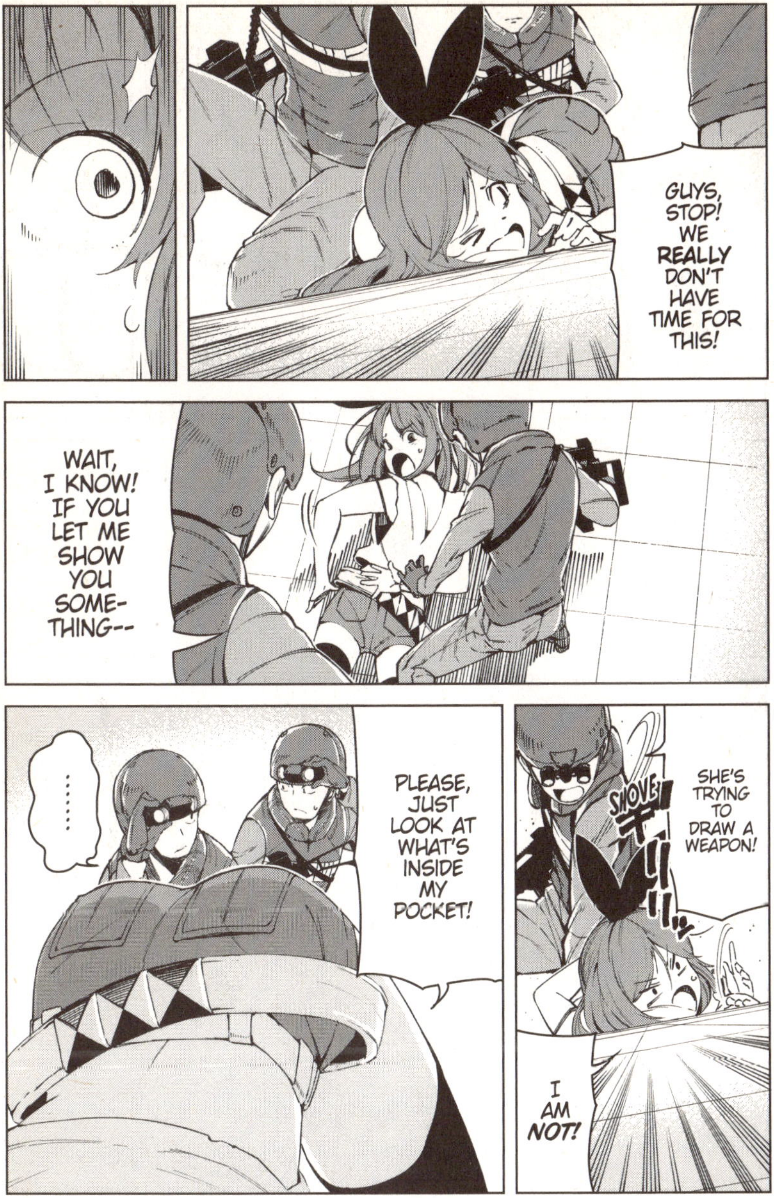
GUYS, STOP! WE REALLY DON'T HAVE TIME FOR THIS!
WAIT, I KNOW! IF YOU LET ME SHOW YOU SOME-THING--
......
PLEASE, JUST LOOK AT WHAT'S INSIDE MY POCKET!
SHE'S TRYING TO DRAW A WEAPON!
SHOVE
I AM NOT!

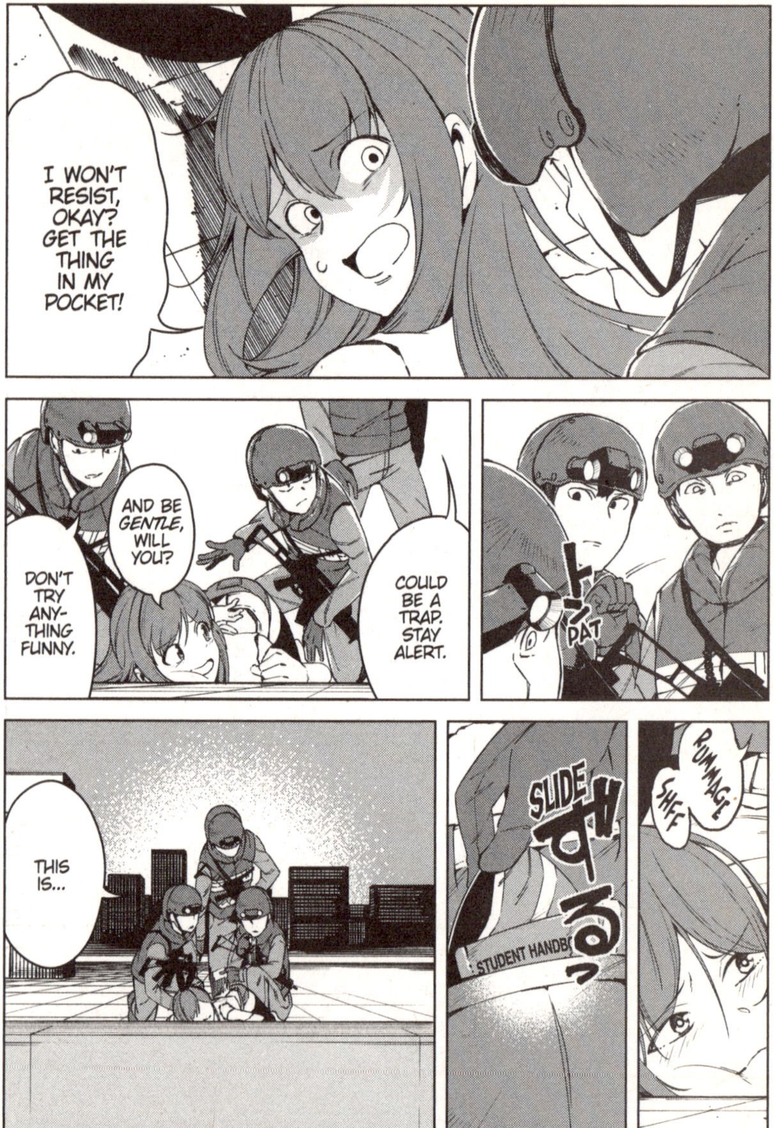
I WON'T RESIST, OKAY? GET THE THING IN MY POCKET!
PAT
COULD BE A TRAP. STAY ALERT.
AND BE GENTLE, WILL YOU?
DON'T TRY ANY-THING FUNNY.
RUMMAGE
SHFF
SLIDE
STUDENT HANDB
THIS IS...

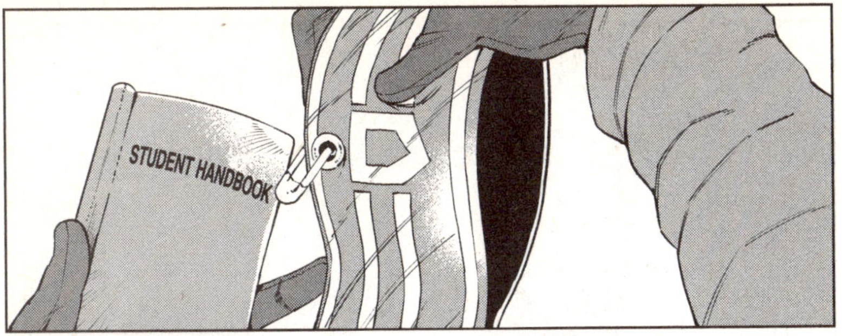
STUDENT HANDBOOK

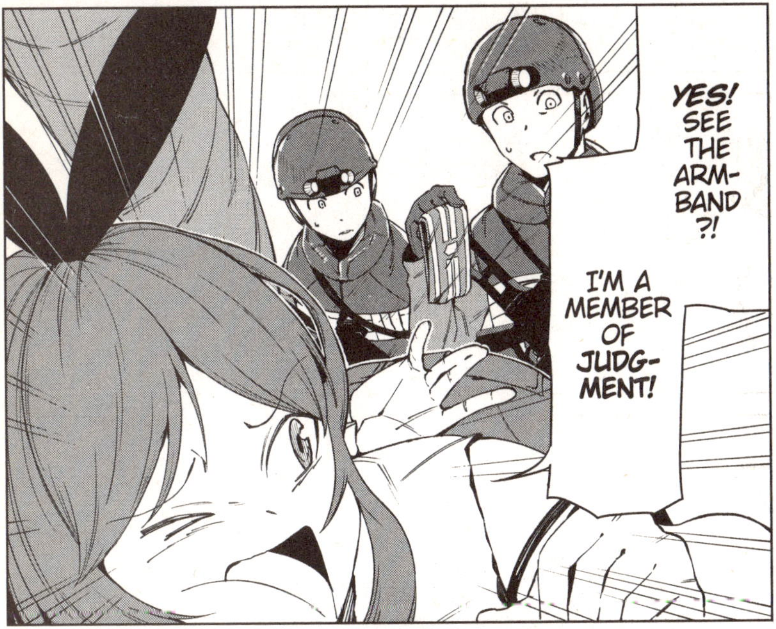
YES! SEE THE ARM-BAND?!
I'M A MEMBER OF JUDG-MENT!

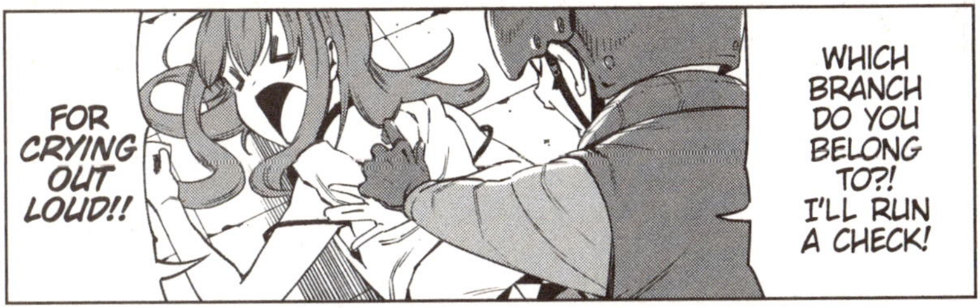
WHICH BRANCH DO YOU BELONG TO?! I'LL RUN A CHECK!
FOR CRYING OUT LOUD!!

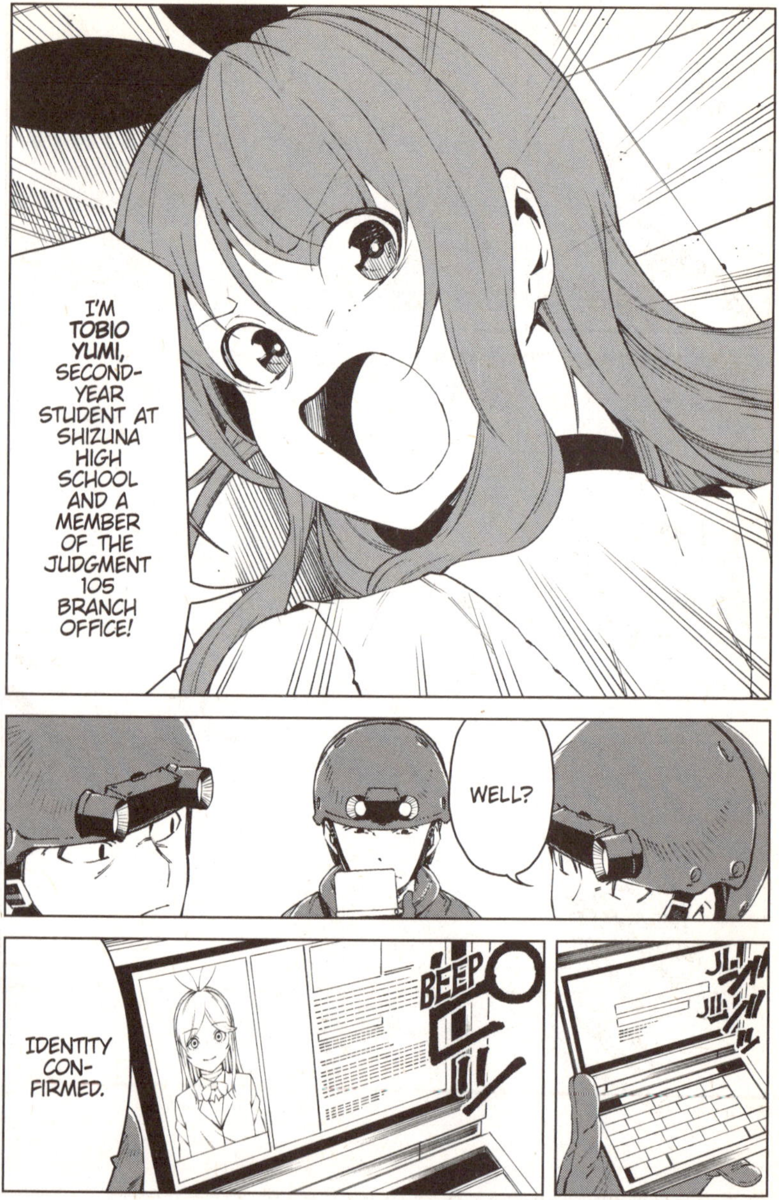
I'M TOBIO YUMI, SECOND-YEAR STUDENT AT SHIZUNA HIGH SCHOOL AND A MEMBER OF THE JUDGMENT 105 BRANCH OFFICE!
WELL?
BEEP
IDENTITY CON-FIRMED.

I STILL DON'T WANT ANY RECKLESS MOVES OUT OF YOU.

GLEAM

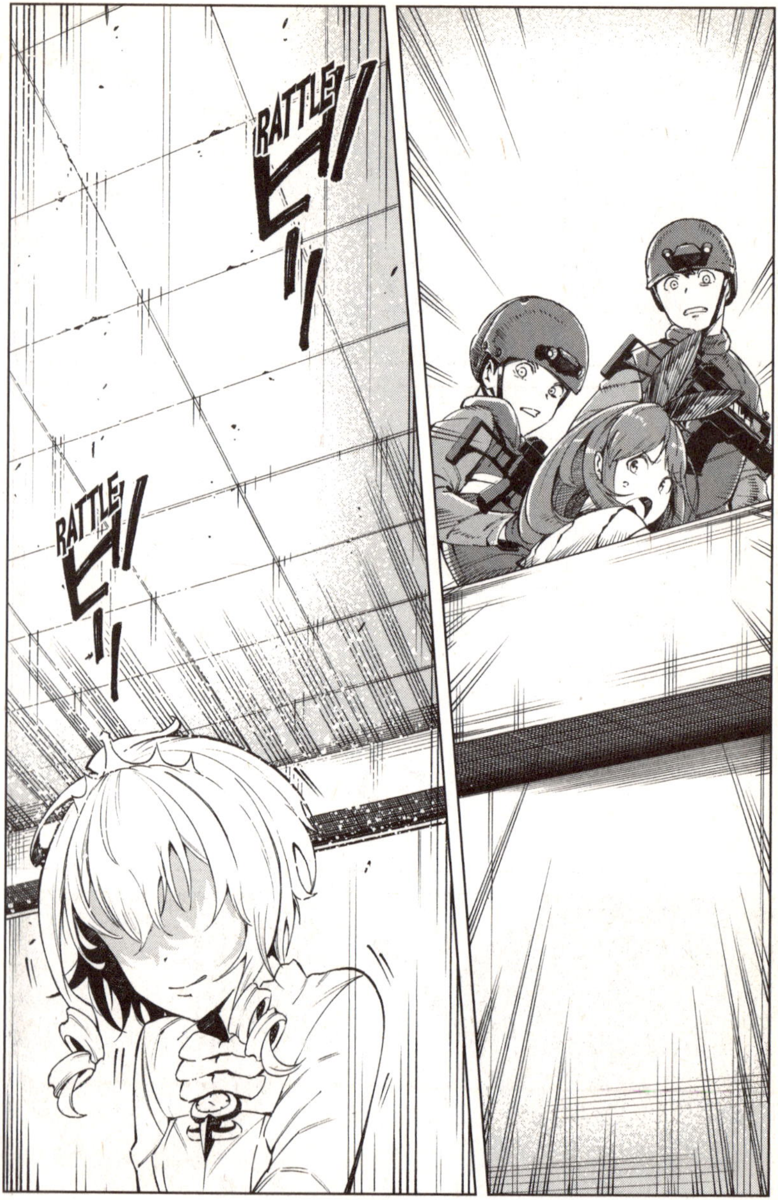
RATTLE
RATTLE

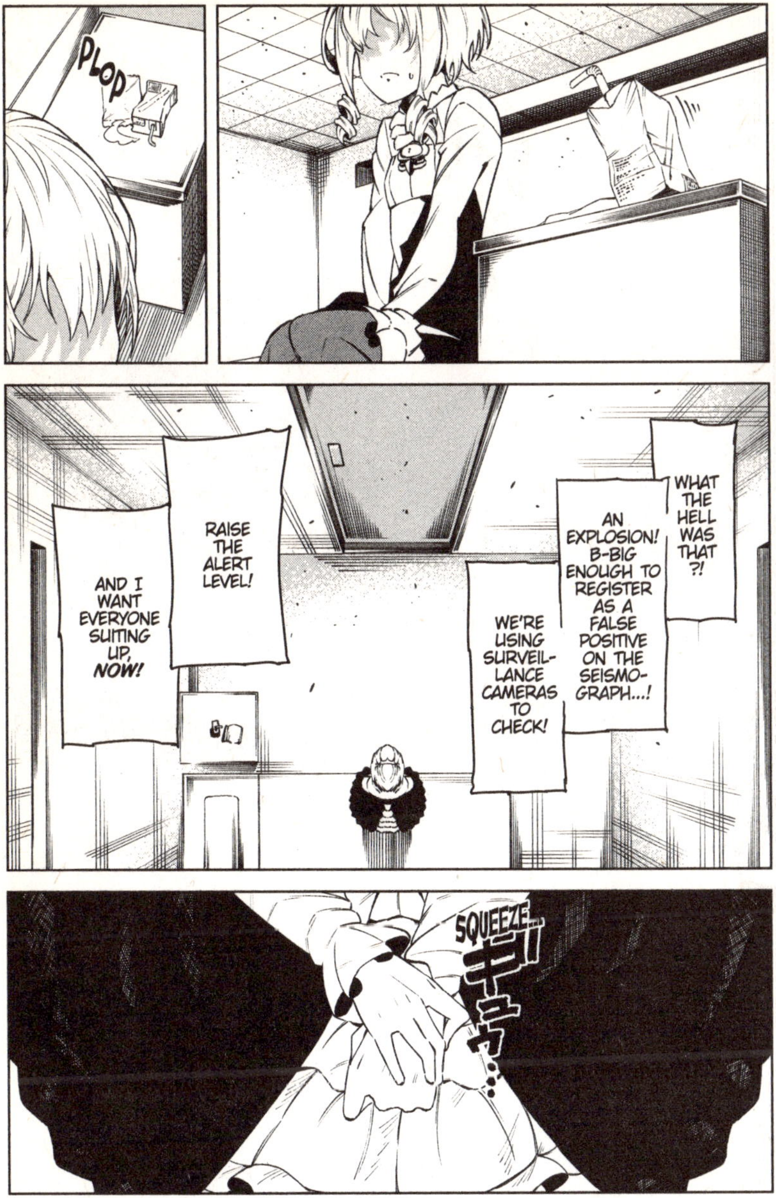
PLOP
WHAT THE HELL WAS THAT?!
AN EXPLOSION! B-BIG ENOUGH TO REGISTER AS A FALSE POSITIVE ON THE SEISMOGRAPH...!
WE'RE USING SURVEILLANCE CAMERAS TO CHECK!
RAISE THE ALERT LEVEL!
AND I WANT EVERYONE SUITING UP, *NOW!*
SQUEEZE...
ギュゥ…

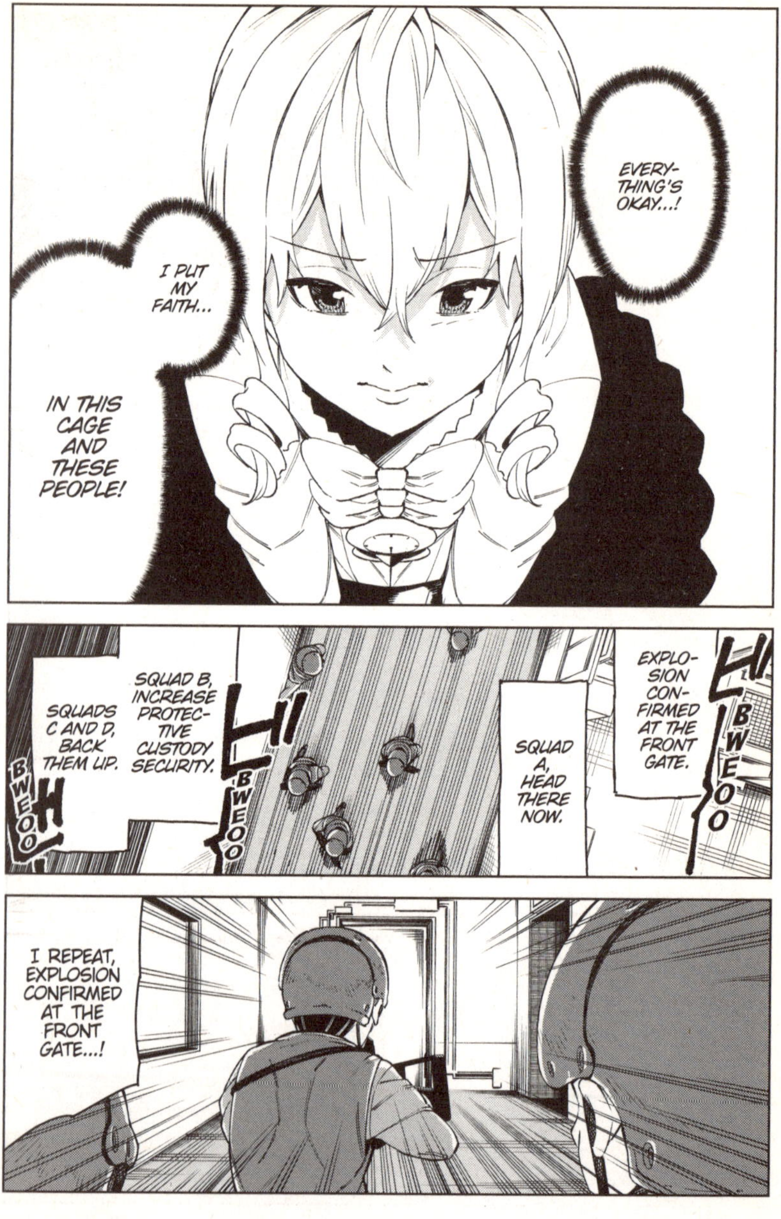
EVERY-THING'S OKAY...!
I PUT MY FAITH...
IN THIS CAGE AND THESE PEOPLE!
EXPLO-SION CON-FIRMED AT THE FRONT GATE.
HI
BWEOO
SQUAD A, HEAD THERE NOW.
HI
BWEOO
SQUAD B, INCREASE PROTEC-TIVE CUSTODY SECURITY.
SQUADS C AND D, BACK THEM UP.
BWEOO
H
I REPEAT, EXPLOSION CONFIRMED AT THE FRONT GATE...!

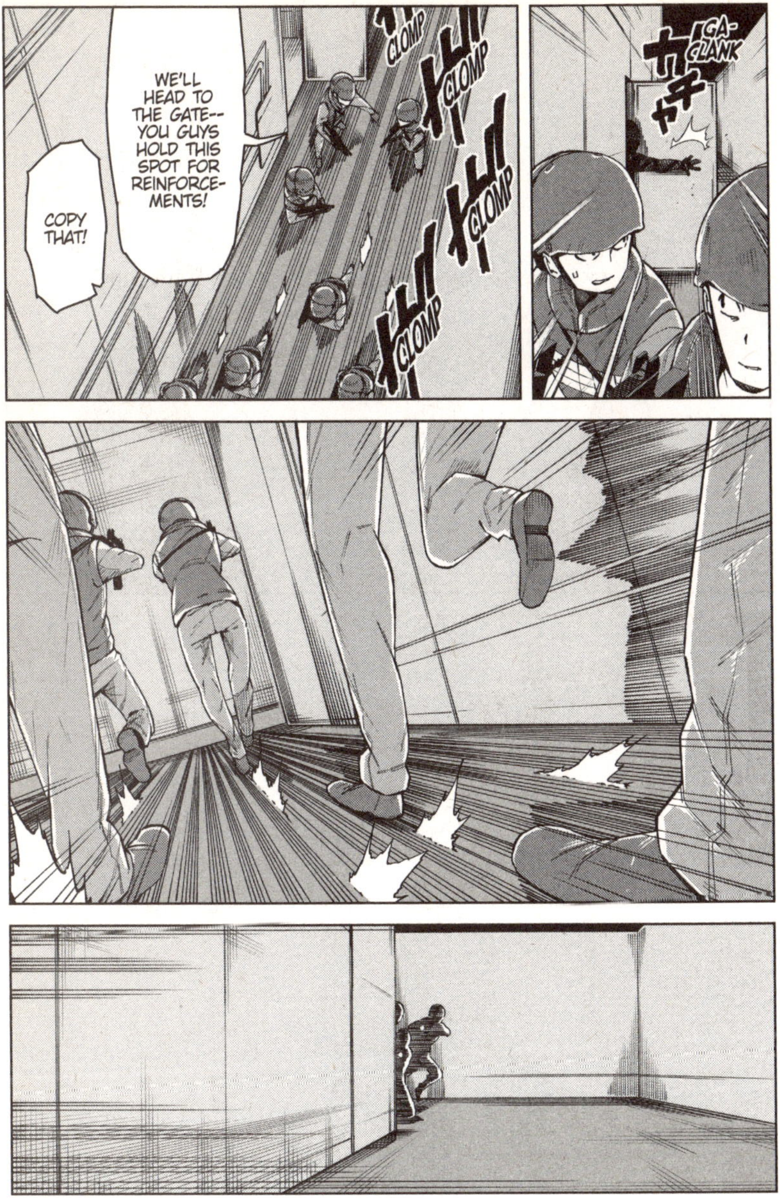
GA-CLANK
CLOMP
CLOMP
CLOMP
CLOMP
CLOMP
WE'LL HEAD TO THE GATE-- YOU GUYS HOLD THIS SPOT FOR REINFORCE-MENTS!
COPY THAT!

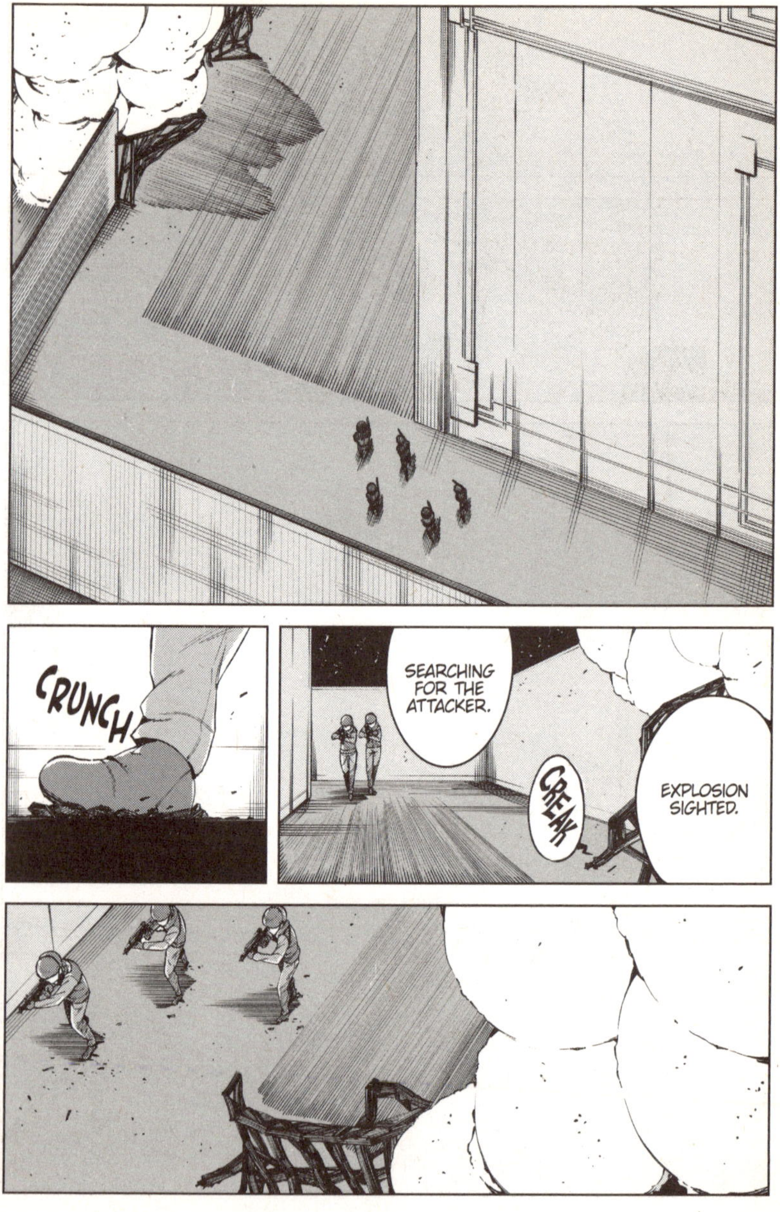
EXPLOSION SIGHTED.
SEARCHING FOR THE ATTACKER.
CREAK
CRUNCH

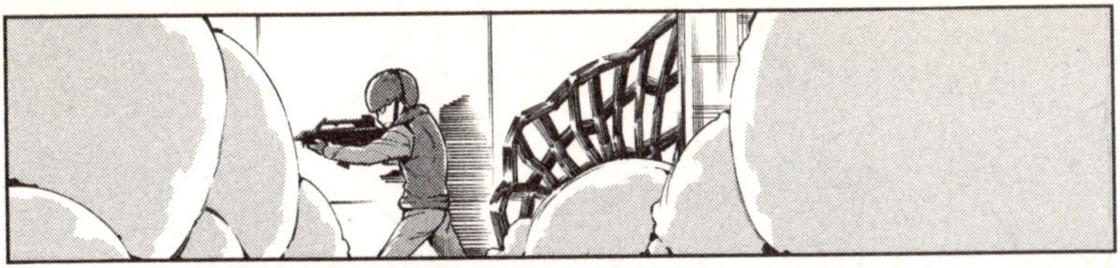
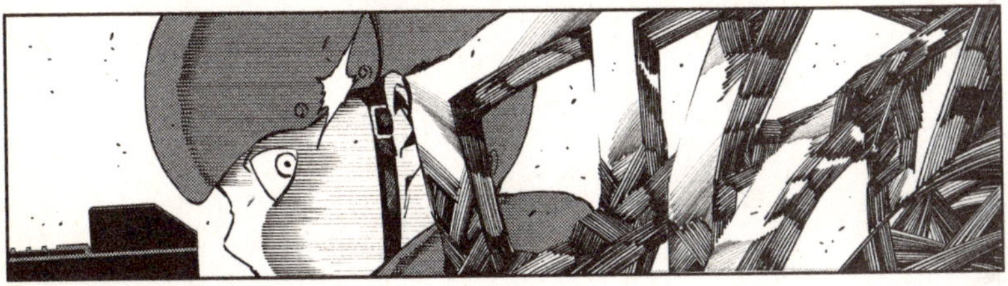
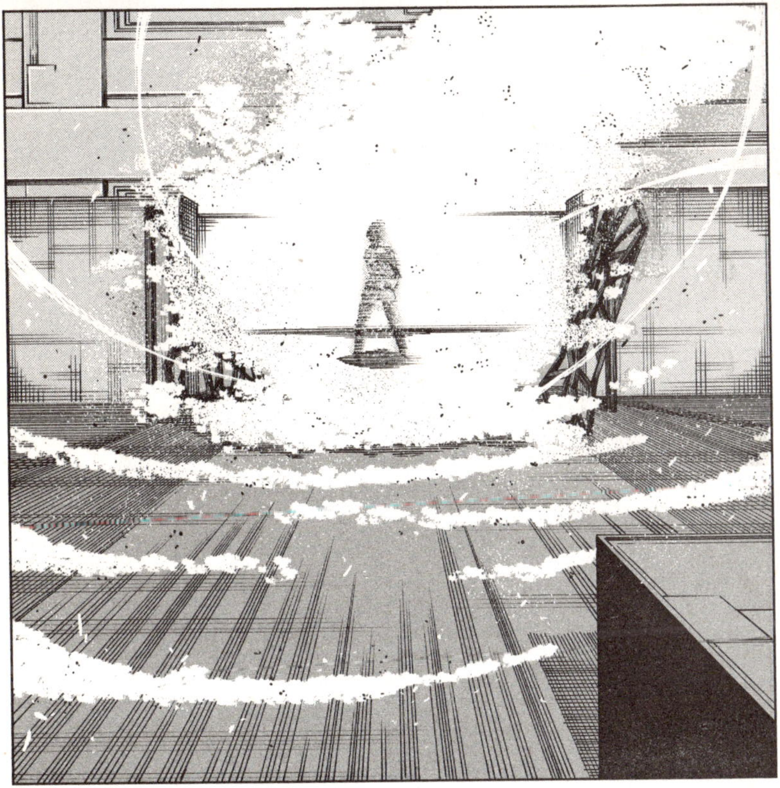

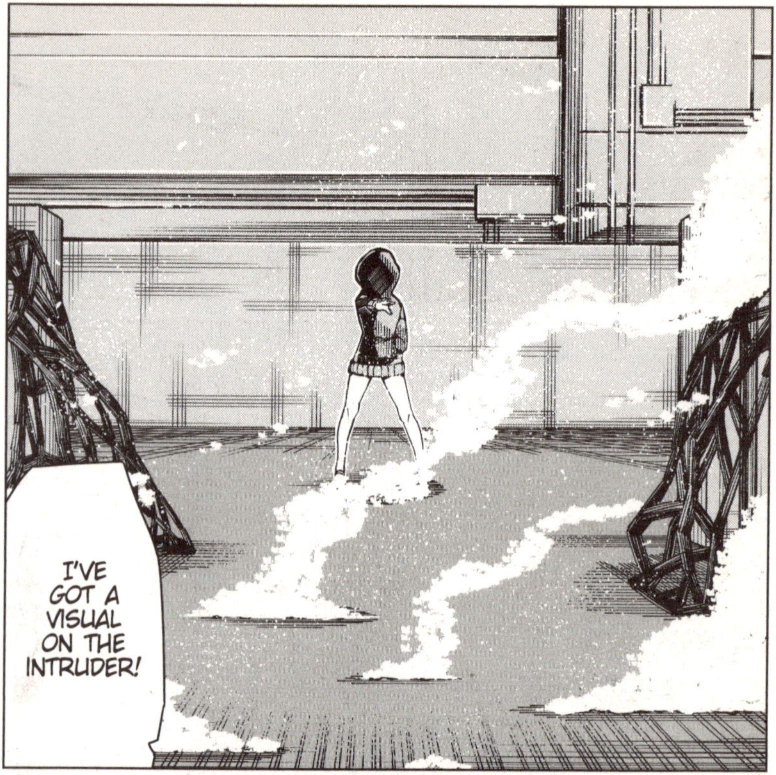
I'VE GOT A VISUAL ON THE INTRUDER!

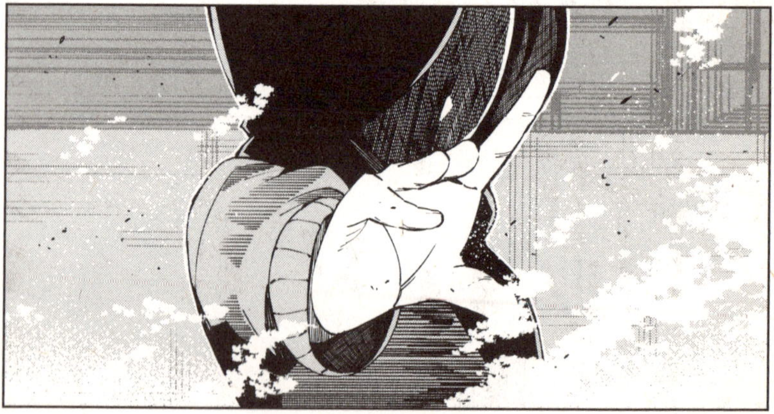

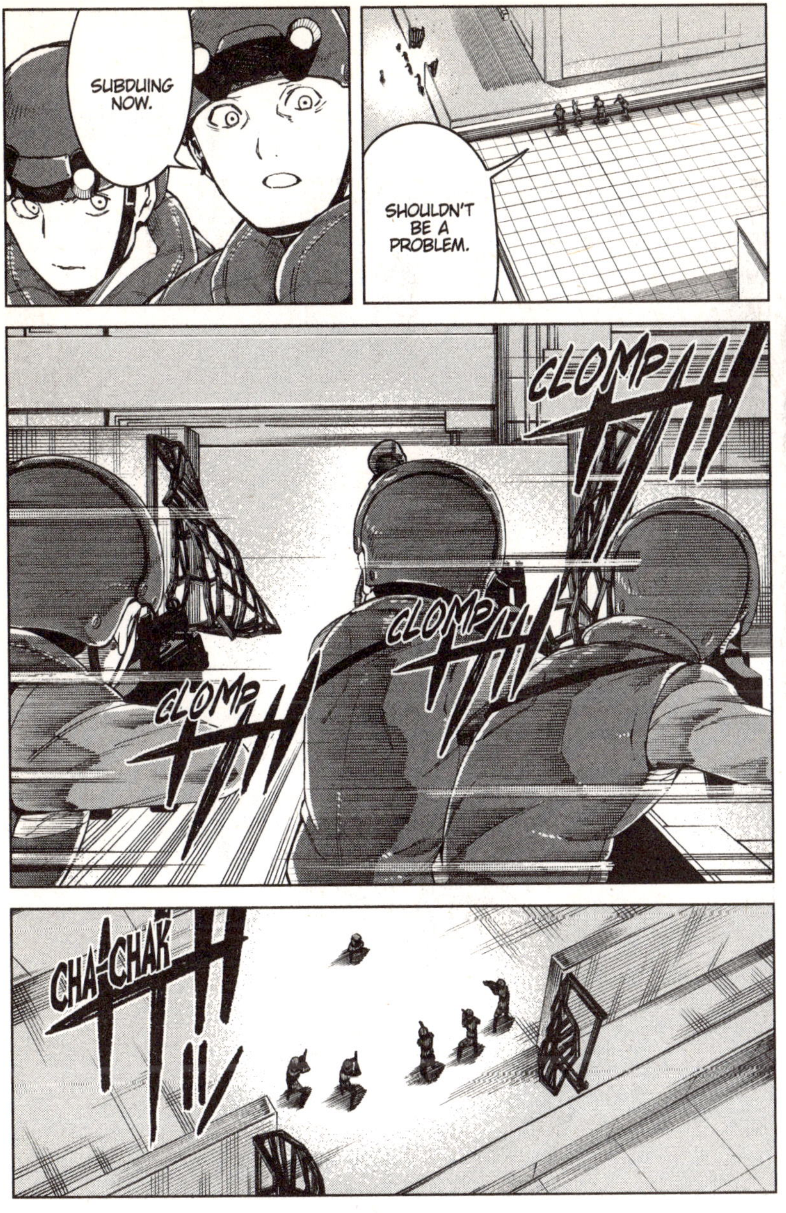
SHOULDN'T BE A PROBLEM.
SUBDUING NOW.
CLOMP
CLOMP
CLOMP
CHA-CHAK

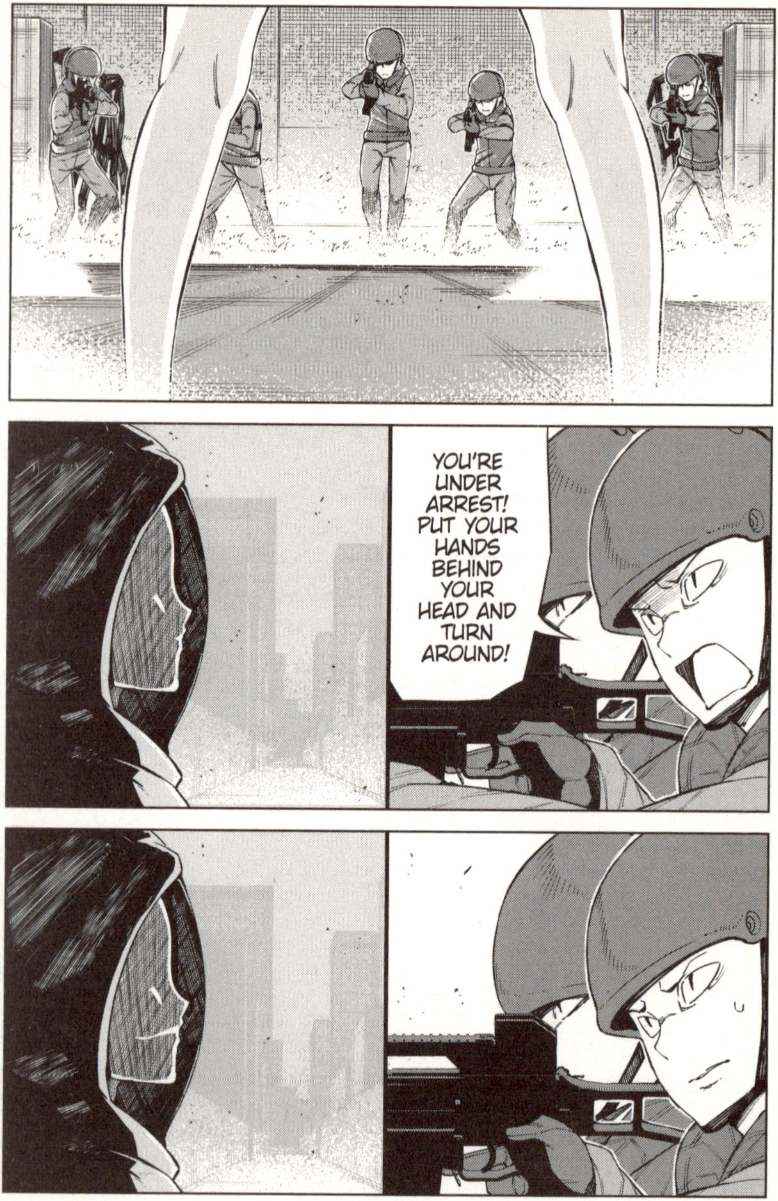
YOU'RE UNDER ARREST! PUT YOUR HANDS BEHIND YOUR HEAD AND TURN AROUND!

I REPEAT, PUT YOUR HANDS BEHIND YOUR HEAD...

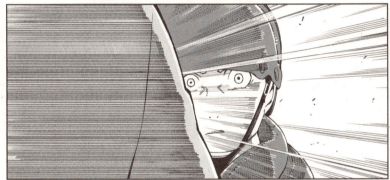

JYA-KI

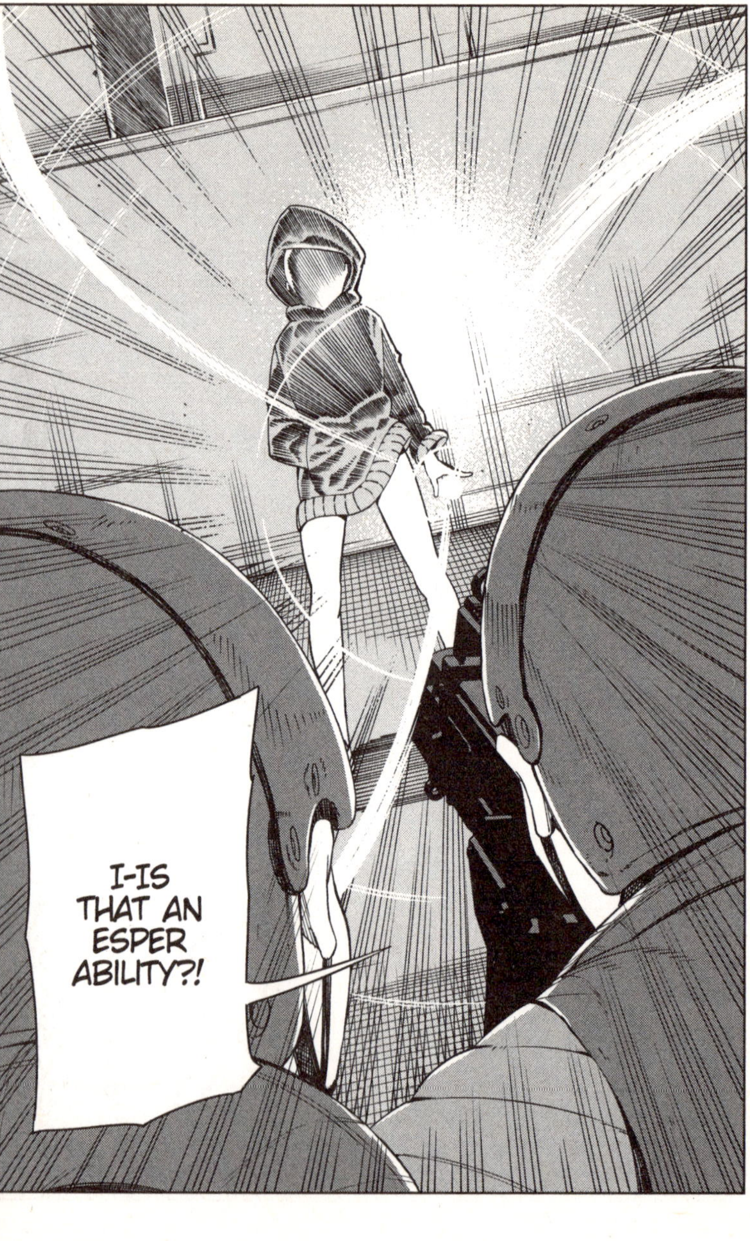
I-IS THAT AN ESPER ABILITY?!

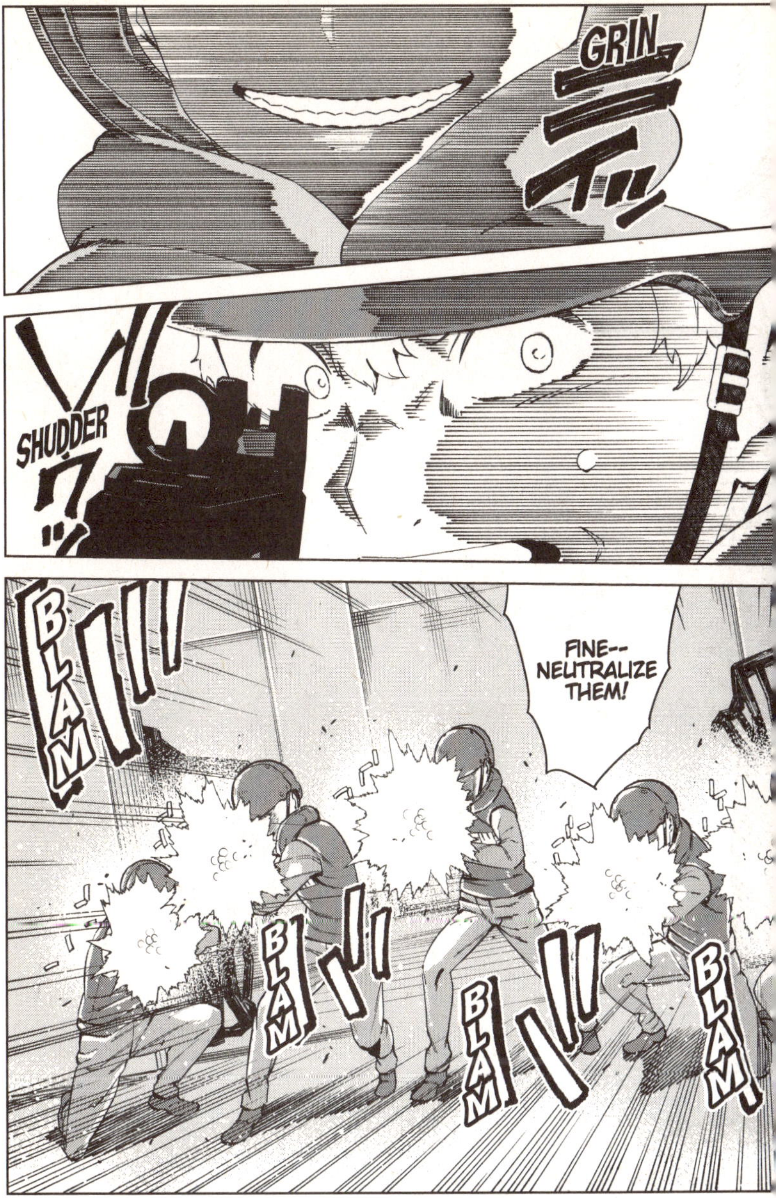
GRIN
SHUDDER
FINE--NEUTRALIZE THEM!
BLAM
BLAM
BLAM
BLAM

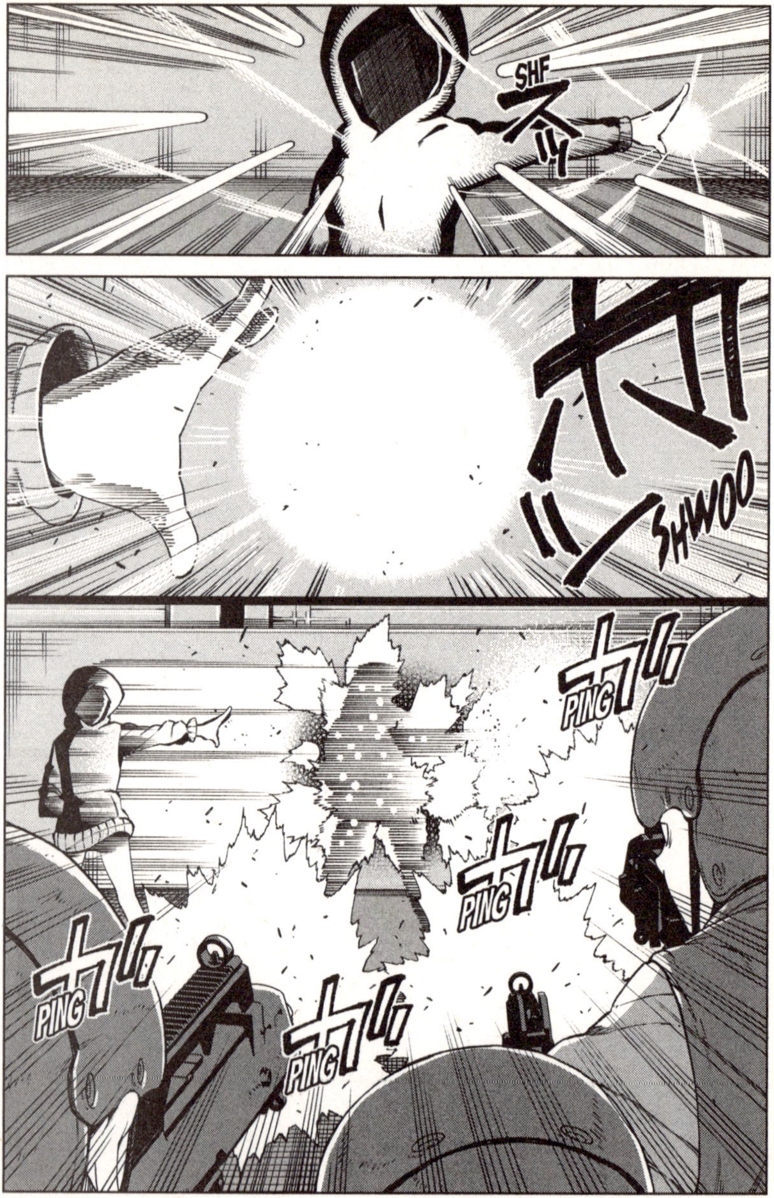
SHF
SHWOO
PING
PING
PING
PING

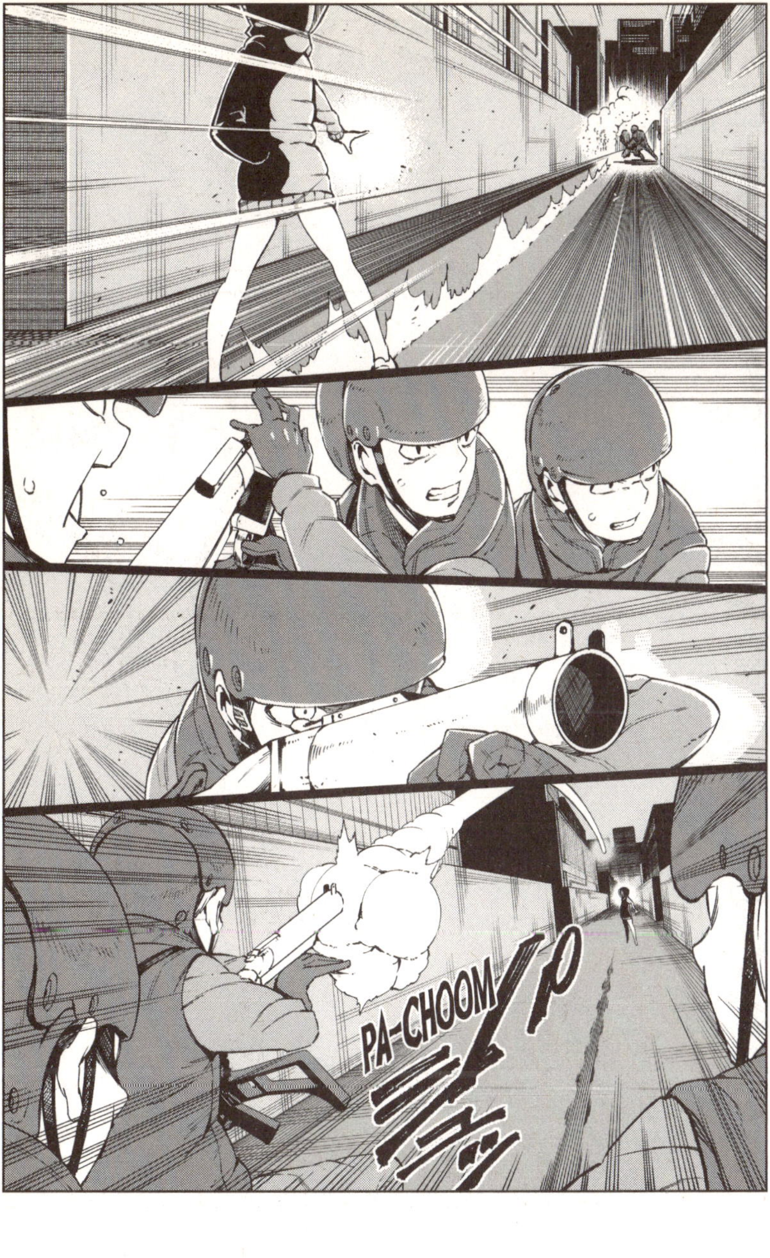
PA-CHOOM

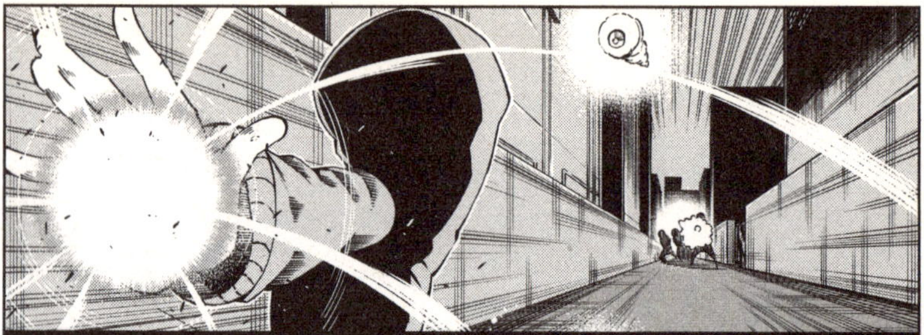
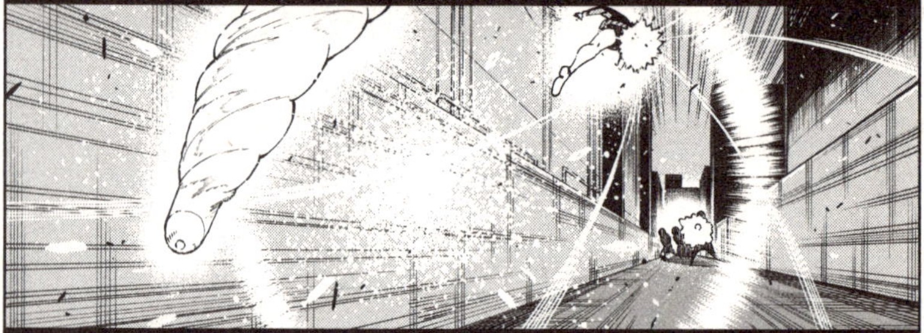
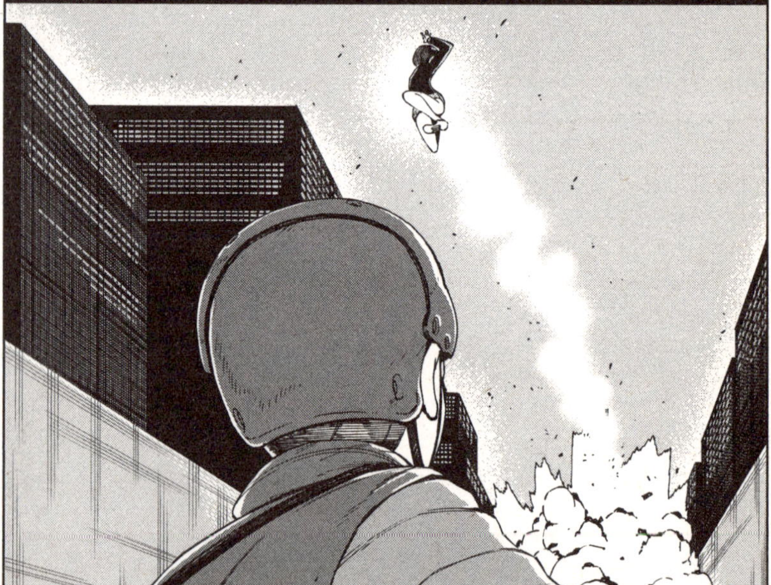

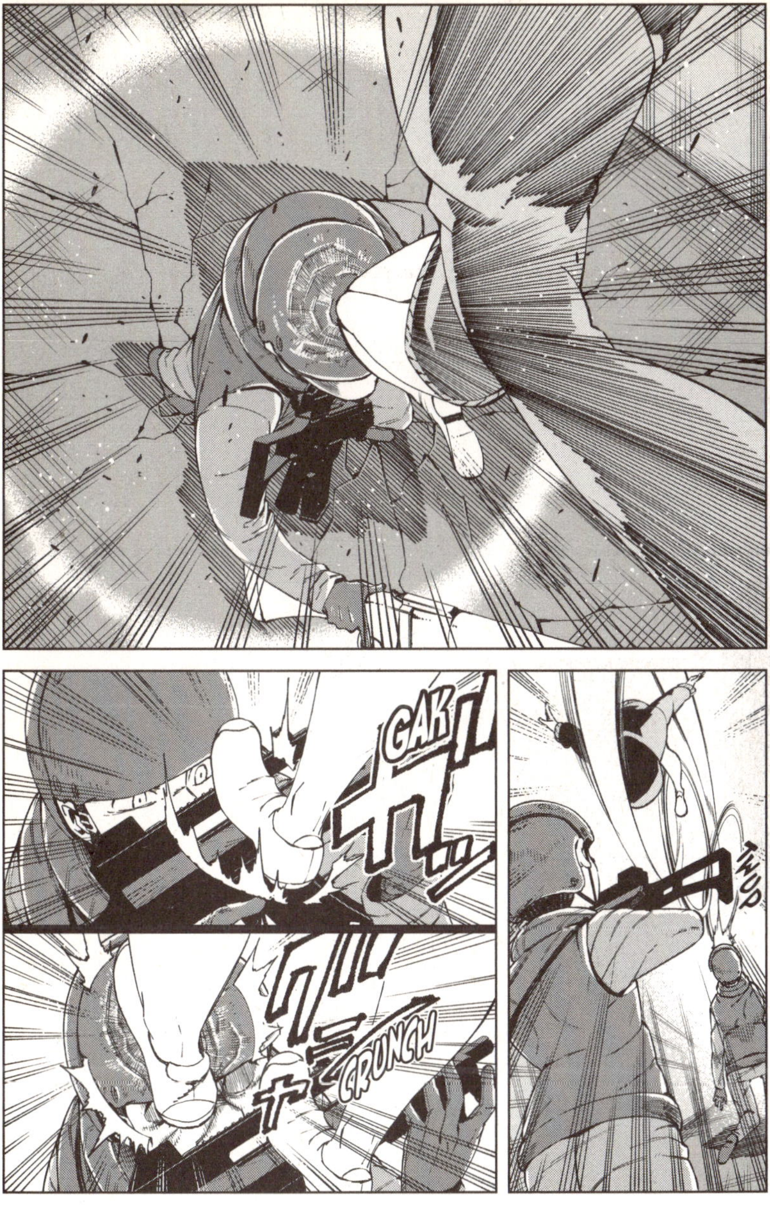
TWUP
GAK
CRUNCH

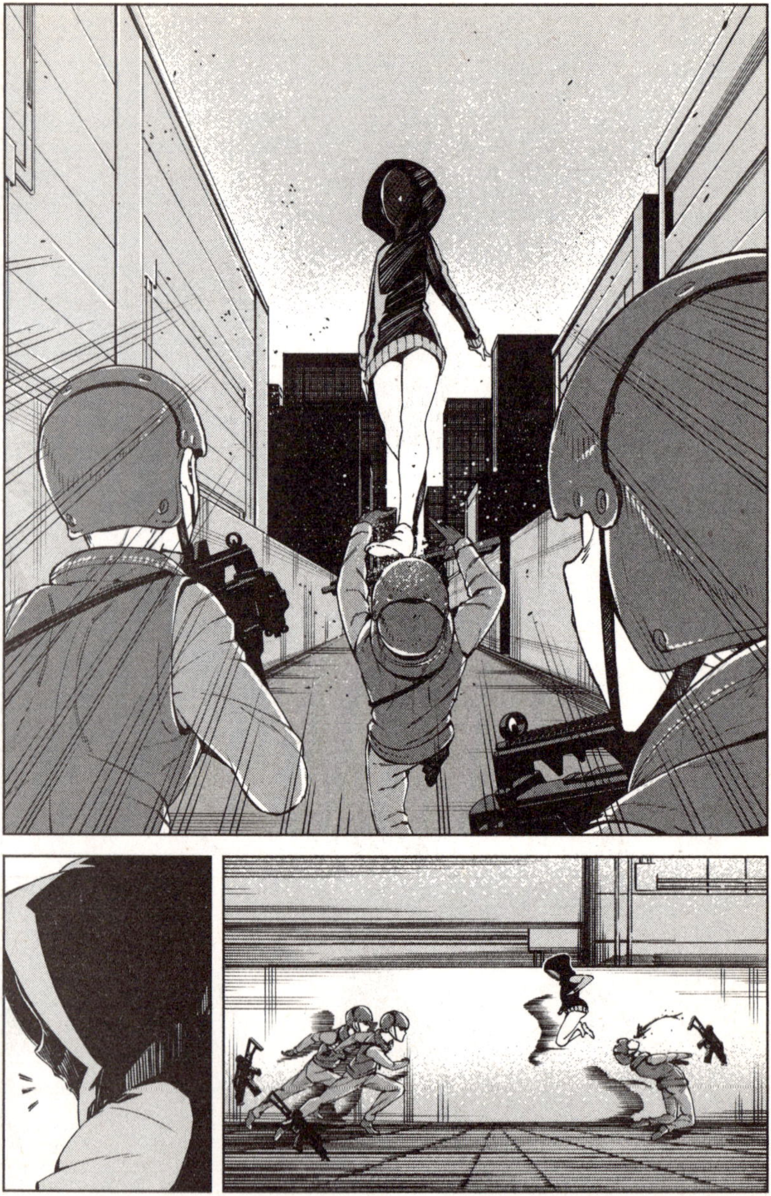

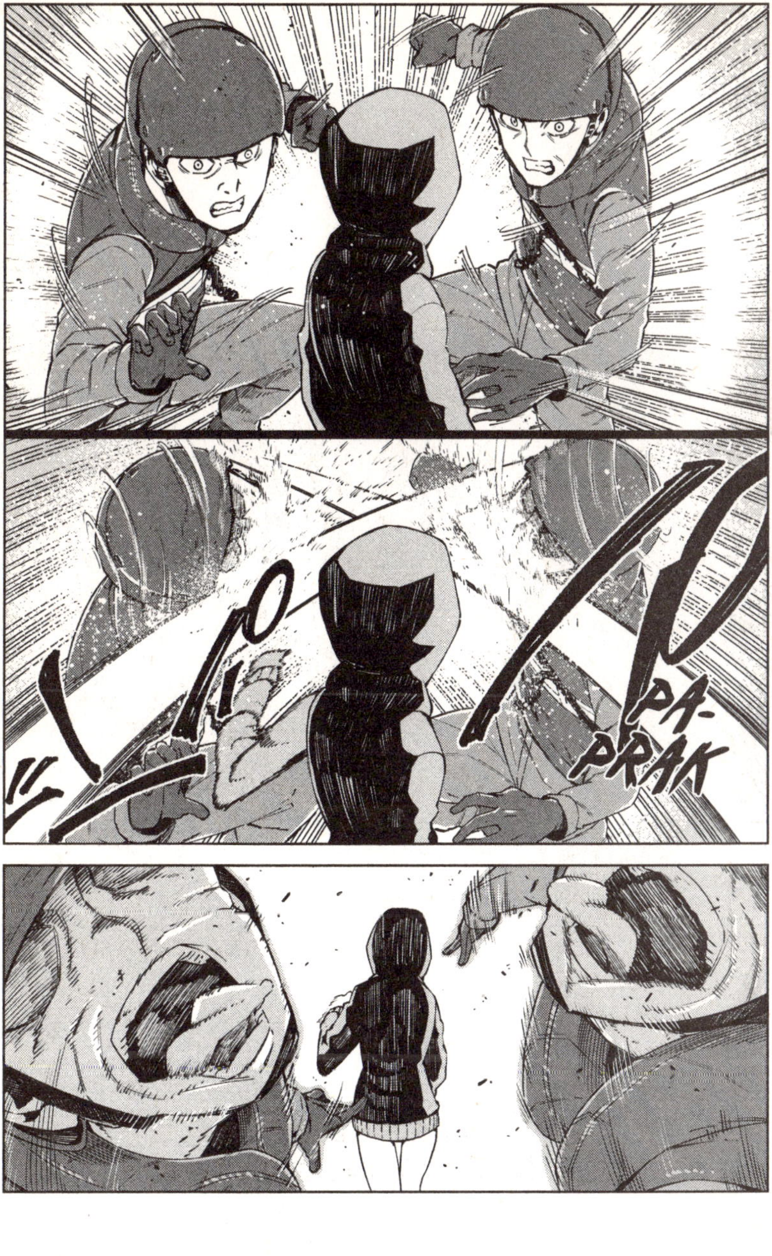
PA-
PRAK

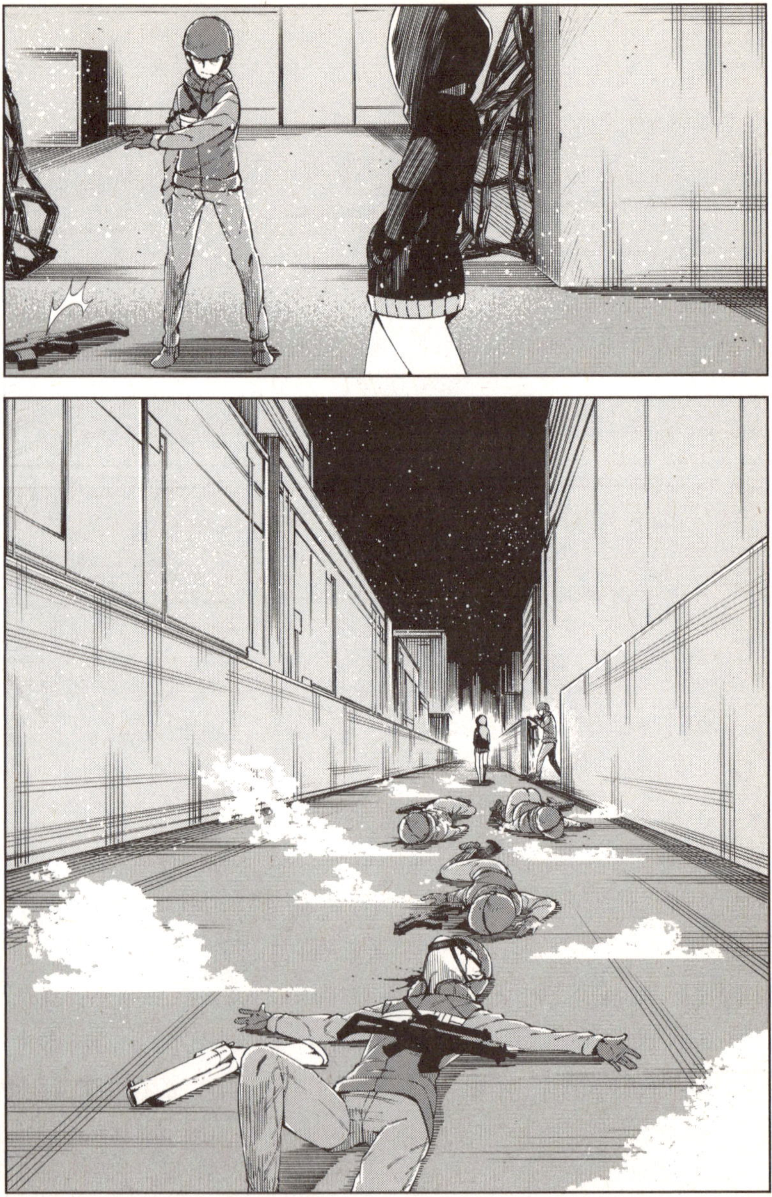

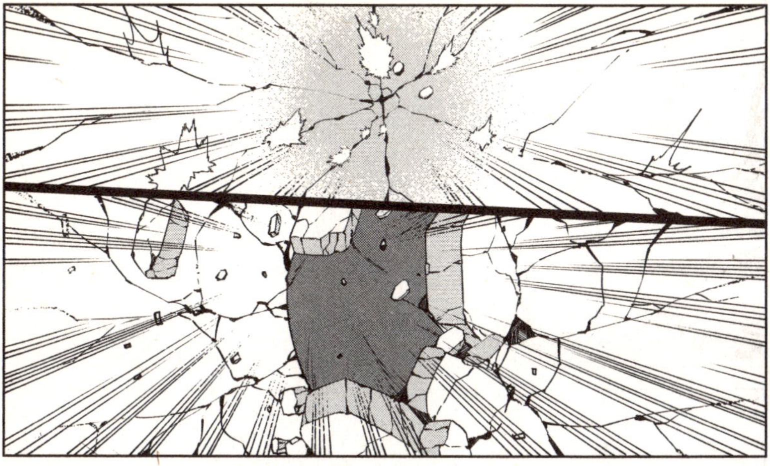

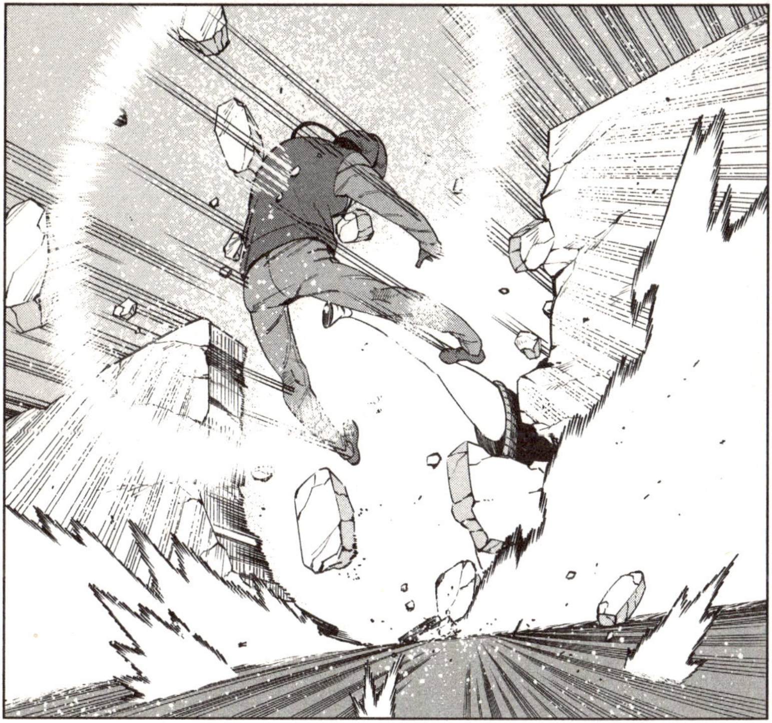

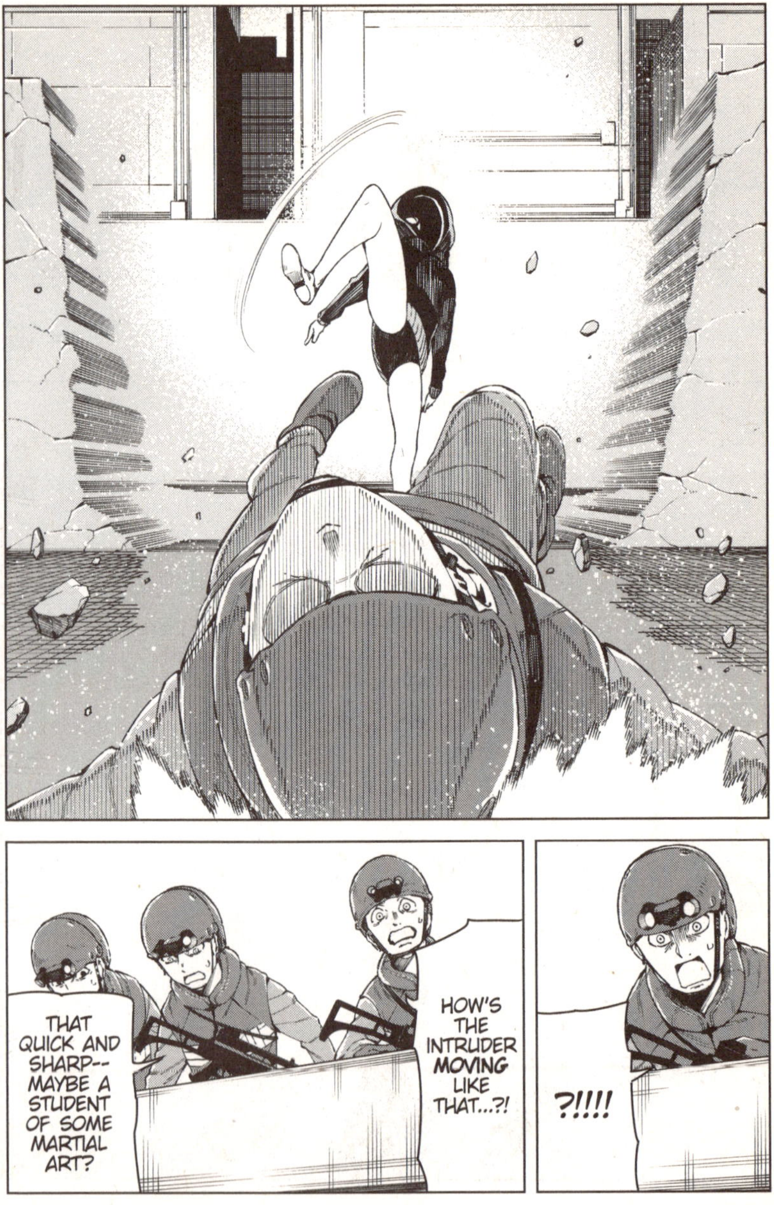
?!!!!
HOW'S THE INTRUDER MOVING LIKE THAT...?!
THAT QUICK AND SHARP-- MAYBE A STUDENT OF SOME MARTIAL ART?

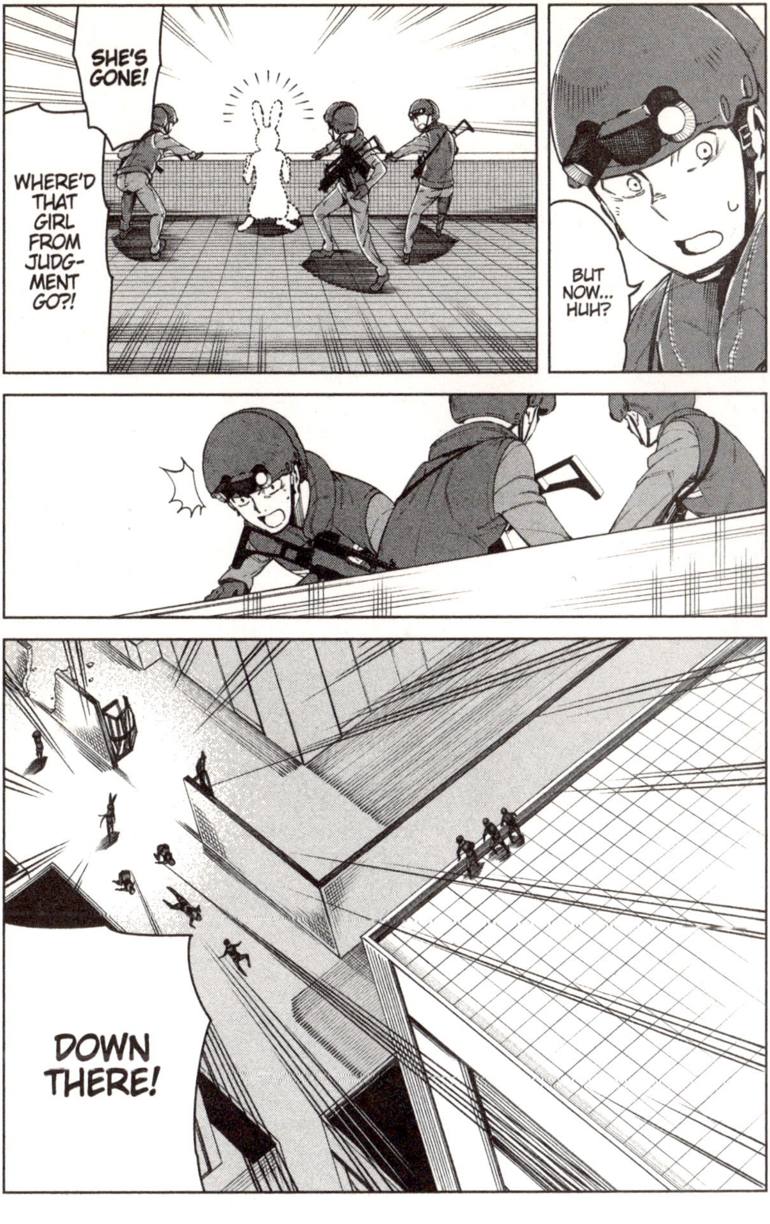
BUT NOW... HUH?
SHE'S GONE!
WHERE'D THAT GIRL FROM JUDGMENT GO?!
DOWN THERE!

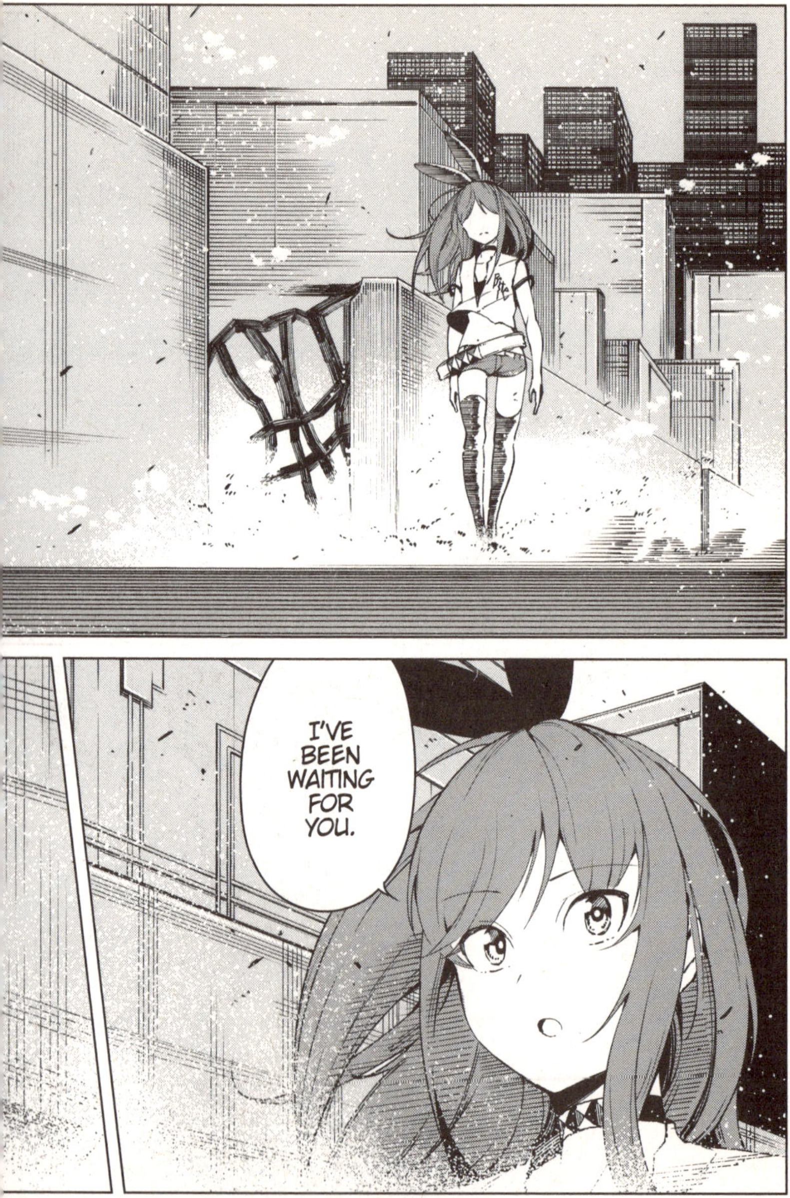
I'VE BEEN WAITING FOR YOU.

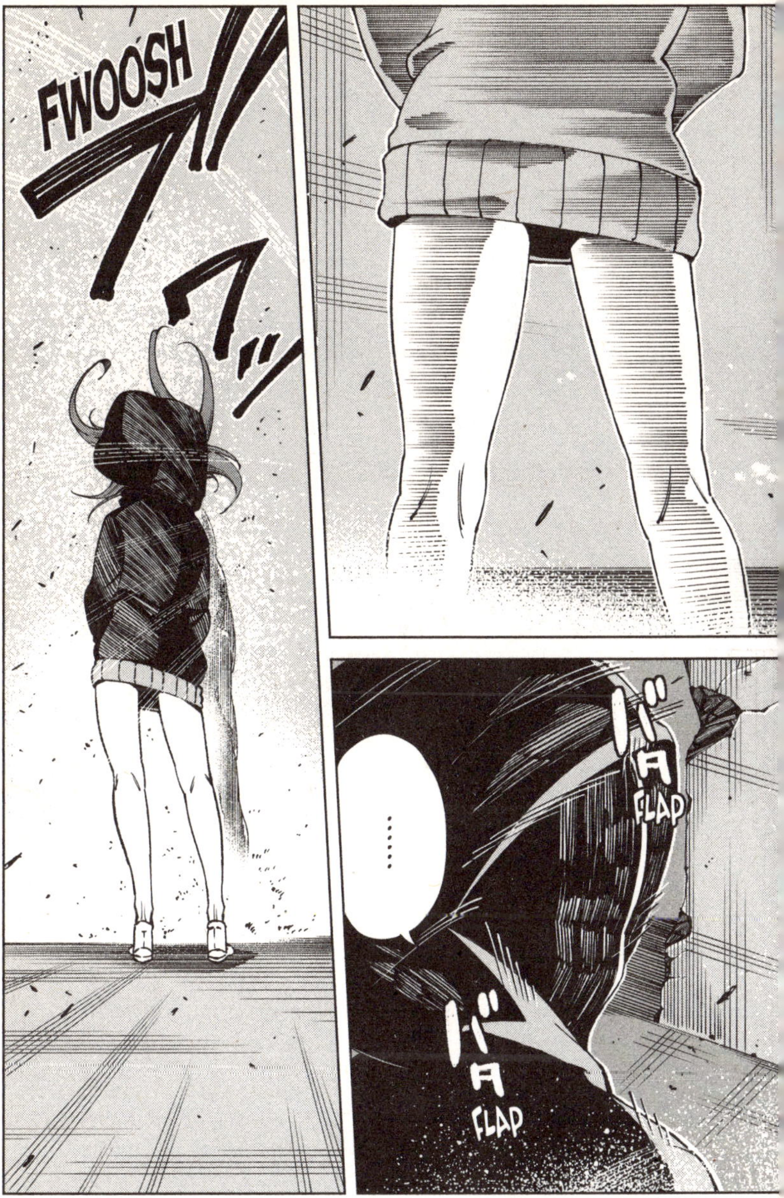
......
FLAP
FLAP
FWOOSH

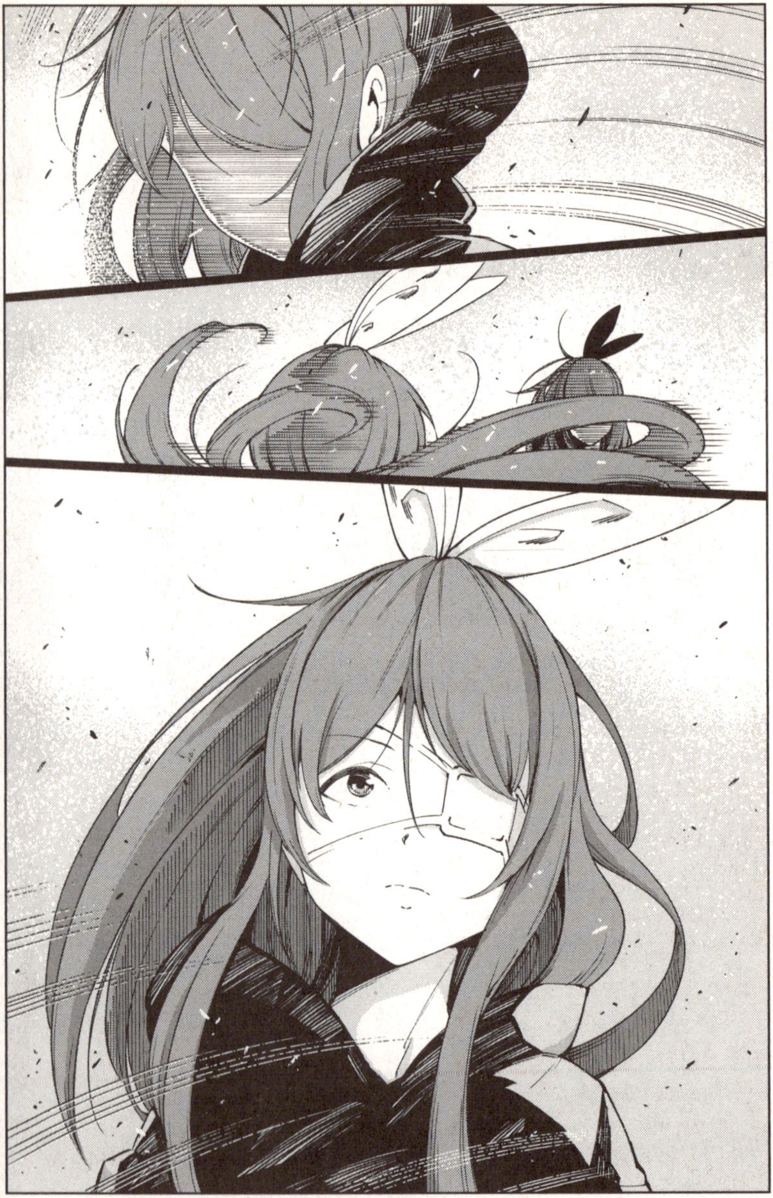

a certain
SCIENTIFIC
ACCELERATOR

とある科学の一方通行

アクセラレータ

とある魔術の禁書目録外伝

# CHAPTER 46

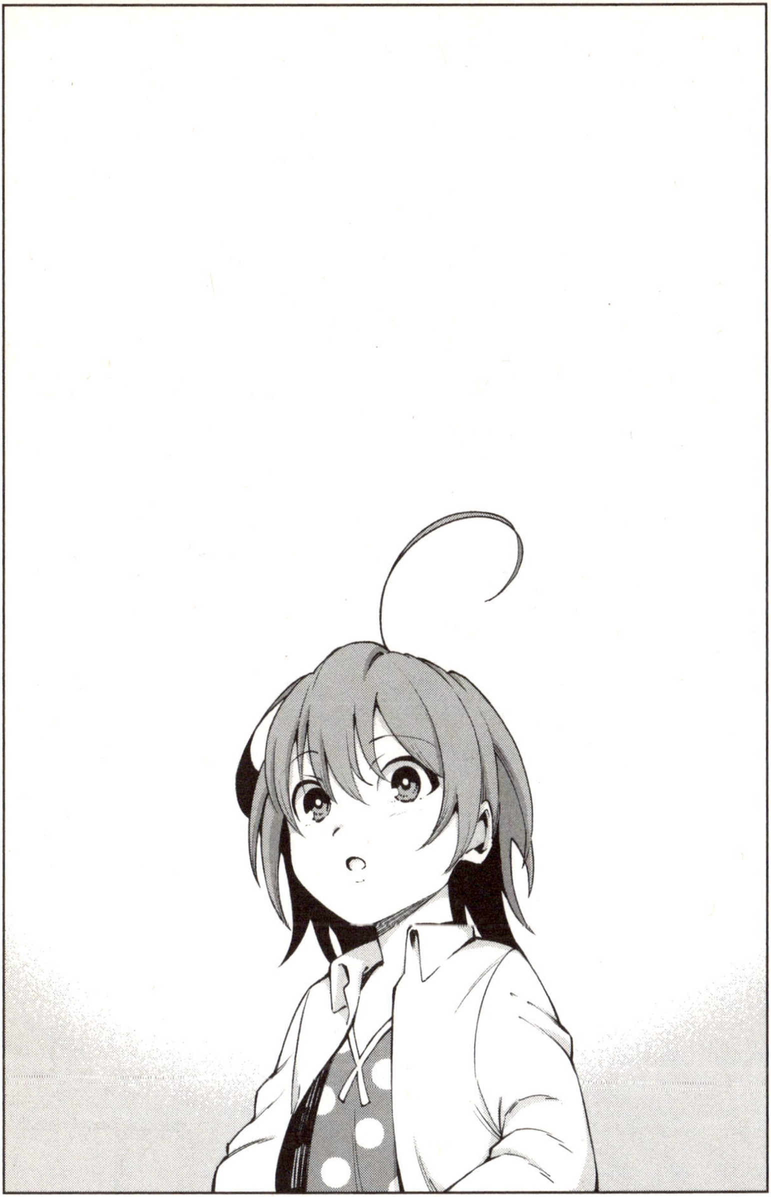

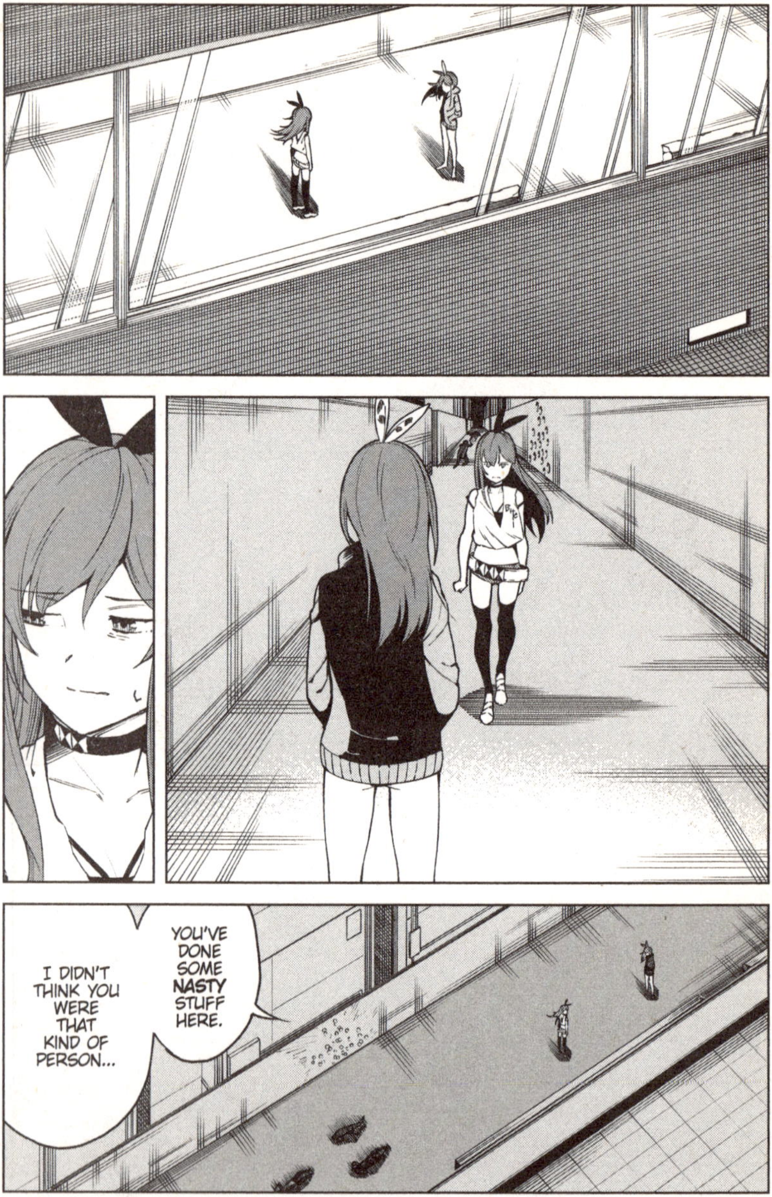
YOU'VE DONE SOME NASTY STUFF HERE.
I DIDN'T THINK YOU WERE THAT KIND OF PERSON...

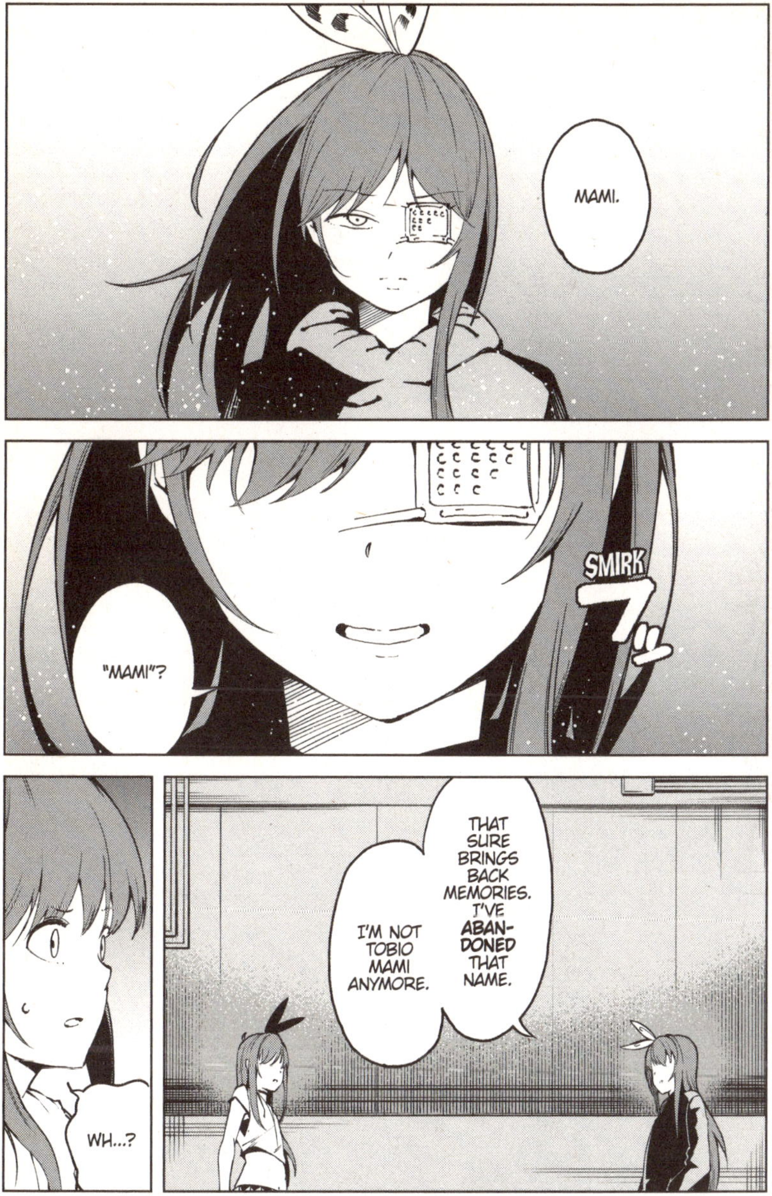
MAMI.
SMIRK
"MAMI"?
THAT SURE BRINGS BACK MEMORIES. I'VE ABANDONED THAT NAME.
I'M NOT TOBIO MAMI ANYMORE.
WH...?

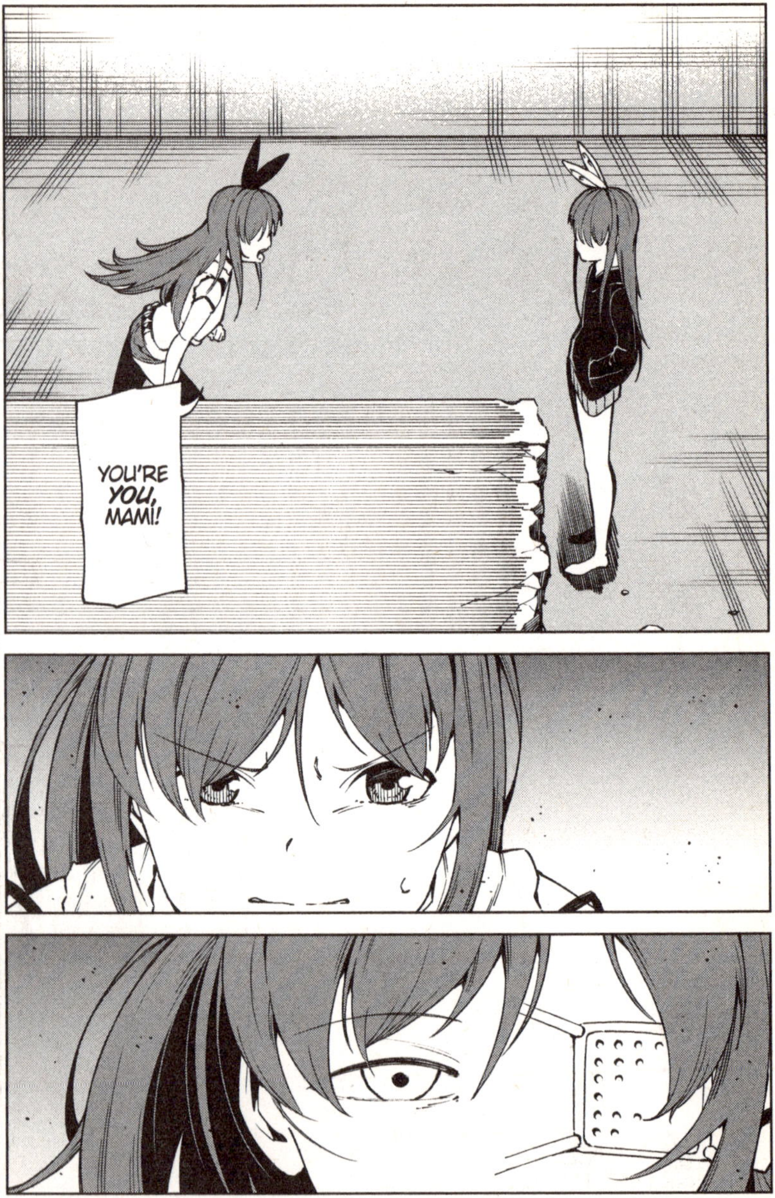
YOU'RE *YOU*, MAMI!

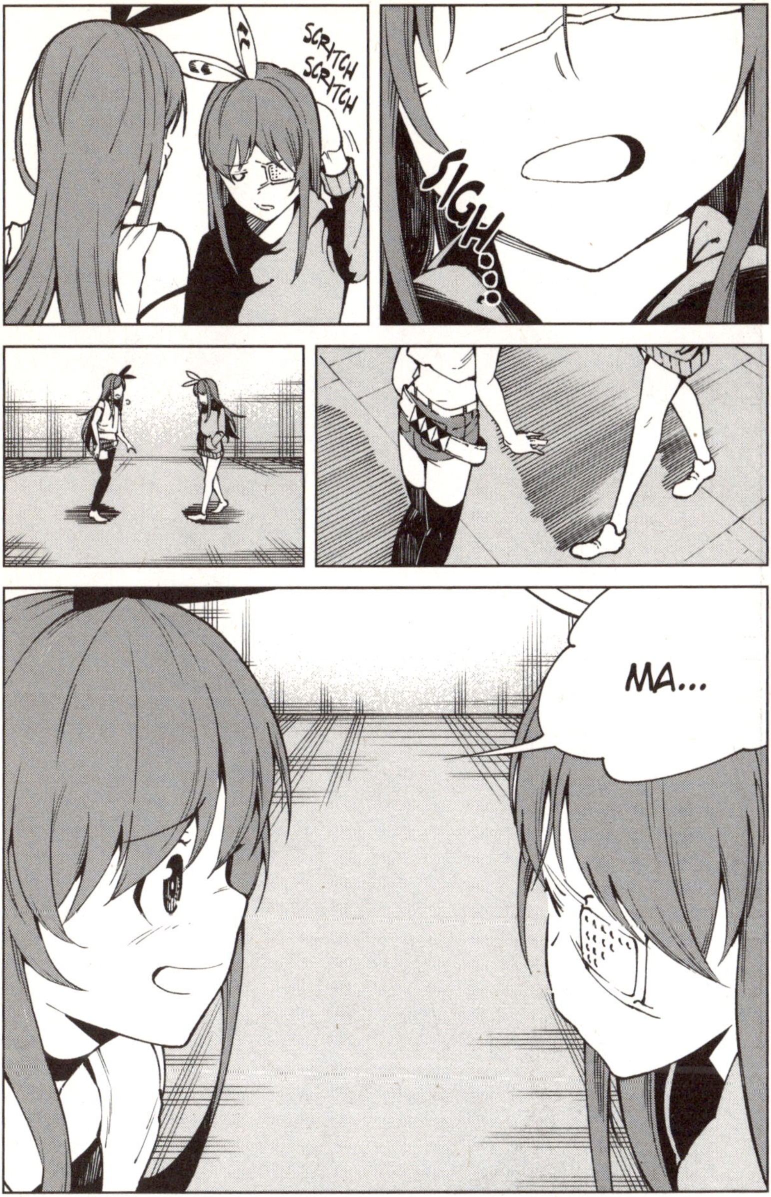
SIGH...
SCRITCH SCRITCH
MA...

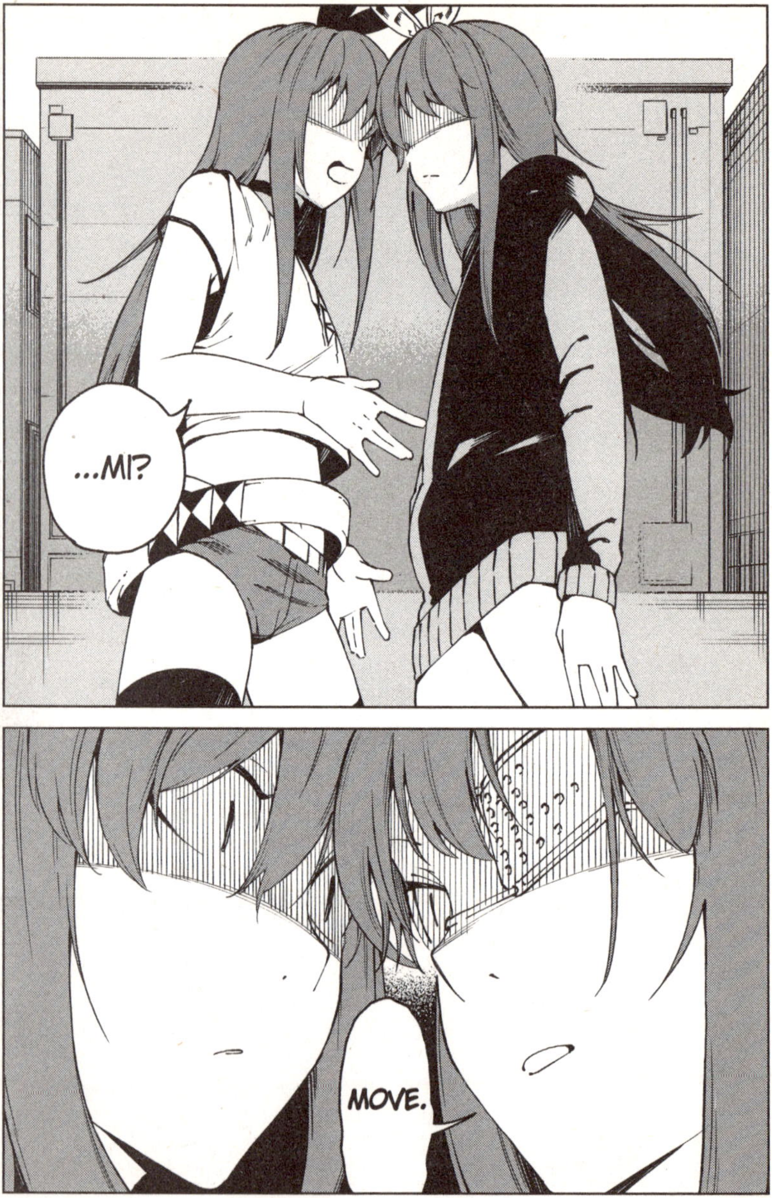
...MI?
MOVE.

I'LL STOP YOU!

NO.
IF YOU'RE GONNA *HURT* PEOPLE, THEN...

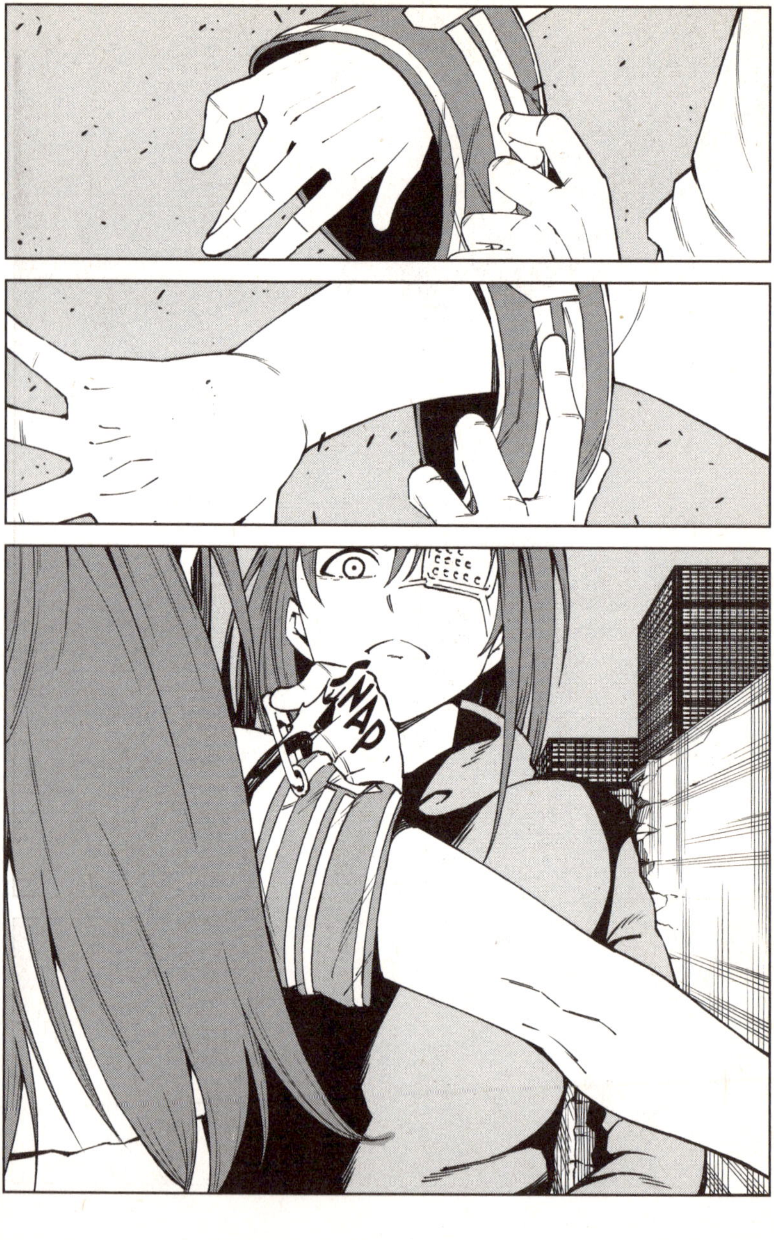
SNAP

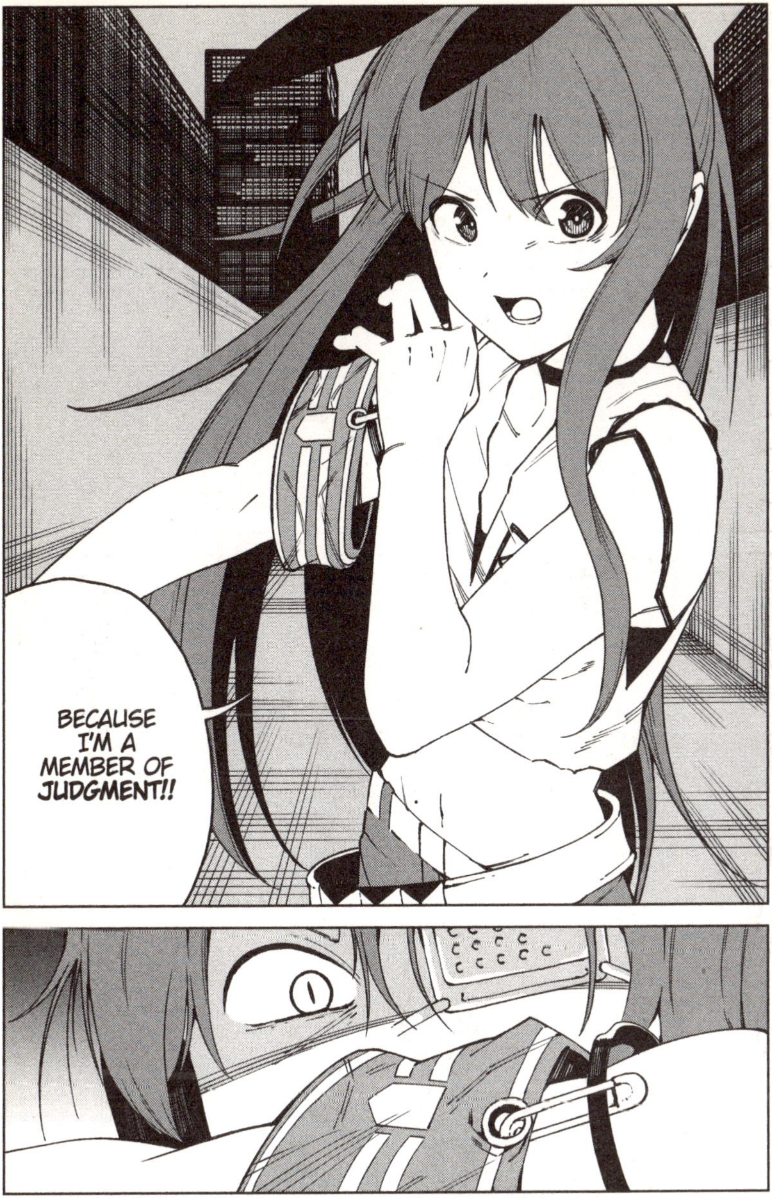
BECAUSE I'M A MEMBER OF JUDGMENT!!

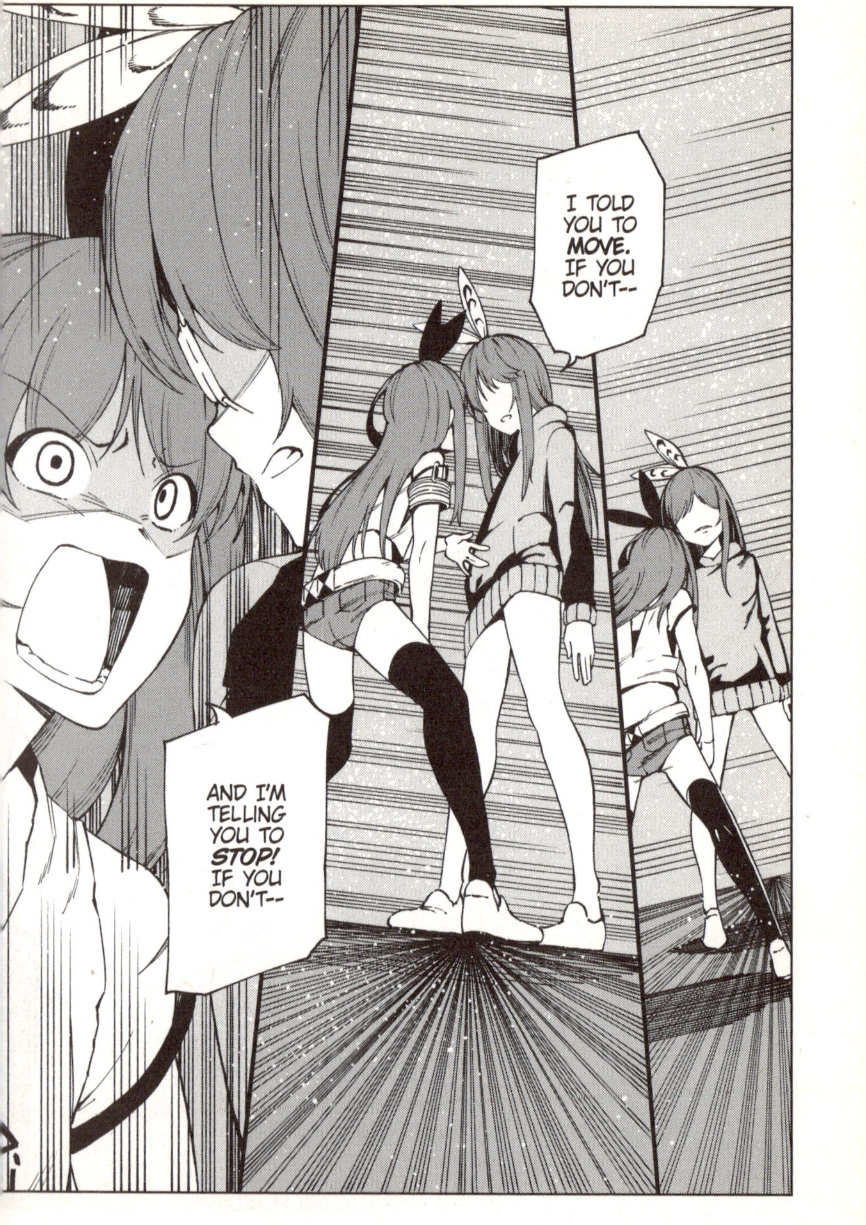
I TOLD YOU TO MOVE. IF YOU DON'T--
AND I'M TELLING YOU TO STOP! IF YOU DON'T--

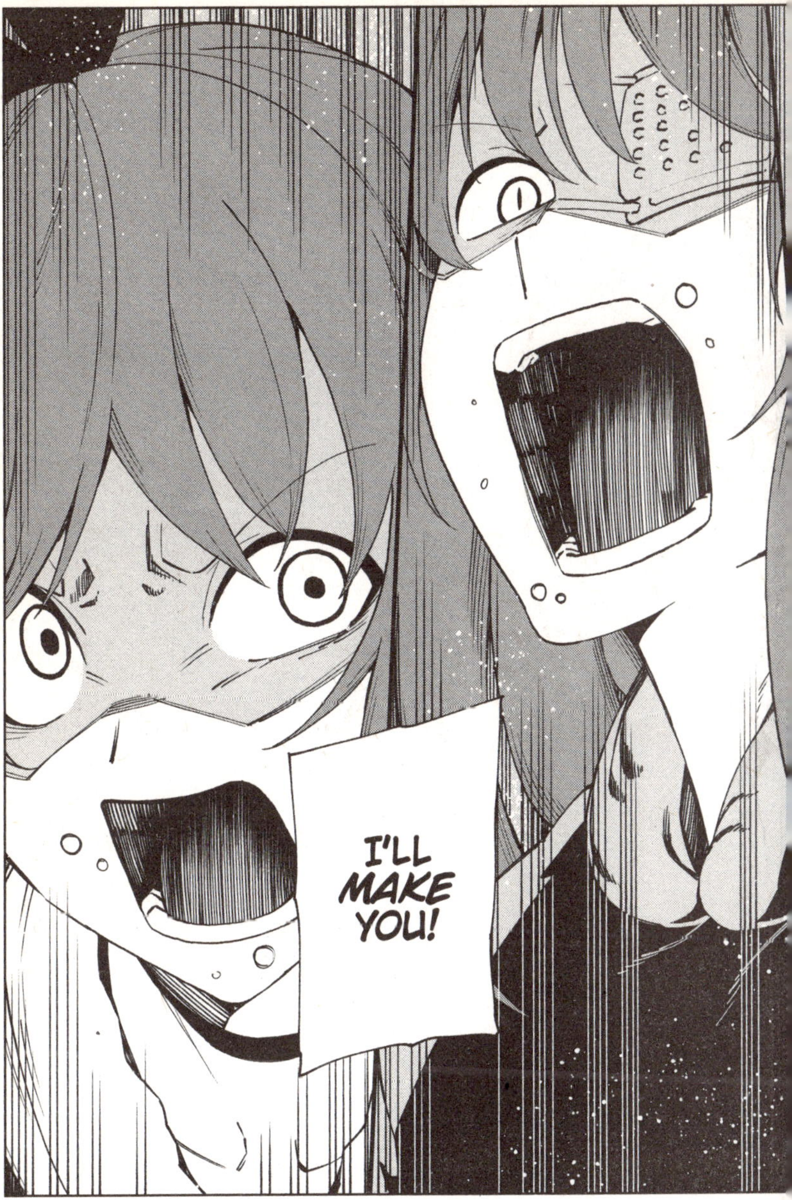
I'LL MAKE YOU!

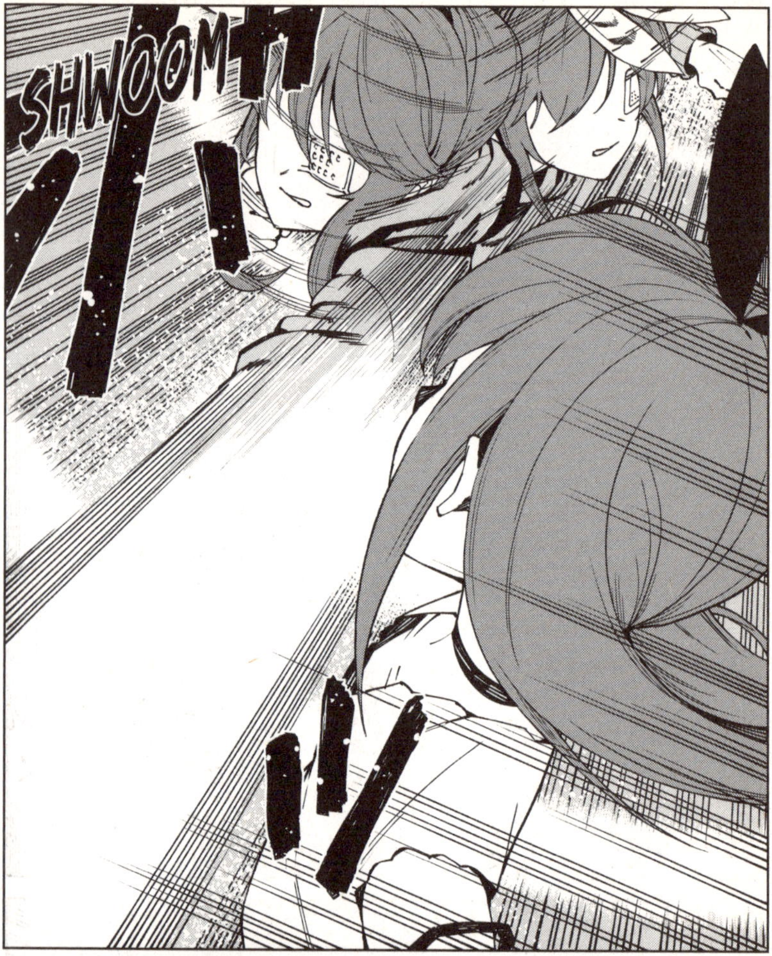
SHWOOM
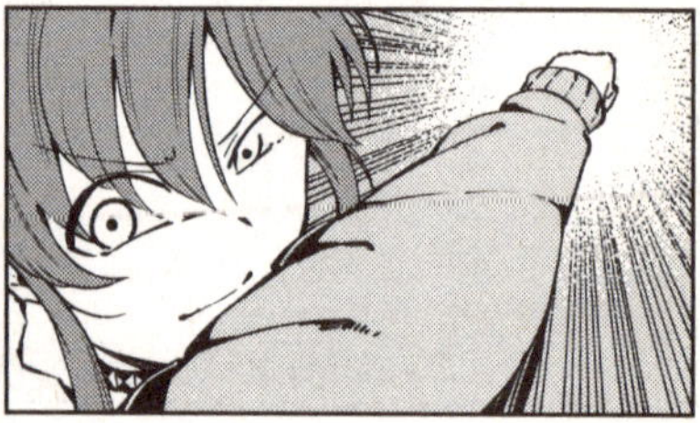
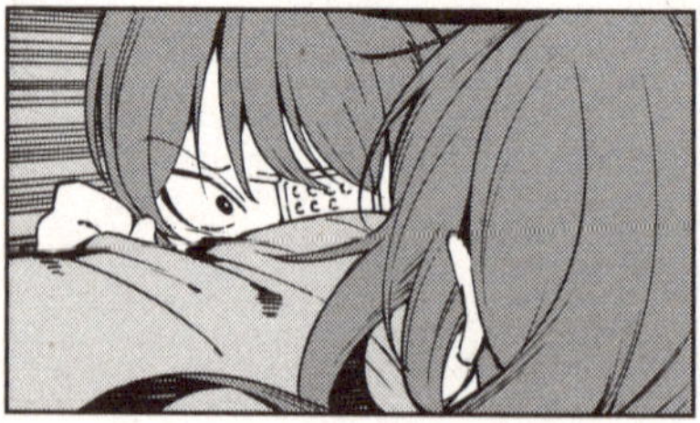

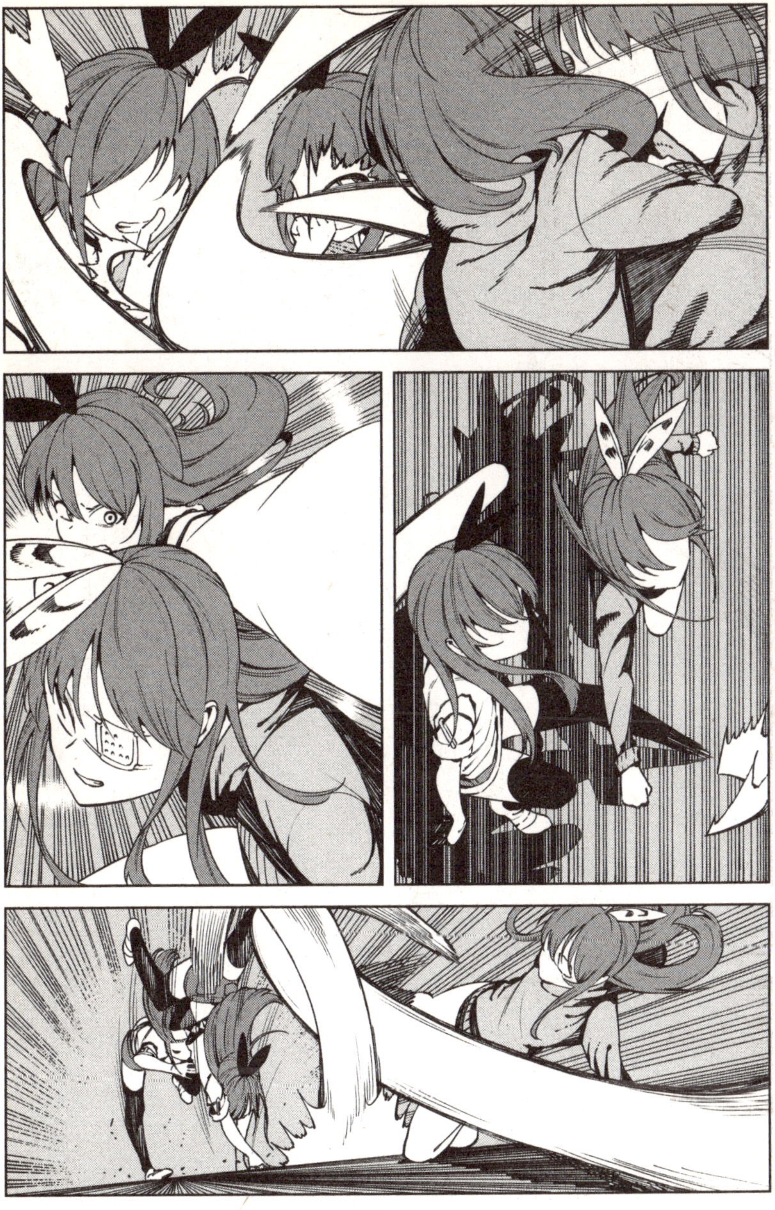

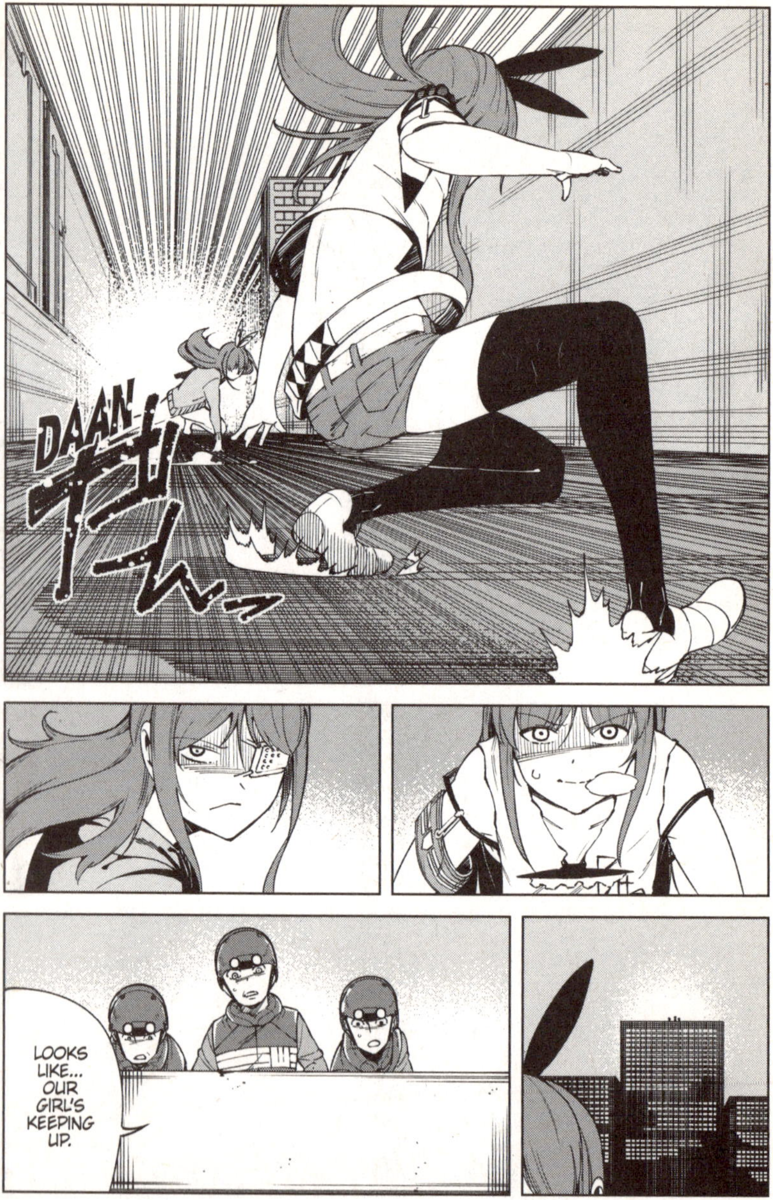
DAAN
LOOKS LIKE... OUR GIRL'S KEEPING UP.

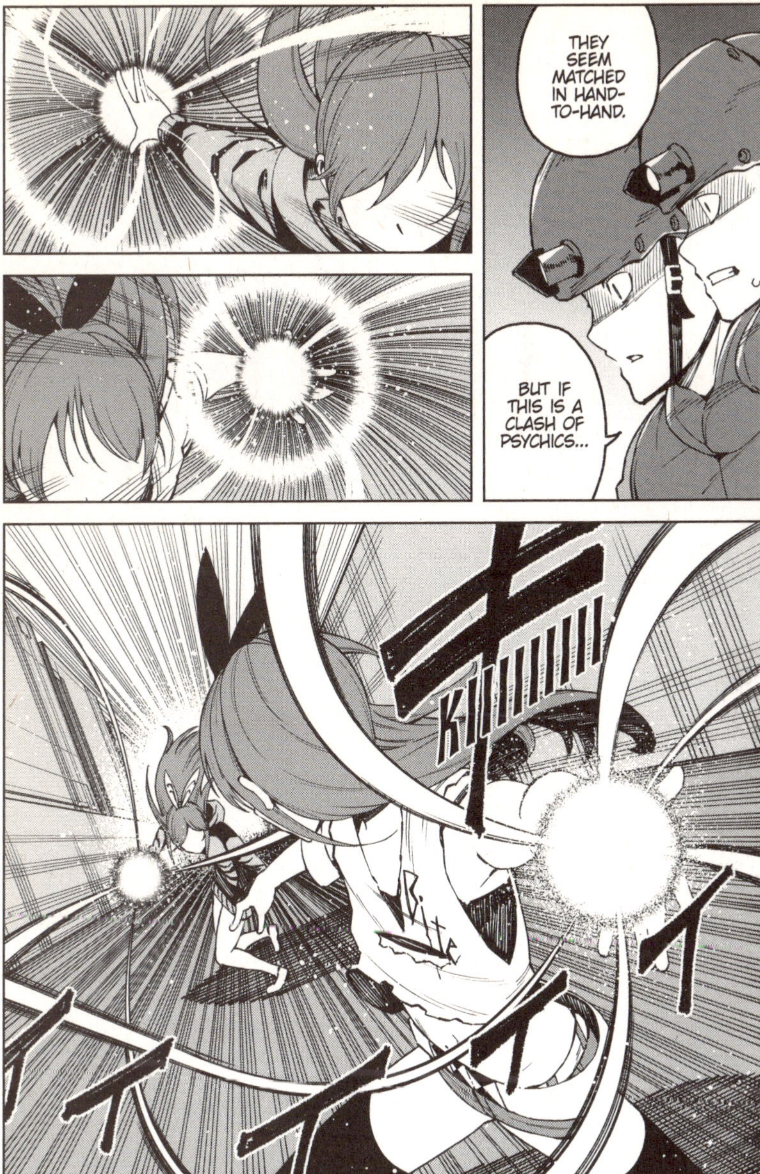
THEY SEEM MATCHED IN HAND-TO-HAND.
BUT IF THIS IS A CLASH OF PSYCHICS...
KIIIIIIII

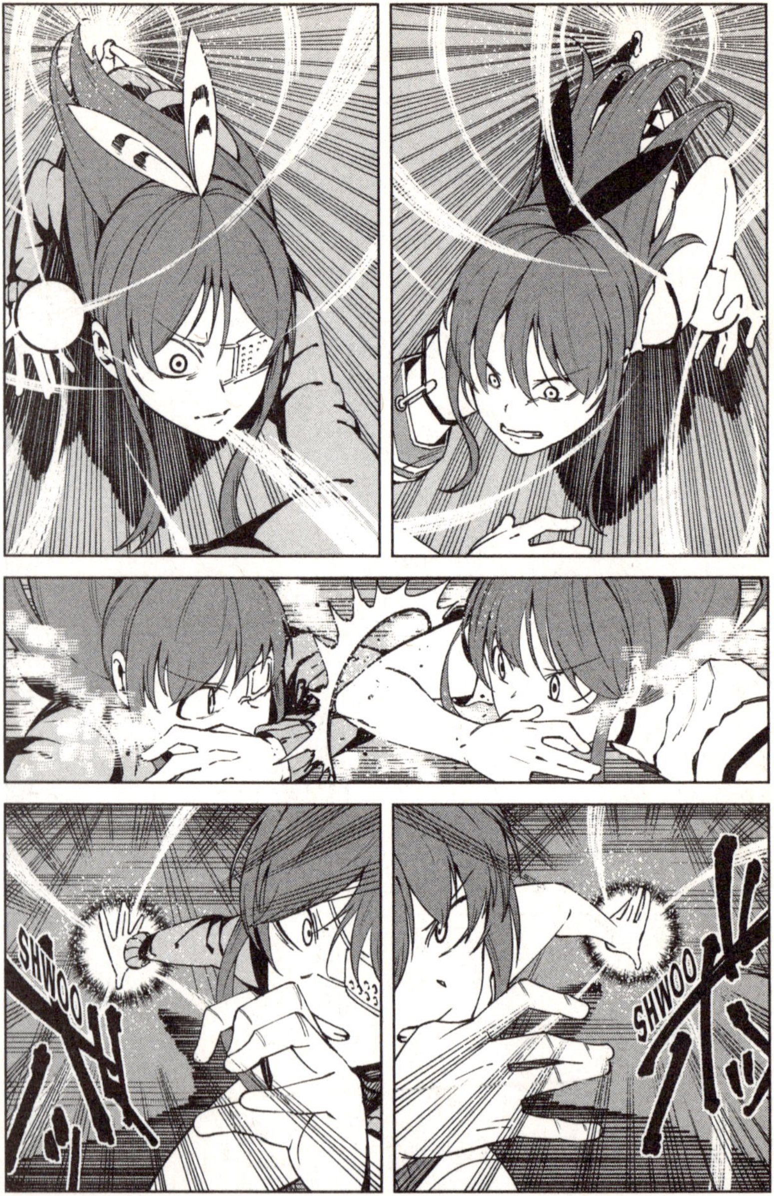
SHWOO
SHWOO

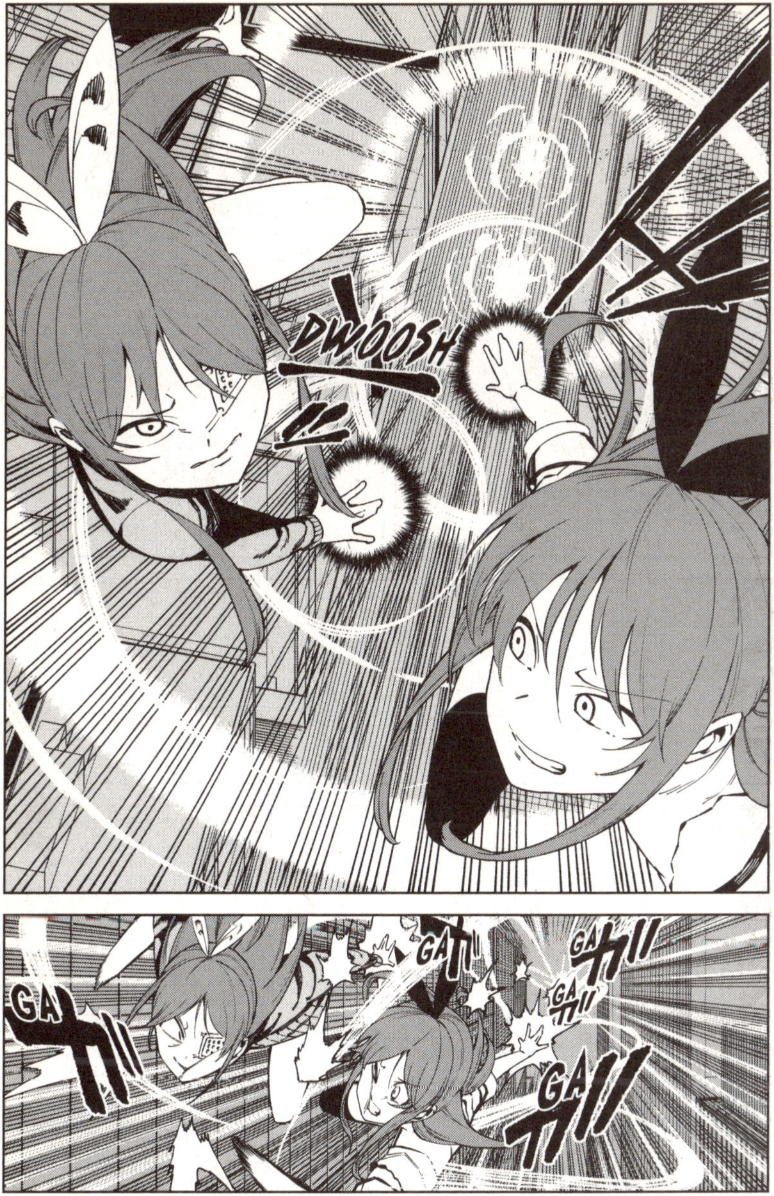
DWOOSH
GA
GA
GA
GA
GA

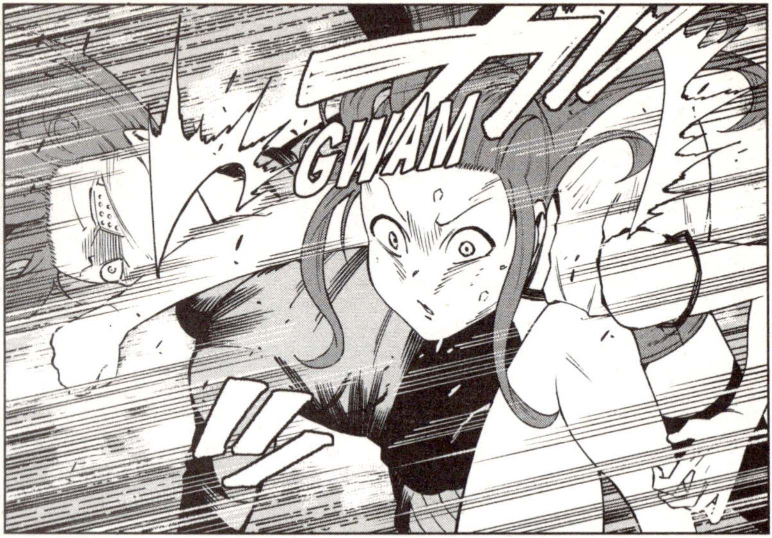
GWAM

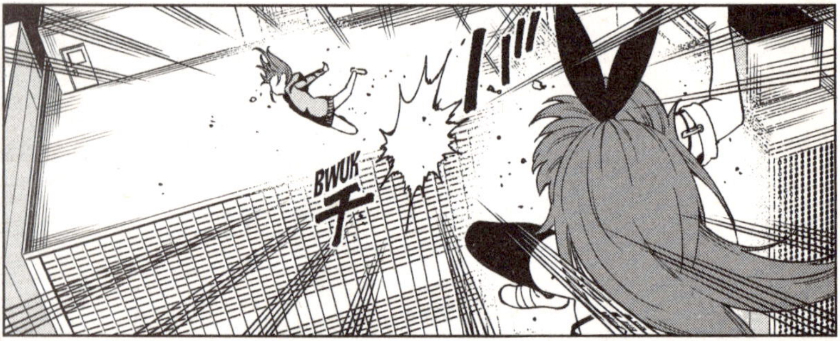
BWUK

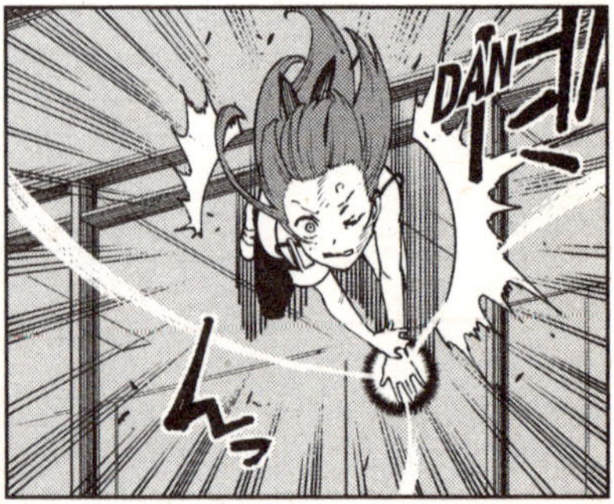
DAN

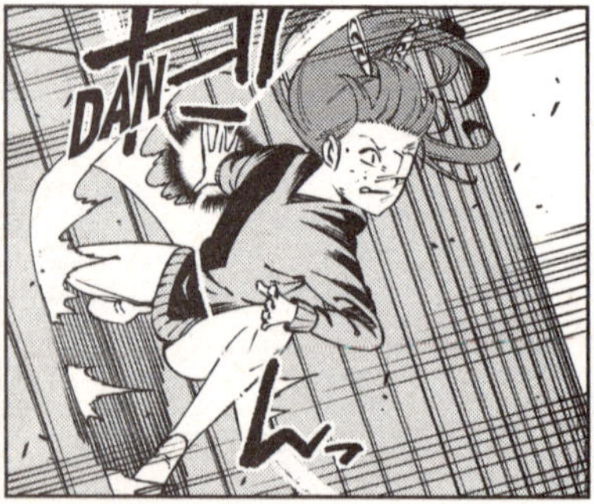
DAN

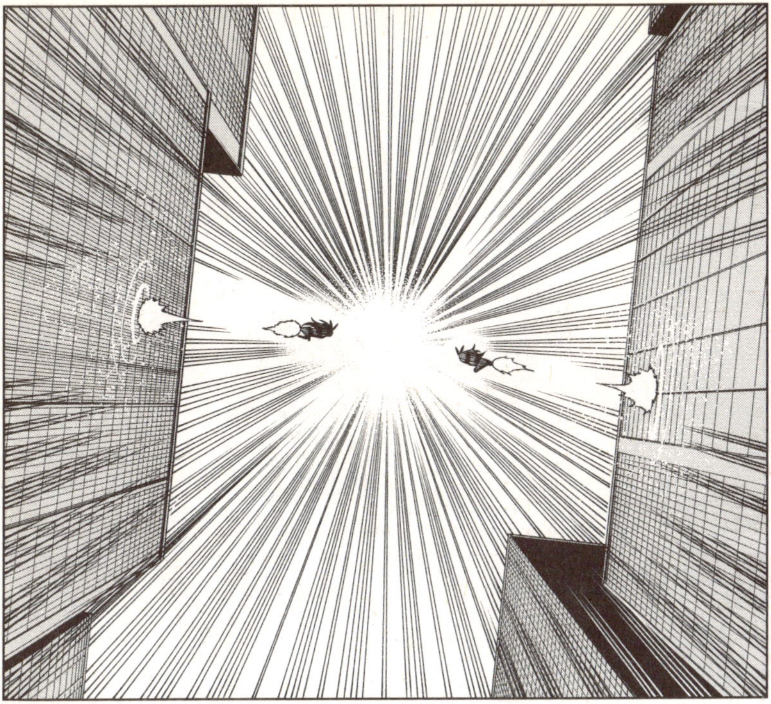

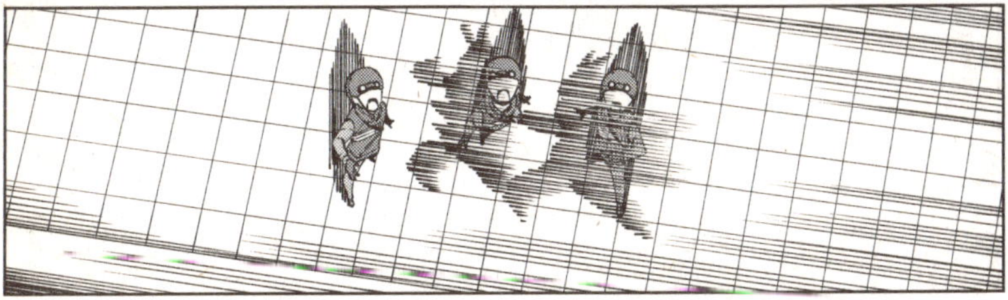

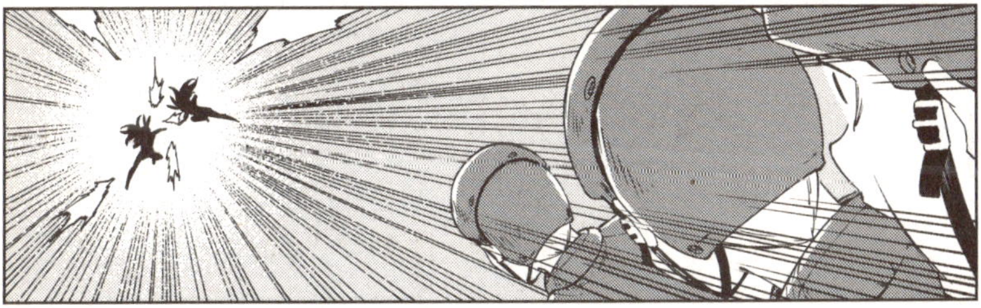

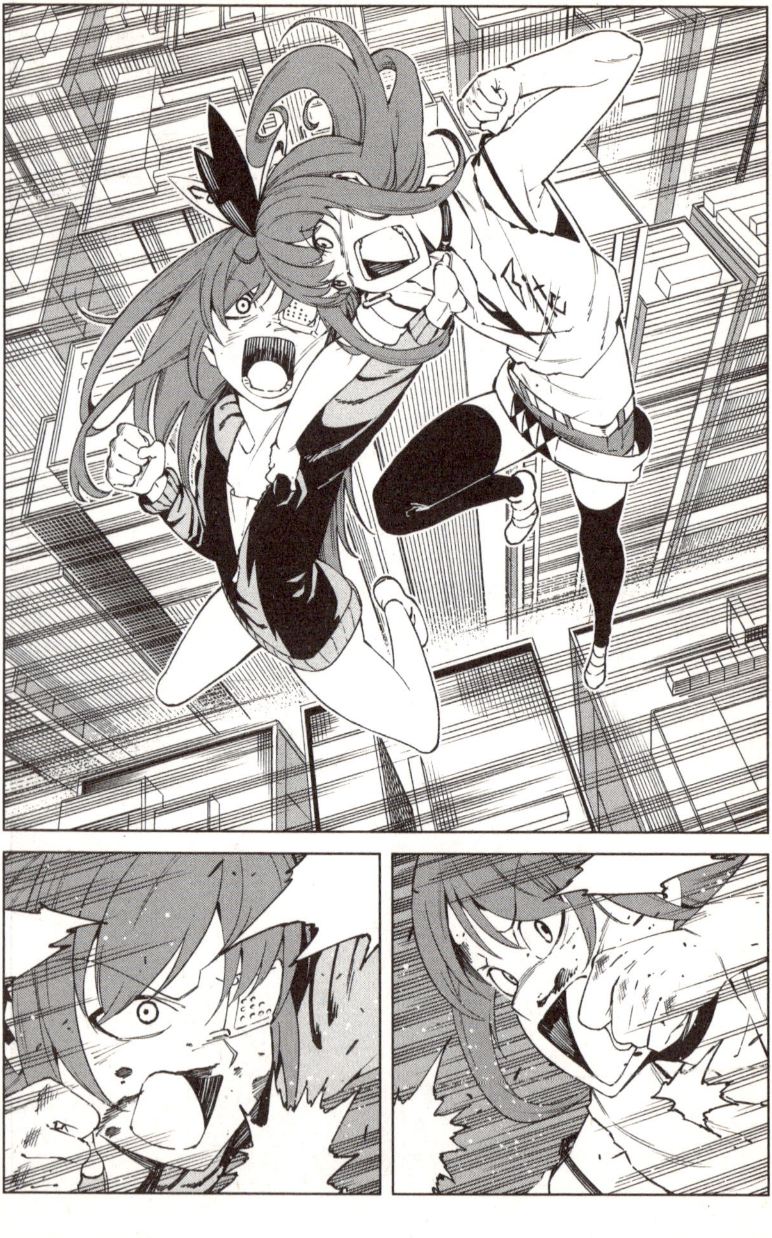

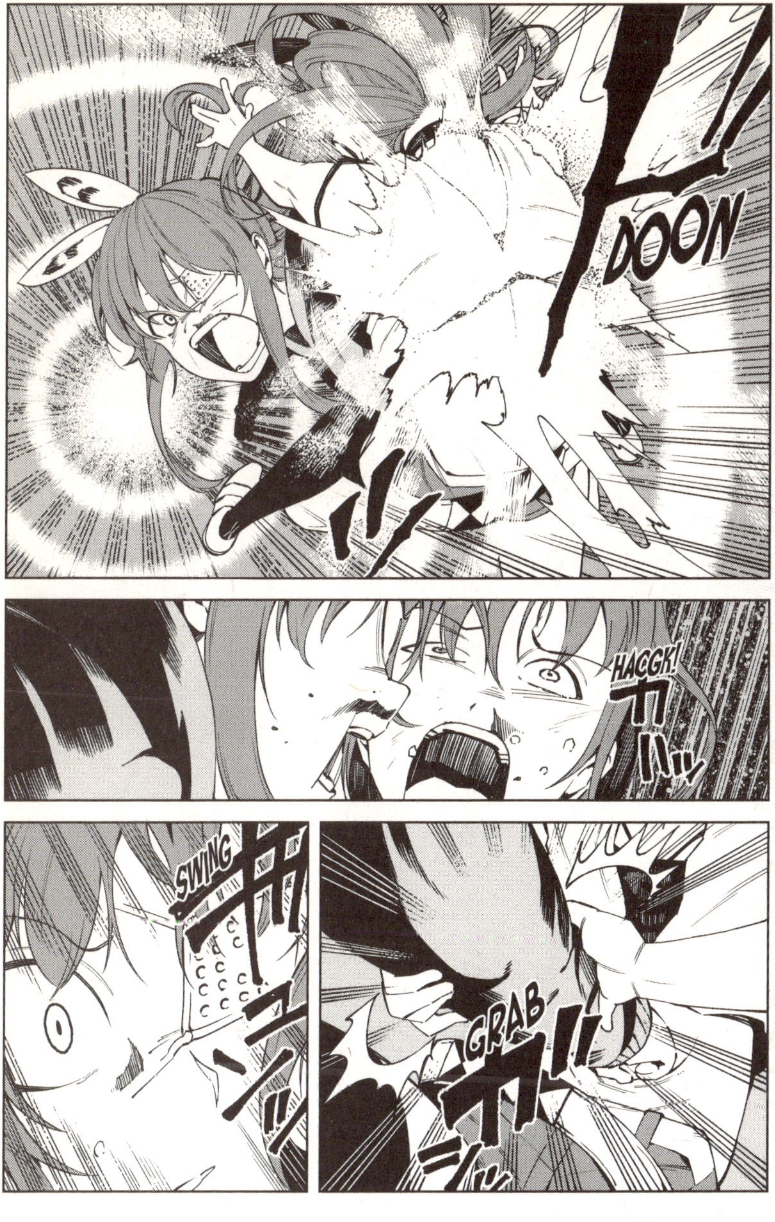
DOON
HACGK!
GRAB
SWING

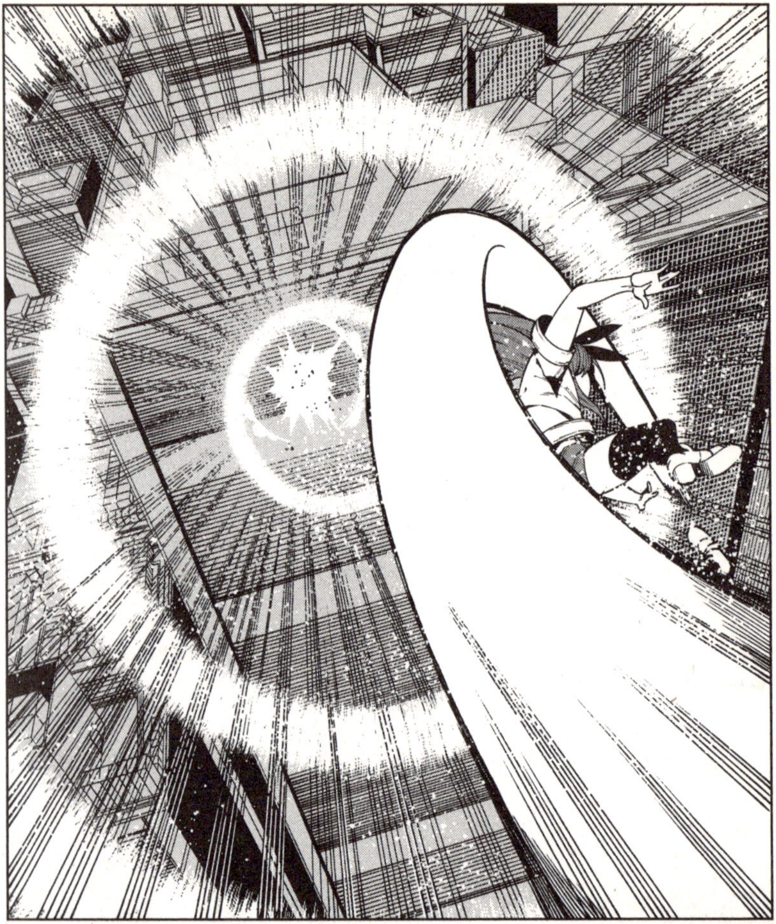
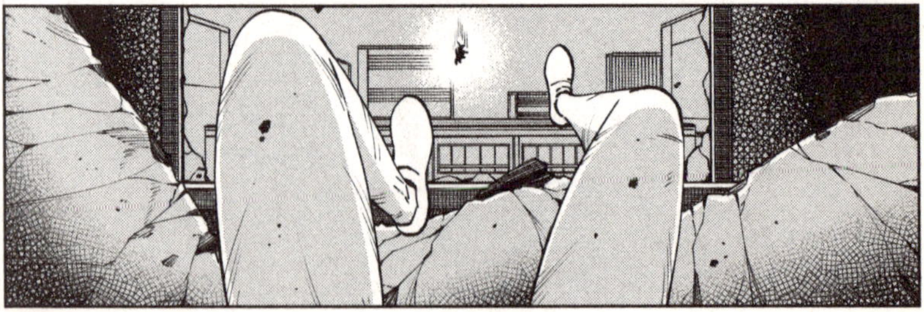

SPLORT!

AIR

BLORP!

FII

THUN

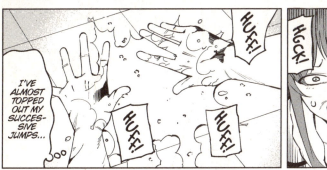

HUFF!

HUFF!

HUFF!

I'VE ALMOST TOPPED OUT MY SUCCESSIVE JUMPS...

HGCK!

HAAH!

MAMI USES THE SAME VOLCANIC BALL ABILITY AS ME-- TRAPPING THE FLOW OF AIR INTO A SPHERE, COMPRESSING, AND STRENGTHENING IT BEFORE UNLEASHING IT ALL AT ONCE.

WE CAN PROBABLY ONLY USE IT ONCE OR TWICE MORE, MAX. IF I FORCE HER TO DO THAT WITH ME, WE'LL BOTH BE OUT OF WEAPONS.

SO I NEED TO RESTRAIN MAMI WHILE I CAN STILL USE IT, OR...

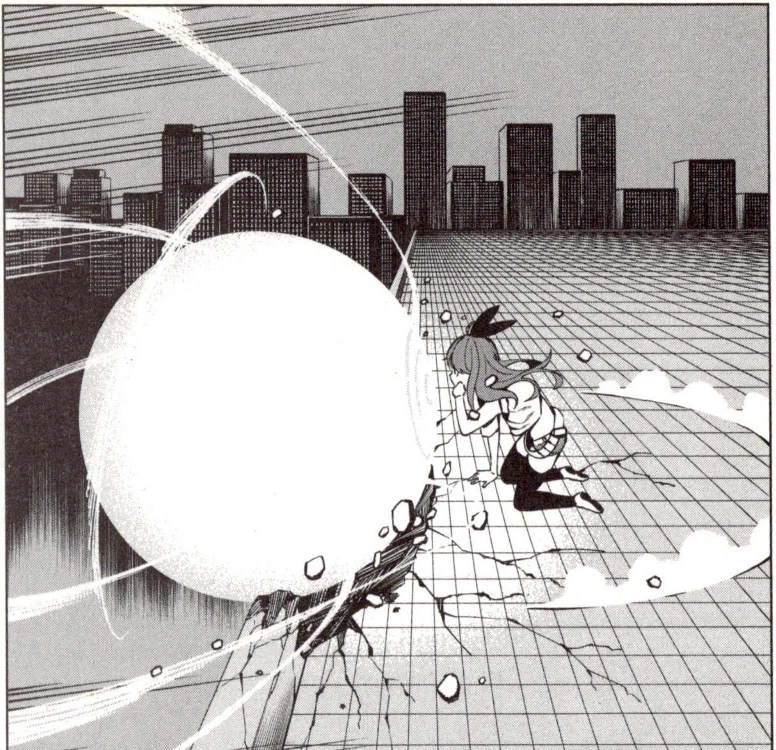

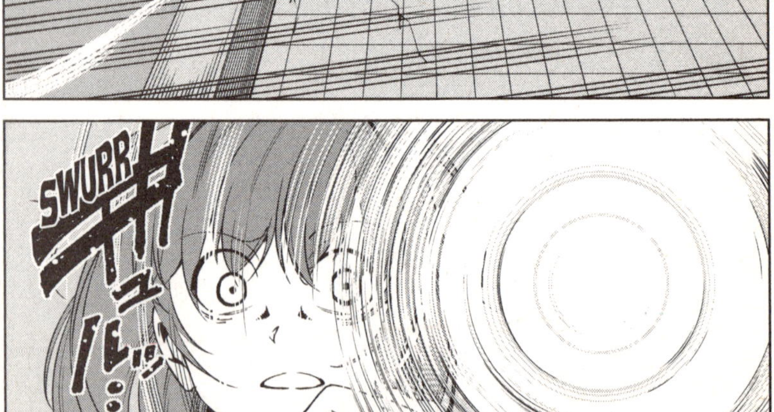
SWURR

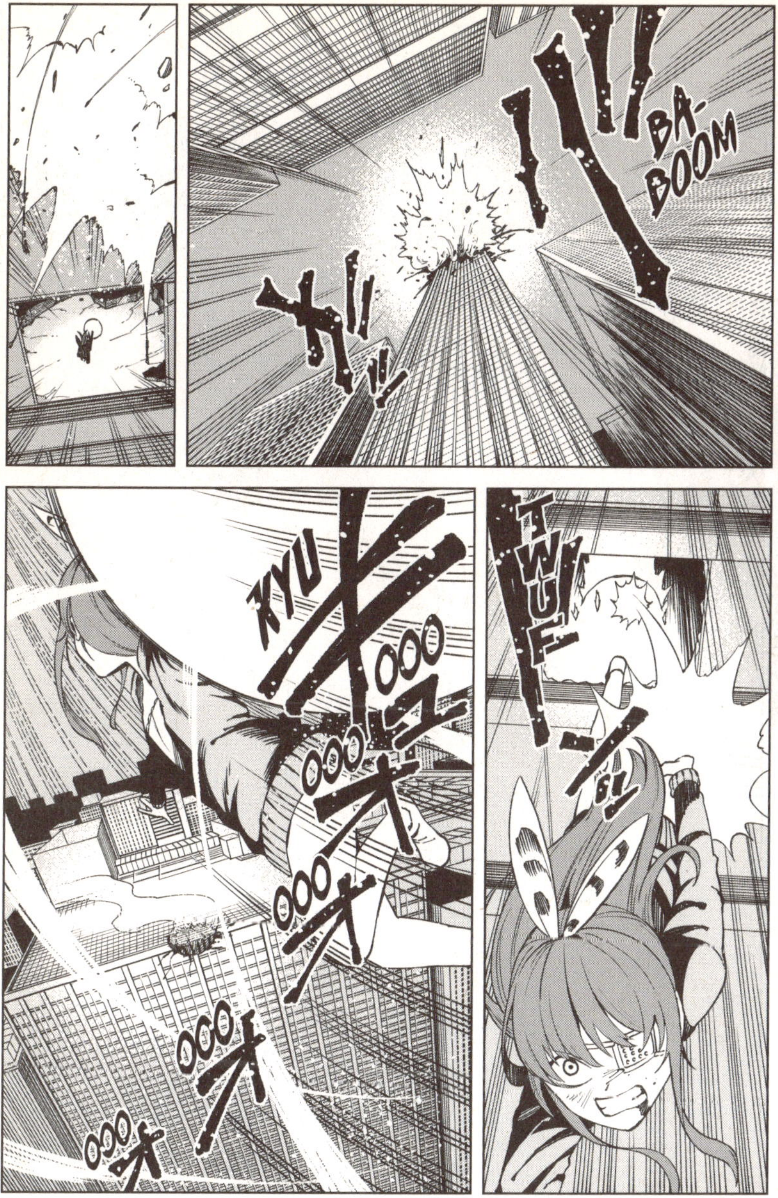
BA-
BOOM
TWUF
KYU

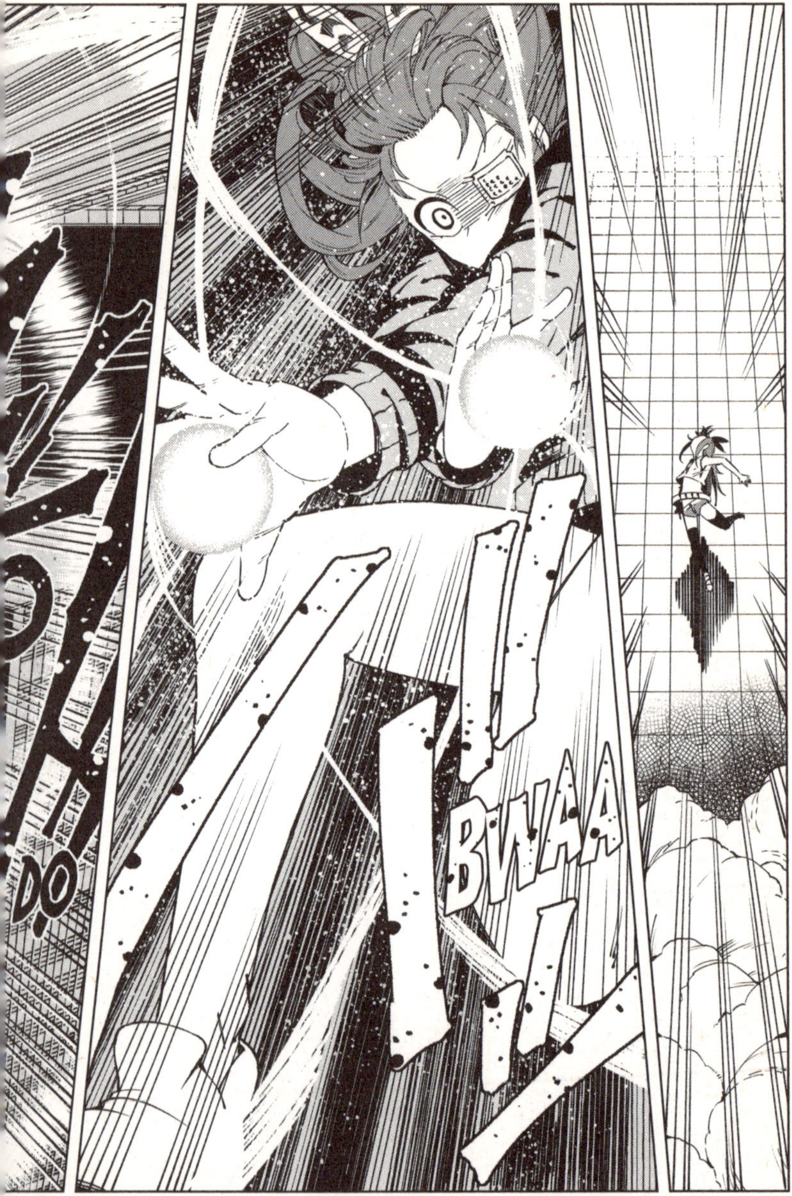
BWAA
DO

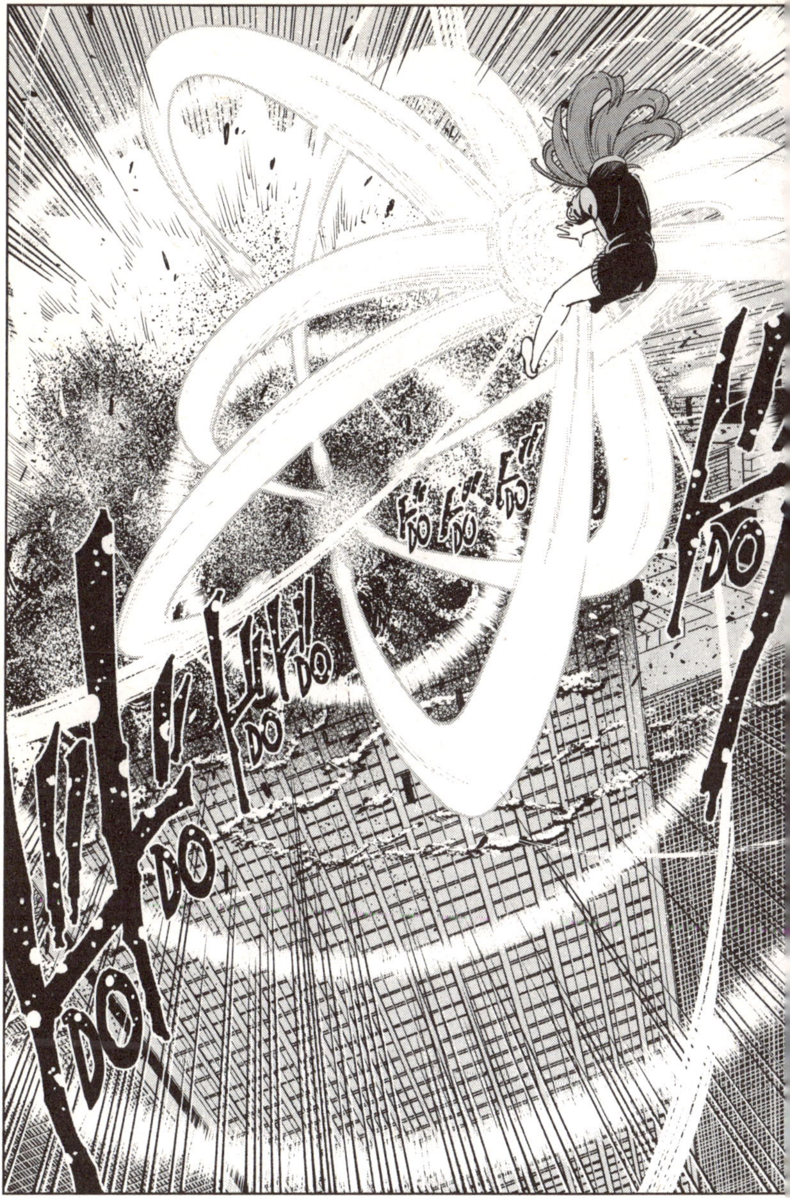
DO
DO
DO
DO
DO
DO
DO
DO

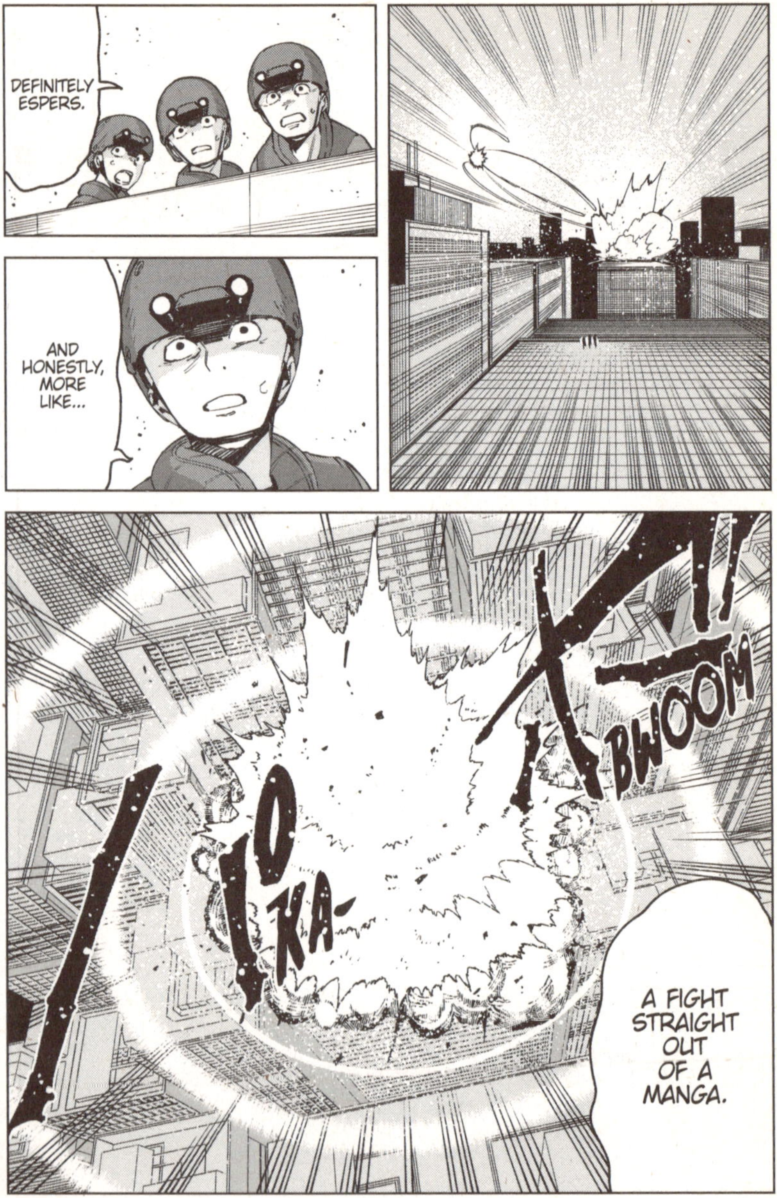
DEFINITELY ESPERS.
AND HONESTLY, MORE LIKE...
BWOOM
KA-
A FIGHT STRAIGHT OUT OF A MANGA.

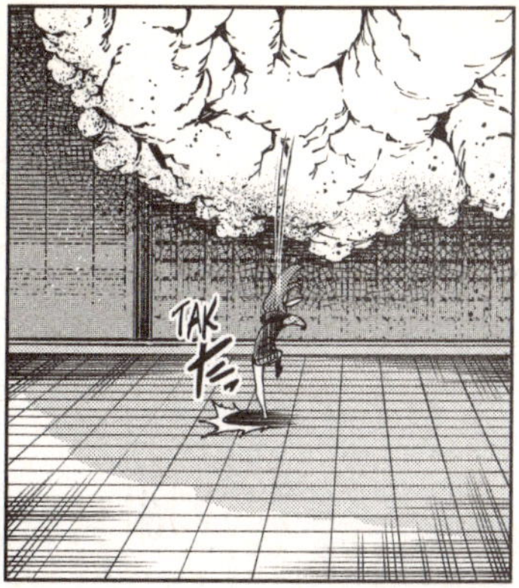
TAK
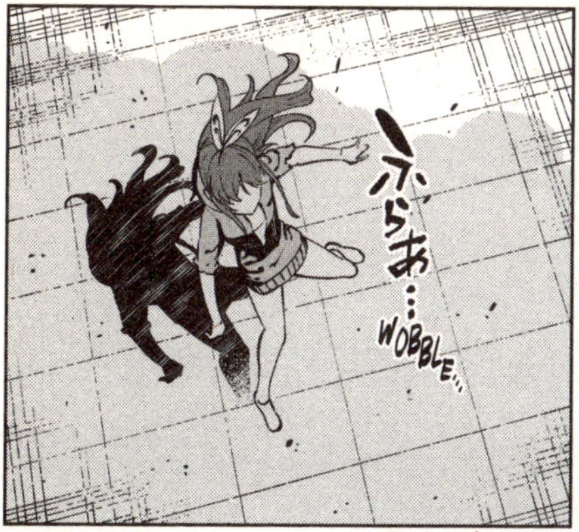
ふらぁ…
WOBBLE...
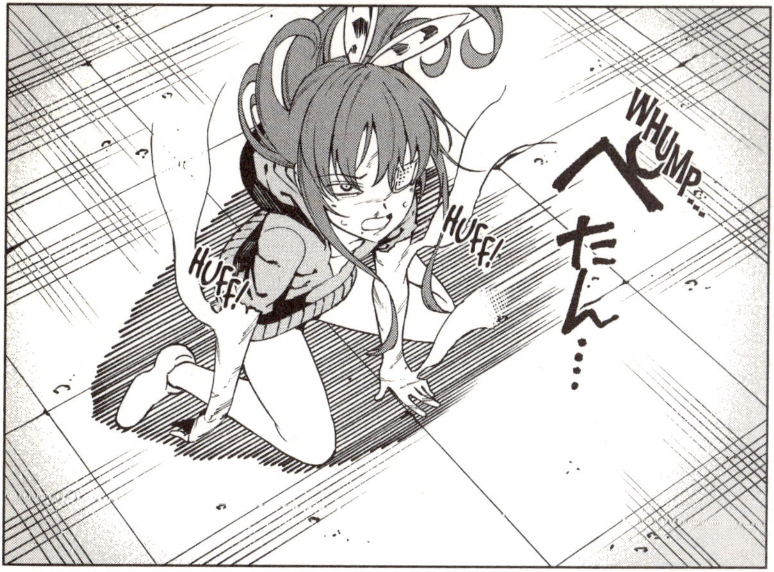
WHUMP...
へたん…
HUFF!
HUFF!
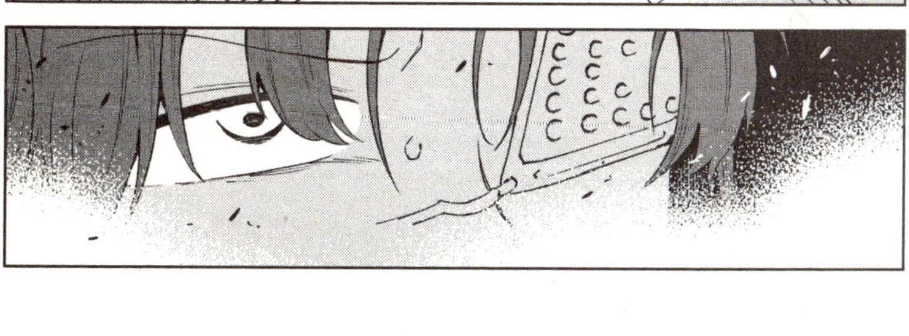

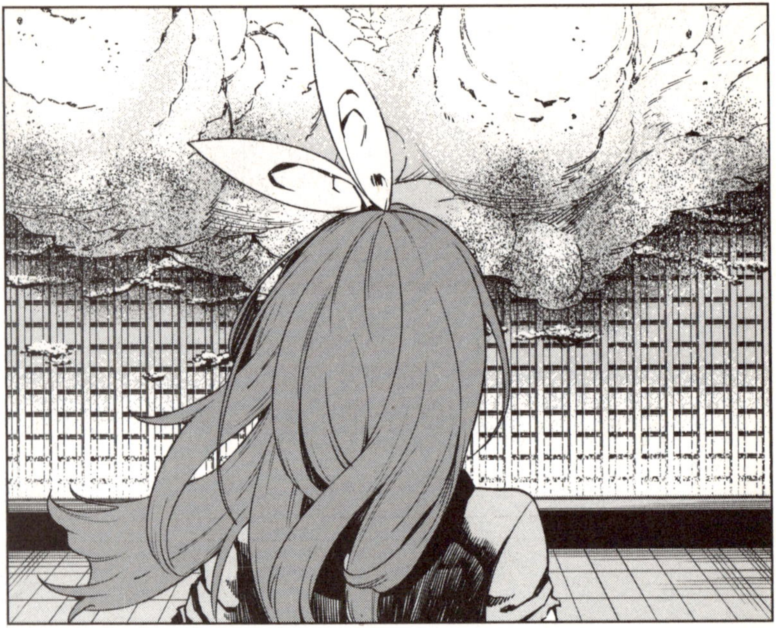
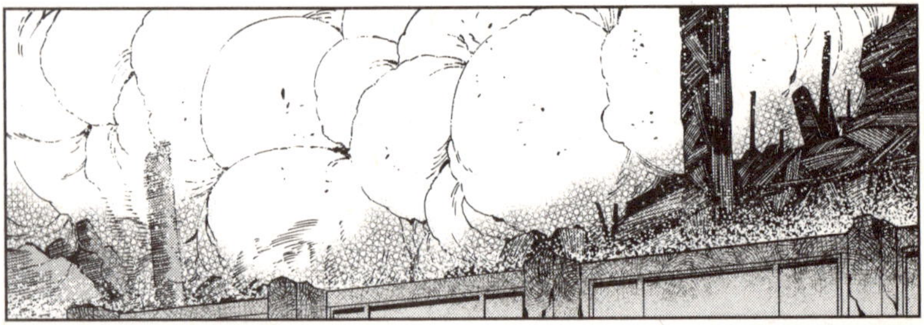
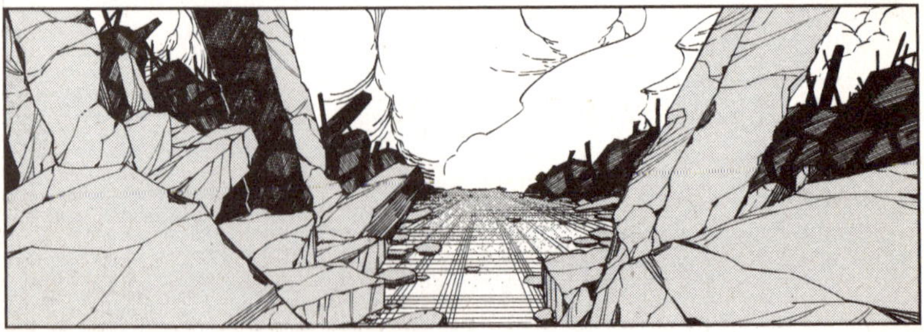

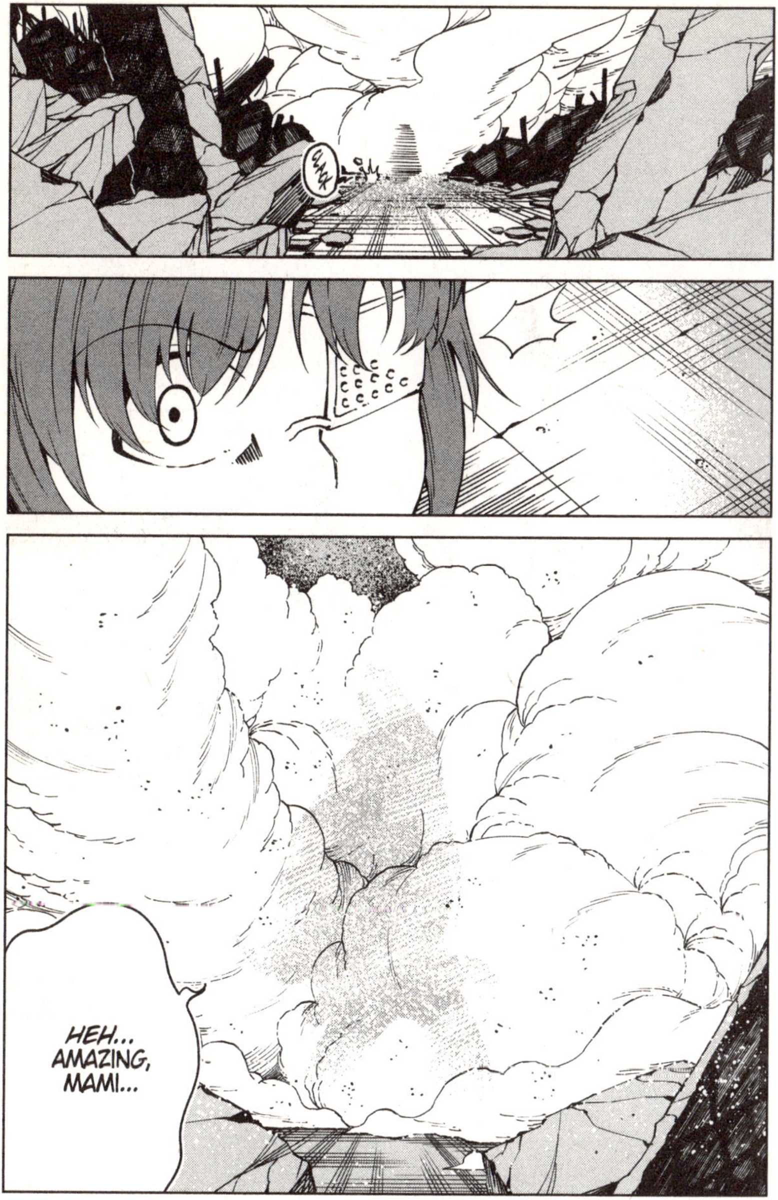
HEH... AMAZING, MAMI...

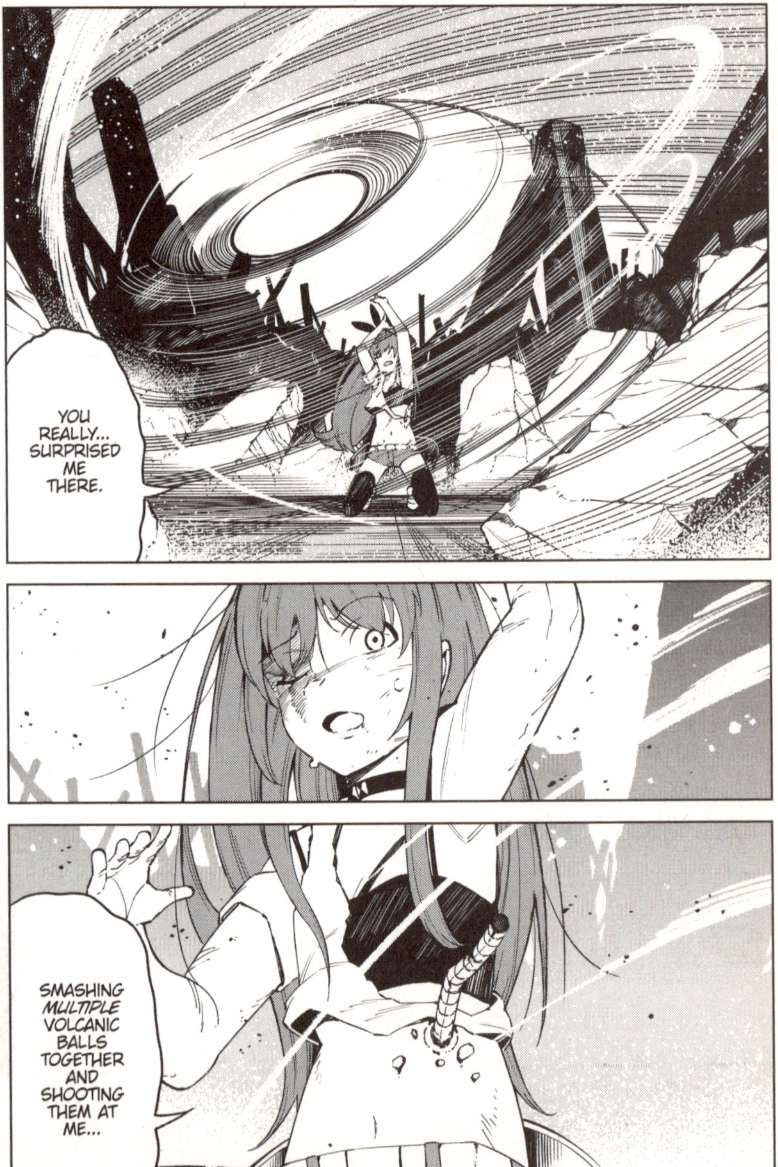
YOU REALLY... SURPRISED ME THERE.
SMASHING *MULTIPLE* VOLCANIC BALLS TOGETHER AND SHOOTING THEM AT ME...

BUT NOW YOU'VE HIT YOUR LIMIT, HUH?

I KNOW YOU HAVE. I KNOW YOU HAVE...

BECAUSE YOU'RE ME.

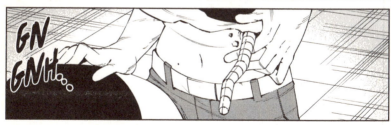

GN GNH...

NOW... CAN WE ACTUALLY TALK?

ず ず SLIIIDE! ず

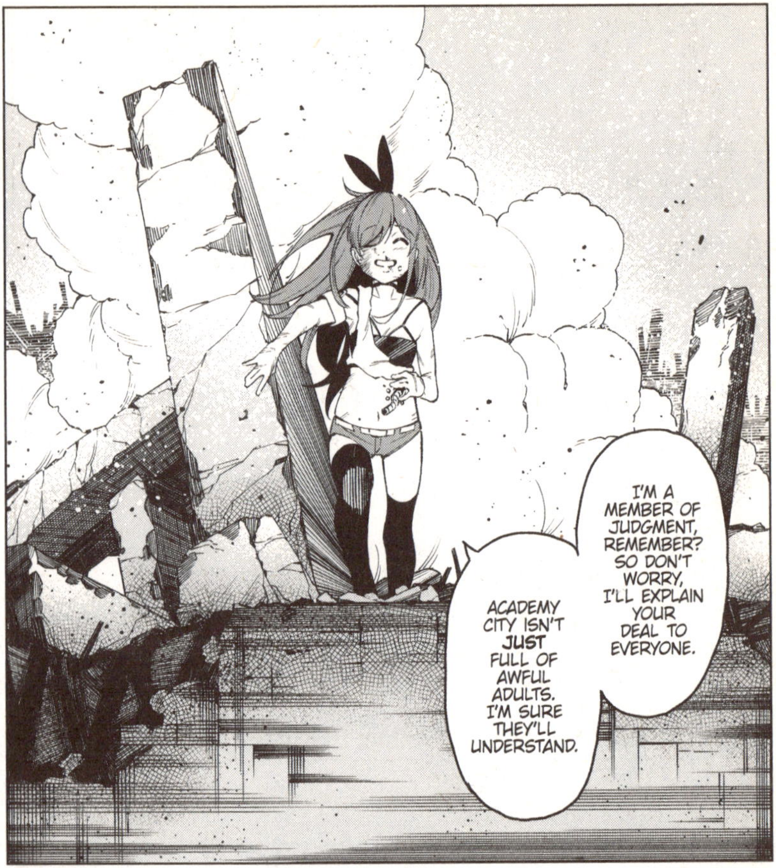
I'M A MEMBER OF JUDGMENT, REMEMBER? SO DON'T WORRY, I'LL EXPLAIN YOUR DEAL TO EVERYONE.
ACADEMY CITY ISN'T **JUST** FULL OF AWFUL ADULTS. I'M SURE THEY'LL UNDERSTAND.

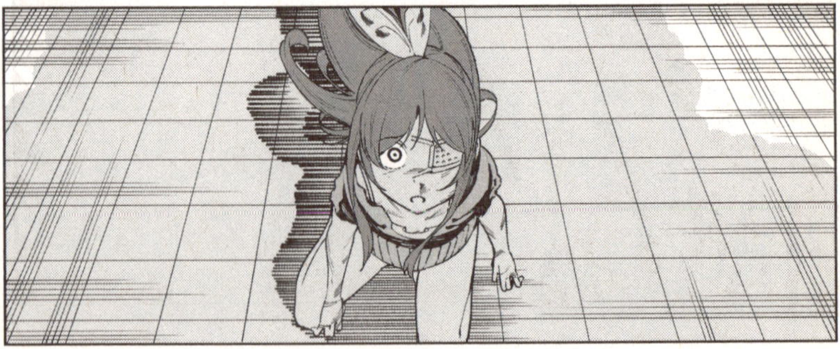

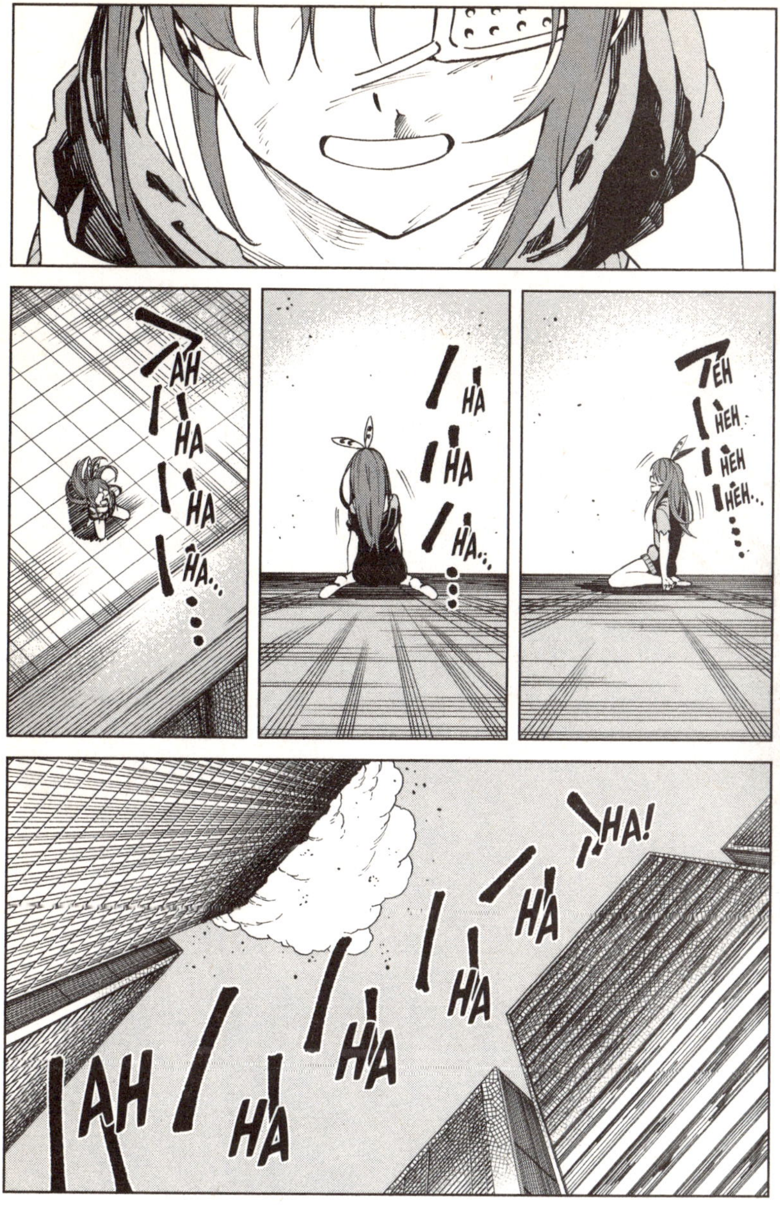
EH HEH HEH HEH...
HA HA HA...
AH HA HA HA...
AH HA HA HA HA HA!

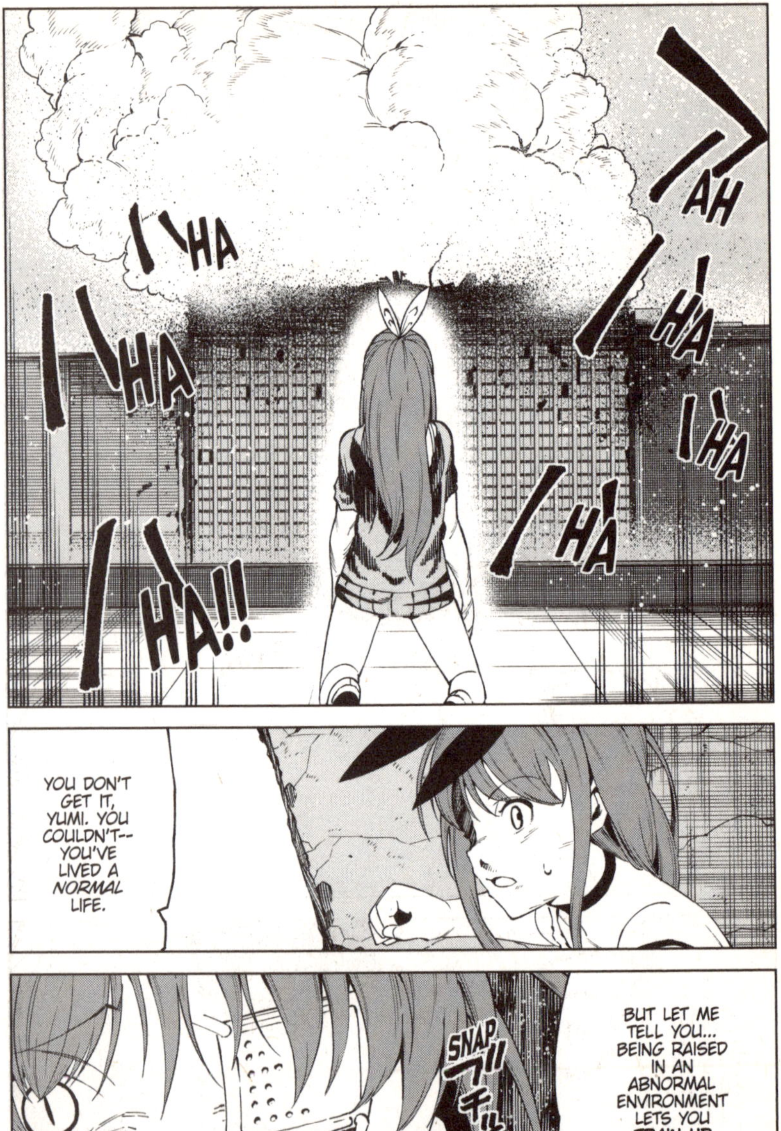
AH
HA
HA
HA
HA
HA
HA
HA!!
YOU DON'T GET IT, YUMI. YOU COULDN'T-- YOU'VE LIVED A *NORMAL* LIFE.
BUT LET ME TELL YOU... BEING RAISED IN AN ABNORMAL ENVIRONMENT LETS YOU **TRAIN UP** YOUR ABILITY.
SNAP

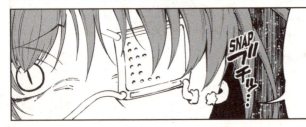

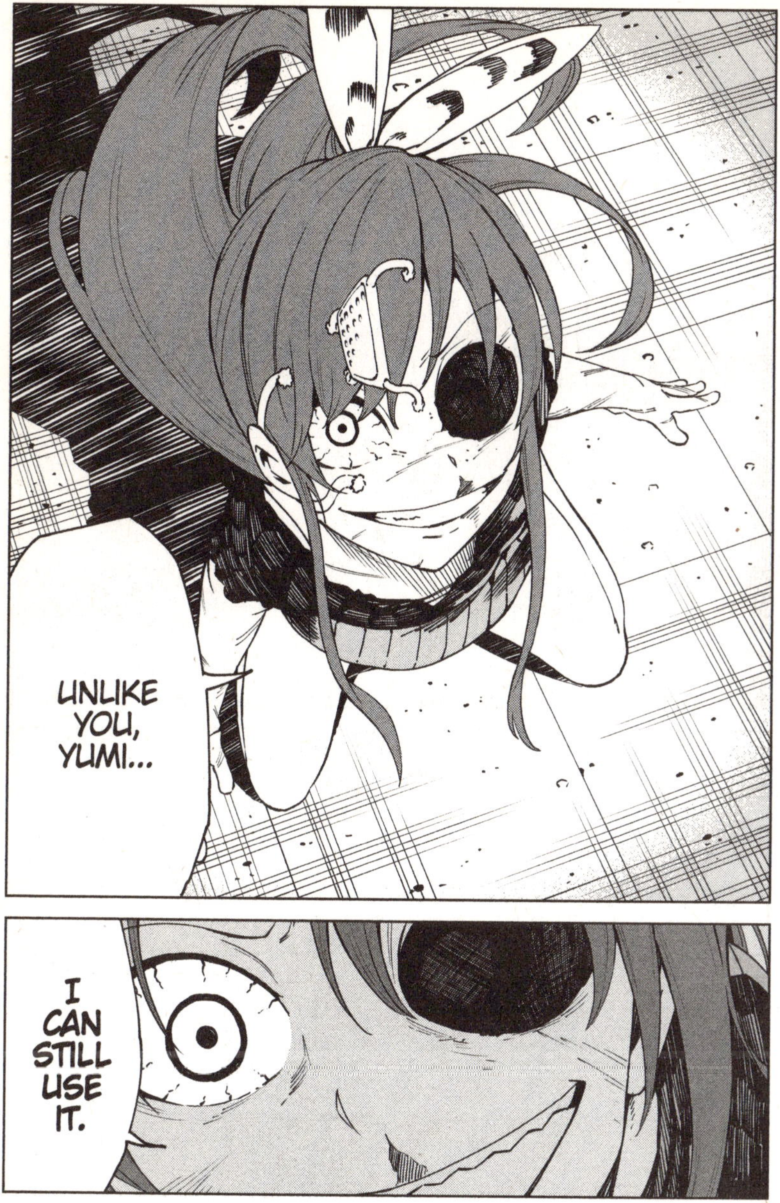
UNLIKE YOU, YUMI...
I CAN STILL USE IT.

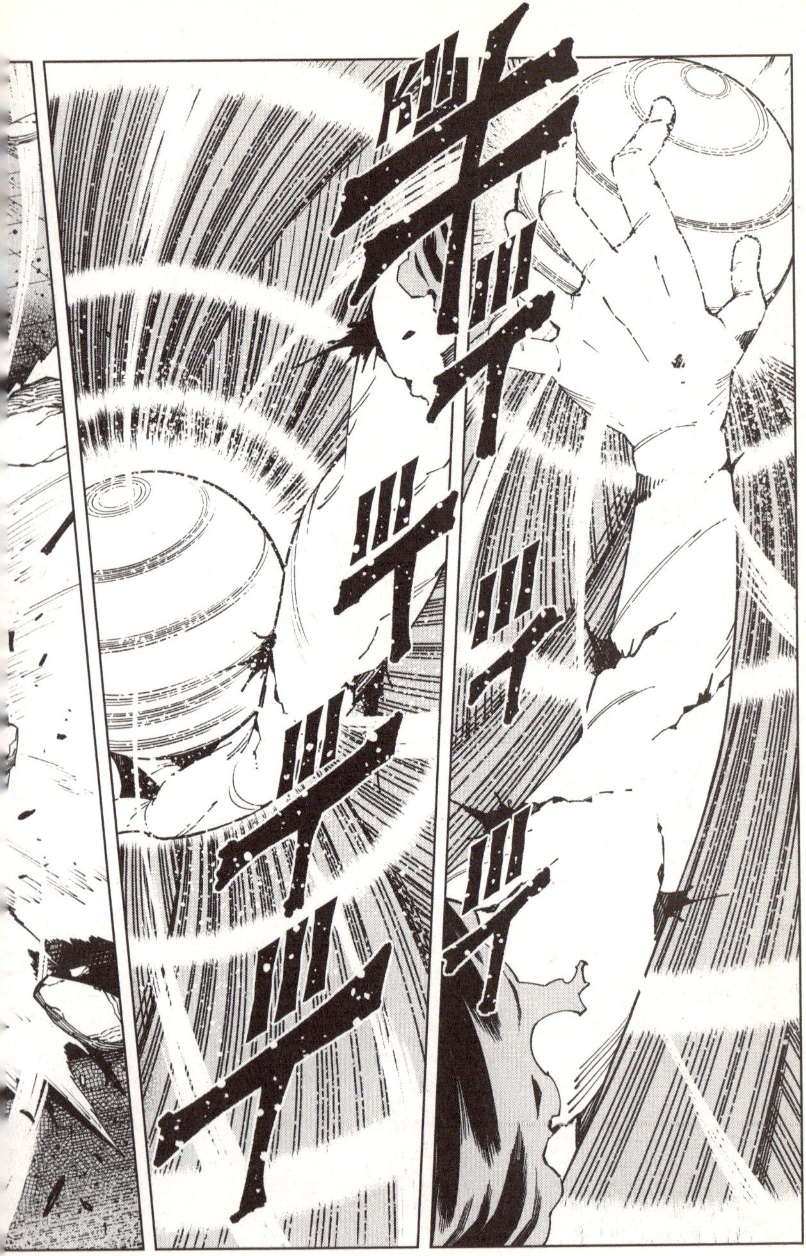
KRII

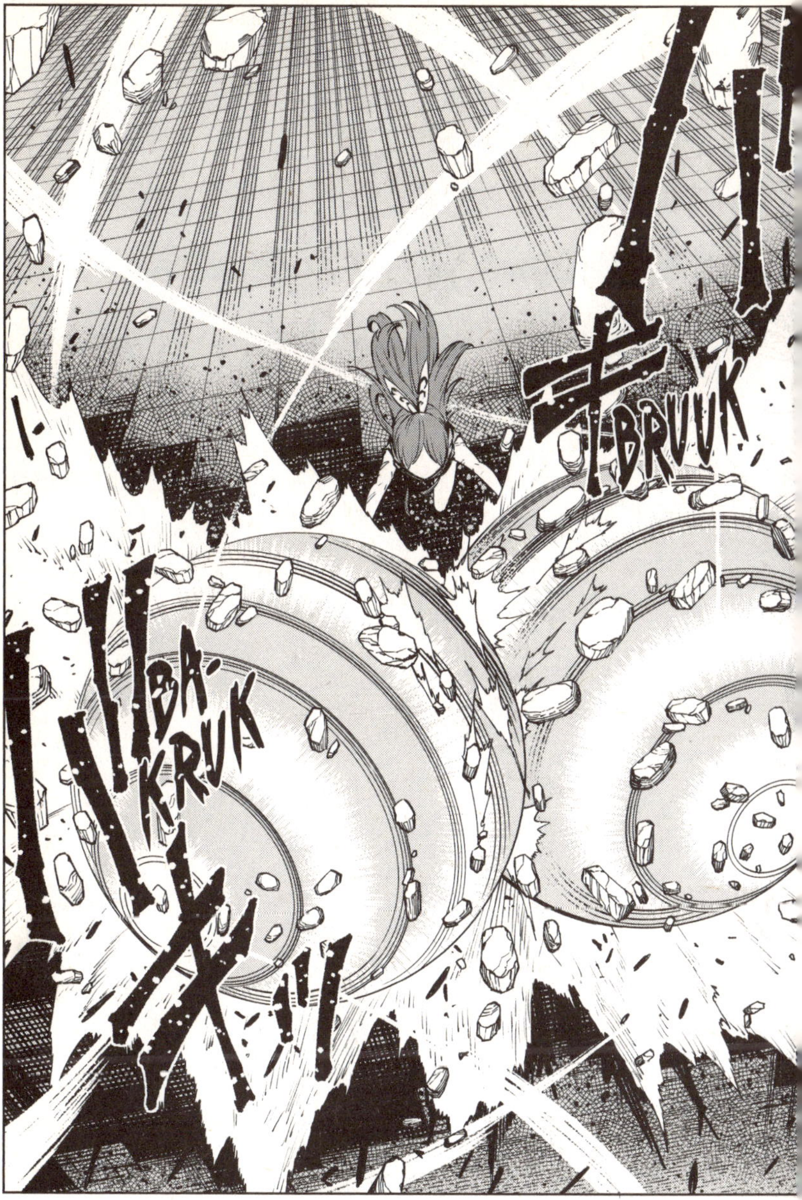
BRUUK
BA-KRUK

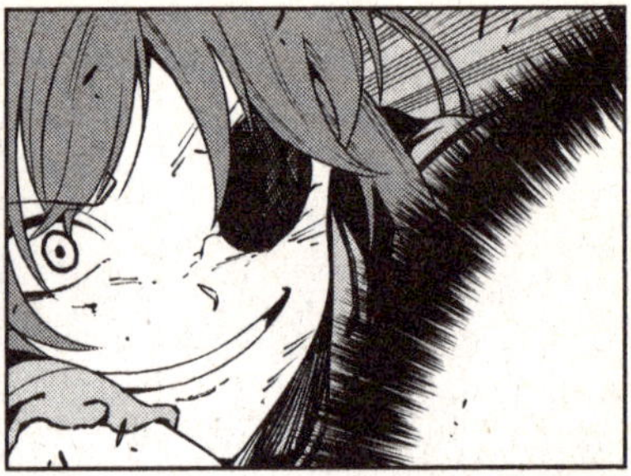
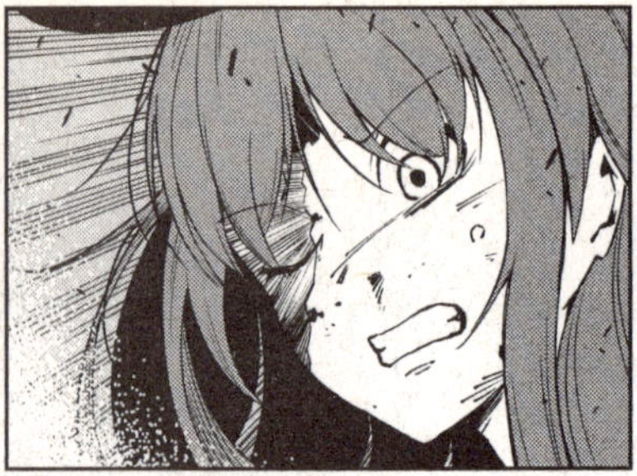
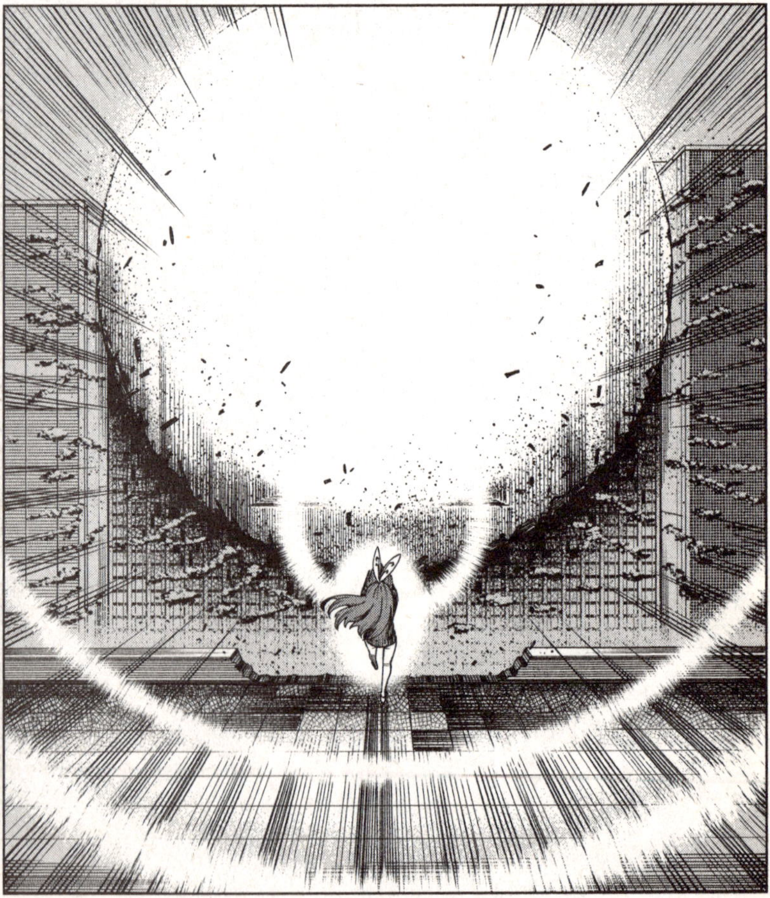

a certain
SCIENTIFIC
ACCELERATOR

とある科学の一方通行

アクセラレータ

とある魔術の禁書目録外伝

# CHAPTER 47

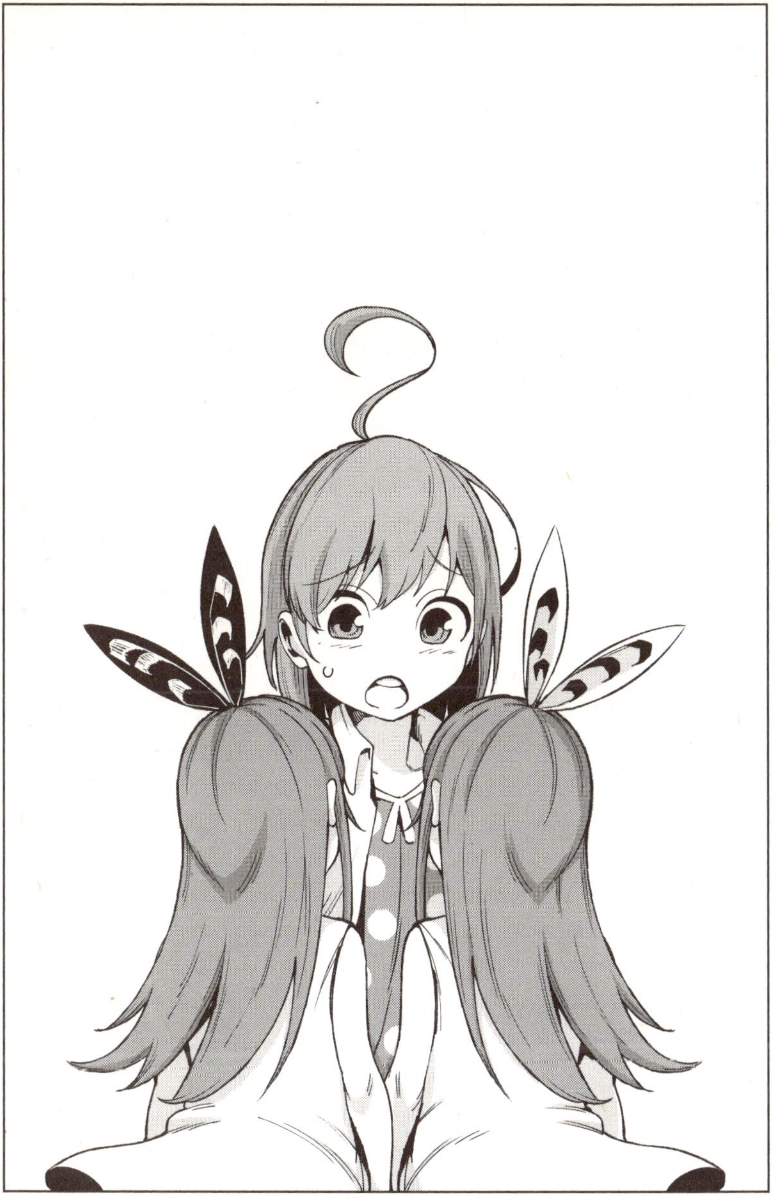

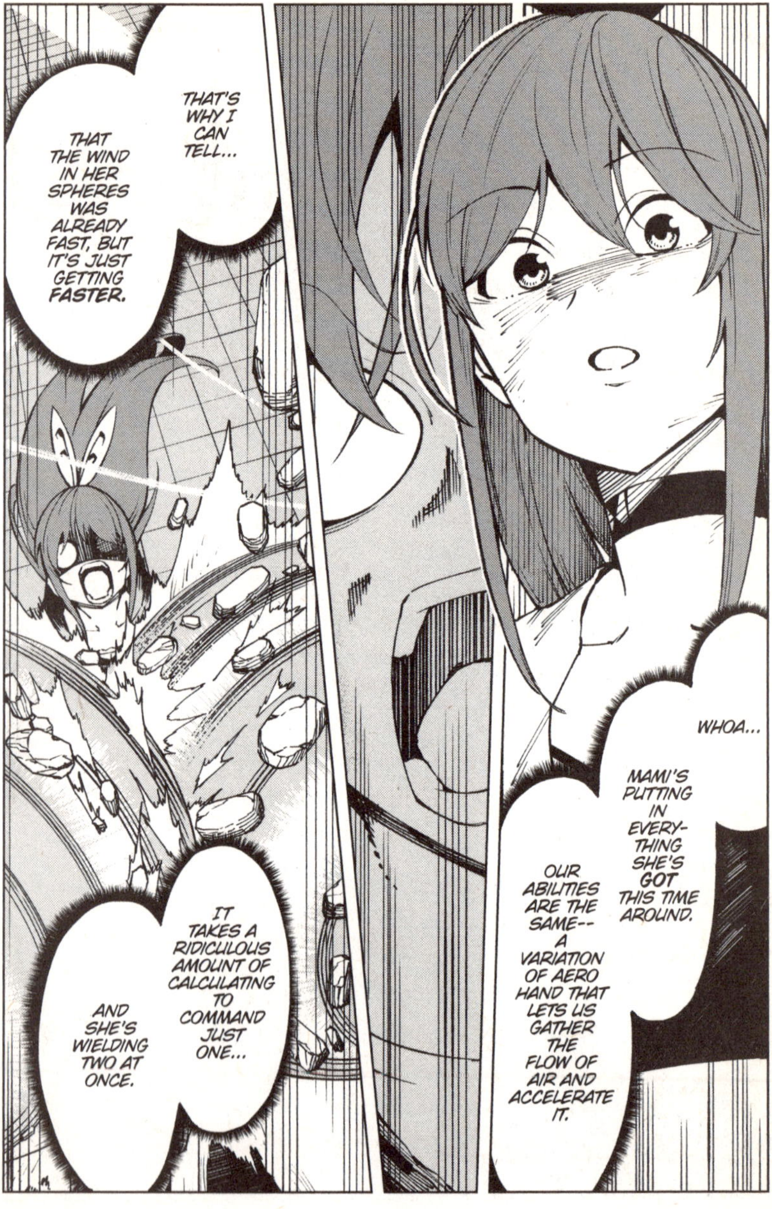
WHOA...
MAMI'S PUTTING IN EVERYTHING SHE'S GOT THIS TIME AROUND.
OUR ABILITIES ARE THE SAME-- A VARIATION OF AERO HAND THAT LETS US GATHER THE FLOW OF AIR AND ACCELERATE IT.
THAT'S WHY I CAN TELL...
THAT THE WIND IN HER SPHERES WAS ALREADY FAST, BUT IT'S JUST GETTING FASTER.
IT TAKES A RIDICULOUS AMOUNT OF CALCULATING TO COMMAND JUST ONE...
AND SHE'S WIELDING TWO AT ONCE.

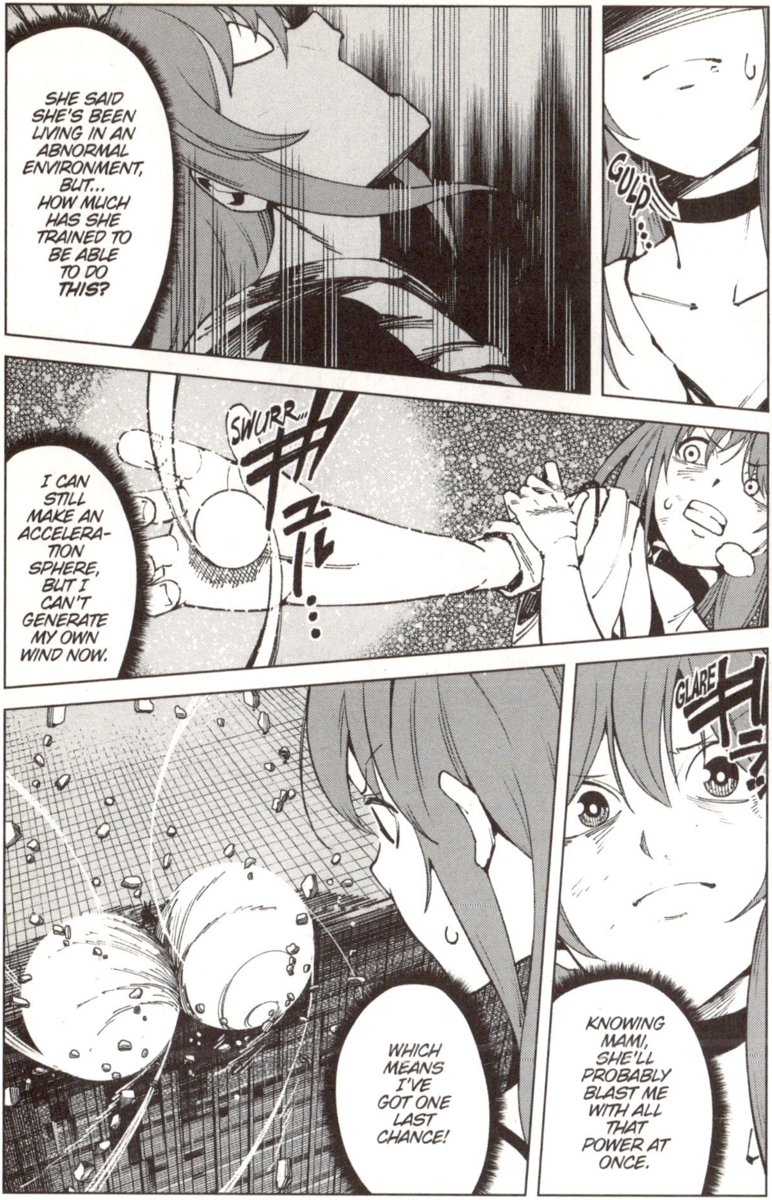
GULP...
SHE SAID SHE'S BEEN LIVING IN AN ABNORMAL ENVIRONMENT, BUT... HOW MUCH HAS SHE TRAINED TO BE ABLE TO DO THIS?
SWURR...
I CAN STILL MAKE AN ACCELERATION SPHERE, BUT I CAN'T GENERATE MY OWN WIND NOW.
GLARE
KNOWING MAMI, SHE'LL PROBABLY BLAST ME WITH ALL THAT POWER AT ONCE.
WHICH MEANS I'VE GOT ONE LAST CHANCE!

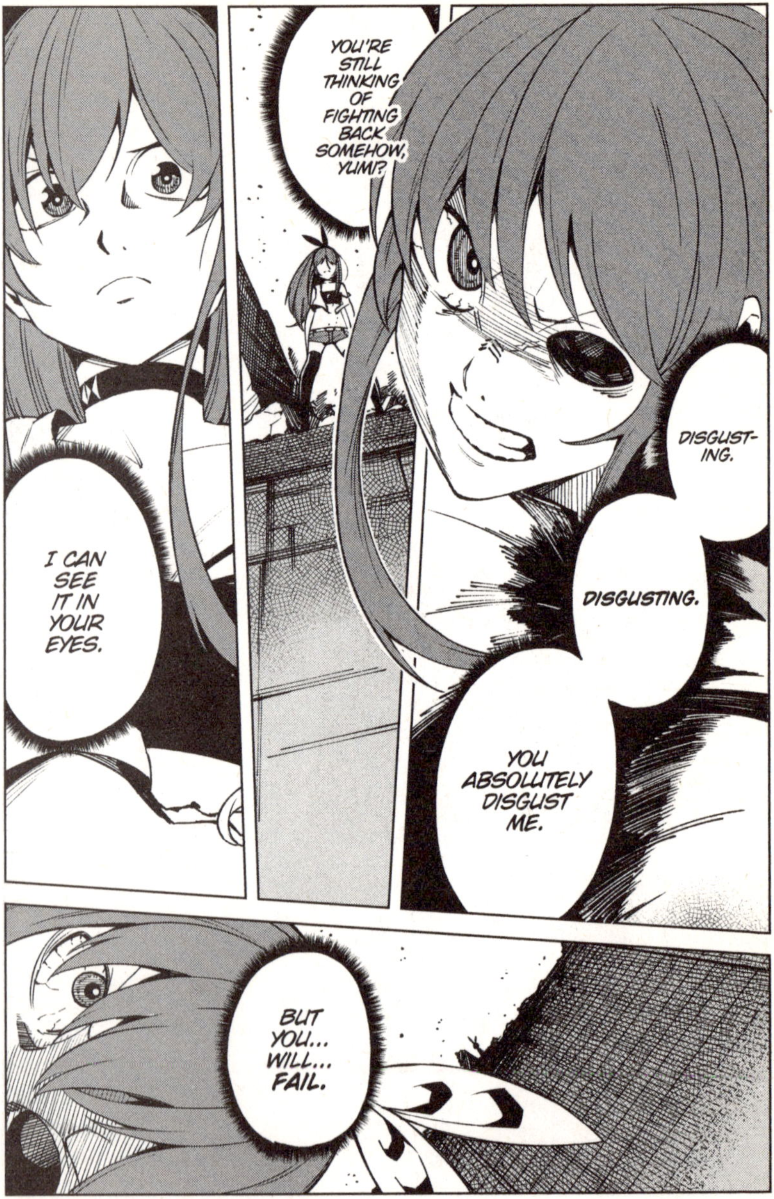
YOU'RE STILL THINKING OF FIGHTING BACK SOMEHOW, YUMI?
DISGUST-ING.
DISGUSTING.
YOU ABSOLUTELY DISGUST ME.
I CAN SEE IT IN YOUR EYES.
BUT YOU... WILL... FAIL.

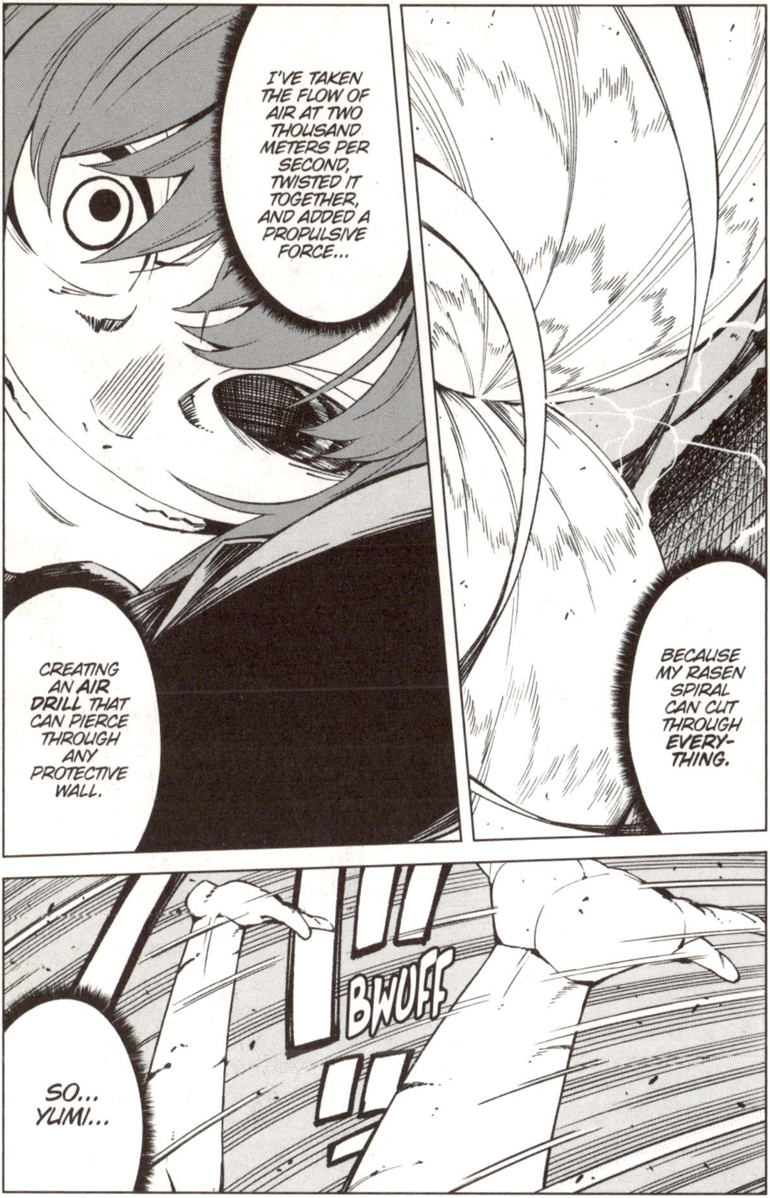
I'VE TAKEN THE FLOW OF AIR AT TWO THOUSAND METERS PER SECOND, TWISTED IT TOGETHER, AND ADDED A PROPULSIVE FORCE...
CREATING AN AIR DRILL THAT CAN PIERCE THROUGH ANY PROTECTIVE WALL.
BECAUSE MY RASEN SPIRAL CAN CUT THROUGH EVERYTHING.
BWUFF
SO... YUMI...

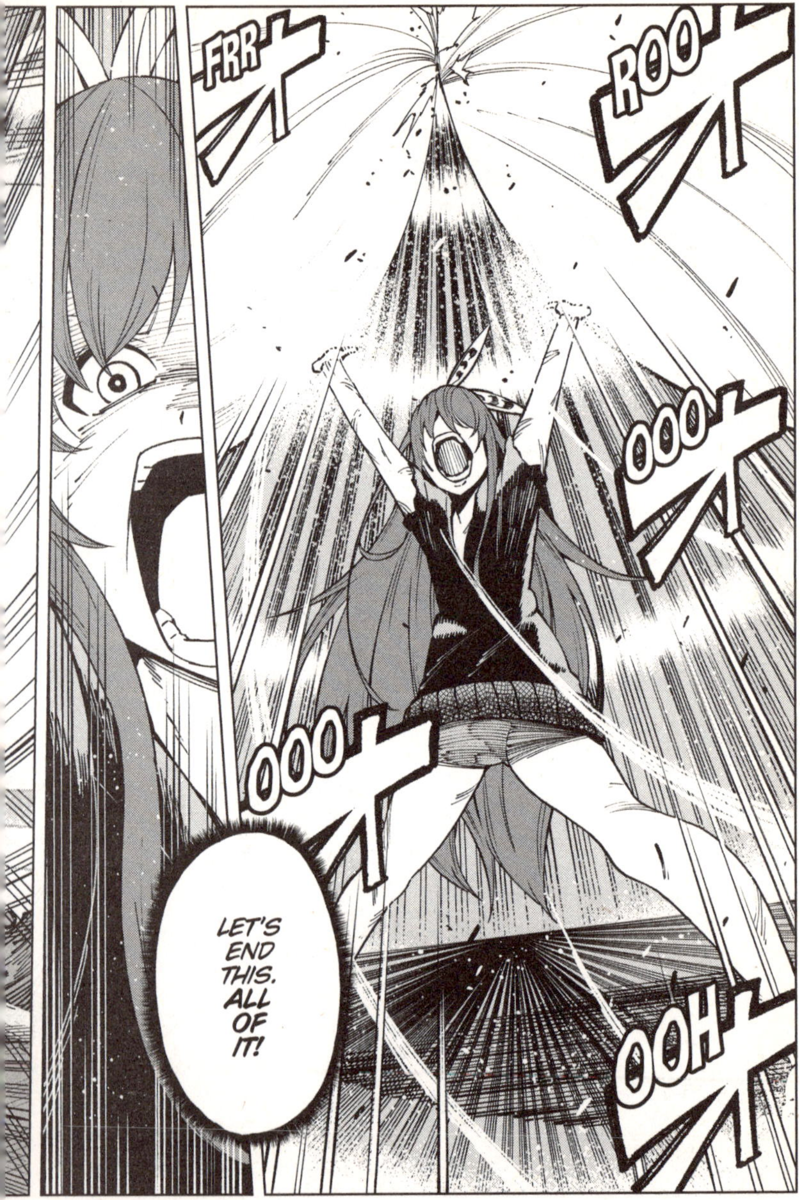
FRR
ROO
OOO
OOO
OOH
LET'S END THIS. ALL OF IT!

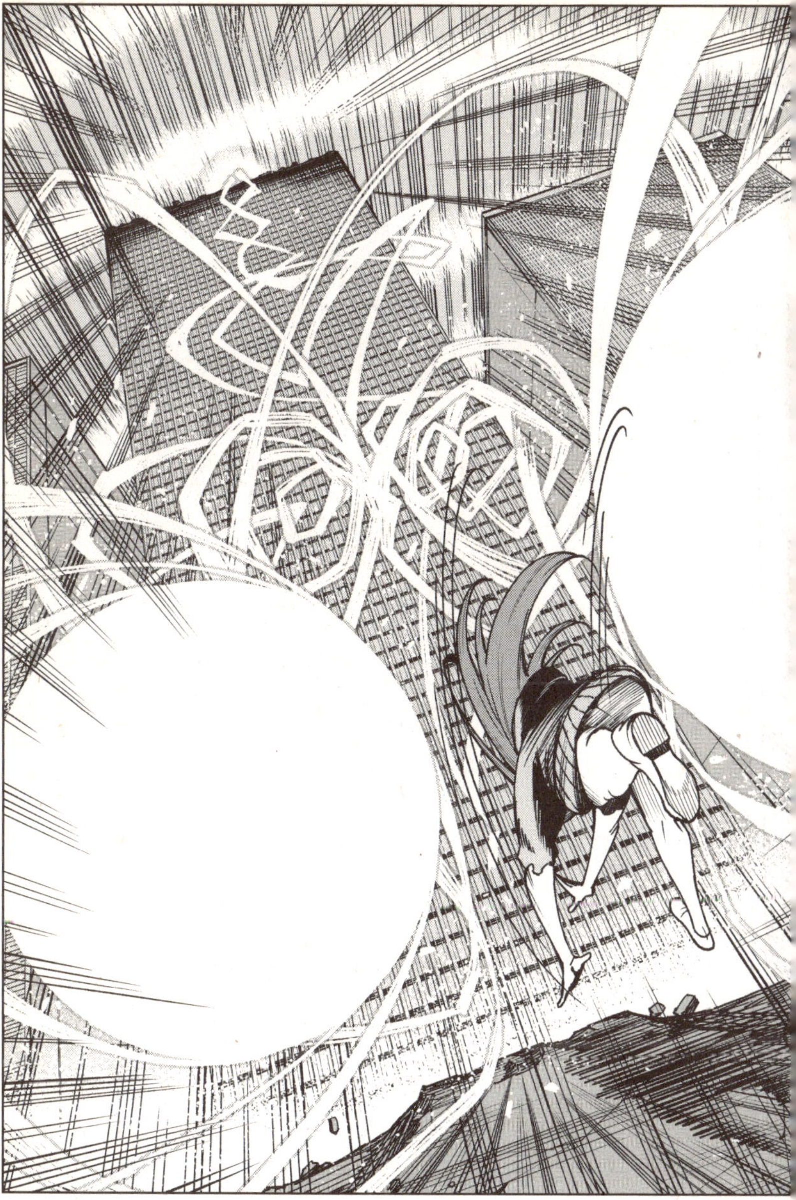

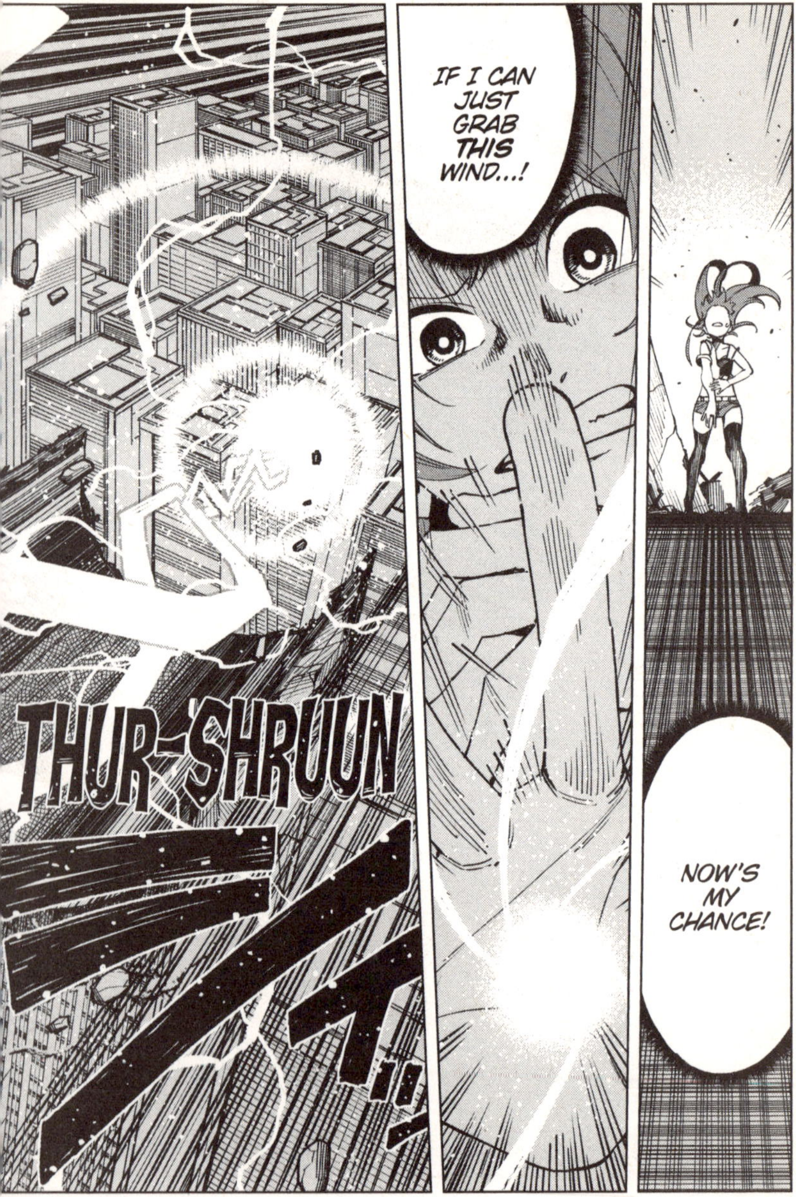
NOW'S MY CHANCE!
IF I CAN JUST GRAB THIS WIND...!
THUR-SHRUUN

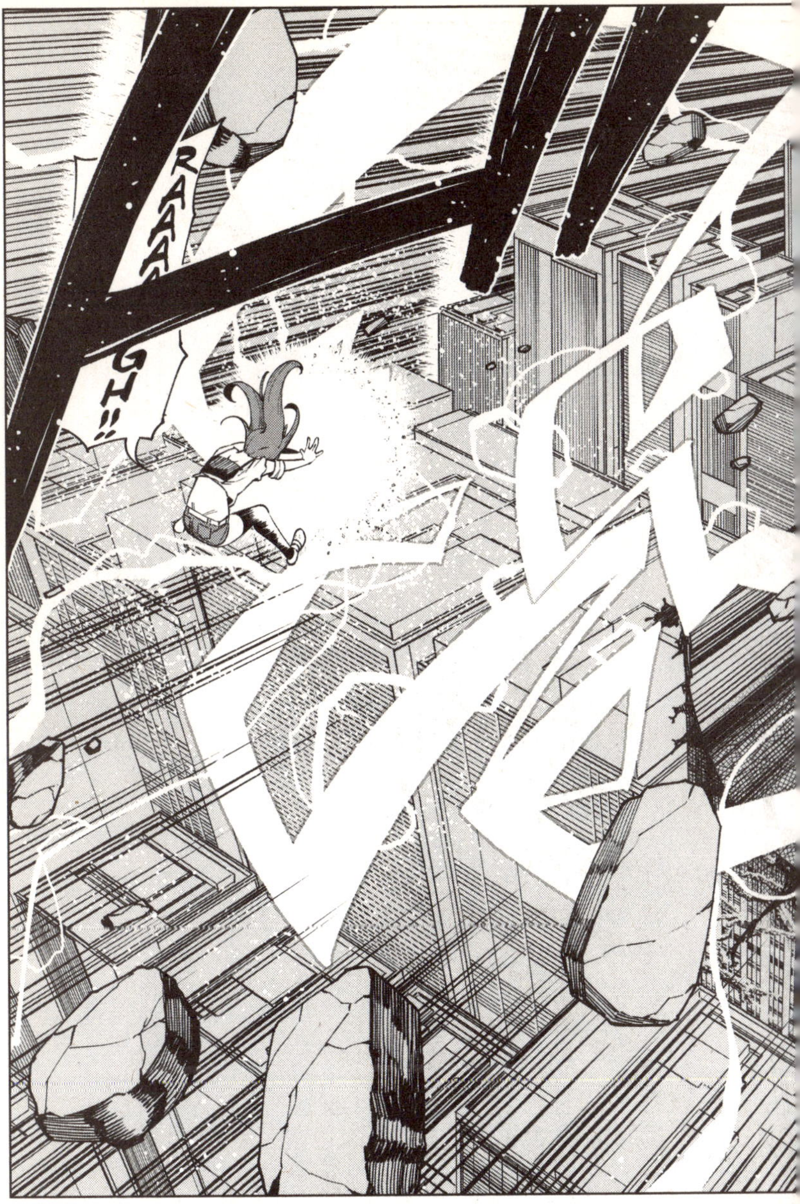
RAAAA
GH!!

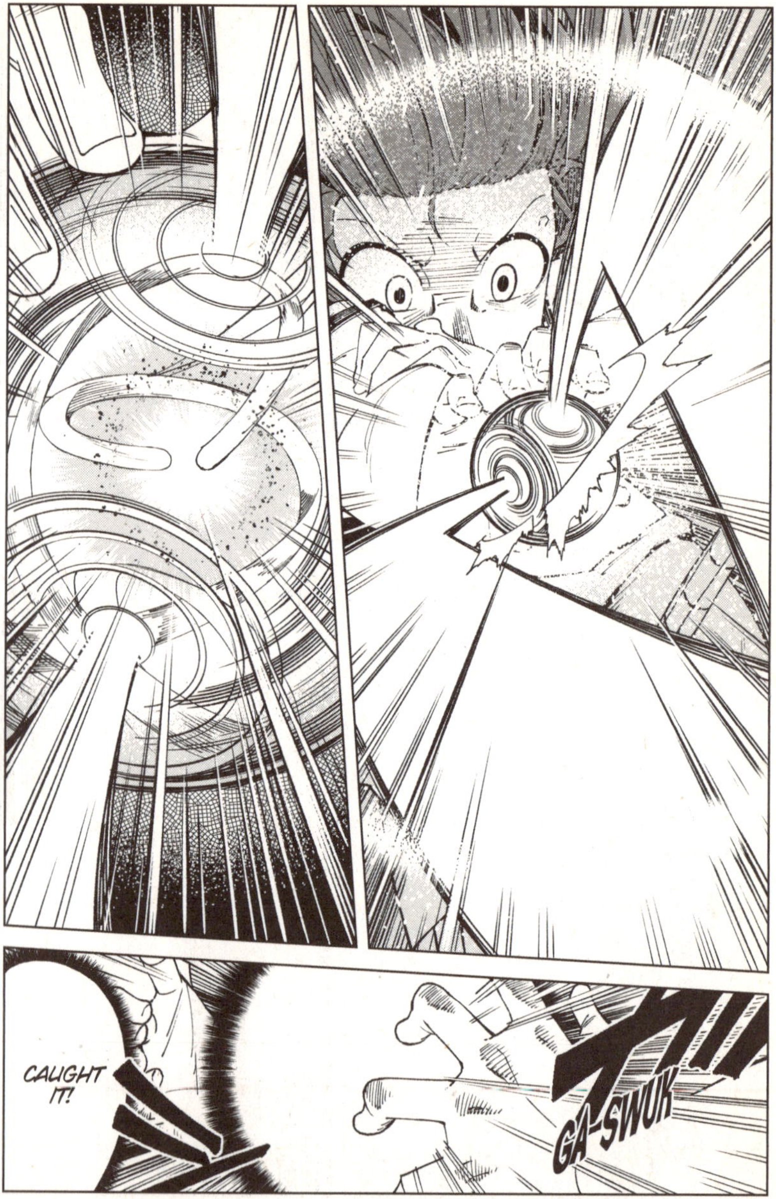
GA-SWUK
CAUGHT IT!

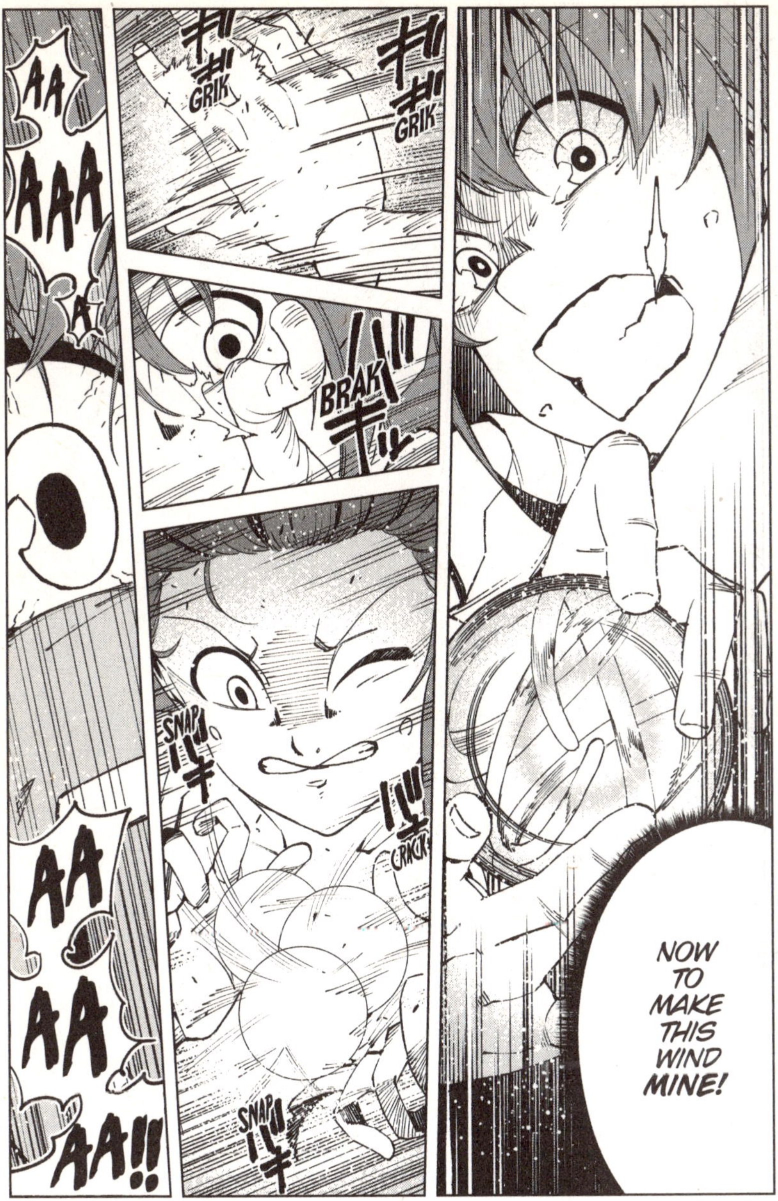
NOW TO MAKE THIS WIND MINE!
GRIK
GRIK
BRAK
SNAP
CRACK
SNAP
AA AAA A
AA AA AA!!

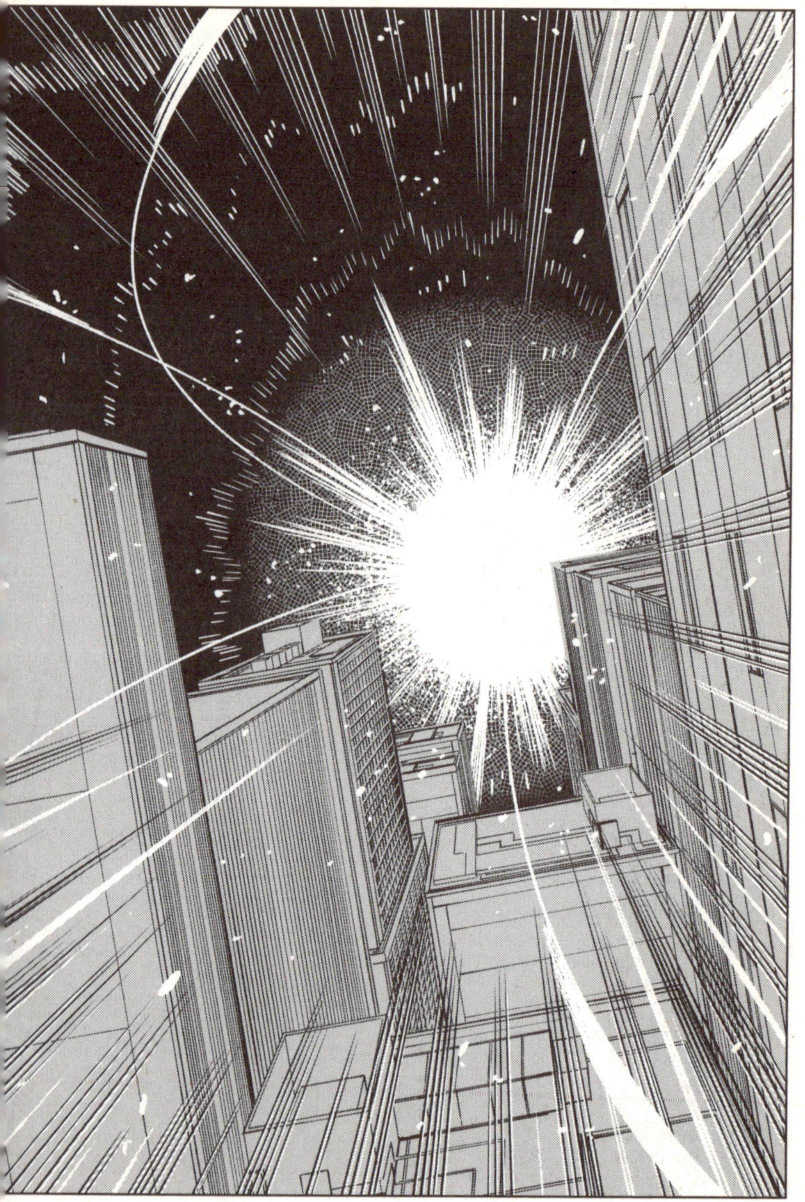

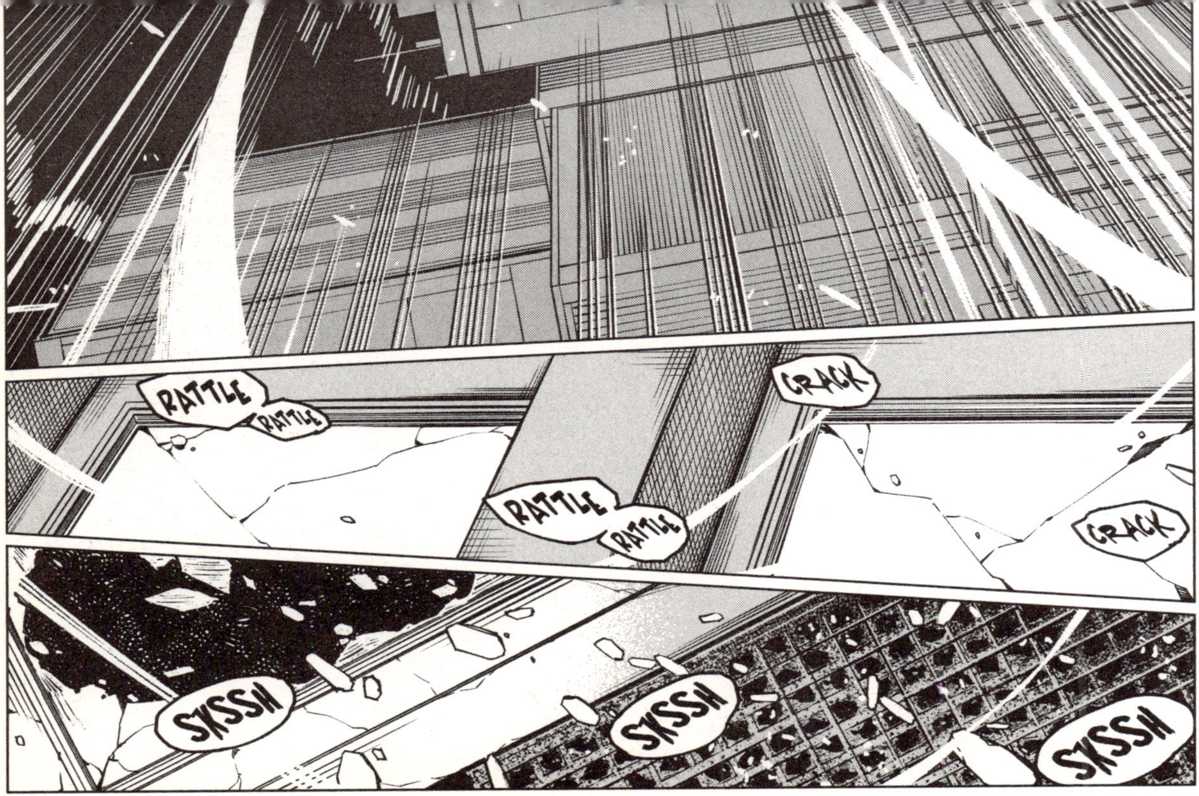
CRACK
CRACK
RATTLE RATTLE
RATTLE RATTLE
SKSSH
SKSSH
SKSSH

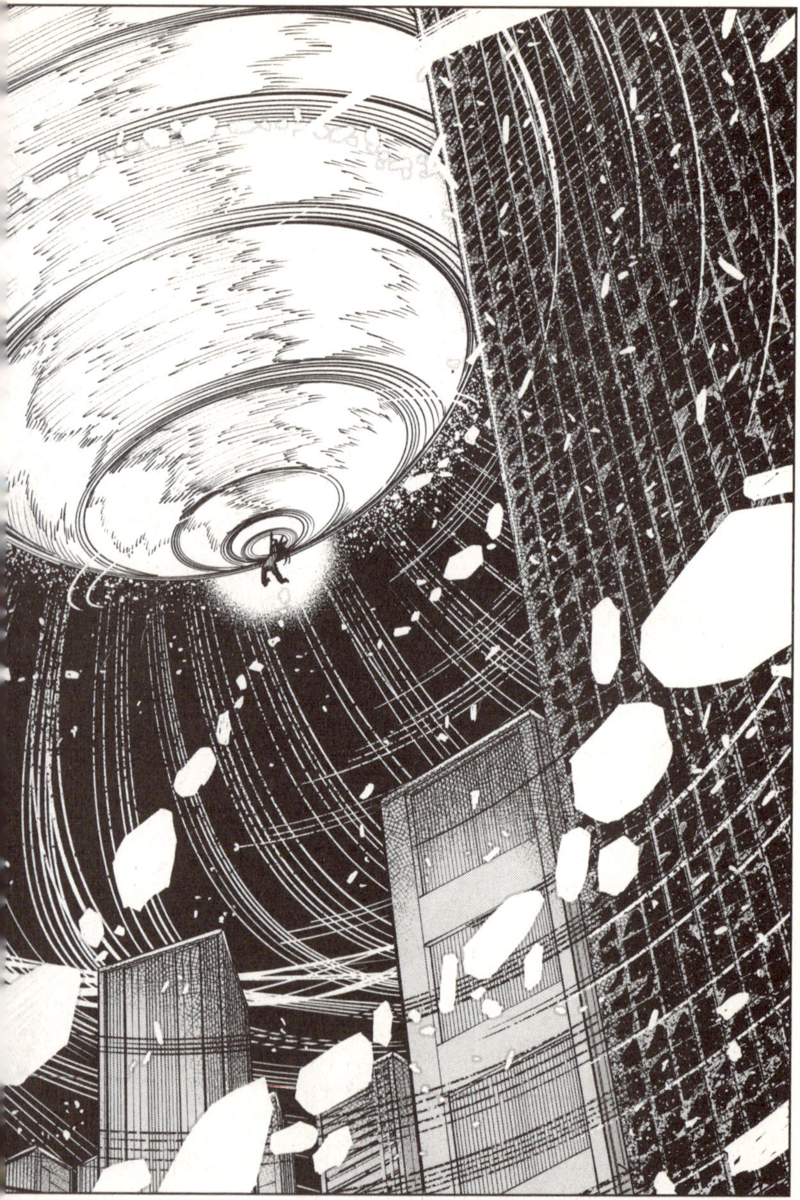

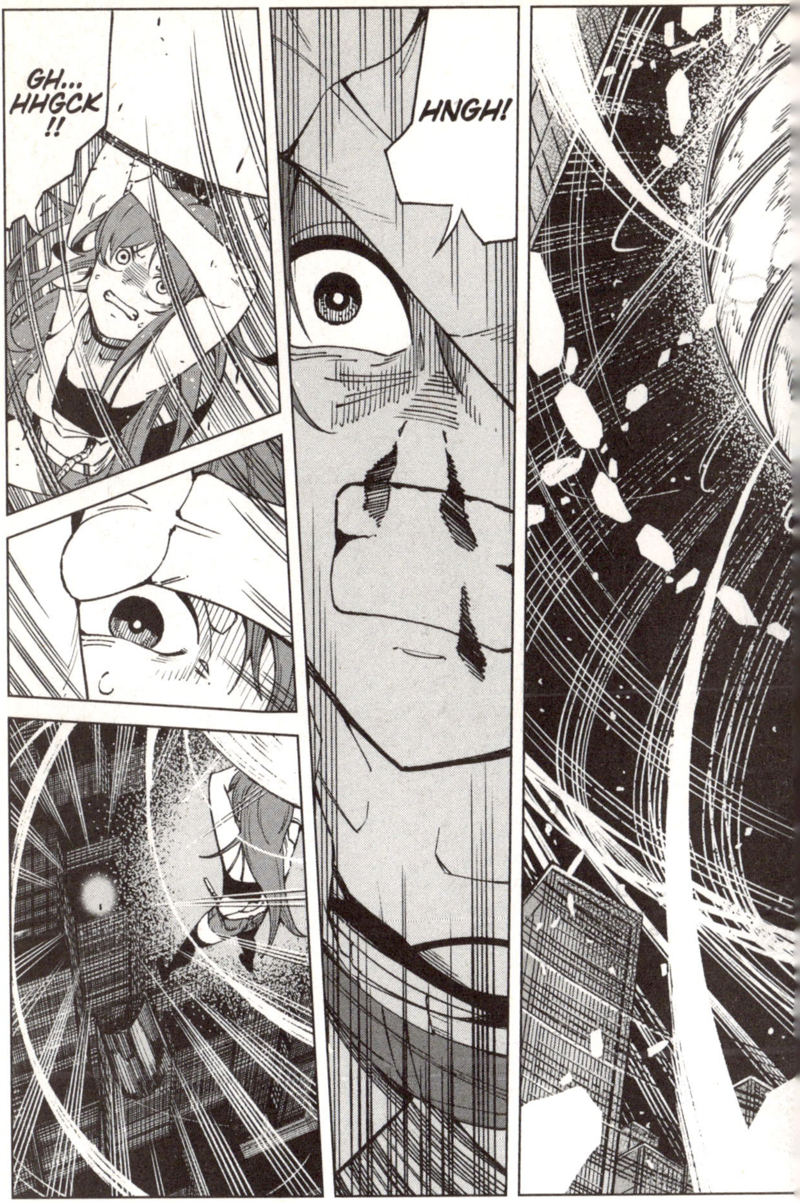
HNGH!
GH... HHGCK !!

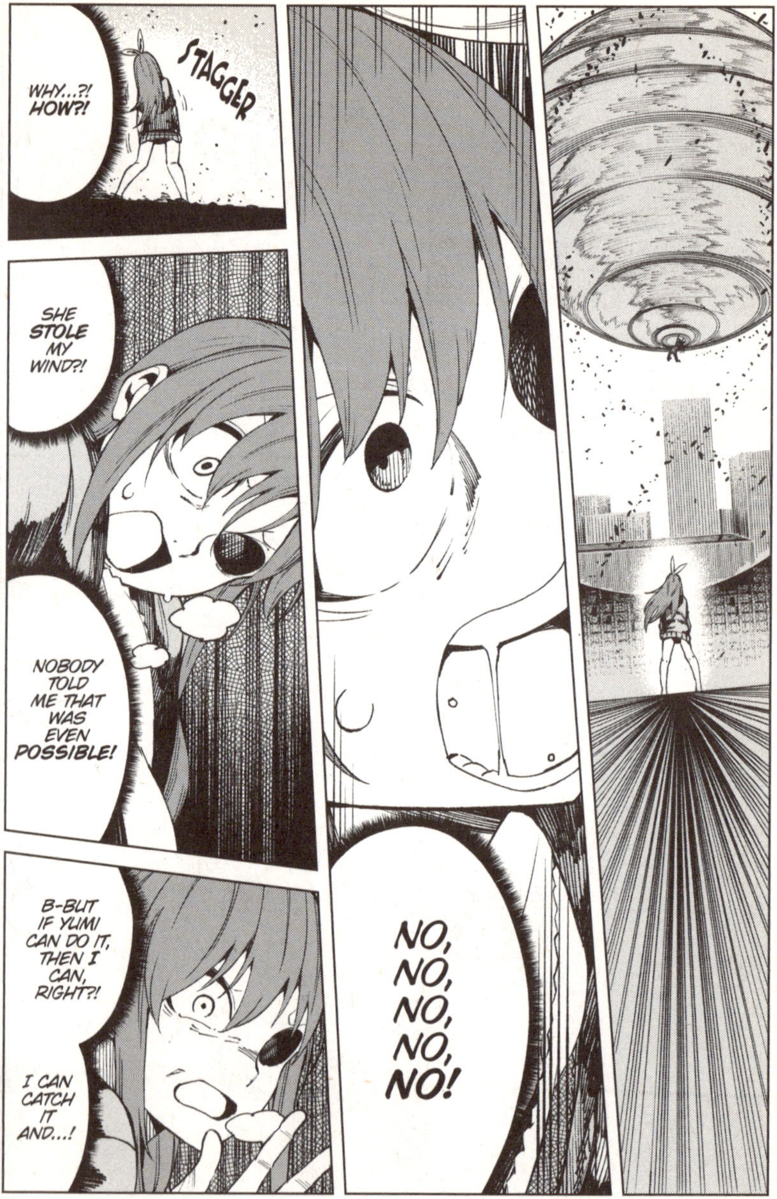
NO, NO, NO, NO, NO!
WHY...?! HOW?!
STAGGER
SHE STOLE MY WIND?!
NOBODY TOLD ME THAT WAS EVEN POSSIBLE!
B-BUT IF YUMI CAN DO IT, THEN I CAN, RIGHT?!
I CAN CATCH IT AND...!

PWOK

I DON'T HAVE THE ARMS OR THE ABILITY TO CALCULATE SOMETHING LIKE THAT RIGHT NOW!

I CAN'T, I CAN'T!

THUD...

HUFF!

HUFF!

HUFF!

HUFF!

HAA...

HUFF!

HUFF!

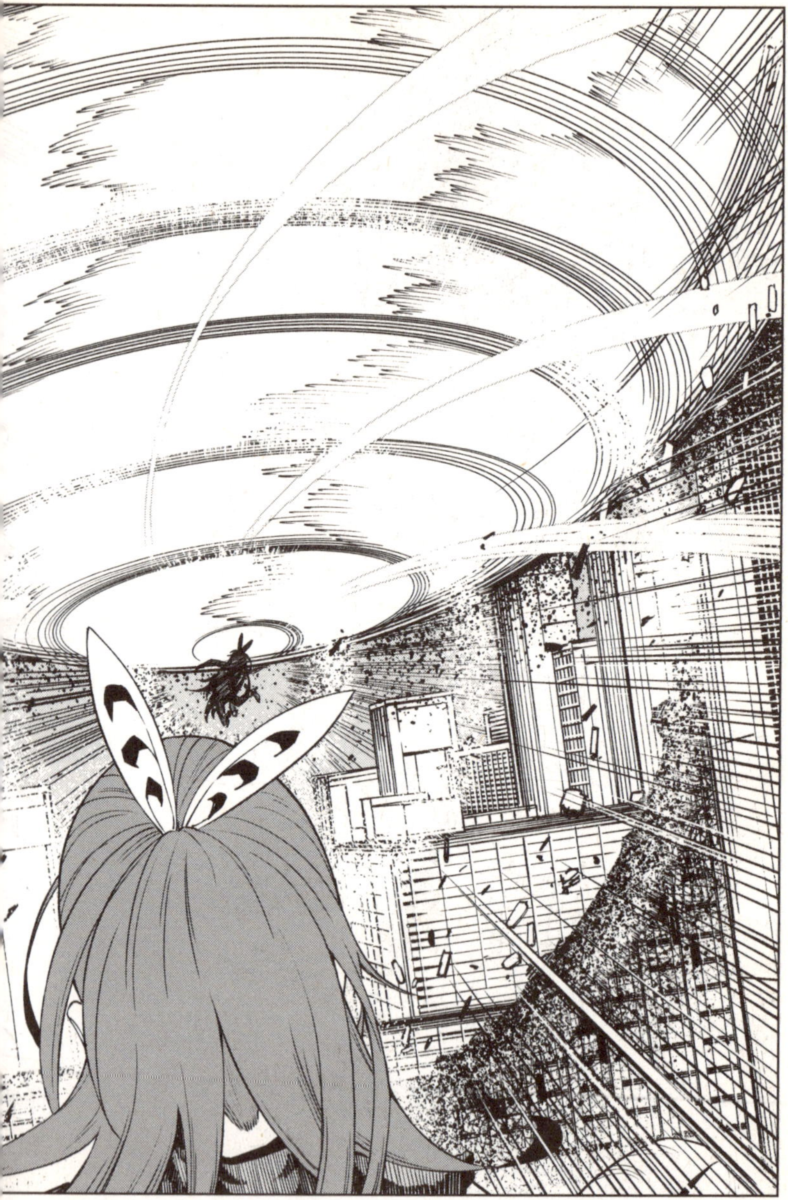

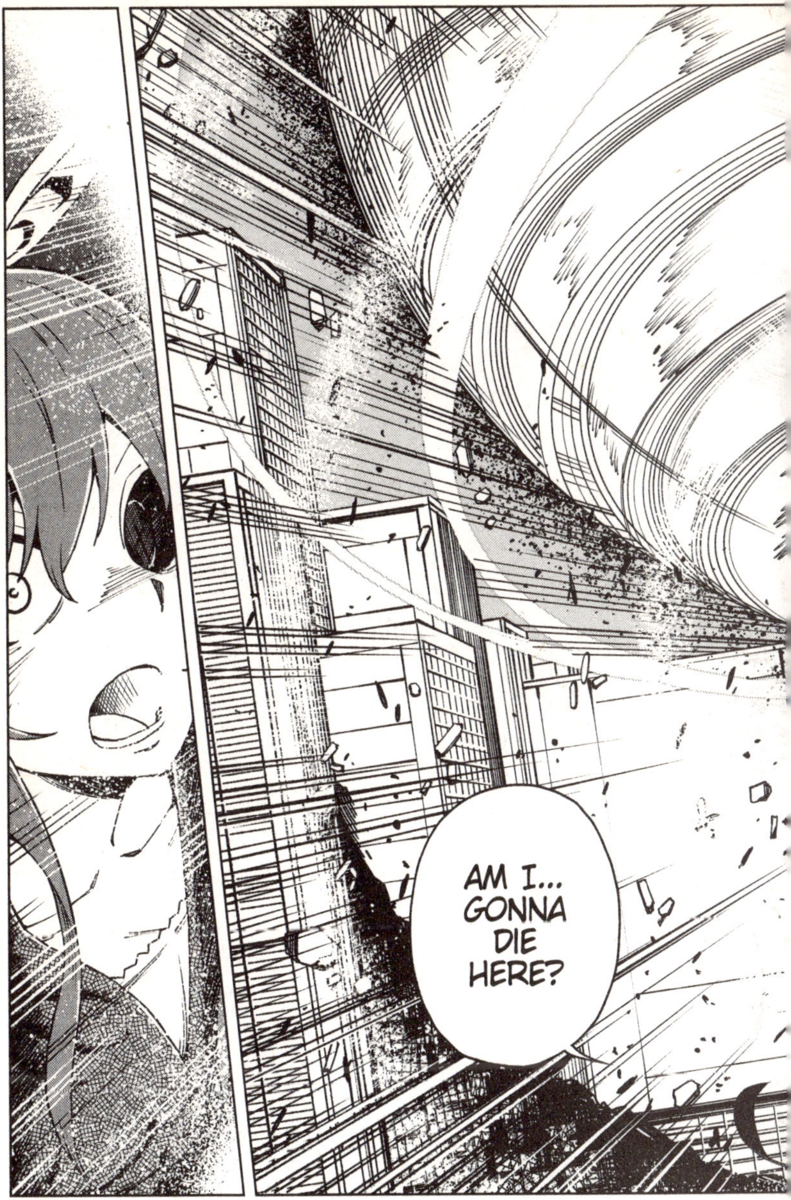
AM I... GONNA DIE HERE?

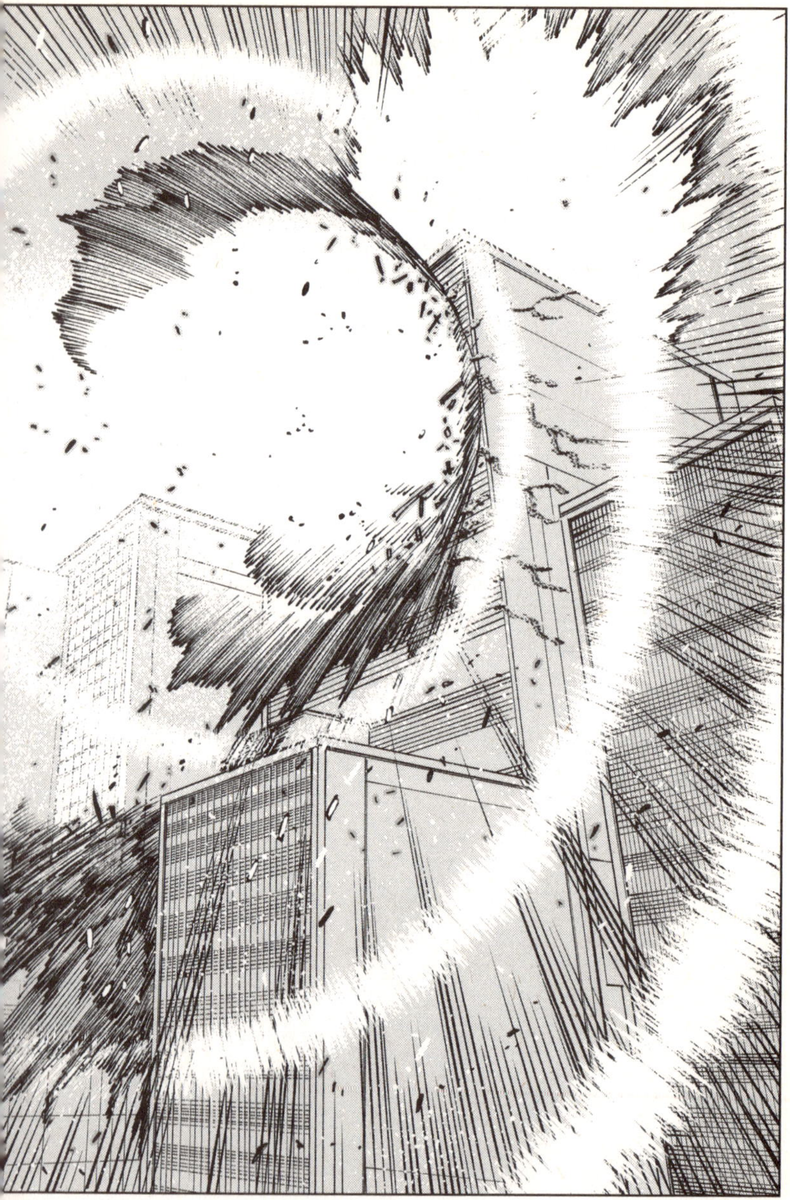

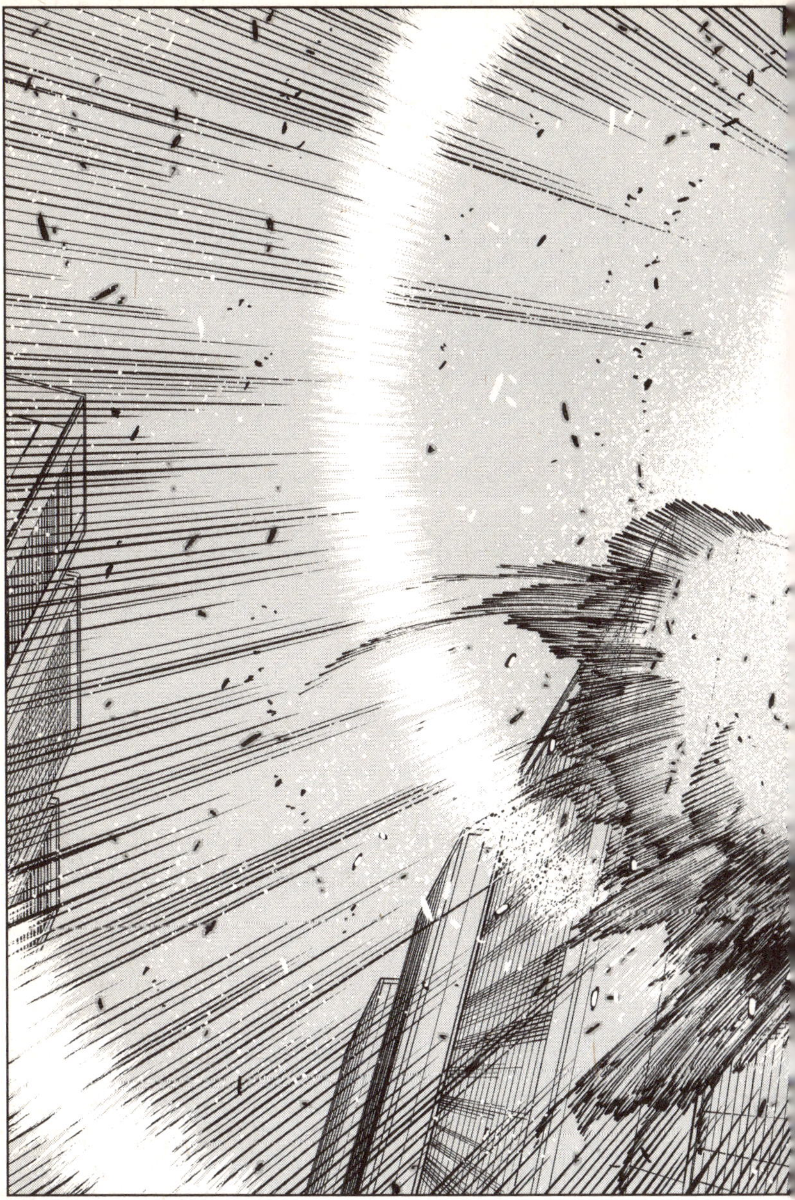

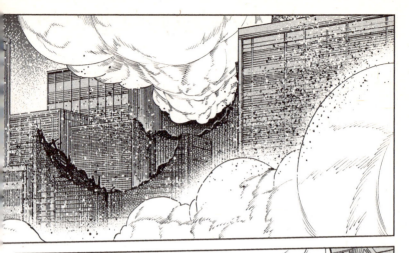

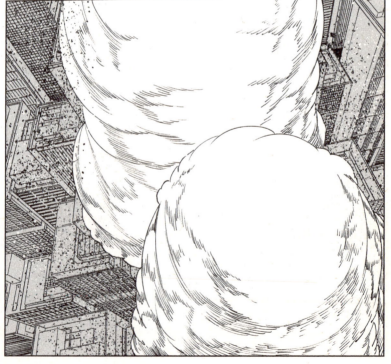

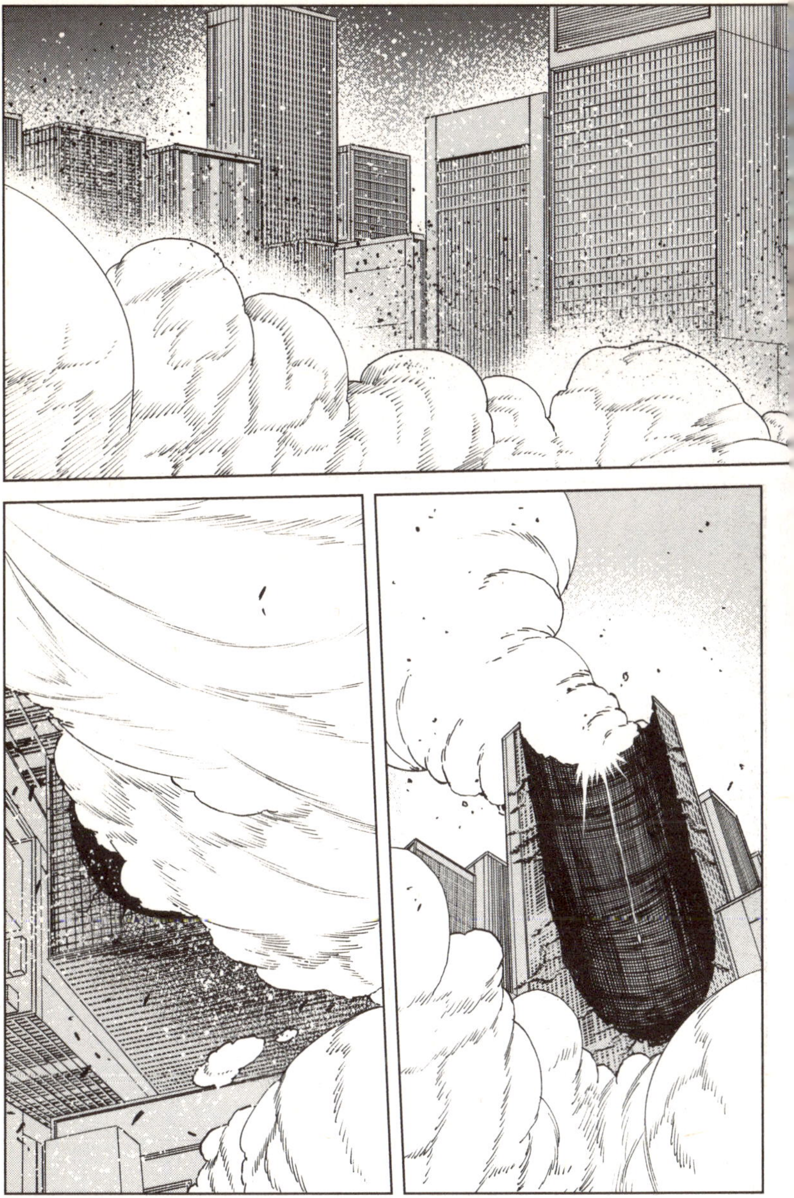

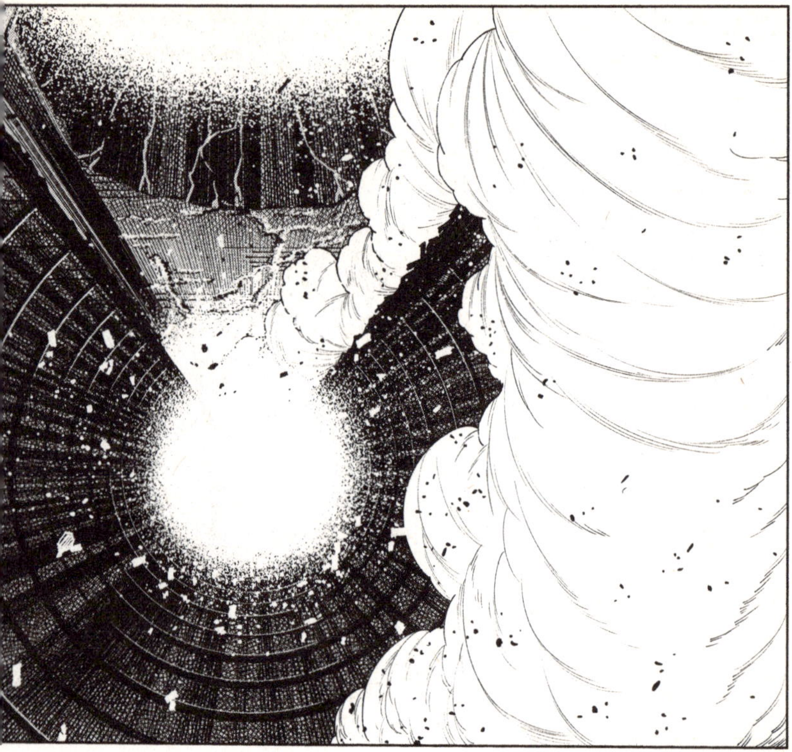

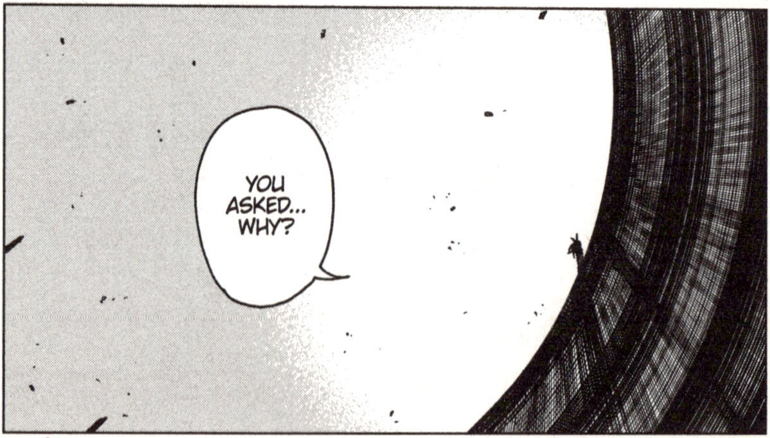
YOU ASKED... WHY?

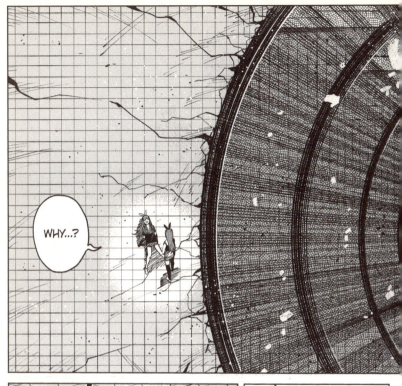

WHY...?

TH-WUMP

B-BE-CAUSE...

WOBBLE

WOBBLE

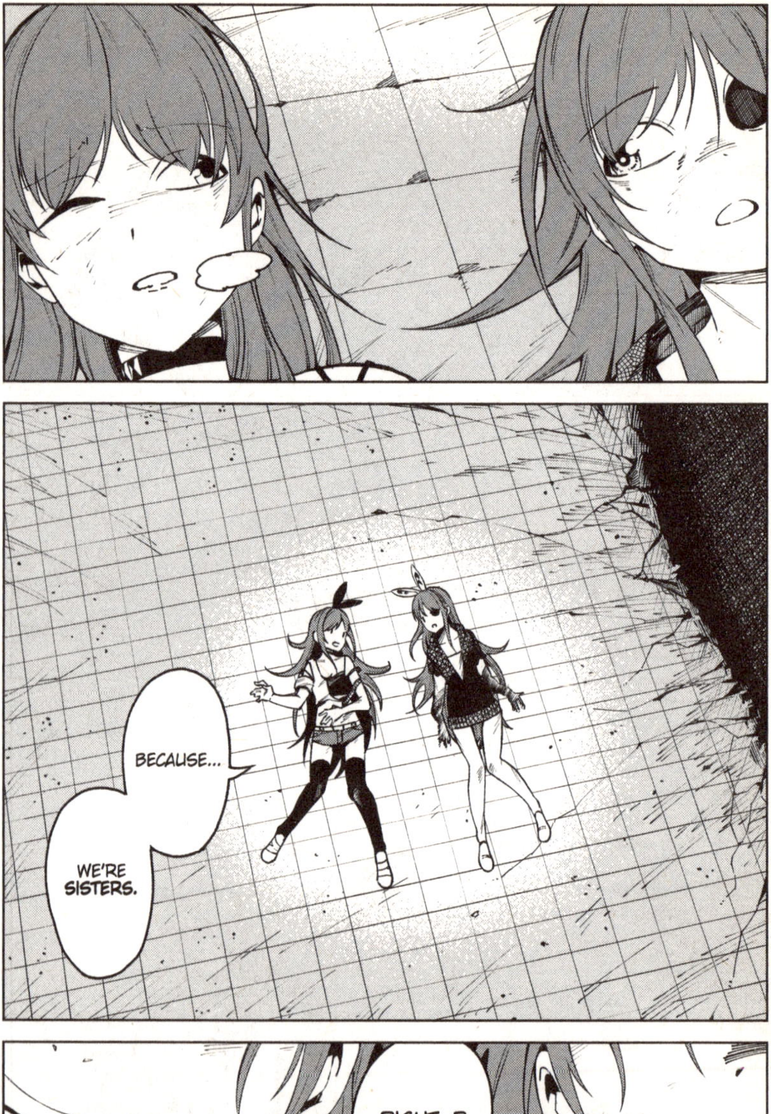
BECAUSE...
WE'RE SISTERS.
RIGHT...?

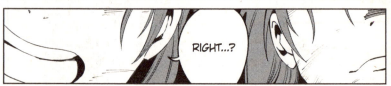

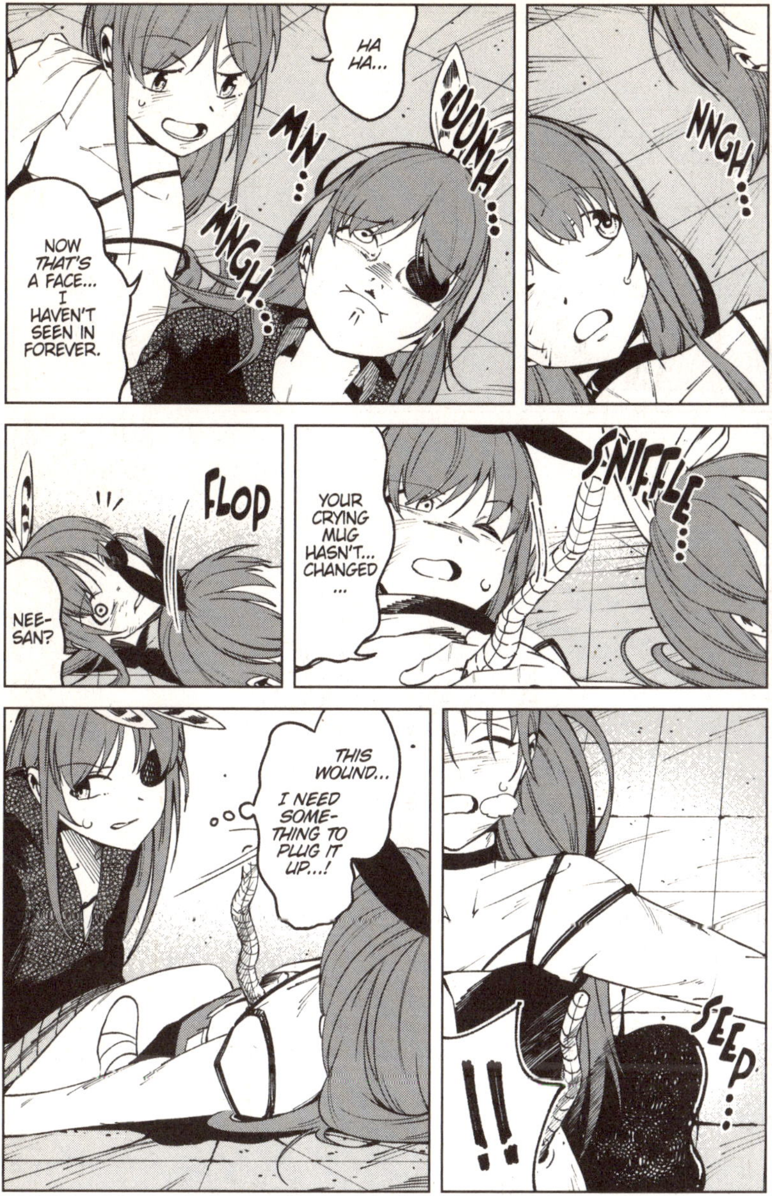
NNGH...
UUNH...
HA HA...
MN...
MNGH...
NOW THAT'S A FACE... I HAVEN'T SEEN IN FOREVER.
SNIFFLE...
YOUR CRYING MUG HASN'T... CHANGED...
FLOP
NEE-SAN?
SEEP...
!!
THIS WOUND...
I NEED SOME-THING TO PLUG IT UP...!

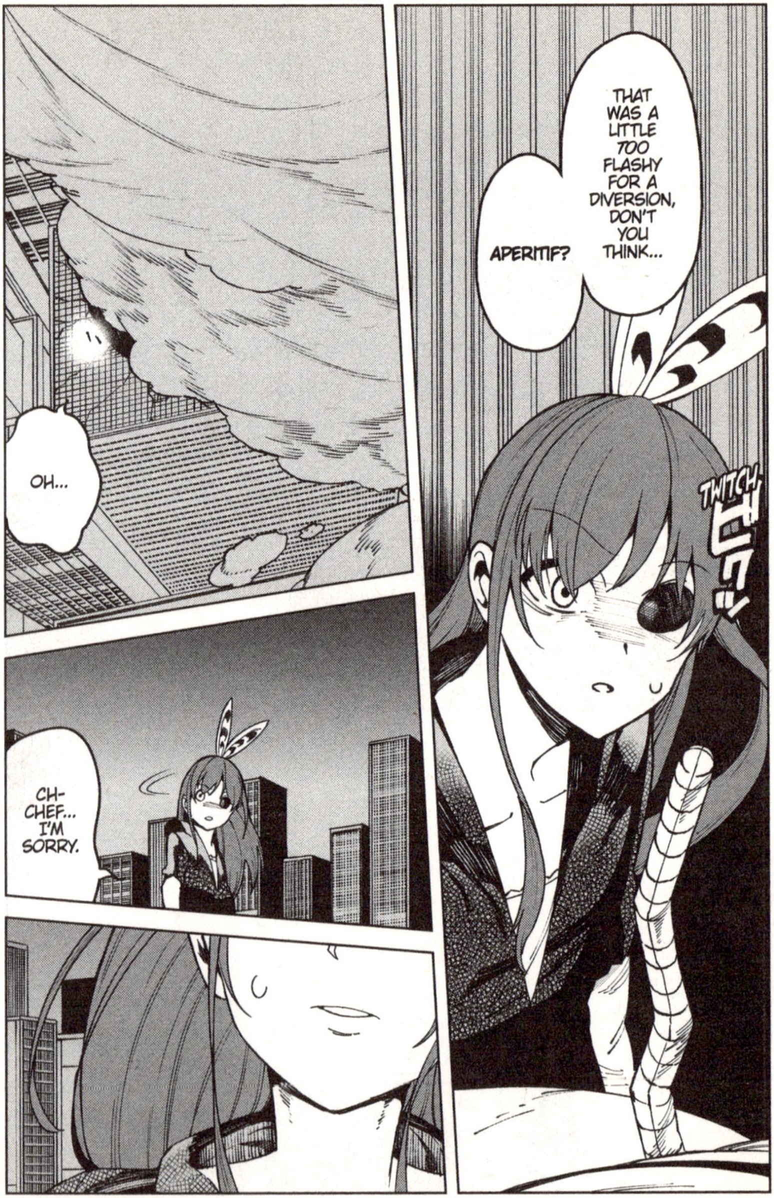
THAT WAS A LITTLE *TOO* FLASHY FOR A DIVERSION, DON'T YOU THINK...
APERITIF?
TWITCH
OH...
CH-CHEF... I'M SORRY.

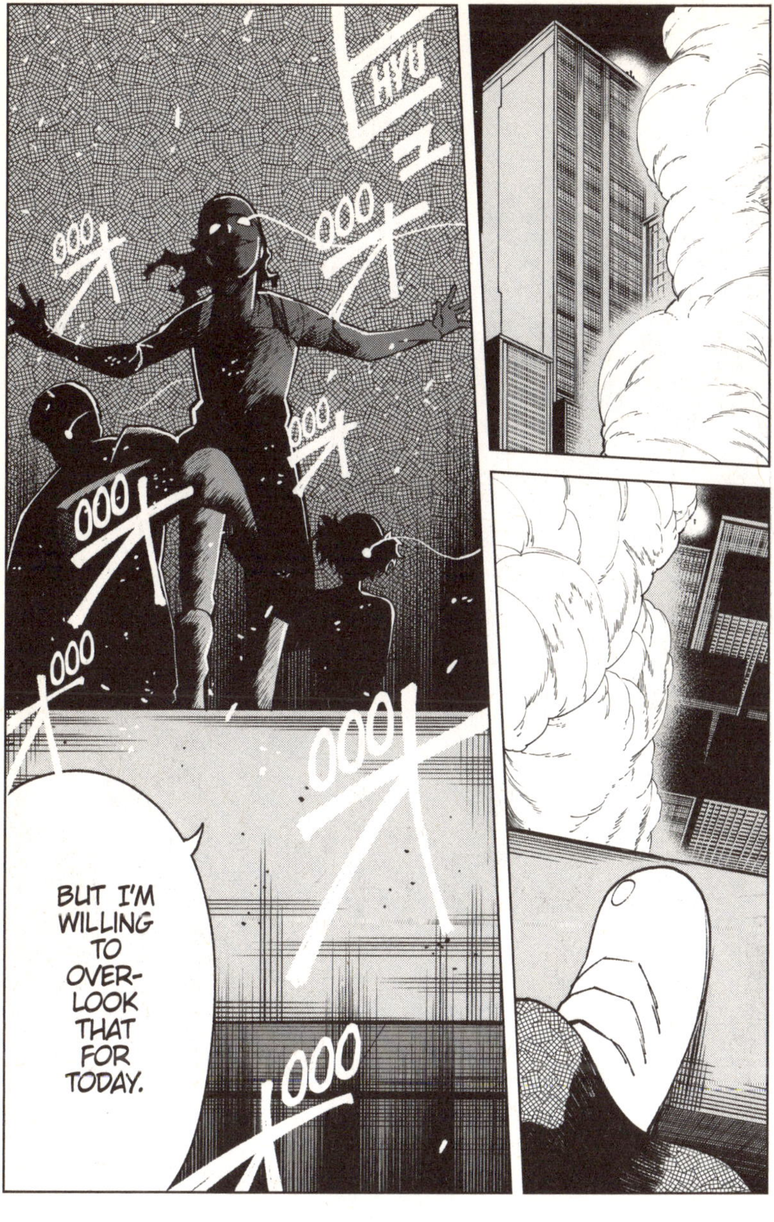
HYU
OOO
OOO
OOO
OOO
OOO
OOO
OOO
BUT I'M WILLING TO OVER-LOOK THAT FOR TODAY.

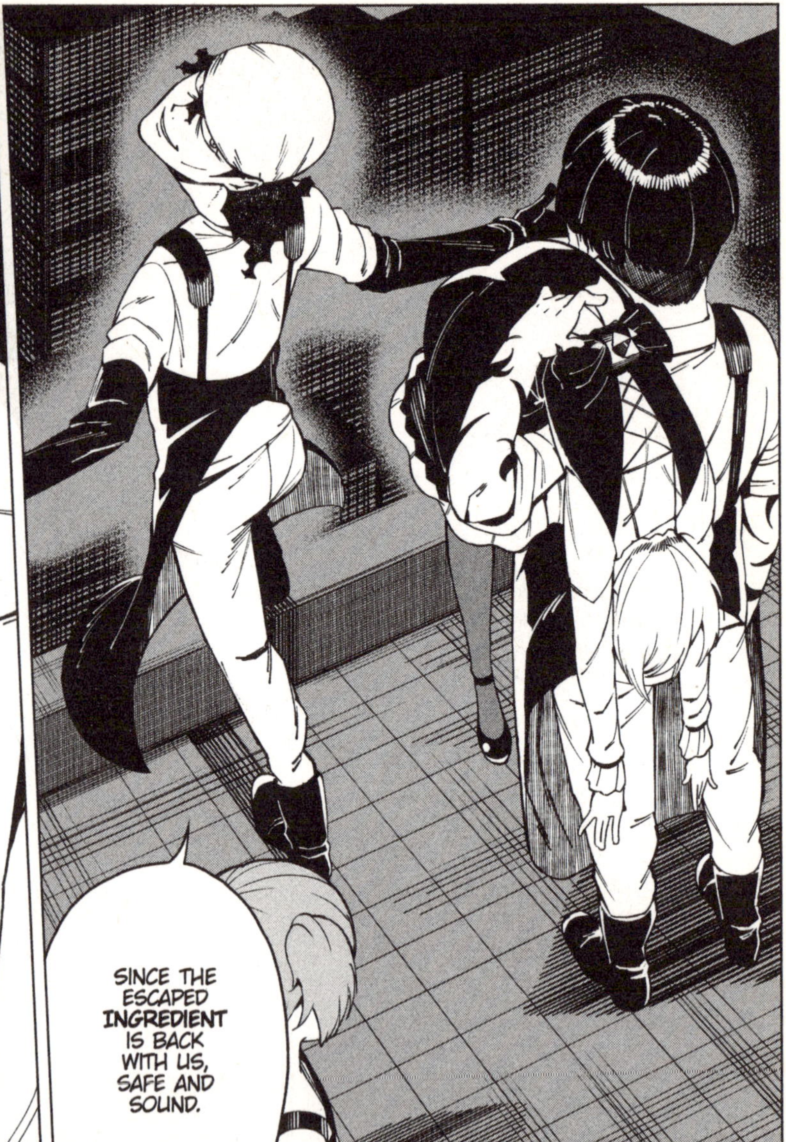
SINCE THE ESCAPED **INGREDIENT** IS BACK WITH US, SAFE AND SOUND.

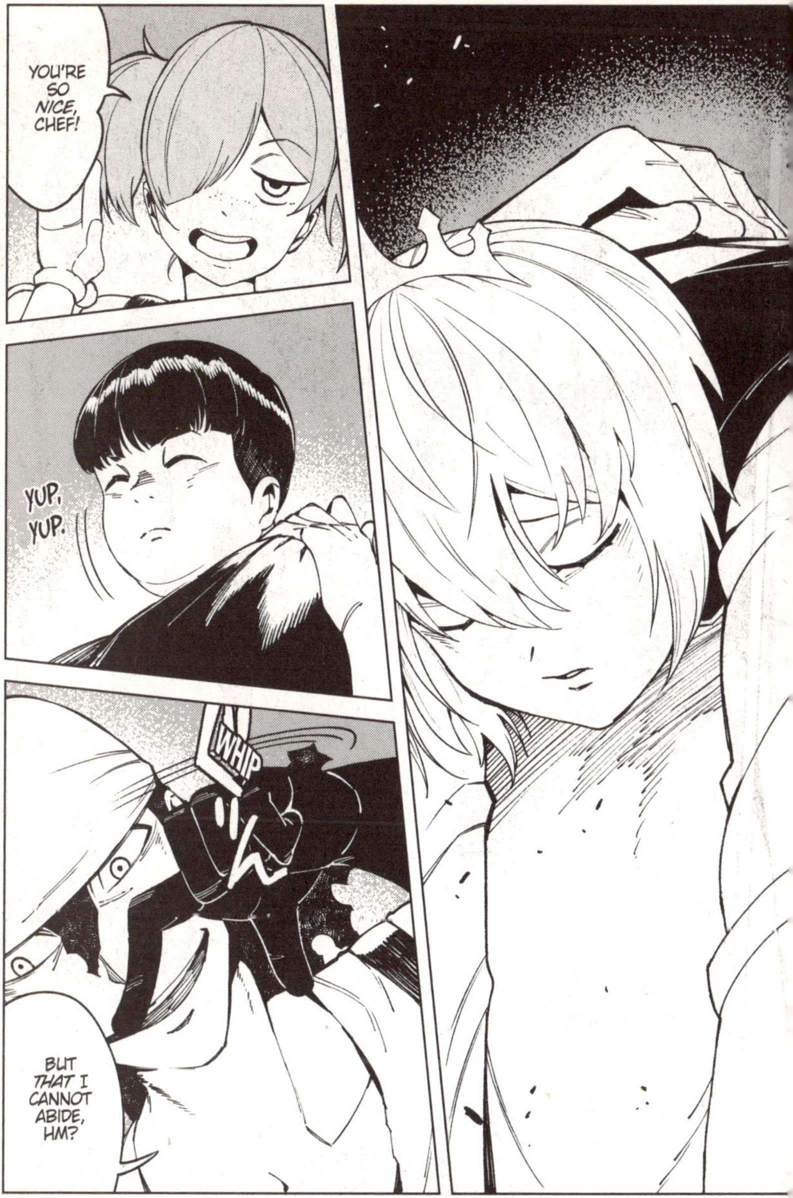
YOU'RE SO NICE, CHEF!
YUP, YUP.
WHIP
BUT *THAT* I CANNOT ABIDE, HM?

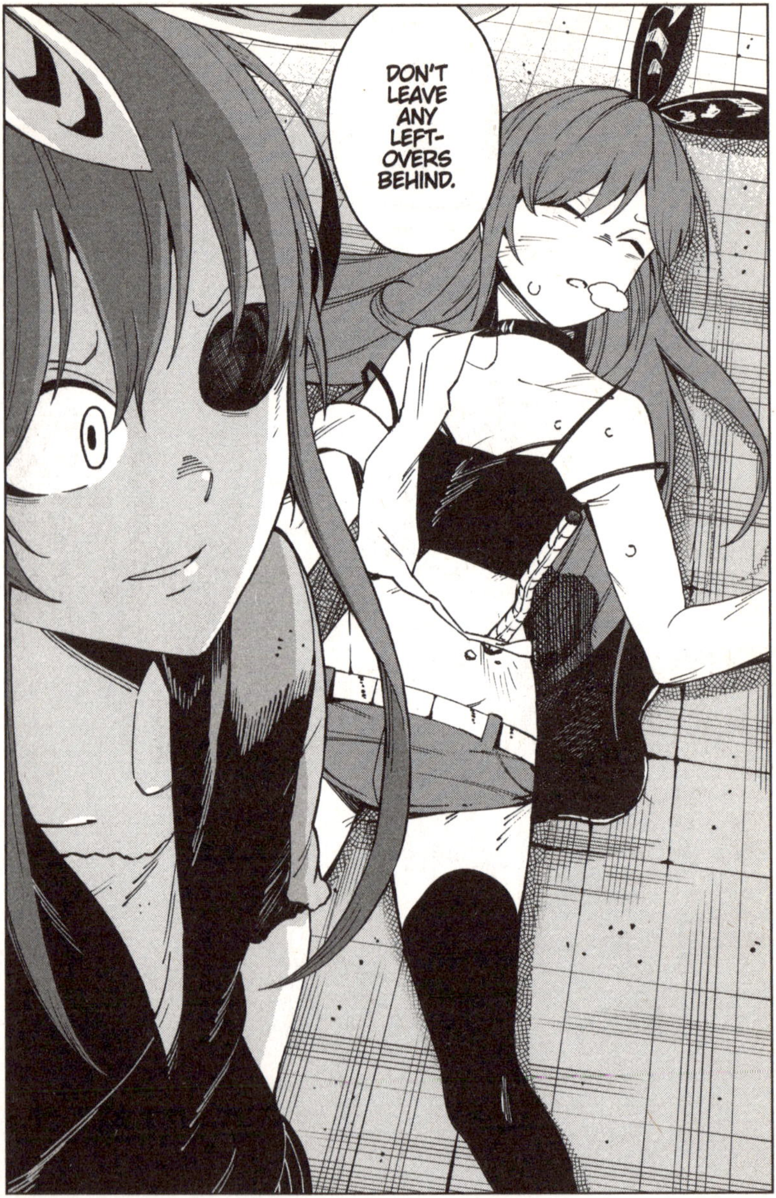
DON'T LEAVE ANY LEFT-OVERS BEHIND.

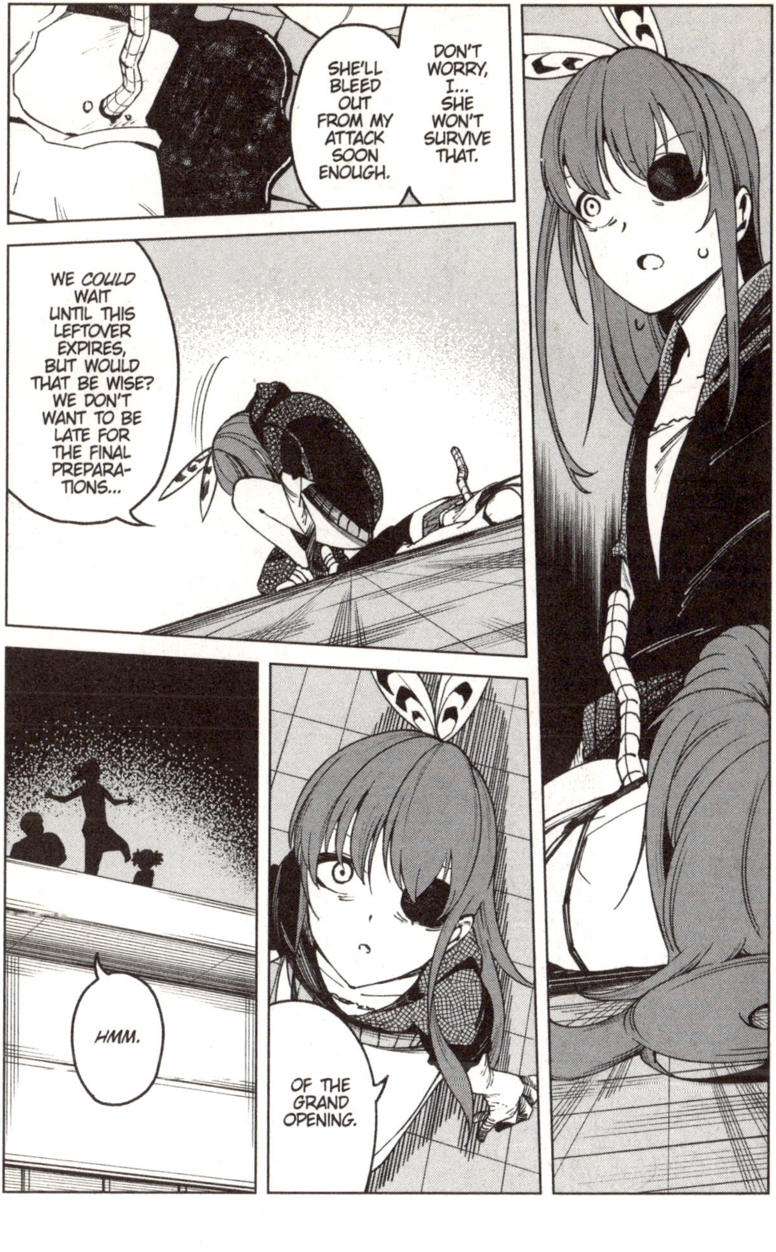
DON'T WORRY, I... SHE WON'T SURVIVE THAT.
SHE'LL BLEED OUT FROM MY ATTACK SOON ENOUGH.
WE *COULD* WAIT UNTIL THIS LEFTOVER EXPIRES, BUT WOULD THAT BE WISE? WE DON'T WANT TO BE LATE FOR THE FINAL PREPARA-TIONS...
OF THE GRAND OPENING.
*HMM.*

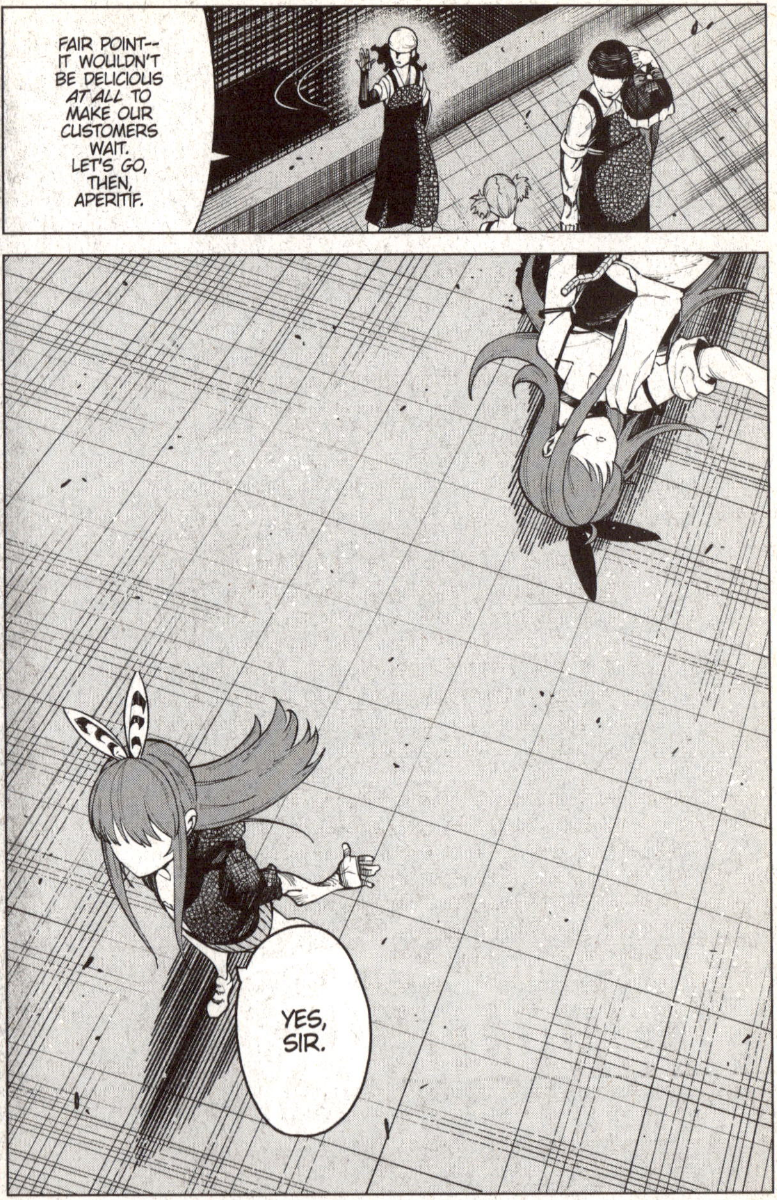
FAIR POINT-- IT WOULDN'T BE DELICIOUS AT ALL TO MAKE OUR CUSTOMERS WAIT. LET'S GO, THEN, APERITIF.
YES, SIR.

a certain
SCIENTIFIC
ACCELERATOR

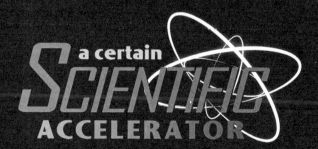

とある科学の一方通行
アクセラレータ

とある魔術の禁書目録
外伝

# CHAPTER 48

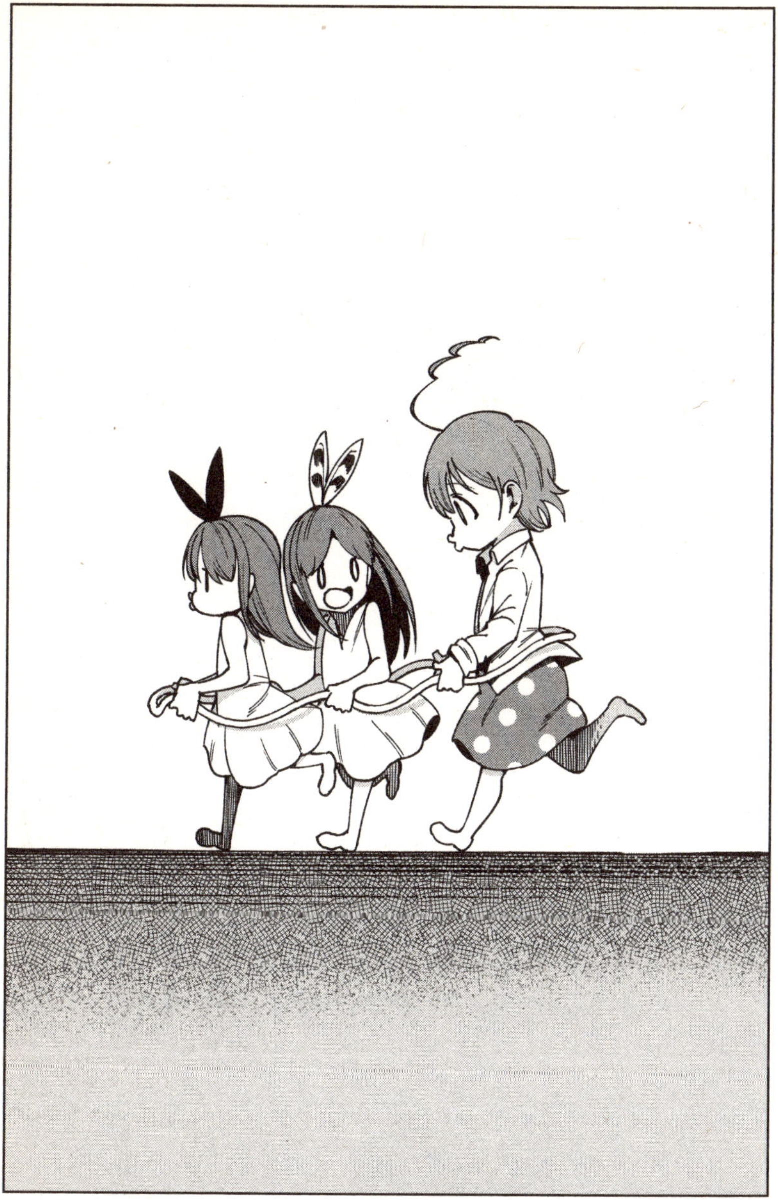

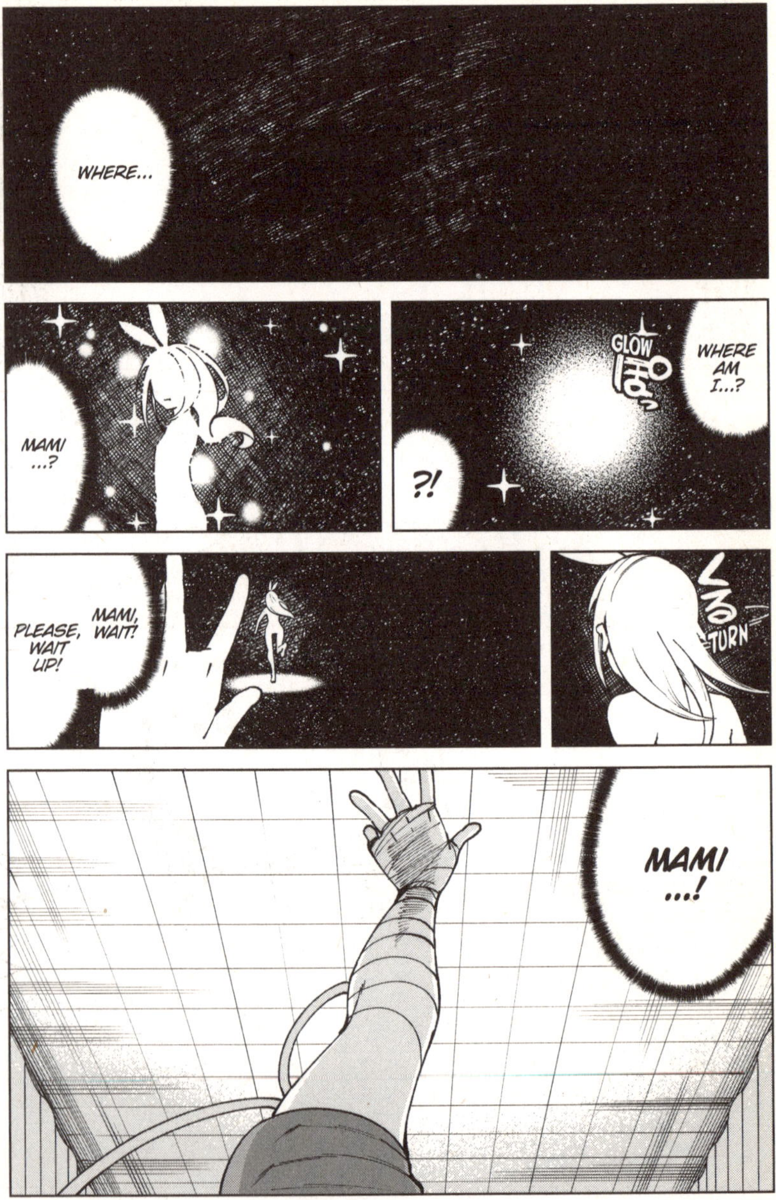
WHERE...
WHERE AM I...?
GLOW ぽっ
?!
MAMI ...?
くる TURN
MAMI, WAIT!
PLEASE, WAIT UP!
MAMI ...!

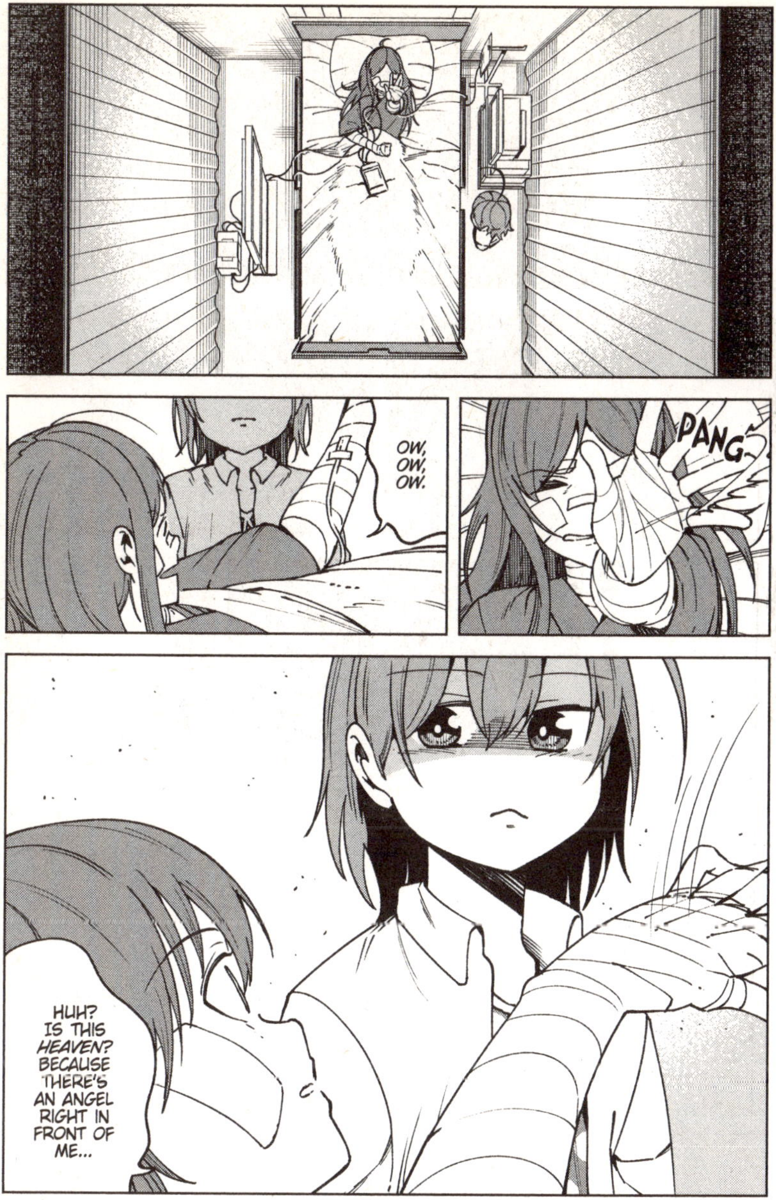
PANG
OW, OW, OW.
HUH? IS THIS *HEAVEN?* BECAUSE THERE'S AN ANGEL RIGHT IN FRONT OF ME...

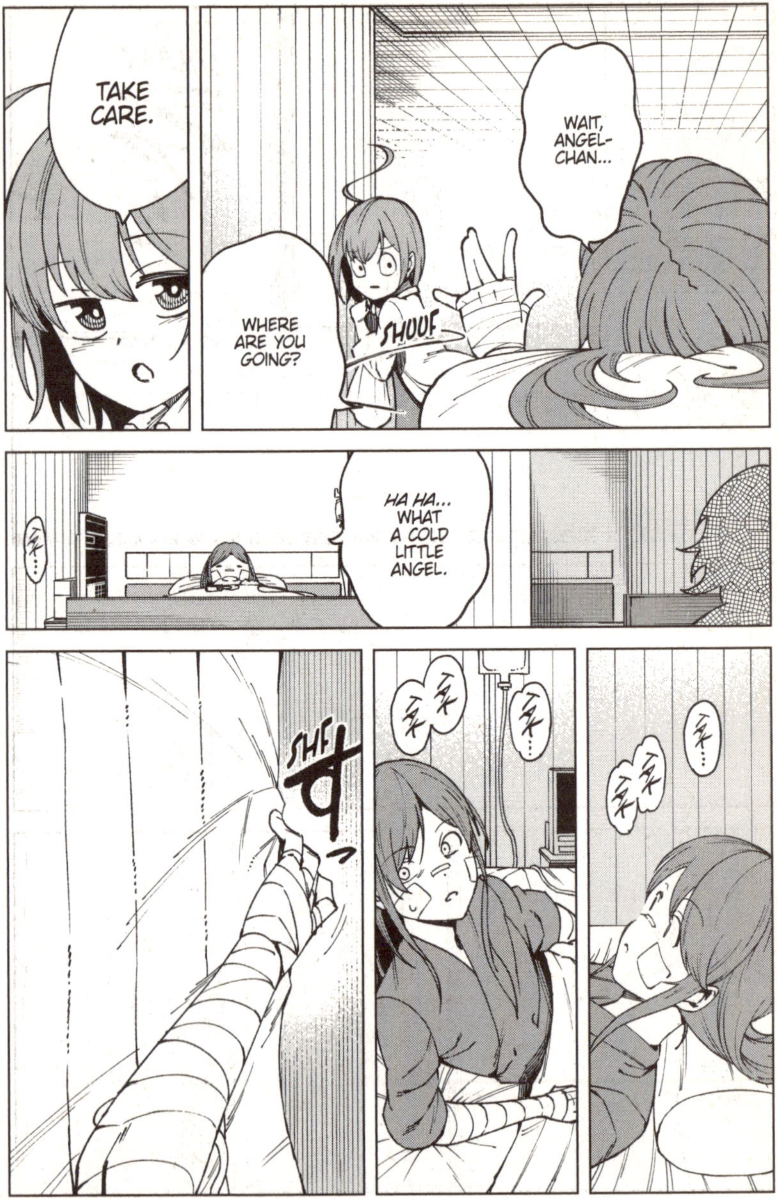
WAIT, ANGEL-CHAN...
WHERE ARE YOU GOING?
SHUUF
TAKE CARE.
HA HA... WHAT A COLD LITTLE ANGEL.
SHF
す

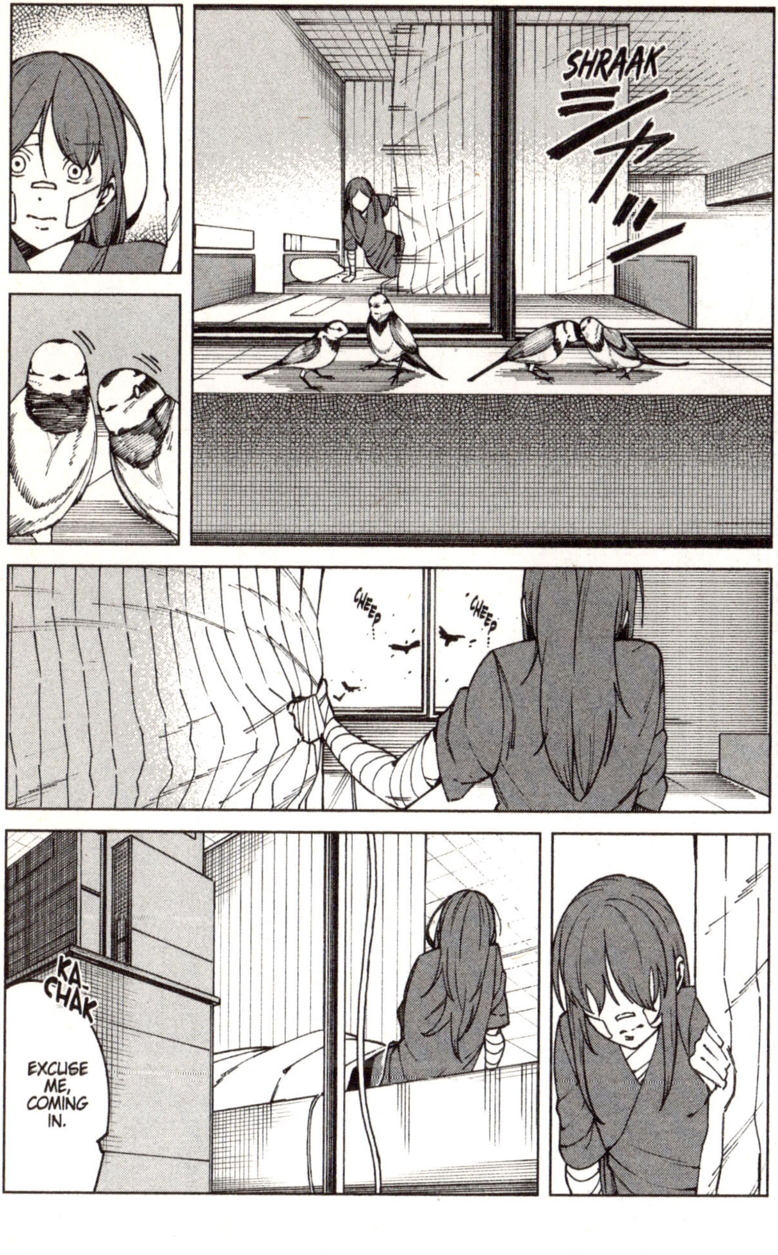
SHRAAK
CHEEP
CHEEP
KA-CHAK
EXCUSE ME, COMING IN.

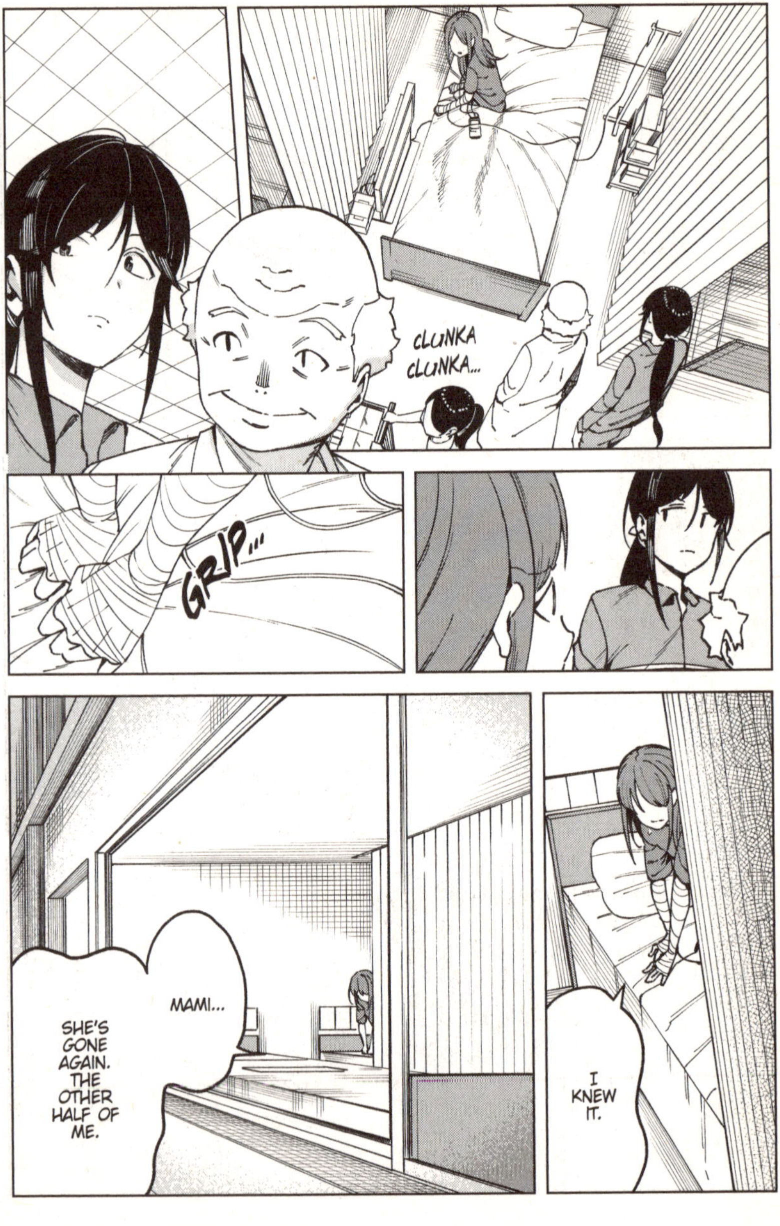
CLUNKA CLUNKA...
GRIP...
I KNEW IT.
MAMI...
SHE'S GONE AGAIN. THE OTHER HALF OF ME.

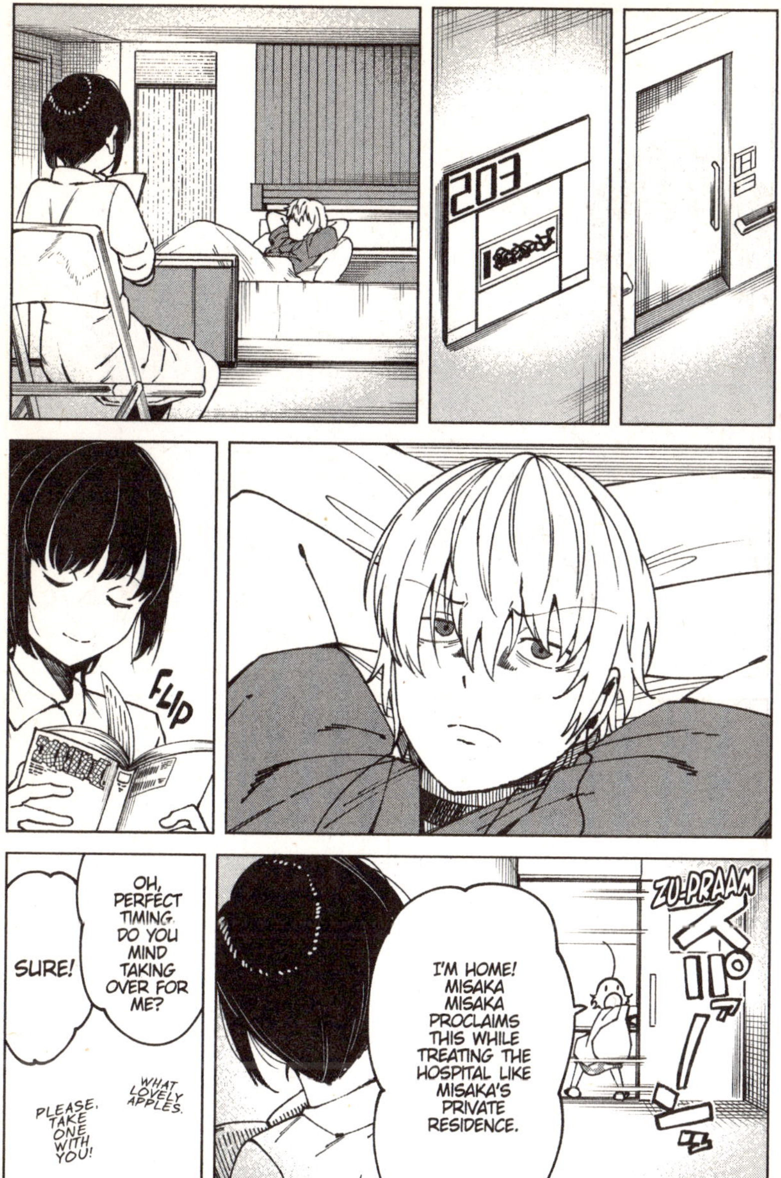
FLIP
ZU-PRAAM
I'M HOME! MISAKA MISAKA PROCLAIMS THIS WHILE TREATING THE HOSPITAL LIKE MISAKA'S PRIVATE RESIDENCE.
OH, PERFECT TIMING. DO YOU MIND TAKING OVER FOR ME?
SURE!
WHAT LOVELY APPLES.
PLEASE, TAKE ONE WITH YOU!

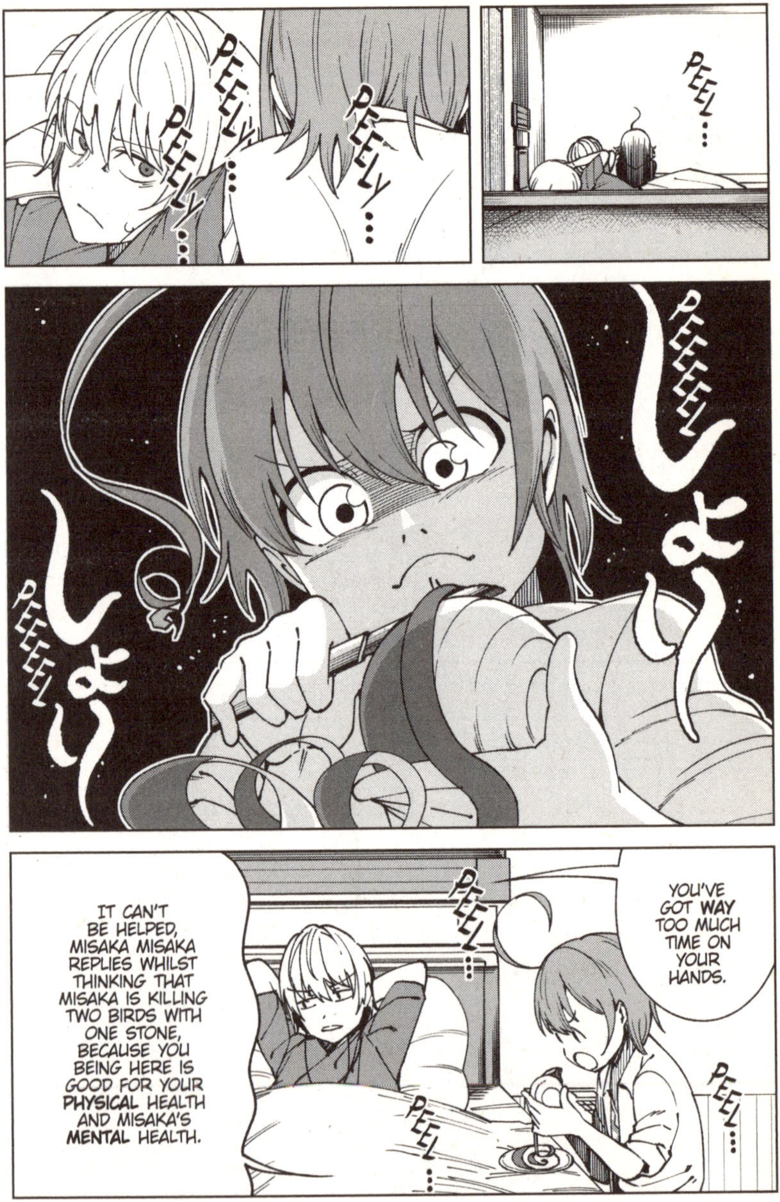
PEEL...
PEELY...
PEELY...
PEELY...
PEEEEL
PEEEEL
YOU'VE GOT **WAY** TOO MUCH TIME ON YOUR HANDS.
PEEL...
IT CAN'T BE HELPED, MISAKA MISAKA REPLIES WHILST THINKING THAT MISAKA IS KILLING TWO BIRDS WITH ONE STONE, BECAUSE YOU BEING HERE IS GOOD FOR YOUR **PHYSICAL** HEALTH AND MISAKA'S **MENTAL** HEALTH.
PEEL...
PEEL...

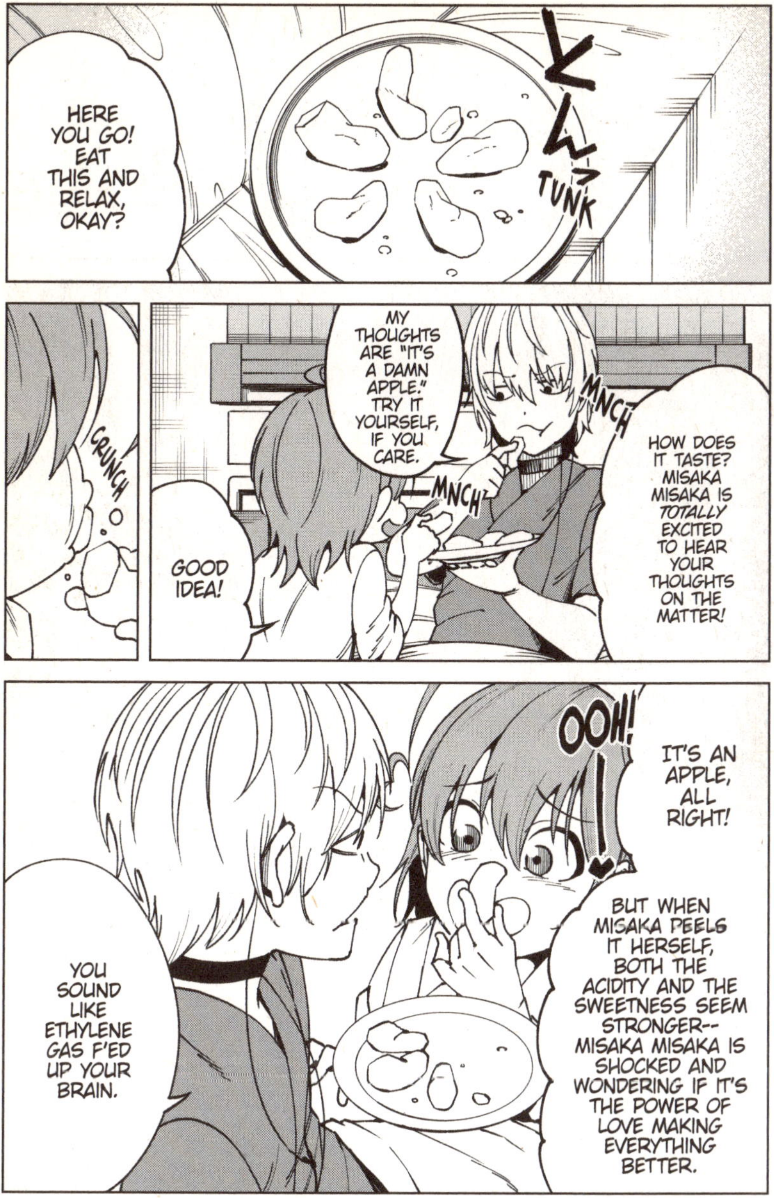
TUNK
HERE YOU GO! EAT THIS AND RELAX, OKAY?
HOW DOES IT TASTE? MISAKA MISAKA IS *TOTALLY* EXCITED TO HEAR YOUR THOUGHTS ON THE MATTER!
MNCH
MY THOUGHTS ARE "IT'S A DAMN APPLE." TRY IT YOURSELF, IF YOU CARE.
MNCH
GOOD IDEA!
CRUNCH
OOH!!
IT'S AN APPLE, ALL RIGHT!
BUT WHEN MISAKA PEELS IT HERSELF, BOTH THE ACIDITY AND THE SWEETNESS SEEM STRONGER-- MISAKA MISAKA IS SHOCKED AND WONDERING IF IT'S THE POWER OF LOVE MAKING EVERYTHING BETTER.
YOU SOUND LIKE ETHYLENE GAS F'ED UP YOUR BRAIN.

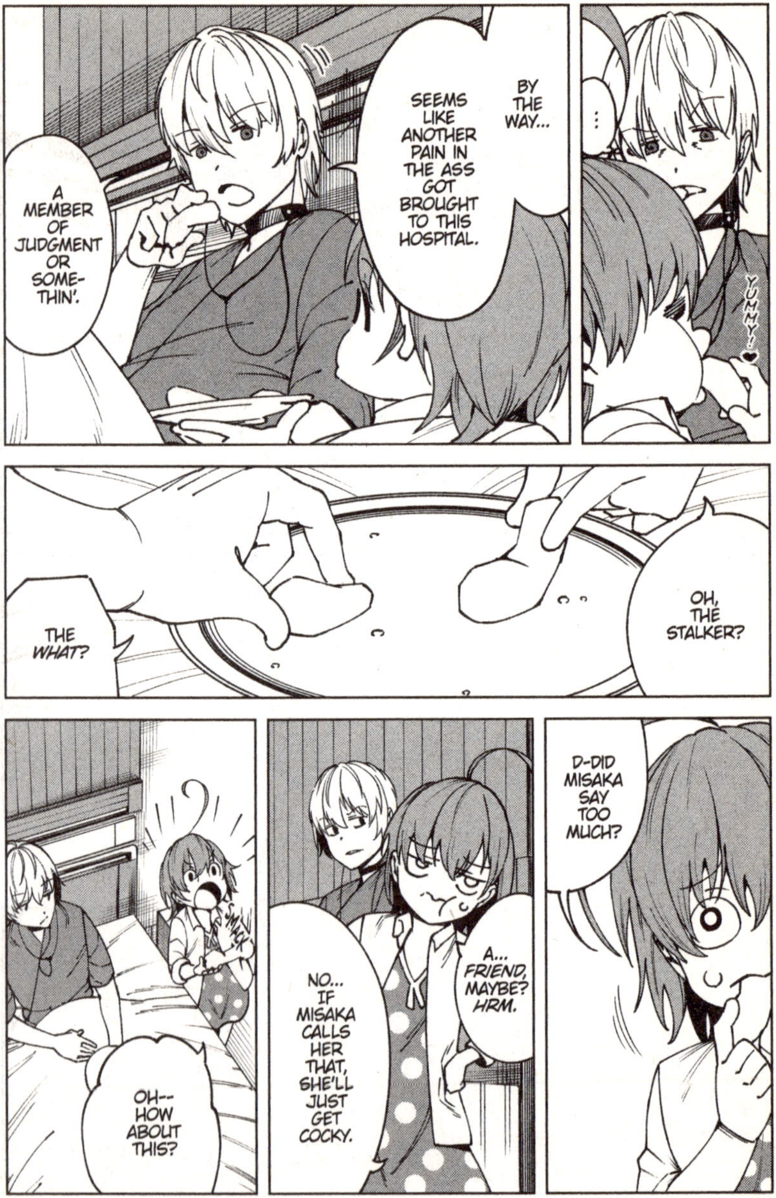
...
YUMMY! ♥
BY THE WAY...
SEEMS LIKE ANOTHER PAIN IN THE ASS GOT BROUGHT TO THIS HOSPITAL.
A MEMBER OF JUDGMENT OR SOMETHIN'.
OH, THE STALKER?
THE *WHAT?*
D-DID MISAKA SAY TOO MUCH?
*A... FRIEND, MAYBE? HRM.*
NO... IF MISAKA CALLS HER THAT, SHE'LL JUST GET COCKY.
SMACK
OH-- HOW ABOUT THIS?

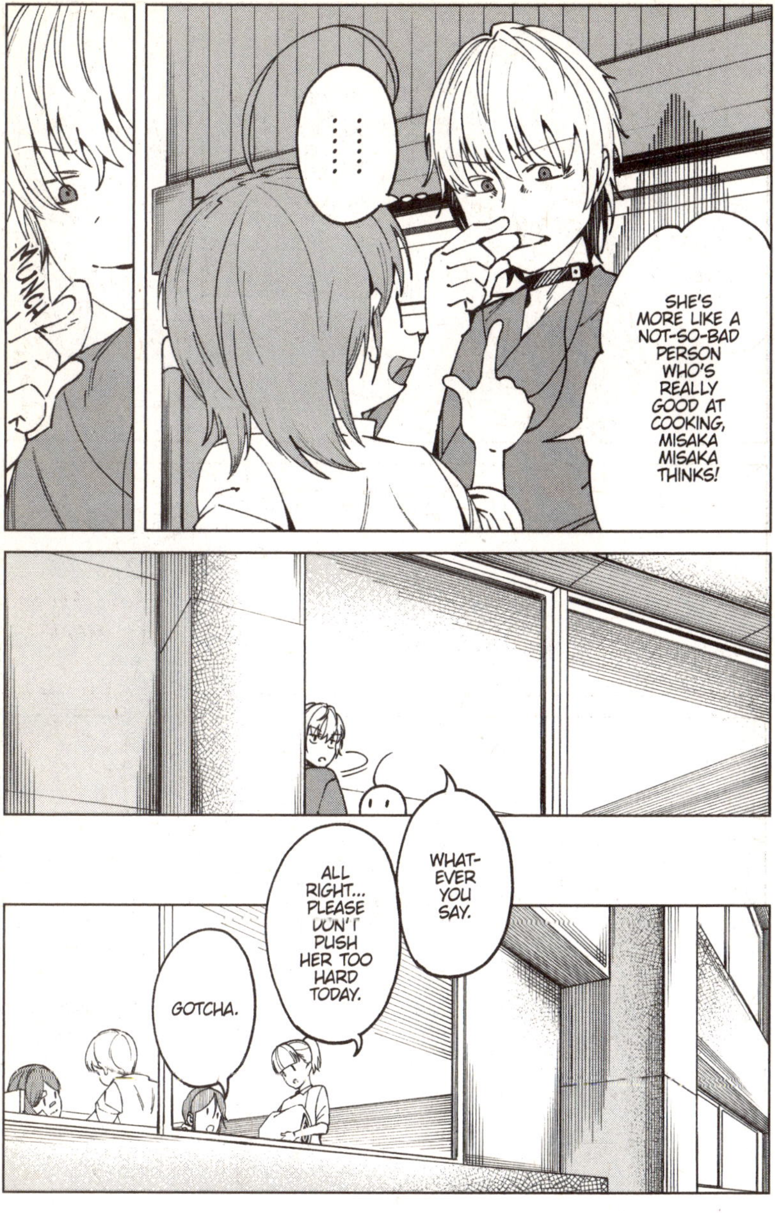
......
SHE'S MORE LIKE A NOT-SO-BAD PERSON WHO'S REALLY GOOD AT COOKING, MISAKA MISAKA THINKS!
MUNCH
WHAT-EVER YOU SAY.
ALL RIGHT... PLEASE DON'T PUSH HER TOO HARD TODAY.
GOTCHA.

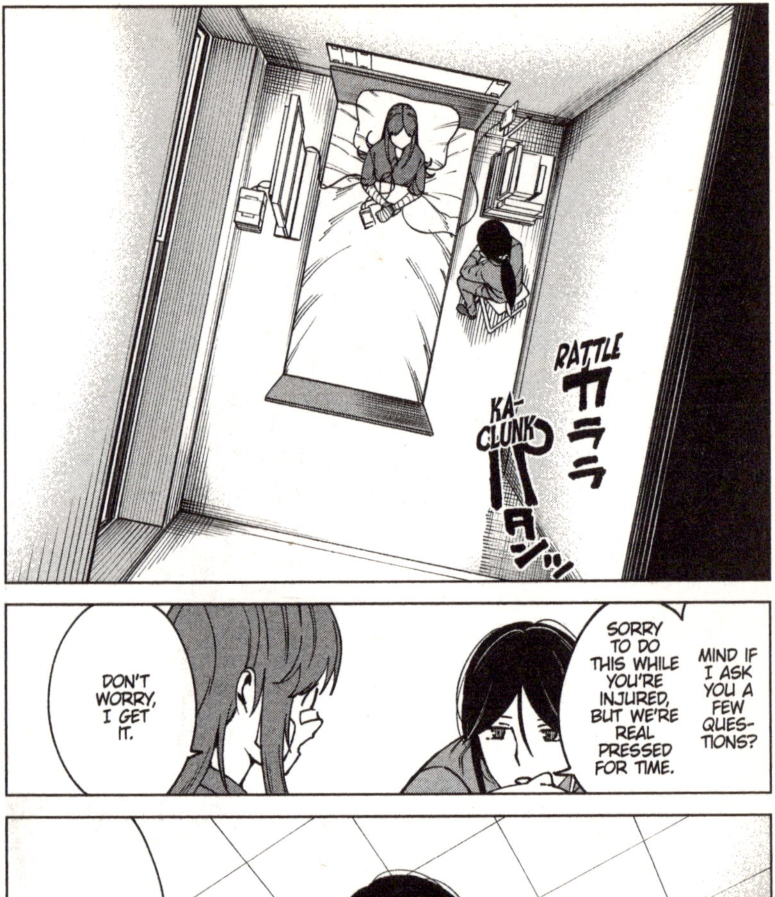
RATTLE
カララ
KA-CLUNK
バタンッ
MIND IF I ASK YOU A FEW QUES-TIONS?
SORRY TO DO THIS WHILE YOU'RE INJURED, BUT WE'RE REAL PRESSED FOR TIME.
DON'T WORRY, I GET IT.
THEN I'LL GET STRAIGHT TO THE POINT.
THE PERSON WHO ATTACKED THAT FACILITY. WAS SHE...?

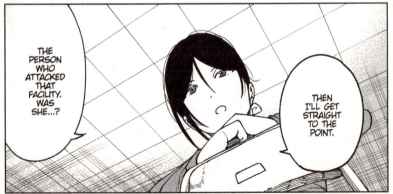

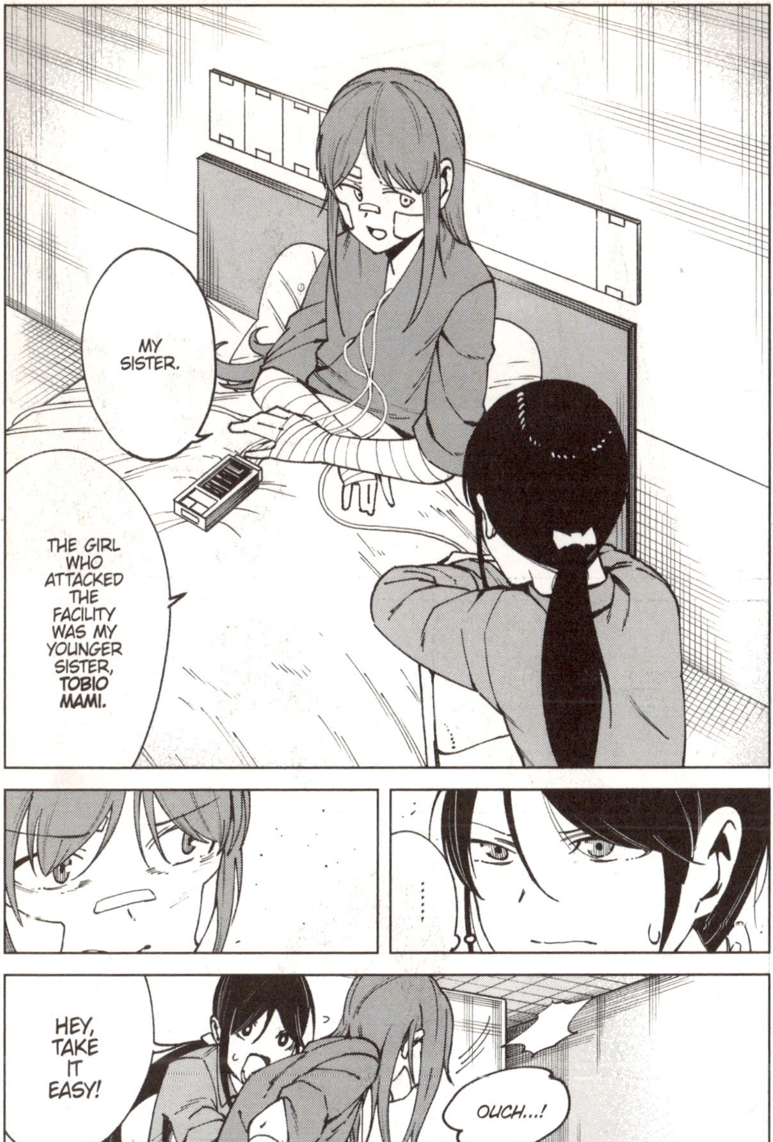
MY SISTER.
THE GIRL WHO ATTACKED THE FACILITY WAS MY YOUNGER SISTER, TOBIO MAMI.
OUCH...!
HEY, TAKE IT EASY!

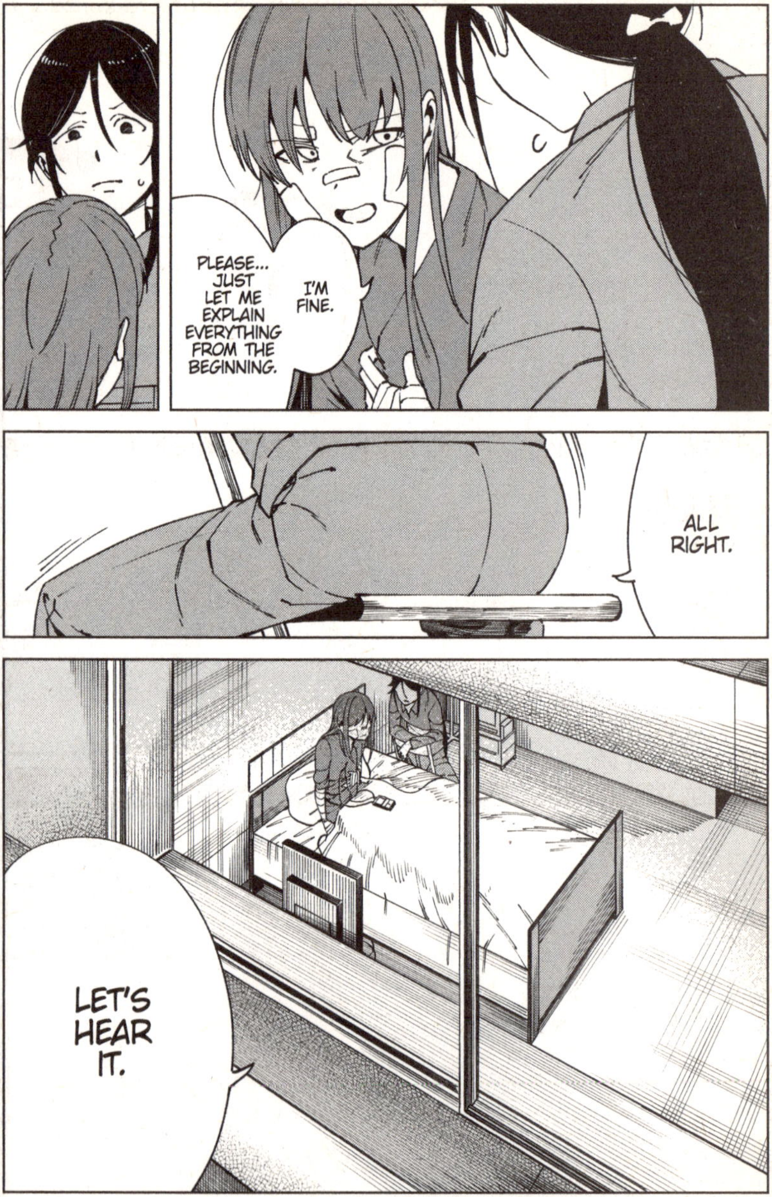
I'M FINE.
PLEASE... JUST LET ME EXPLAIN EVERYTHING FROM THE BEGINNING.
ALL RIGHT.
LET'S HEAR IT.

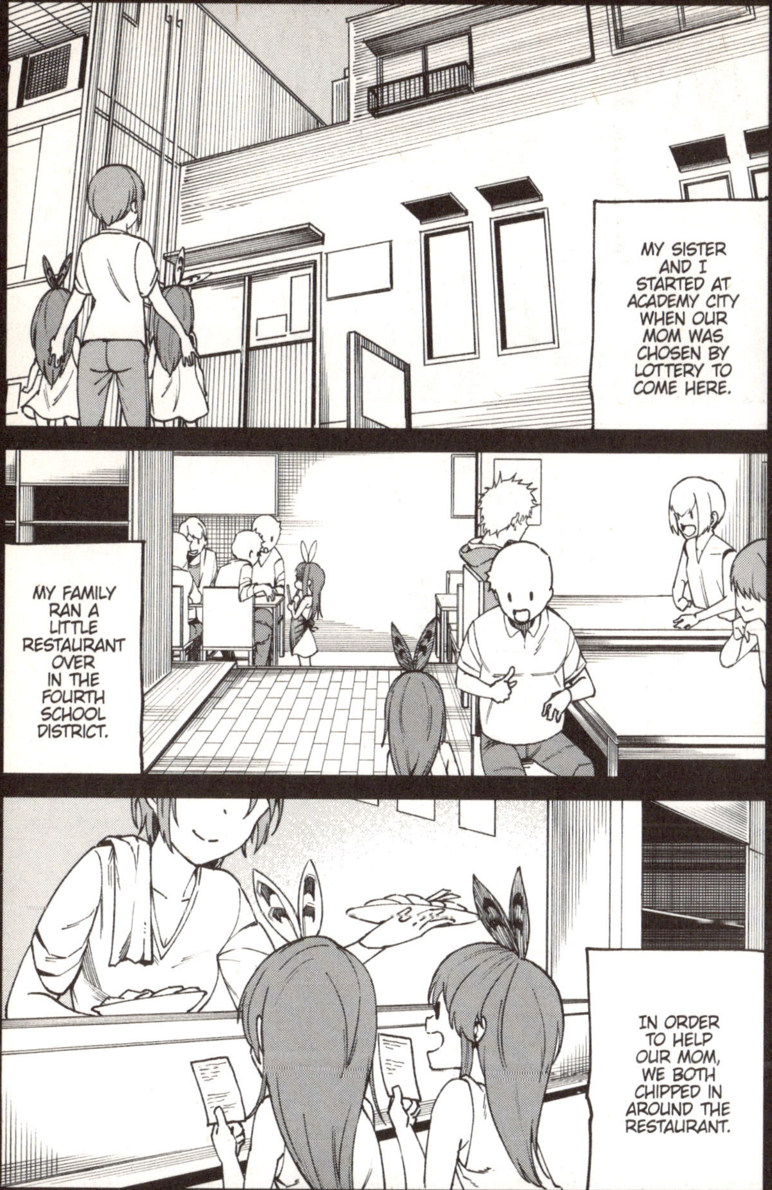
MY SISTER AND I STARTED AT ACADEMY CITY WHEN OUR MOM WAS CHOSEN BY LOTTERY TO COME HERE.
MY FAMILY RAN A LITTLE RESTAURANT OVER IN THE FOURTH SCHOOL DISTRICT.
IN ORDER TO HELP OUR MOM, WE BOTH CHIPPED IN AROUND THE RESTAURANT.

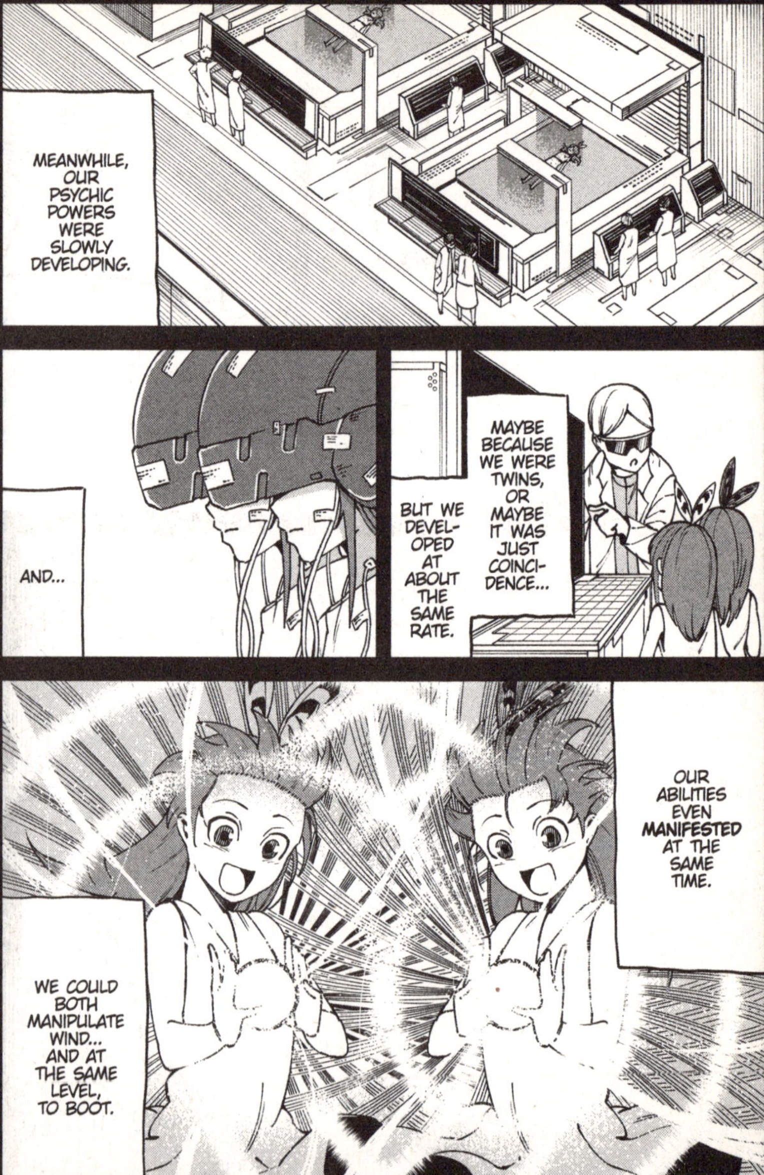
MEANWHILE, OUR PSYCHIC POWERS WERE SLOWLY DEVELOPING.
MAYBE BECAUSE WE WERE TWINS, OR MAYBE IT WAS JUST COINCIDENCE...
BUT WE DEVEL-OPED AT ABOUT THE SAME RATE.
AND...
OUR ABILITIES EVEN **MANIFESTED** AT THE SAME TIME.
WE COULD BOTH MANIPULATE WIND... AND AT THE SAME LEVEL, TO BOOT.

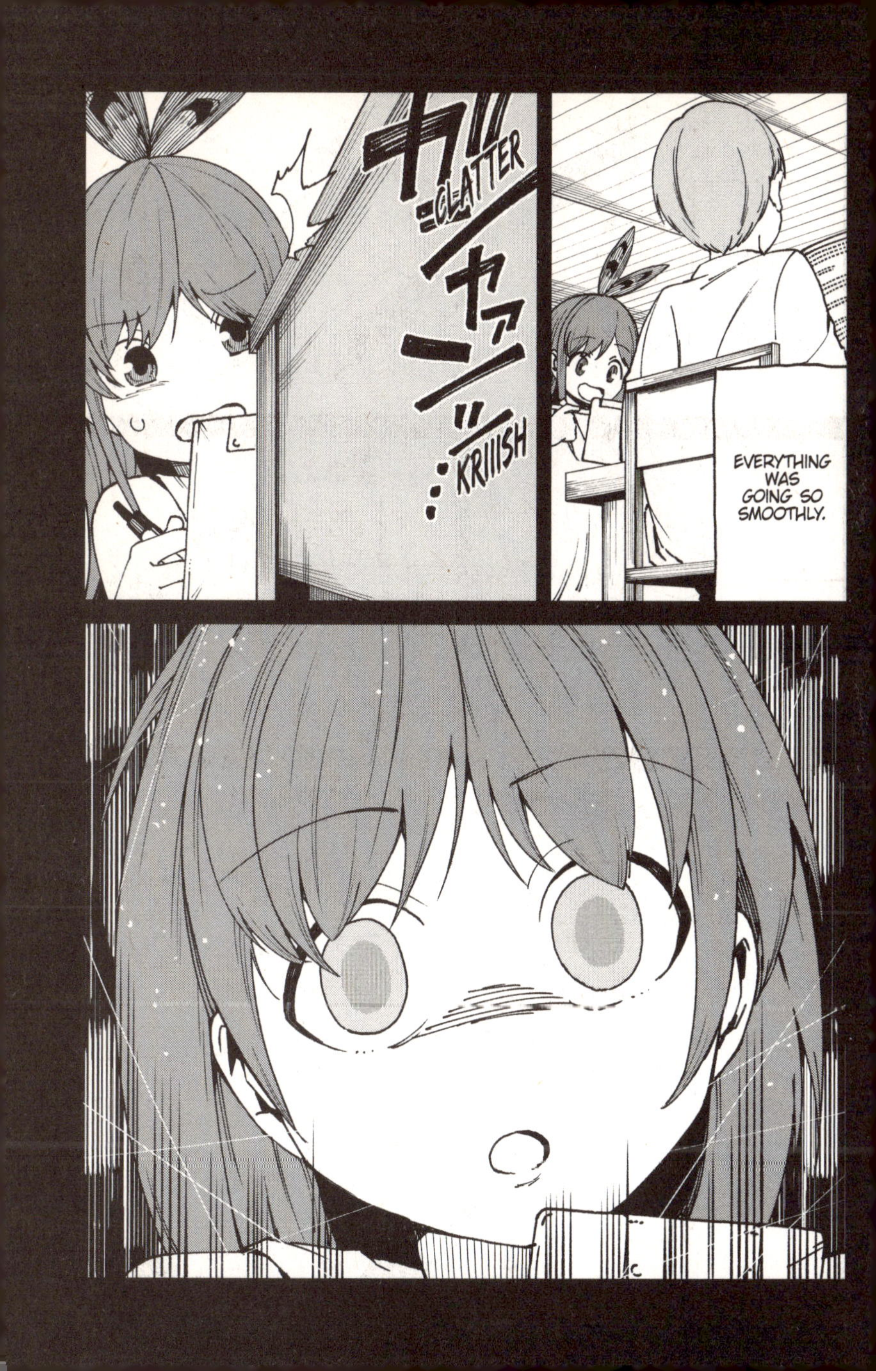
EVERYTHING WAS GOING SO SMOOTHLY.
CLATTER
KRIIISH

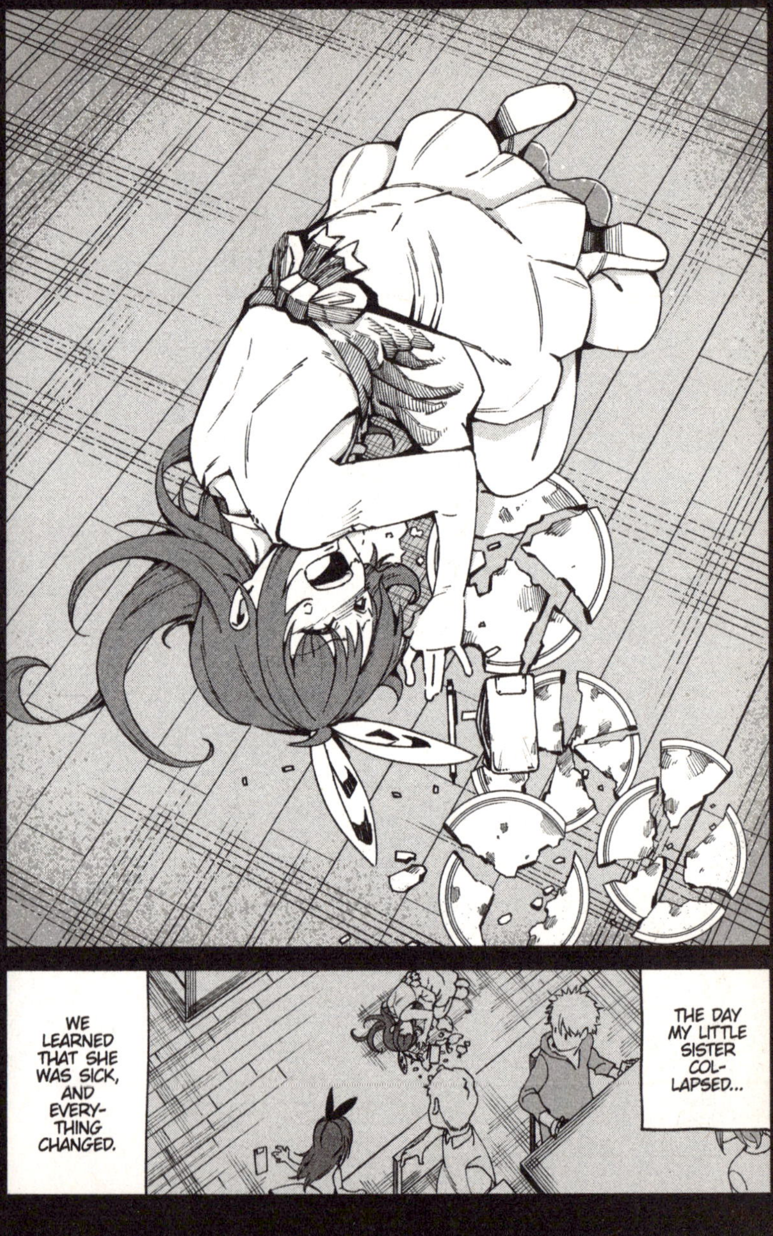
THE DAY MY LITTLE SISTER COL-LAPSED...
WE LEARNED THAT SHE WAS SICK, AND EVERY-THING CHANGED.

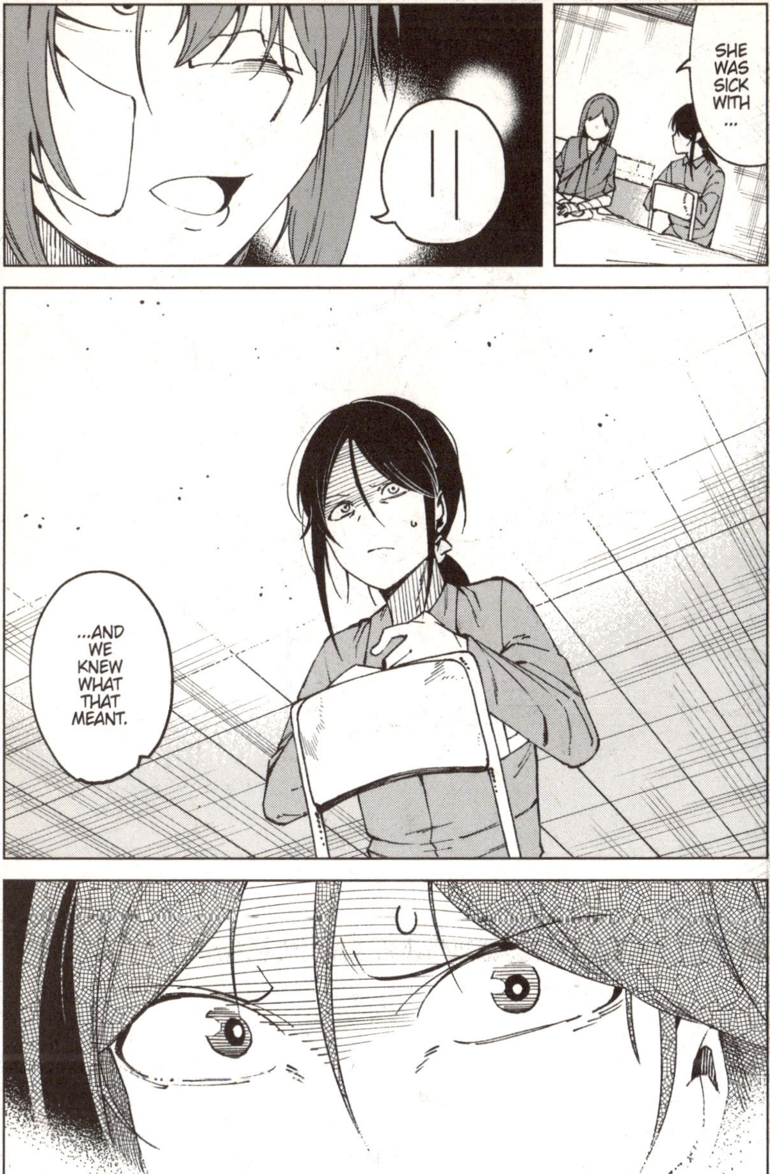
SHE WAS SICK WITH ...
...AND WE KNEW WHAT THAT MEANT.

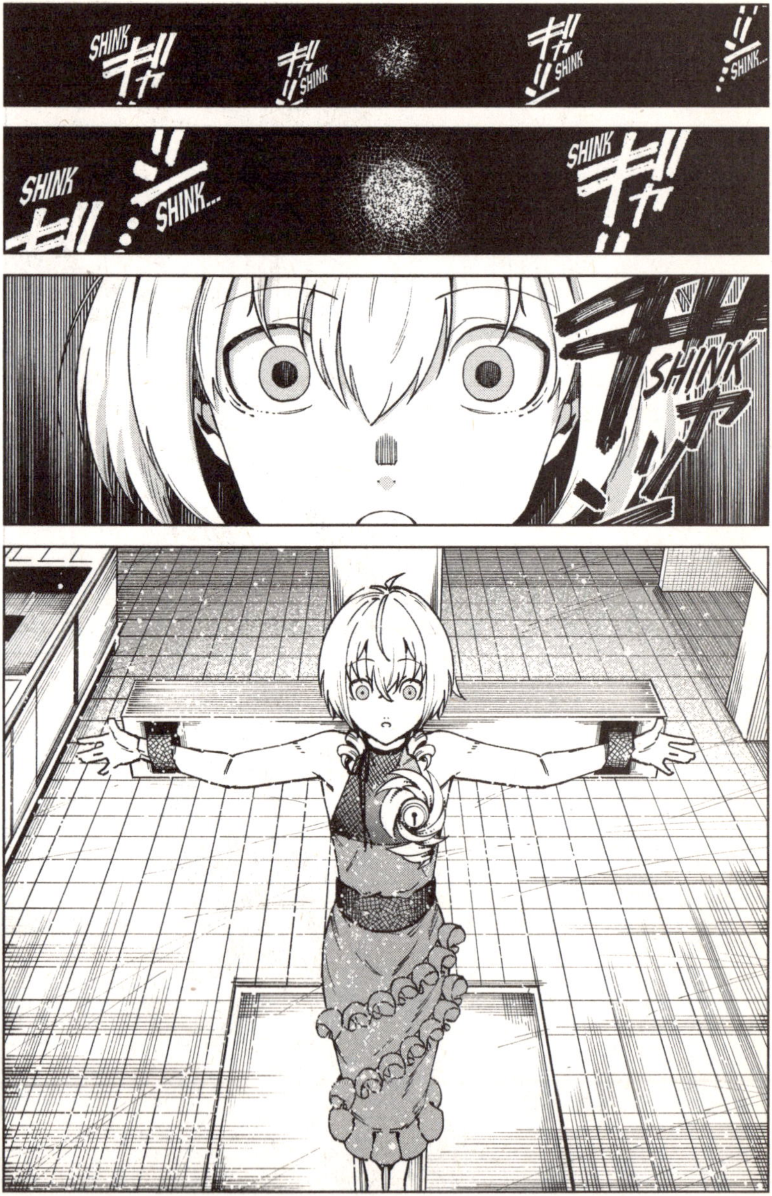
SHINK...
SHINK
SHINK
SHINK
SHINK
SHINK...
SHINK
SHINK

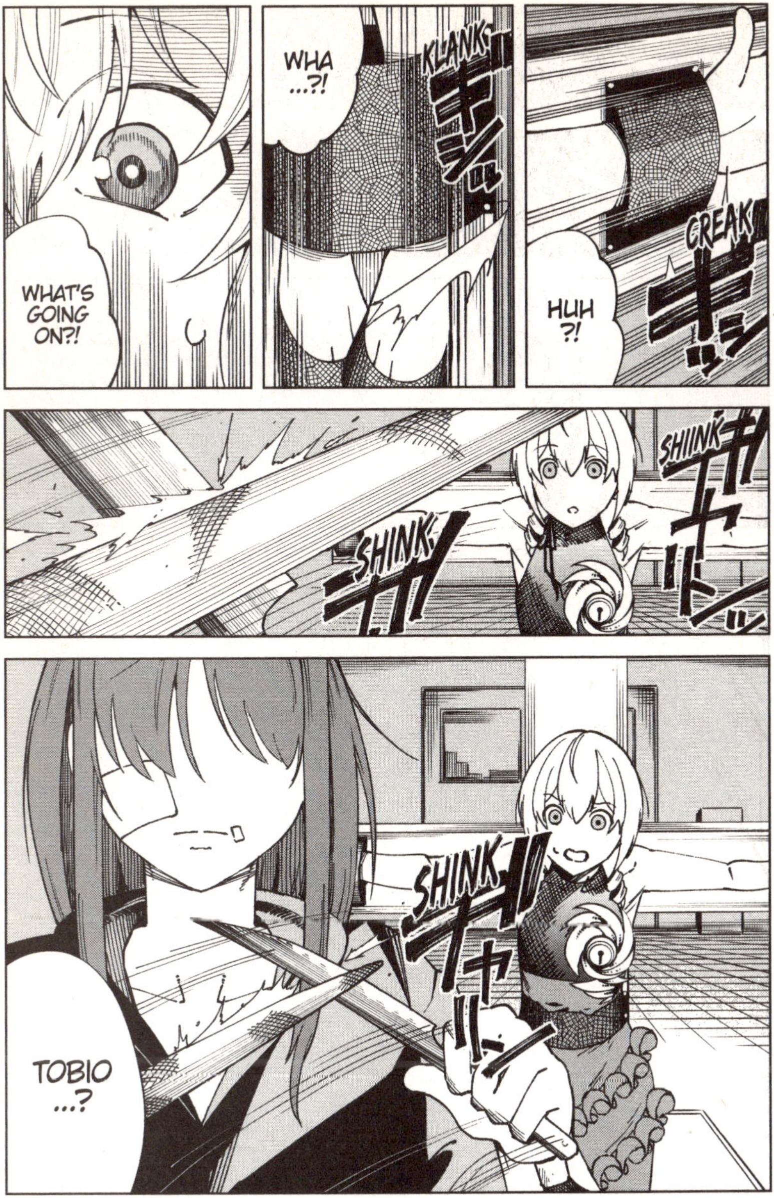
HUH ?!
CREAK
WHA ...?!
KLANK
WHAT'S GOING ON?!
SHIINK
SHIINK
SHINK!!
TOBIO ...?

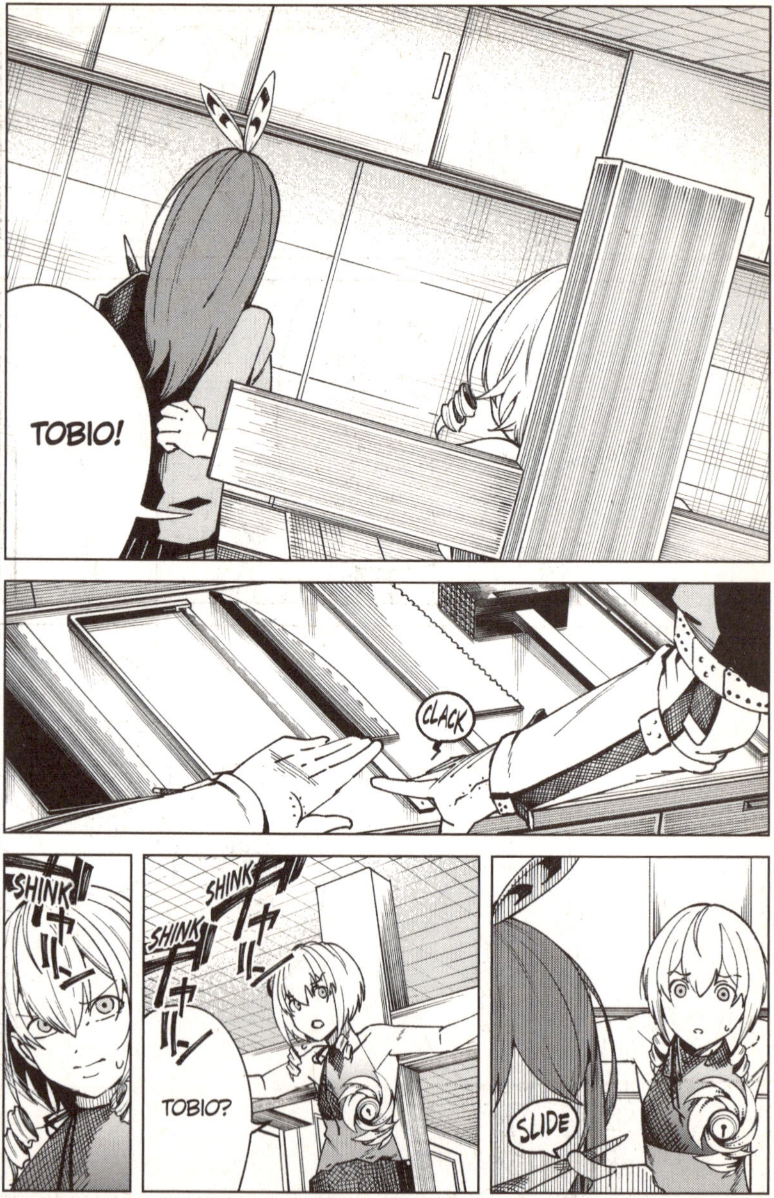
TOBIO!
CLACK
SLIDE
SHINK
SHINK
TOBIO?
SHINK

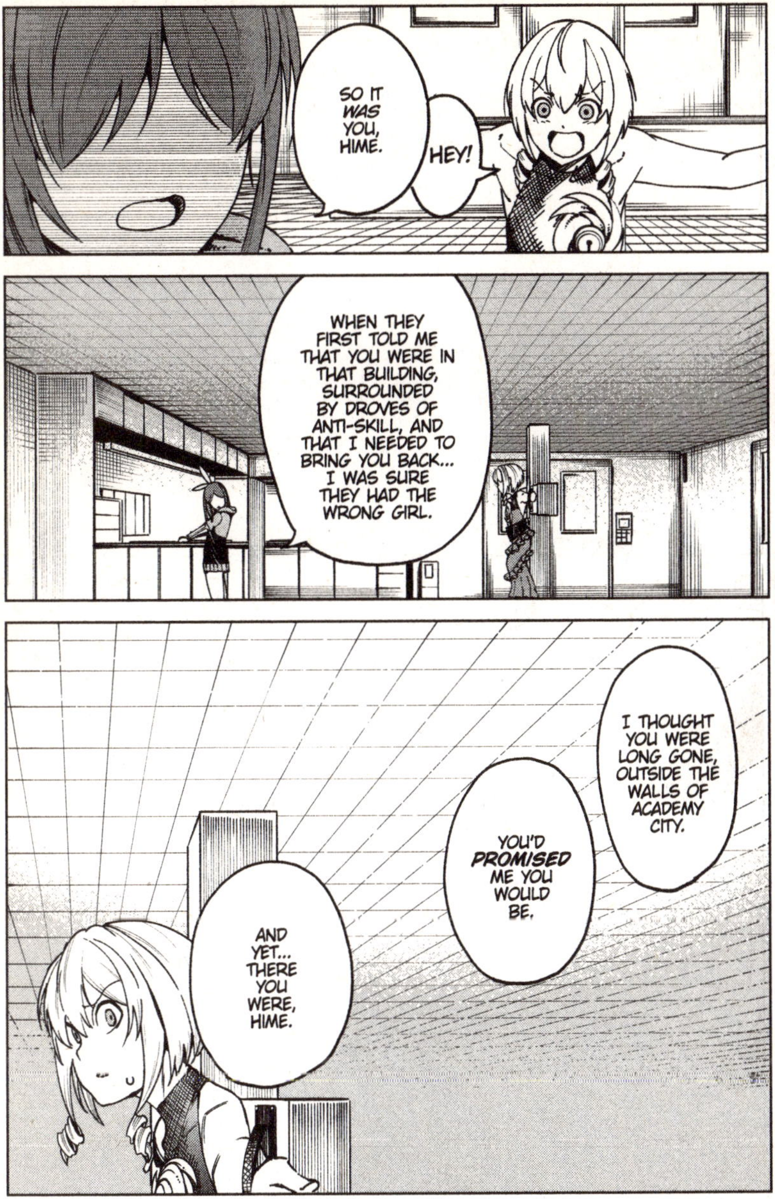
HEY!
SO IT WAS YOU, HIME.
WHEN THEY FIRST TOLD ME THAT YOU WERE IN THAT BUILDING, SURROUNDED BY DROVES OF ANTI-SKILL, AND THAT I NEEDED TO BRING YOU BACK... I WAS SURE THEY HAD THE WRONG GIRL.
I THOUGHT YOU WERE LONG GONE, OUTSIDE THE WALLS OF ACADEMY CITY.
YOU'D PROMISED ME YOU WOULD BE.
AND YET... THERE YOU WERE, HIME.

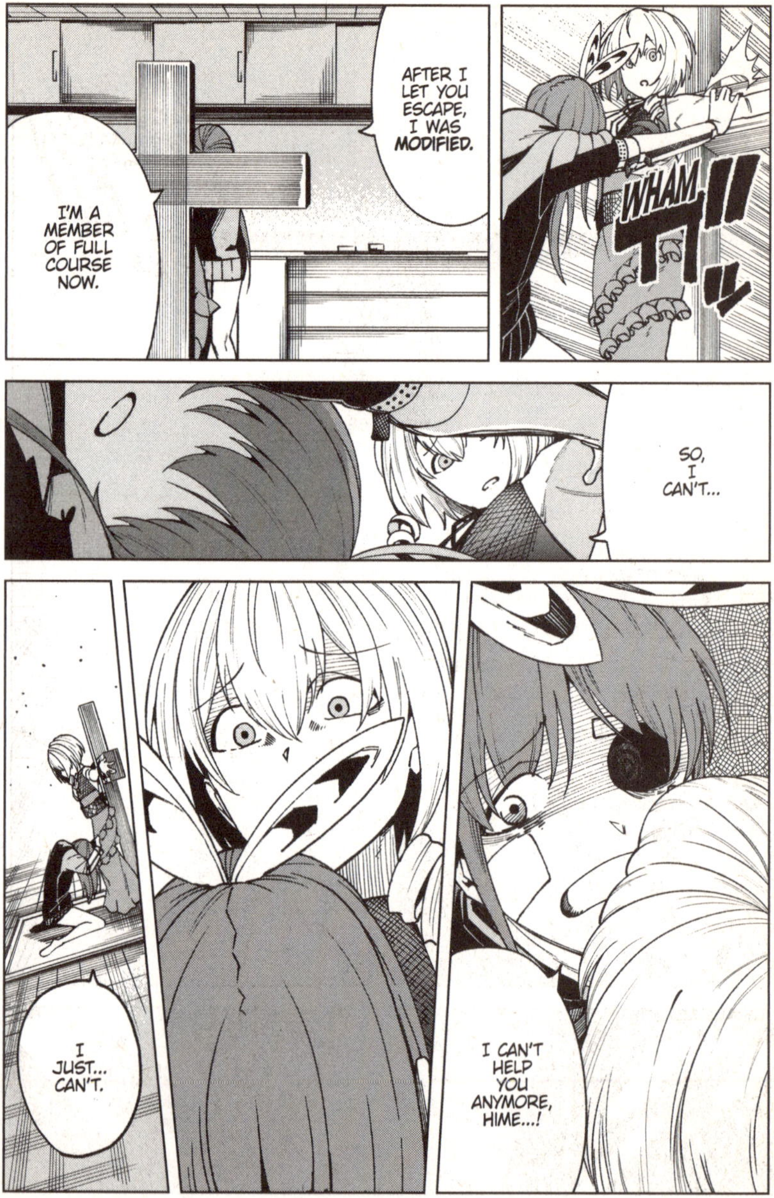
WHAM
AFTER I LET YOU ESCAPE, I WAS MODIFIED.
I'M A MEMBER OF FULL COURSE NOW.
SO, I CAN'T...
I CAN'T HELP YOU ANYMORE, HIME...!
I JUST... CAN'T.

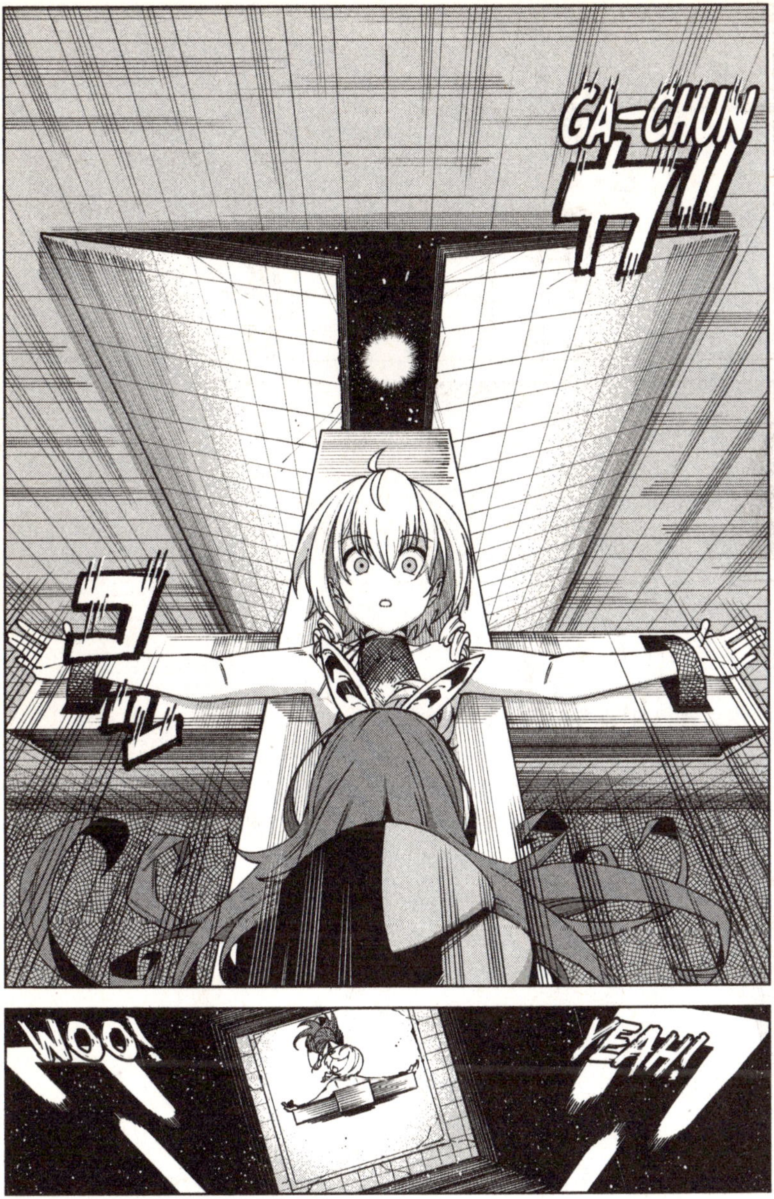
GA-CHUN
YEAH!
WOO!

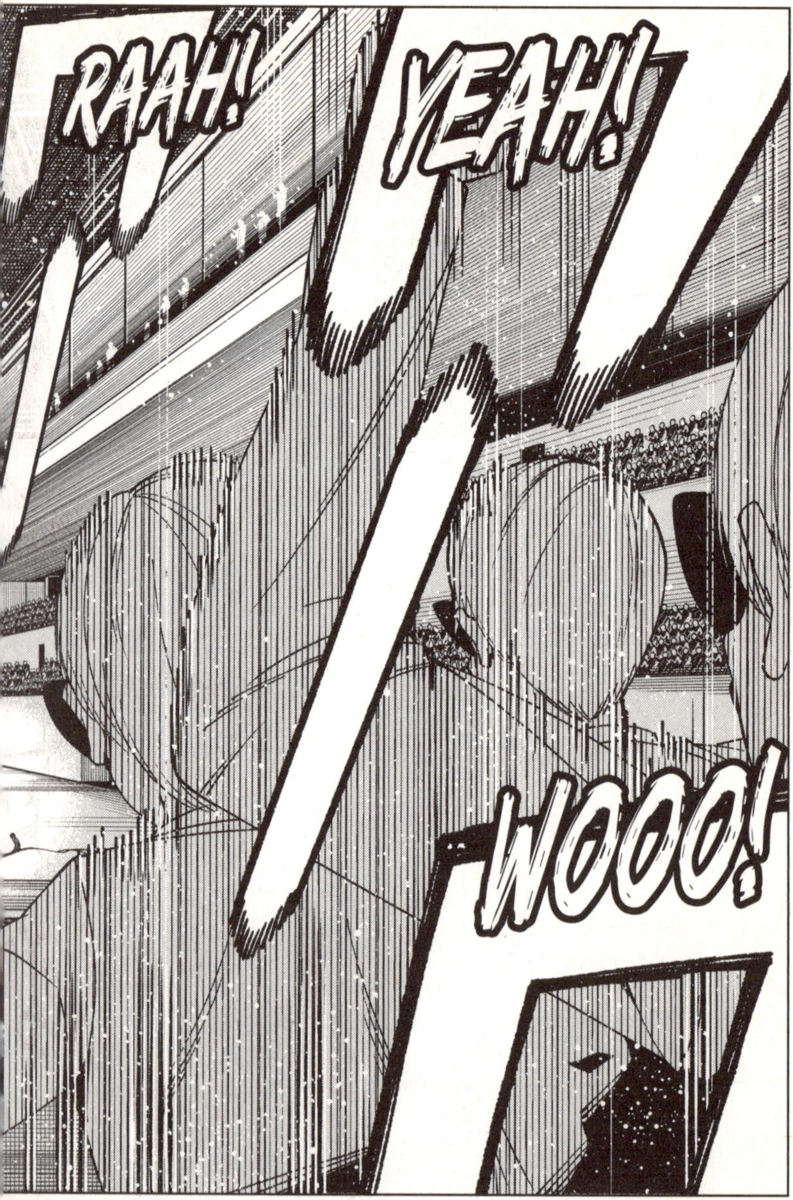
YEAH!
RAAH!
WOOO!

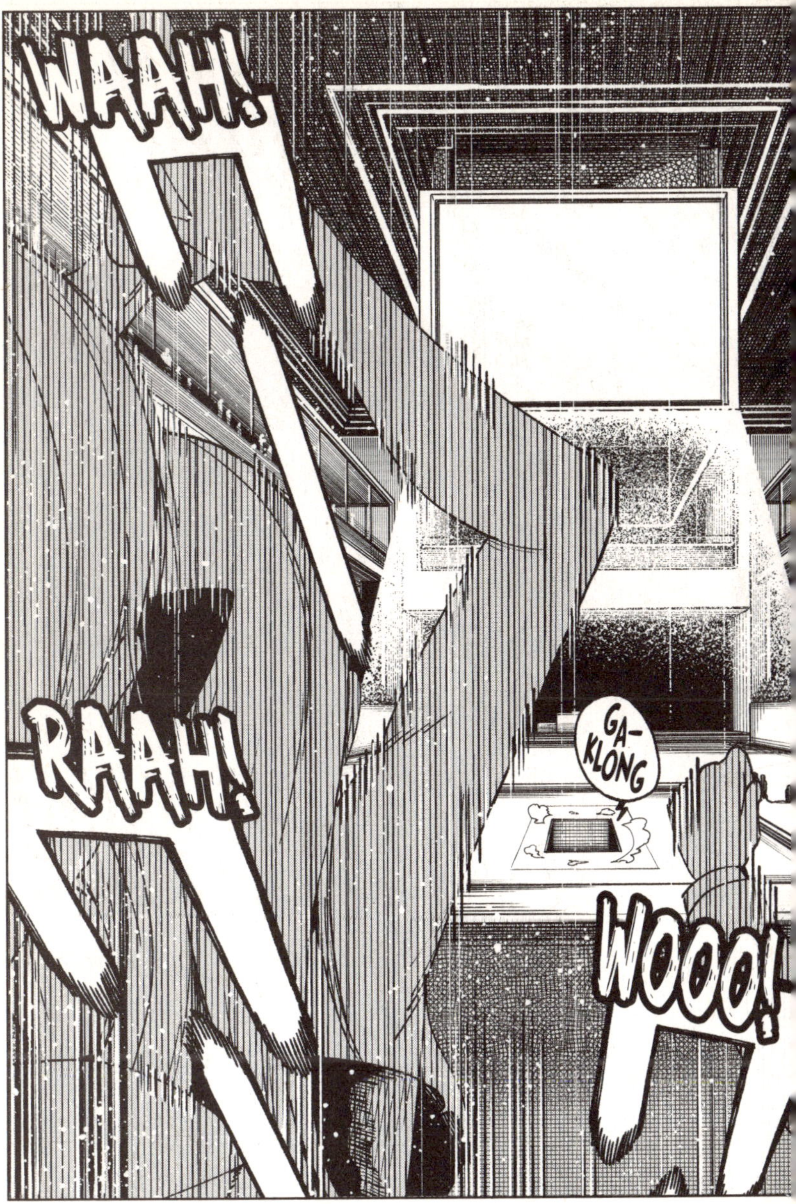
WAAH!
GA-KLONG
RAAH!
WOOO!

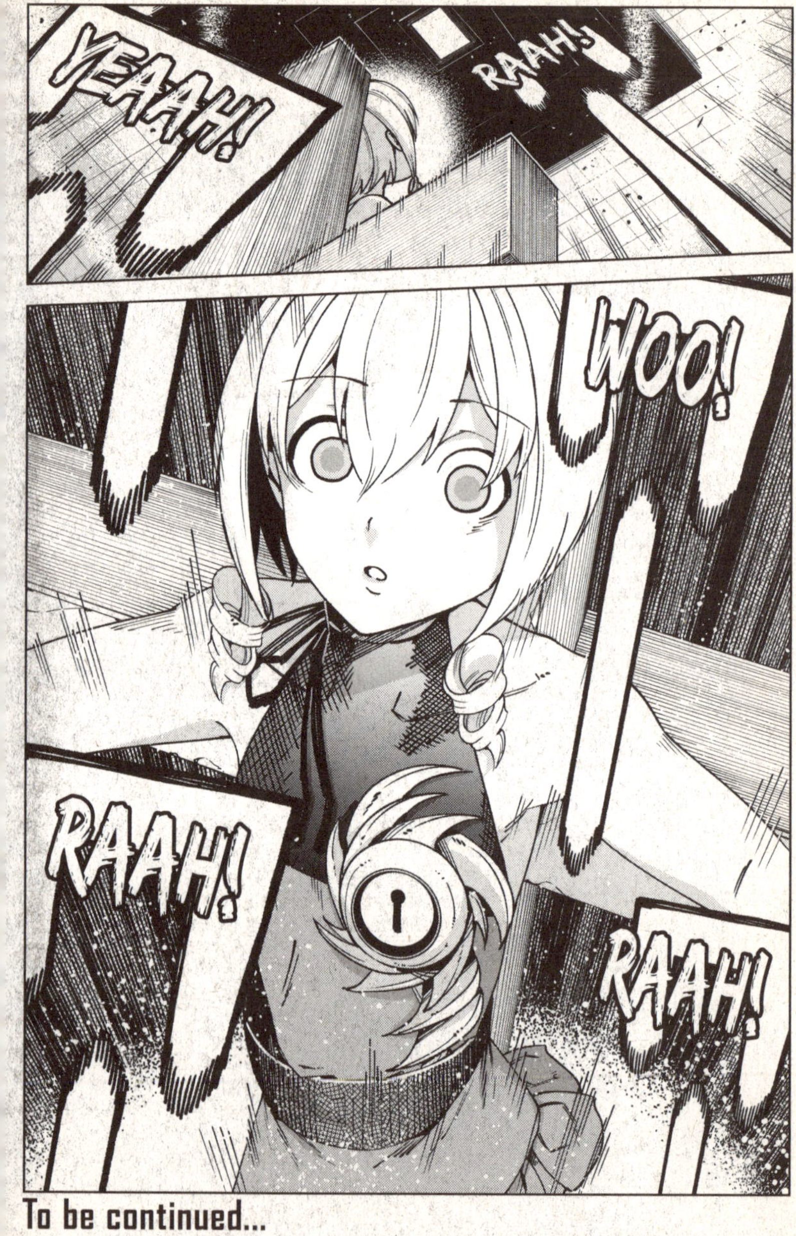
RAAH!
YEAAH!
WOO!
RAAH!
RAAH!

To be continued...

THIS IS THE STORY OF THE HERO OF THE WORST DEFEATS THE EVIL

# A Certain Scientific
# ACCELERATOR

Story by Kazuma Kamachi
Art by Arata Yamaji

Character Design by
Kiyotaka Haimura & Arata Yamaji

# PREVIEW OF NEXT VOLUME

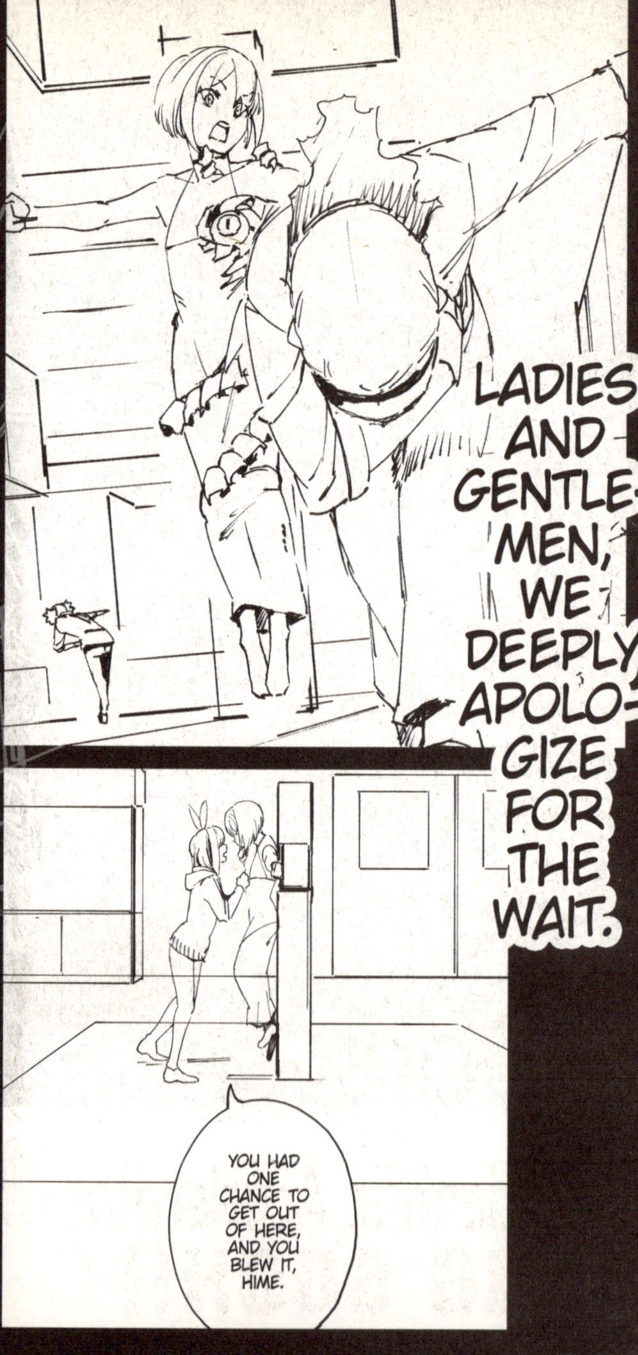
LADIES AND GENTLEMEN, WE DEEPLY APOLOGIZE FOR THE WAIT.
YOU HAD ONE CHANCE TO GET OUT OF HERE, AND YOU BLEW IT, HIME.

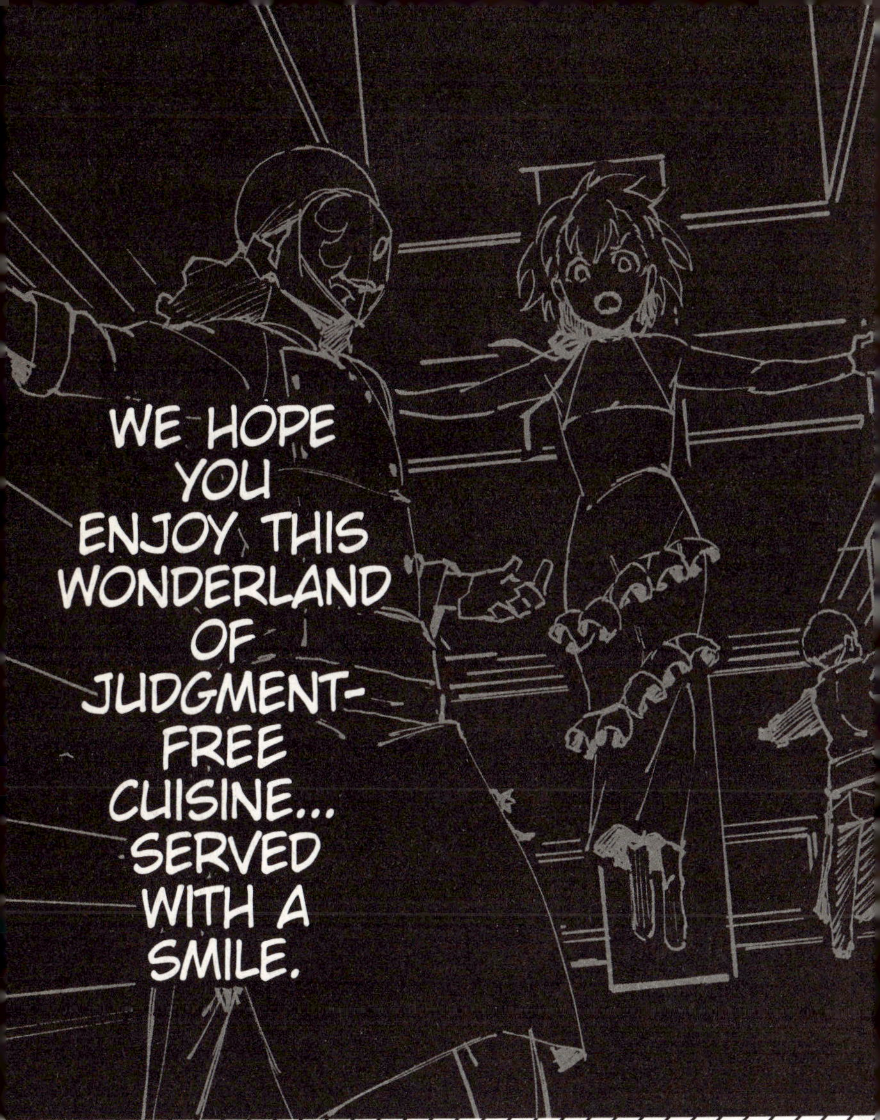
WE HOPE YOU ENJOY THIS WONDERLAND OF JUDGMENT-FREE CUISINE... SERVED WITH A SMILE.

A Certain Scientific Accelerator 10

**COMING SOON!!**

SEVEN SEAS ENTERTAINMENT PRESENTS



# a certain SCIENTIFIC ACCELERATOR



volume 9

story by **KAZUMA KAMACHI** / art by **ARATA YAMAJI**

TRANSLATION
**Nan Rymer**

ADAPTATION
**Maggie Danger**

LETTERING AND RETOUCH
**Roland Amago**
**Bambi Eloriaga-Amago**

COVER DESIGN
**Nicky Lim**

PROOFREADER
**Rebecca Schneidereit**

ASSISTANT EDITOR
**Shannon Fay**

PRODUCTION MANAGER
**Lissa Pattillo**

MANAGING EDITOR
**Julie Davis**

EDITOR-IN-CHIEF
**Adam Arnold**

PUBLISHER
**Jason DeAngelis**


First published in 2018 by KADOKAWA CORPORATION, Tokyo.
English translation rights arranged with KADOKAWA CORPORATION, Tokyo.



Seven Seas press and purchase enquiries can be sent to Marketing Manager Lianne Sentar at press@gomanga.com. Information regarding the distribution and purchase of digital editions is available from Digital Manager CK Russell at digital@gomanga.com.



ISBN: 978-1-64275-088-1

Printed in Canada

First Printing: June 2019

10 9 8 7 6 5 4 3 2 1





## READING DIRECTIONS

This book reads from ***right to left***, Japanese style. If this is your first time reading manga, you start reading from the top right panel on each page and take it from there. If you get lost, just follow the numbered diagram here. It may seem backwards at first, but you'll get the hang of it! Have fun!!

1
2
3
4
5
6
7
8
9

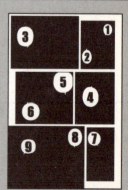